SAY YES TO THE DEATH

A CLAIRE HARTLEY ACCIDENTAL MYSTERY

MADISON SCORE

That's What She Said Publishing, Inc.

Say Yes to the DEATH

To Mom. For my first library card, for believing in me, and for decades of apple goodie.

To Do:
- Hunt for antique frames
- Take Rosie to the groomer

THE BLAST OF A HORN ROUSED HER FROM SLEEP.

What was happening? Where was she? This was wrong. All wrong. Claire Hartley's heart hammered in her chest. The neon lights of the city blinded her as she leaned against the trunk of a white sedan. She bent at the waist, breath coming in hitches. Her head was fuzzy, and her ears were ringing like someone had just hit a gong with a sledgehammer. The concrete sidewalk was warm beneath her bare feet. Something heavy and wet hit the ground beside her.

Was that a taco?

"Ma'am? Are you okay? That truck almost hit you." A teenage boy with an afro and beat-up basketball sneakers knelt on the ground next to her, fighting with the buttons on his flannel shirt.

A truck? That must have been the source of the noise and light that had snapped her back to consciousness.

"I—I don't know how I got here." Dread snaked into her stomach, hot and heavy like molten steel. She glanced at her watch. It was one in the morning. What was that smell —moussaka? She scanned the city block. A Greek restaurant four blocks from her apartment stood on the corner. How in the hell had she gotten four blocks from her apartment in the middle of the night with no memory of leaving?

She hadn't been this disoriented since she woke up in a parking garage tied to a pillar. At least this time there was a Good Samaritan standing in front of her instead of a knife-wielding maniac.

The teenager removed his shirt and handed it to Claire. She glanced down. She was totally wearing a shirt. Thank god. A startling number of people had seen her blood-drenched yet somehow still extremely pale breasts a few days ago. She wasn't eager to add another to the list.

"You're not wearing any pants," he explained.

She glanced down again. Sure enough, she was standing in the middle of the city of West Haven, Pennsylvania, wearing her oldest, most comfortable underwear. Everyone on Market Street had an unimpeded view of her granny panties. Goosebumps ran down the length of her legs.

Luke was not going to be happy about this. But maybe he hadn't noticed that she was missing.

"Thank you so much," Claire said, taking the shirt and wrapping it around her waist. It didn't cover as much as she had hoped, but it was probably enough to keep her from being arrested for indecent exposure. "Is this your taco?"

"No, ma'am, you were holding it when I pulled you off the street. Are you okay? Can I call someone for you?"

"I'm fine. I think I was sleepwalking." She glared at her legs. They had completely betrayed her. She had a meeting with a new client in the morning, and she needed to have her wits about her. Midnight sleepwalk tacos were not on the agenda.

"Pretty impressive that you bought Mexican food in your sleep," the boy remarked. He chuckled, a warm sound in the breezy night.

How had she gotten the taco, anyway? Her purse wasn't with her. Was she a kleptomaniac as well as a sleepwalker? Or worse, was it a dumpster taco? Her stomach churned. There was no point in worrying about it now.

She shook her head. "Priorities. What's your address? I'll have your shirt dry-cleaned and sent back to you." Wait, was it creepy to ask a minor for his address? It was too late.

He shook his head. The afro didn't budge an inch. "You can keep it."

"Please, I insist. Why are you out here at this time of night, anyway? Does your mother know where you are?"

"Relax, lady. I work the closing shift at the Greek place."

"Claire?" A panicked voice came from down the street.

Claire and the teenager turned.

There he was. Luke Islestorm. Six feet and two inches of hunky, grumpy filmmaker. The gray sweatpants he wore rode low on his hips as he jogged up to them. She hadn't had the chance to find out what lay beneath those sweatpants since getting stabbed by a serial killer last week, but her desire to find out was quickly eclipsing her body's need to heal.

"What the hell are you doing?" Luke bent at the waist and put his hands on his knees. His arms rippled under the moonlight as he caught his breath. "I woke up and you were gone. I've been looking for you for twenty minutes. I almost called the police to see if Barney broke out of prison. And who's this?" His sea-green eyes blazed under the streetlight.

"Oh, this is—" She hadn't even asked the teen's name. So embarrassing. Her mother, Alice, would be horrified at her lack of tact.

"Jemarcus. I pulled your girl off the street so she didn't get hit by a truck."

She bristled at his use of the phrase "your girl." She didn't belong to anyone. She and Luke weren't even officially together. Were they?

Luke grasped Jemarcus's hand. "Thank you. Claire, let's go."

Oh boy, he was pissed.

"Jemarcus, thank you so much. I'll bring your shirt back to the restaurant." She turned, but he was already gone.

"What the hell were you thinking? It's the middle of the night. It's a miracle no one recognized you. And where are your pants?"

"I was sleepwalking." She crossed her arms over her chest.

Her picture—thankfully a flattering one taken from the "About Me" page on her proposal planning blog—had been plastered over the news for the last week. People recognized her in the grocery store, and the press had been stalking her like she was a celebrity buying Ben and Jerry's without a bra on. It was exhausting. "It's not like I did it on purpose."

"Sleepwalking?" His brow furrowed. "Is that something you've always done?"

"No. This is new," she admitted.

Why now, after twenty-five years of normal sleeping habits, would she suddenly start sleepwalking? Maybe it had something to do with the fact that she was abducted and stabbed the week before. She didn't need to pay a shrink $200 an hour to figure that one out for her, despite her friends' incessant, heavy hinting about therapy.

Luke shook his head. "Great, I'm going to have to invest in shackles now. Come on, I should change your bandage anyway."

"Before we go back, do you have your wallet on you?"

"Yes, but we're not going to Sephora."

She shot him a dirty look. "Obviously not, they close at seven. Can we hit the taco truck? There's a chance unconscious Claire may have stolen some goods."

Luke sighed. "Never a dull moment."

CHAPTER TWO

"I'M GOING TO NEED YOU TO STEAL AS MANY PAINTINGS AS possible," Claire said as she led a bespectacled, owlish-looking man between two rows of industrial shelving. She shook her mass of blonde curls over one shoulder and stifled a yawn. She should have stopped for coffee. Her midnight escapade had definitely compromised her beauty sleep.

"I'm sorry?" He cocked his head to the side and stepped over a disembodied mannequin arm.

"Watch your step, Aaron. I need you to start smuggling Jane's paintings away. Ones she won't notice are missing. I'll store them here at the warehouse."

"All right," he said, clearly perplexed. "What are we going to do with her paintings?"

They emerged at the far end of Claire's cavernous warehouse, where a projector stood next to a conference table. She pressed a button on the top, and an image of a studio flickered to life on a nearby screen. The glow from the projector illuminated the large bandage above her left collarbone, a constant, inescapable reminder in her peripheral vision. She shifted the hem of her shirt until it was covered. Her recent trauma was not invited to the discussion of Aaron's happily ever after.

"My friend owns a photography studio downtown. We're going to temporarily turn her space into an art gallery and give your soon-to-be fiancée her very first showing."

His face lit up, and his chocolate-colored eyes crinkled behind horn-rimmed glasses. He stepped closer to the screen. "I never would have thought of that. She'll love it."

"That's what I'm here for." She clicked through several slides showing the studio. "Based on my estimation, we need about twenty-five pieces for the space. All different sizes. Can you get that many?"

He nodded, and his glasses slid down the brim of his nose. "Definitely. She has dozens of paintings in our storage shed."

"Perfect. I trust your judgment, so bring me whatever you think she would be most proud of. Now, to make it look more legitimate." She paused, flipping open the binder on the conference table. "We'll need to secure a caterer and bar service. I don't want Jane to be suspicious until the last second. If that works for you, I'll get some quotes and check in with you."

Aaron nodded and put his hands in his pockets, his gaze shifting to the studio once again. "It's perfect. She won't even know what to say. I mean, hopefully she says yes. You know. To the proposal."

Claire laughed. "She would be crazy not to. I had one other thought. Are you an artist yourself, Aaron?"

The man shrugged and fiddled with the bottom point of his paisley tie. "Not like Jane. I used to draw cartoons when I was a kid, but that's about the extent of it."

Claire smiled, bouncing on her toes in excitement. She'd bet anything he was being modest. "Perfect. I want you to draw a sketch of the proposal before it happens, and then I want to blow it up as a huge print and hang it in a closed room at the back of the gallery."

His face flushed. "Oh, no. I couldn't."

"You can. And you will. Now I don't know about your creative process, but I would suggest—"

"Claire?" Footsteps echoed from the back of the warehouse.

Her heart leapt into her throat.

She wasn't expecting another appointment. Her shoulders hunched up as she flipped on a light switch. She reached underneath the conference table and tugged at a strap. *Krrrrshhhh.* A Taser fell into her hand. Her mother had sent her a half dozen after the abduction, and they all had unique homes.

Aaron jumped backward like she had suddenly transformed into an armed assassin. He bumped against a shelving unit, jostling a row of glass vases.

She pointed the weapon toward the door. "Who is it? If you're a member of the press, I'm only going to tell you once that you are trespassing on private property, and unless you have a scheduled appointment, you will be strung up by your toes and dangled over a tank of piranhas."

Jason Goldman, the last man she expected to see today,

stepped into the pool of fluorescent lighting. A manila envelope was clutched under one arm. His gaze darted around the room as if he expected to be attacked by a mannequin or a length of ribbon. He was built like the football player he once was, but he must have gained thirty pounds since they broke up nearly a year ago—now more bowling ball shape than linebacker.

"What do you want?" Claire stared her ex-fiancé down even as her stomach lurched like she was aboard a broken carnival ride. "I'm in a meeting."

"I just wanted to talk to you about something. It won't take long."

Aaron checked his watch. "We're just two minutes short of an hour anyway, Claire. Email me the updated quote when you talk to the caterers?"

"Of course. Sorry about this." Her cheeks were hot. Jason had already single-handedly ruined her ability to trust, and now he was storming into a client meeting. Would he ever leave her alone?

"I'll send you the breakdown of my other ideas, and we'll schedule the next meeting." She flashed a bright smile at Aaron.

Aaron waved as he disappeared into the maze of matrimonial paraphernalia.

Jason shuffled closer and cleared his throat. A sheen of sweat covered his forehead. It wasn't *that* hot outside. What had her ex so hot and bothered? She wrinkled her nose. His musky cologne hadn't changed a bit since college.

"How have you been?" The envelope crinkled in his meaty fists. He seemed to be addressing an organizer full of drywall screws over Claire's shoulder. Apparently, he could leave her thirty singing voicemails begging to take him back, but he couldn't maintain eye contact for a fifteen second conversation.

The side door closed, signaling Aaron's exit, and the customer service smile slipped from her face like a mask. "You mean since you cheated on me with my nemesis? Or since I was abducted and stabbed? You'll have to be more specific—it's been a busy year."

She didn't have time for whatever this was. Jason had stalked her for eight months after their breakup. Constant phone calls, flowers, even visits to her apartment. She had finally succeeded in getting him to leave her alone after she had given the police his name as a suspect for a break-in that had occurred in her apartment the previous month. But now here he was, with shifty eyes and holding a curious envelope.

He took a deep breath and reached for her hand. Oh *hell* no. She snatched her hand back as if his was dripping with fire ants.

"Claire, we were close once. I just wanted to make sure you were okay. I heard that the hearing is coming up and today was supposed to be—"

"Don't," she said sharply. "We are not going to talk about what today was supposed to be. Why are you really here? And what's that?" She gestured to the envelope. "Are you going to ask me if I have a minute to hear the word of our Lord and Savior Wendy Flutter?"

Wendy and Claire had a long history. Almost four years ago, they had been pitted against each other for Event Planner of the Year at the West Haven Chamber of Commerce Small Business Awards. Claire won. From that night on, Wendy had made it her personal mission to ruin Claire both personally and professionally. She had slandered her on public television, slept with her fiancé, and tampered with the biggest proposal Claire had ever orchestrated. Nevertheless, Claire kept winning.

Jason handed her the envelope. "Not exactly. But these are some legal documents. They're for you. I have to go." He turned and scurried back through the warehouse.

Legal documents? The envelope was heavy in her hands. She turned it over and ripped it open. A pile of papers slid out. She skimmed the first few lines. Her mouth dropped open.

"*Are you freaking kidding me*?" She slammed the pile of papers down on the conference table and picked up her phone. For an instant, her vision blurred and the numbers swam in front of her eyes. Every breath burned in her chest, and her heart beat so hard and fast she swore she could hear it.

"Mindy? You're never going to guess what just happened. Jason just came to the warehouse and served me papers. Wendy is suing me over the fight at Nicole's engagement party. *Suing me. For five million dollars.*"

"What do you mean? On what grounds? Get off for a second, Gavin, it's Claire," Mindy said, slightly muffled. There was a shuffling sound as her assistant and best friend presumably disentangled herself from her British boyfriend.

Claire glanced over the first few lines of the summons. "For 'aggravated battery.' There are doctor bills and pictures of her bruises in this file. Mindy, what do I do? I don't have five million dollars."

She collapsed onto a chair and hunched forward, massaging her temples. Apparently, getting abducted and stabbed was just the beginning of her bad luck this summer.

There was more shuffling and the jingling of keys on Mindy's end of the line. "This is ridiculous. I am so slashing that bitch's tires. I'll call Kyle. Do you want me to come over? I'll bring ice cream and a lock pick. We could pay Wendy a visit. I know a guy who can get us some termites."

Claire gave a weak laugh. "Thanks, but no thanks. I'm not going to stoop to her level. I'm going to beat her fair and square at the award ceremony in a few weeks, and then I guess I'll beat her in court. I'm headed to Luke's after this anyway. Could you take my last appointment for the day and pick up the giant custom box from The Box Store? It won't fit in my car, and I need to figure this out."

"Of course. I'll let you know what I find. And Claire— maybe don't check our general email tonight."

Her insides shriveled. "Are there more?"

"Dozens, just in the past hour alone. Somebody from Dubai is offering 500k plus travel expenses, it's absolutely—"

"Okay. I don't need to hear any more." Claire's heart was pounding again. There was no way she was capable of making a decision about expanding the business right now. She needed a glass of wine and some vitamin D. Whether that would come from sunshine or Luke remained to be seen.

"We're going to have to start making some decisions about expanding or—"

"Mindy, I'm getting sued. And I got stabbed a hot minute ago. I can't do this right now. Can we talk about it tomorrow?"

Mindy paused. "Are you sure tomorrow is going to be better? Don't you have a super important dinner?"

Dammit. She had foolishly insisted on making dinner for Luke and his mother. It was an integral part of her wooing routine for meeting parents for the first time— thoughtful gift, homecooked dinner, intelligent conversation. She and Rachel hadn't met, but she was an attorney and had a reputation for being equally unpleasant in and out of court.

"Thanks for reminding me. At least this will be fodder for dinner conversation. Maybe Rachel will have some advice. I have to go."

"Okay. Don't worry. Everything is going to be fine. Call Luke. He'll want to know."

Claire hung up and slumped in her chair, staring at the stack of papers. All she wanted was some Chinese takeout and a blanket to hide under. Now she was being sued by her ex-fiancé's new girlfriend, who also happened to be her biggest nemesis, *and* the wretched hag was going after Claire for five million dollars. Were the scales of justice broken this summer?

She flipped open her day planner and scanned the month of June. Thanks to Barney Windsor, the former client who abducted and stabbed her last week, her calendar was filling up with unplanned events. Lawyer meetings and a sure-to-be-hellish preliminary hearing all before Father's Day. *Ugh.* Father's Day.

She secured her Taser (Taser #2, to be exact) to the underside of the table. She whistled, and nails skittered excitedly somewhere in the warehouse. An extremely dusty corgi rounded the corner and arrived at Claire's side with a violent sneeze.

"Bless you. How would you feel about running away and starting a new life in Cancun, RoRo? We could change our names. I'll be Catalina and you be Rosalita."

Rosie whined softly.

Claire sighed. "You're right. I'd miss Nicole and Mindy."

Rosie yipped.

"Luke, too, I guess. They could come along, though. We

could start a destination proposal business! Proposals in Paradise. I can see it now."

Rosie put her paw on Claire's shoe and looked at her skeptically.

"Fine." Claire stood and rummaged through her purse. "Where did I put your leash?" While Rosie was a loveable dog, she was poorly trained. One sighting of an errant squirrel and she would bolt down the streets of West Haven, never to be seen again.

The new HDTV that Luke had installed in the corner of the warehouse (because apparently the existing projector didn't meet bougie Luke's screening standards) changed from an erectile dysfunction commercial to a local newscaster.

"Thank you for joining us for a special afternoon edition of *Marnie in the Morning*," said a light, clear voice Claire had last heard during her TV debut. "You are watching history being made, ladies and gentlemen."

The camera panned out, revealing another chair.

Claire swallowed hard. Rosie whined and put her front paws on her knee.

"Here with us today is Victoria Wolfgang, the former fiancée of the alleged serial killer the West Haven Widowmaker, otherwise known as Barney Windsor, CEO of the Heirloom Hotel chain."

Barney's mugshot appeared behind the two women. His normally slicked-back brown hair was unkempt. A sheen of sweat covered his forehead, and his steel-gray eyes burned with malice.

Claire's hands shook like she had just gripped a live wire. Papers scattered to the floor as she swept them aside. Where the hell was the remote? She didn't want to listen to this conversation. *Couldn't* listen to it.

Rosie growled.

"Victoria, how are you coping?" Marnie asked onscreen.

Something drew Claire's eyes back to the screen. Victoria looked shrunken almost, smaller and timider than Claire had last seen her. Her brown eyes were glassy, skin extra pale. On the night of her proposal, she had exuded warmth from every pore. Now she looked like a prisoner of war.

"As well as anyone who was engaged to a serial killer could be, I guess."

Marnie reached out and patted her on the hand. Victoria flinched.

"I can't imagine. Victoria, did you ever have any inclination that Barney was more sinister than he seemed? What did your friends and family think of him?"

Victoria sighed and tugged at the hem of her pencil skirt. She must have asked herself this question a million times.

"He was kind, honest, a perfect gentleman. I truly believed that he loved me. And maybe he did, in his own way. As much as a murderer is capable of love. My family adored him. He was so good with my niece and nephew. Everyone was overjoyed that we were getting married."

The camera zoomed in on her left hand, focusing on her bare ring finger.

"That's right. And the woman who planned your engagement was Barney's last attempted victim."

"Yes, Claire," Victoria said softly. She wrung her hands, rubbing a thumb over the place where the four-carat diamond ring no longer rested. "She sent me a lovely sympathy basket."

Claire's stomach twisted. A basket could never make up

for facilitating a marriage proposal to a killer. She really needed to call her. But what could she say?

"How kind. Now tell me, Victoria, did you ever notice him doing anything suspicious, like disappearing for long periods of time?"

Victoria brushed a lock of brown hair behind her ear. "He always attributed his absences to work. He owns hotels all over the state, so I believed him."

Marnie leaned forward. "Was there anything else? Did you ever catch him doing something, or trying to cover something up?"

Damn, Marnie. Give the girl a break.

Victoria stared out into the crowd, but it was clear she wasn't really looking at anything. She was so drawn that her features had retreated into her face like a corn husk doll.

"He came home with blood on his shirt once. Looking back now, I think it was right before Courtney Stevens's disappearance was announced. He said he had gotten a nosebleed. I helped him wash the blood out." Victoria gasped, starting to shake.

Claire shuddered, and the wounds all over her body pulsated and burned. She took a deep breath, which made it worse.

Marnie appeared to make eye contact with someone offstage, and she straightened up. "I understand that you haven't visited him in prison."

"No, I haven't. And I won't."

Who could blame her?

"Is there anything that you want to say to him today?" Marnie asked, gesturing to the cameras.

Victoria took a deep breath and sat taller in the beige chair. "Barney, if any part of you ever truly loved me, I wish you would cooperate with the police. Tell them where the girls are. Give their families some closure. Let them be laid to rest."

Marnie shifted her attention back to the camera. "The bodies of the five missing women attributed to the West Haven Widowmaker have never been recovered. Anyone with information is urged to contact the Pennsylvania State Police or the FBI tip line."

Pictures of the five known victims filled the screen, all with bright eyes and wide smiles. None of them knew of the horror who had watched them, waited for them to have everything they ever dreamed. Claire had spent hours staring at pictures of those girls last month when she and Luke had tried to identify the killer. She shivered. Why the hell was the past sniffing around her doorstep so aggressively today?

She turned the TV off and snapped a leash on Rosie. "Let's get out of here."

Something about the interview was odd. The way Marnie glanced offstage. Victoria's reluctance to answer questions. Something told Claire it wasn't Victoria's idea to appear on the show.

Claire pulled a floppy black hat from a hook by the warehouse door and slid on a pair of sunglasses. She pressed her ear to the crack of the door. Silence.

"Nice and quick to the car," she muttered and thrust the door open. "Oh, shit."

CHAPTER THREE

To Do:
- *Get quote for bar service*
- *Grocery shopping*
- *Burn Wendy's apartment to the ground*

Just outside the warehouse, Jason stood in a circle of reporters. Half a dozen microphones were thrust into his face. There was an audible gasp from the crowd, followed by an immediate frantic shuffling as the press rushed past him. An anchorman from *Channel Six News* shoved Jason and knocked him to the ground as if Claire was a big screen TV on Black Friday. Jason moaned, cheek resting on a faded white parking line as reporters and cameramen descended from everywhere, stepping over and occasionally on him to block Claire's path to her Audi convertible.

"Miss Hartley, what can you tell us about the ongoing investigation?" A toothy woman with bulging eyes bearing a striking resemblance to a beaver demanded. A lily that Claire had painstakingly planted in the bed around the warehouse was crushed under her Jimmy Choos. She clenched her fists.

Rosie barked fiercely. Her ears went back, and her teeth were bared. Claire reached down to pick her up as she side-stepped a reporter. If they trampled her dog, they would get way more on camera than they had bargained for.

"No comment," she muttered, not as forcefully as she intended.

"Claire, how does it feel to be the only survivor of the West Haven Widowmaker?" A reporter with a handlebar mustache shoved a microphone in her face.

"Is it true that Mr. Windsor dressed you in your wedding dress and tied you to a pillar in the parking garage? The wedding dress you were supposed to wear today?"

That stopped her dead in her tracks, and she stared at a weaselly looking gentleman with an old-school press hat.

The police had never revealed that piece of information to the public. Her eyes swung to Jason, who had gotten to his feet and seemed to be struggling to open his car door. The back of his neck was bright red. That son of a bitch.

The reporters crushed around her, jostling her. Rosie continued to bark, trying to wiggle out of her grasp.

"How do you respond to the allegations that you assaulted your ex-fiancé's girlfriend at an event last week?"

Claire edged around another reporter. Her purse dug into her shoulder blade, twice as heavy as usual because of the thick packet of legal papers stuffed inside. Had Jason told them about the lawsuit? Every face before her was desperate for a story. And they were everywhere lately—outside her business, her apartment, waiting for her as she left Luke's.

Her throat closed, and her insides twisted like she had just swallowed a bag of jacks. She needed to get away, to find air. The stink of their desperation nearly drowned her.

The midday sun was warm and the dreamy blue sky was dotted with cottony clouds, giving her something to focus on for a moment. She took a deep breath and pressed the panic button on her key fob.

Her Audi set off a shrill, piercing alarm. The startled reporters backed away long enough for Claire to break through their masses.

They rushed after her, expensive shoes smacking against the asphalt. She fumbled her keys and almost dropped them, then wrenched the driver's seat forward and deposited Rosie in the back seat. The dog seatbelt was twisted. Flashbulbs popped over her shoulder as she struggled to buckle Rosie in. Desperate shouts surrounded her. Maybe it was time to buy a four-door car. She climbed into the driver's seat and buckled her seatbelt, hands shaking as she tried to jam the key into the ignition. Angry metal music blasted out of her speakers.

Rosie barked from the back seat as Claire threw her car into reverse. A news anchor dove out of the way as she squeezed out of her parking spot.

She floored it, tires squealing on the asphalt. As she lurched onto Market Street, the vice grip on her chest loosened. The warehouse grew smaller in her rearview mirror before disappearing entirely. She drove three more blocks with no one behind her. Maybe she had lost them.

As she braked for an elderly woman at a crosswalk, Claire glanced behind her. A news van with a satellite dish idled behind her.

"Shit." She smacked her steering wheel. Could this old lady cross the street any slower? She must have been weighed down by the metric ton of cat food in her shopping bag. Maybe Claire should offer her a piggyback ride.

She took a deep breath and pressed a button on her console.

"Call Luke," she ordered. He picked up almost immediately.

"Hey, you. How was your meeting?"

"Fine. Aaron liked the ideas." The old woman inched her way onto the sidewalk, and Claire stomped on her gas pedal. The car shot forward and away from the news van. She was normally a painfully safe driver, but this was no day to dawdle.

"Are you still sold on the whole having-him-sketch-the-proposal-thing, because instead you could—"

"Not now." She turned without signaling at the next intersection. The news van blew past her. Success! Suck it, *Channel Eight News*.

"Geeze, okay. Are you on your way home?" Luke's voice, as sweet and hot as molasses in July, poured out of the speaker.

"To your house, yes," Claire said, noting the distinction. With the exception of the previous evening, she had barely been in her apartment since she was abducted. But that didn't mean Luke's sprawling country estate had earned the title of "home." He didn't even have a laminator.

"You've been there almost every night since the incident. What's the harm in calling it—"

"Luke, they're chasing me again," she interrupted. She swung into the left lane and glanced in her rearview mirror. Another news van was hot on her tail.

He swore. "Which street are you on?"

"Astor, by the park."

"Try losing them in the underground parking garage

beneath the Wilmington. Then you can take Fourth Street to Susquehanna Ave. If that doesn't work, let me know and I'll call Detective Smith to escort you. Do you still have your gate opener?"

Claire glanced at the button that was clipped to her visor. "I do."

"Good. I'm on my way back from Harrisburg now, but it'll be at least an hour till I'm there. I'll bring dinner."

"Thank you," she said, feeling slightly better. "Chinese?" Surely the sweet sting of General Tso's could erase the tide of horrific memories that had been dredged up today.

"Of course. Did you change your bandage today?"

"No, Luke. You insist that I keep doing it wrong, so I didn't bother." She rolled her eyes as she swung back into the right lane. The Wilmington Hotel—thankfully not a business owned by the hotel tycoon who had stabbed her—loomed large on the next block.

"That's probably for the better."

"Shut up. How was your day? Did Mrs. Rathfon agree to the interview?" Carly Rathfon, the mother of Widowmaker victim Shawna DeLong, had been ignoring Luke's phone calls for a week.

"We don't have to talk about it. Your day sounds shitty enough already."

Claire bit her lip. The hotel was half a block away. "I'm still interested. It's not your fault that the subject of your next documentary tried to kill me." It was, however, Luke's fault that he suspected Claire was the next intended victim of the West Haven Widowmaker and neglected to tell her about it, but she was over that. Well, almost.

She swerved into the underground parking lot without signaling. A jolt of fear struck as the sky disappeared, replaced by concrete pillars. Fluorescent lights glowed ominously overhead. The marks on her wrists burned.

Taillights lit up red in her mirror, but she was free. She tore through the parking lot as fast as she dared and out into the afternoon sun. Freedom!

"She did," Luke said calmly, as if Claire wasn't breaking ten traffic rules at once. "I could tell she was ready to slam the door in my face at first. She said the press has been relentless, especially since he got caught. But I explained the premise and gave her Ariel and Kayley's mothers' phone numbers so she could talk to them first. I'm confident that she'll call me back."

"That's great. I'm sure she will." It was hard to be a good (maybe) girlfriend in the middle of a sensationally crappy day and medium-speed car chase.

"Something else is bothering you. Your angry music is playing. Are you nervous about dinner with my mom tomorrow? I don't blame you. She's basically an irritable dragon in a pantsuit. We could pretend you're sick."

It was a tempting offer. A dragon-like mother of her maybe boyfriend was not likely to improve Claire's week. "No, that's not it. We'll talk about it when you get home. I mean, to your house."

He chuckled. "Okay. Are they still following you?"

She flicked her gaze to her rearview mirror. Surely the press weren't hiding in the Amish buggy cantering along behind her. "I think I lost them. I'm leaving town now. Should be there soon."

"Good. I'll see you soon."

She smiled as she hung up. Claire had given up on men after Jason had slept with Wendy in a bathroom at the Chamber of Commerce awards ceremony the previous year. Everything changed when Luke stormed into her apartment eight months later demanding a meeting for their joint project. Despite her best efforts, she was actually developing real feelings for the grumpy filmmaker who disparaged her career path at every turn. But they weren't really together. Were they? There had been some very steamy kisses that ended in a trip to the hospital, but they hadn't defined the relationship.

The apartment buildings and corner convenience stores of West Haven fell away behind her. As much as she loved her little apartment in the city, she couldn't deny the appeal of the wide-open spaces of the country. At Luke's house, no overly sensitive neighbors smacked the ceiling with a broomstick when she dared to watch TV past ten p.m.

She turned onto a state highway and drove past an expansive dairy farm. The cows lay in the field, staring judgmentally at her as she passed. She searched the sky, but there weren't any storm clouds on the horizon.

Rain was supposed to be good luck on your wedding day. And today had nearly been hers. The clock on the dashboard read 1:37. As hard as she tried to put it out of her mind, she had memorized every second of the wedding day schedule. She should have been taking first look photos with Jason right now. Instead, he was headed home to a scheming shrew, and Claire was recovering from a stab wound at the home of a hunky, if grumpy, filmmaker. And her beautiful, one-of-a-kind wedding dress was covered in blood, hanging in an evidence locker.

If she was being honest with herself, she had dodged a bullet by breaking off her engagement. Jason was lazy, unmotivated, and utterly trapped in the past. A football star in high school and college, he had regressed to a chronically underemployed art history major who couldn't even manage to set down the video game controller long enough to order takeout. But apparently Wendy didn't mind.

Claire glanced repeatedly in her rearview mirror as she cruised down the empty stretch of state highway, but the press didn't reappear. Her heart rate had returned to normal by the time she pressed a button and watched the newly installed gate across Luke's driveway swing open.

Guilt settled on her like a stifling flannel blanket. Because of her, a serial killer had broken into Luke's house and stamped Rosie's paw on a threatening note. She had endangered everyone she cared about.

At the end of the winding driveway stood a remarkable country home. Natural wood and stone covered the facade. Turquoise Adirondack chairs sat on the front porch. Flower beds with knockout roses and lilies were in full bloom.

The humid air hung on her as she crawled out of the car. She swatted at a gnat and flinched when a hummingbird buzzed past her ear, aiming for one of the half dozen feeders Luke had stationed around the property.

Rosie leapt out beside her and shook, releasing a cloud of warehouse dust.

"Gross, Roro. I'm going to have to vacuum the car like six times. Do you want to go swimming?"

The dog's ears perked up. Claire lugged her oversized purse on one arm and a tote bag on the other as Rosie bolted for the backyard.

Claire opened the gate, and Rosie darted inside. She pranced excitedly on the concrete edge, barking at an inflatable unicorn that listed lazily in the pool. Claire had purchased it online a few days earlier after indulging in half a bottle of merlot, and Luke had graciously blown it up for her.

"Okay, okay. Hold your horses." She reached into her

tote bag and pulled out a corgi-sized life vest. She stuffed Rosie's tiny legs into it and dodged her sloppy tongue as she strapped her into the vest. Rosie immediately flopped on her back and rolled around on the concrete.

Satisfied with her handiwork, Claire walked into Luke's pool house. She pulled down the blind on the small, square window and scanned the tree line. There weren't any reporters dangling from the trees, but it wouldn't be the first time someone had snuck onto Luke's property through the woods. She quickly changed into a bathing suit. The last thing she needed was her bare bottom on the cover of a tabloid. *Widowmaker Survivor Bares All.* Not today, Satan.

After tucking herself carefully into the triangles of her bikini, she dragged the float to the edge of the pool. Rosie gave a stubby-legged leap and landed squarely in the middle. She rolled over on the unicorn to sun her belly, her tongue flopped out in pure doggie happiness.

Claire snapped a picture before turning her phone on silent and tossing it in her bag. Her clients weren't likely to need her, and she could do with some peace before Luke came home.

She dragged another float out of the pool house and tossed it into the water. It bobbed gently while she carefully lowered herself onto it, frowning at the thick bandage on her chest. Her stab wound was like a new pet with specific rules: keep it dry, change the dressing every twenty-four hours, cover it with petroleum jelly. The alternative, as her self-proclaimed psychic mother advised, was to present a large potato and a penny to an Amish healer.

Claire closed her eyes and slid on her sunglasses, determined to push all thoughts of Wendy and the lawsuit from her mind. She wouldn't get away with this. Sure, Claire had technically beat the crap out of her at Nicole's engagement party. But if sleeping with Claire's fiancé, sabotaging her biggest proposal ever, and insulting the bride-to-be at her own party weren't punchable offenses, what were? What was she supposed to do, rob a bank for five million dollars so she didn't lose her business in case Wendy won? Kyle would figure something out. Wouldn't he?

She released the top tie of her bikini and tucked the strings underneath her, leaving the triangles to cover her bits. There was nothing she could do about the weird tan line she'd have from her massive bandage, but at least she could avoid the strings. She floated her arms out to her side and relaxed in the warmth of the summer sun.

CHAPTER FOUR

To Do:
- Call caterers—not Yuffie!
- Plan Nicole's bachelorette party

AN IRRITATING TAPPING NOISE TUGGED AT CLAIRE'S consciousness. She had been in the middle of a dream in which she had to plan a proposal using only a handful of materials given to her by the Prime Minister of Singapore. A miniature Eiffel Tower had been half-constructed from paper clips and ponytail holders when she jerked awake.

Where was she? Was she sleepwalking again?

She shot upright, and the pool float slid out from under her. The shock of the cold water hit her like an uppercut as she slid into the deep end. Sputtering, she rose to the surface and grabbed blindly for the edge of the pool, a mat of wet hair clinging to her face. Rosie barked from somewhere behind Claire.

She coughed, trying to clear the water from her lungs as she made contact with the concrete edge of the pool and dragged herself up and onto the still warm pavement. Her bikini top was now floating several feet away from the edge. Long shadows stretched across the yard. The air had a chill to it now, and she had gotten her stupid bandage wet. Luke was going to be pissed.

"And who, may I ask, are you?" a sharp, nasal voice inquired.

Claire screamed and grabbed the pool skimmer, whipping it around and knocking a lounge chair over in the process. With her other hand, she struggled to cover as much of her top half as she could.

The source of the tapping noise revealed itself to be a tall, thin brunette woman who looked alert and pissed off, like a great horned owl ready to snatch up some field mice. She stood by the pool gate, one talon-like hand clutching a phone as she stared at Claire with narrowed eyes.

"*Me*? Who the hell are you? This is private property." Was she press? Claire's heart hammered in her chest. She did not need a picture of her looking like a damp mop on the cover of the *West Haven Times*. She held the pool skimmer in front of her like a sword, fairly confident that she could slam the net over the woman's head and thrust her into the pool to make a quick getaway. But what would she do with Rosie? "How did you get through the gate?"

Rosie growled from inside her float, which was spinning. She stood in the center, barking each time she rotated to face the intruder.

The woman's arms were crossed so severely over her torso that it looked like she was trapped in an invisible straight jacket. Gray strands peppered the hair that was wound into a serpentine chignon. Large pearl studs adorned her ears, and the Armani pantsuit she wore flattered her trim figure. She certainly didn't look like a member of the press who had crawled through the woods to harass her. So who was she?

Claire jabbed the skimmer in the woman's direction. She flinched as a droplet of pool water splashed onto her cheek. An expensive pair of Italian shoes tapped impatiently on the concrete as she wiped it off. Fine lines shrouded her mouth despite looking like she had never smiled before.

"I'm Rachel. Lucas's mother," the woman said.

Shit.

"Oh my god. Ms. Islestorm, I am so sorry." The pool skimmer clattered on the concrete. Rachel looked nothing like the carefree woman in the yellow dress in the picture in Luke's den. Her cheekbones were more severe, and the light was gone from her eyes.

"We didn't expect you until tomorrow." Claire's face was hot.

Rachel's perfectly manicured eyebrows raised at the use of the word "we."

Claire turned her back to Rachel and grabbed the beach towel that was draped over the only lounge chair left standing. She wound it around herself, absolutely mortified. She took a deep breath and searched for composure before turning back to the dragon of a woman.

"I'm Claire. Very pleased to meet you. Luke has a lovely picture of you in the den." She shook the hand that was coolly offered. Rachel clutched her hand as though she was trying to squash a bug.

"Lucas never mentioned a Claire."

What the shit? Claire bit her lip. "He didn't?"

"I daresay I would have remembered my son mentioning that he was employing a topless pool girl."

Oh no she *didn't*. Claire drew herself up to her full height of five feet and three inches, but her eye level still only hit Rachel's shoulder pads.

"I am not a pool girl," she said, enunciating very clearly. "I work with Luke, not for him."

Rachel let out a shrill laugh. It was a strange noise, as though she weren't used to making it. "In what capacity?"

"We collaborate on various projects. He assists with the filmmaking portion of my business." Her hands were clenched into fists.

"And what is your business?"

Here we go. Luke's distaste for marriage was clearly learned from somewhere. Something told her this over-sized bird of prey in Prada pumps had something to do with it.

"Event planning. Specifically marriage proposals," Claire said. She squared her shoulders and stared Rachel down.

Rachel blinked in surprise. "Marriage proposals? Is planning really necessary? Aren't they supposed to be quite simple?"

"For some couples, yes. Others prefer a greater degree of thoughtfulness. Rosie, hush," Claire said to her dog, who was still barking in the pool.

Rachel glanced at the dog with disdain. She brushed an imaginary hair from her blouse.

Claire's hands were balled into fists at her side, but her mother's stern instruction on manners floated to the surface. Rachel had already seen her topless. But maybe she could mitigate some of the damage. "Could I get you anything, Rachel? Something to drink?"

"That's quite unnecessary, thank you. I believe I'll wait in the guest room until Lucas comes home."

"Let me help you with your bags," Claire said, picking up a Louis Vuitton weekend bag.

"I'll get that, thank you," Rachel said, snatching it away. She turned in a whirl of CHANEL N°5 and stormed across the patio tiles to the house.

Claire fought the urge to flip her middle finger at Rachel's retreating back.

"Oh my god," she whispered to herself, retrieving her phone. She dialed Luke's number.

"*Lucas Eugene Islestorm.*"

"Oh, shit. What did I do?"

"Remember that time that you told me your very rigid, very stern, perpetual-stick-up-the-ass of a mother was coming for dinner at your house tomorrow?" She glanced behind her, fully expecting to see Rachel rounding on her with a machete.

"Yes?" He sounded clueless.

"Remind me. What day is today? Is this tomorrow?"

"No," he said slowly.

"Then why did a velociraptor disguised as a business-woman named Rachel who claims to be your mother just drop in unannounced? And while we're at it, maybe you could explain why she has no idea who I am." Claire picked up the lounge chair she had flipped over.

"Oh, shit."

"'Oh, shit' doesn't even come close, Luke. I almost assaulted her with the pool skimmer. Your mother has seen my breasts, in broad daylight. But it's okay, because she thinks I'm just your topless pool girl."

"You were topless?"

"So not the point."

He paused. "I was going to call and tell her about you

tonight. Before she met you tomorrow. I guess she decided to come early."

A likely story. Claire righted another lounge chair so aggressively that it almost flipped into the pool. "I have been practically living with you for the past week while I recover from the worst night of my life, and you couldn't tell your mother you were harboring that stab victim who's all over the news? Does she even know what happened?"

"Not exactly."

Claire swore. "I won't be here when you get back. I'll see you for dinner tomorrow." She ended the call and flung her phone into her bag. Her fingers brushed the stack of legal papers, and a knot grew in her stomach. She ignored the phone vibrating in her purse as she scrambled to get her things together.

She dragged the unicorn float to the edge of the pool and picked Rosie up, almost tripping over the edge of the towel that was starting to unwind. Was there a judgmental gaze emanating from the oval-shaped window in the guest bedroom? She shuddered. Tossing on a T-shirt and a pair of shorts, she abandoned her floating bikini and stormed over to her car. Goosebumps prickled her skin as the sun sank below the trees.

A white Infiniti sat in the driveway, as shiny as if it had just been driven off the lot. Claire fought the urge to kick the tires as she skirted around it.

She tucked Rosie into her car seat and pulled her phone out again. Her hand froze on Nicole's contact. One of her best friends was finalizing her flower choices today. No bride needed an emergency call in the middle of that. She dialed Mindy's number instead.

"Yeah?" Mindy answered, sounding distracted.

"Mindy, I need you. This is an emergency. Even worse than the me-getting-sued thing. Can you meet at my place?"

"What the hell happened?"

"I'll explain when you get there," Claire said.

"I'll see you in thirty. I'll bring ice cream." There was the sound of a laptop snapping shut on Mindy's end.

"Thanks. I'll pick up the wine."

"Red or white?"

"Both," Claire said firmly.

"Oh boy. This must be a big one. See you soon."

Claire's face was still hot when she hung up. Rosie whined from the back seat, looking at her inquisitively. Claire practically pulled her arm out of its socket to scratch Rosie behind the ears.

Claire's anxiety slowly died down as the rolling hills of the country turned into a slew of Mexican restaurants and mom-and-pop stores. She pulled into the liquor store on the outskirts of town, leaving Rosie with the car running and the air conditioner on.

She treaded the familiar path through the store, tucking wines into the crook of her arm. When she reached for a top-shelf cabernet sauvignon, a camera shutter sound came from the cashier's desk. Claire whipped around, expecting to see a reporter. Instead she saw a sheepish looking twenty-something woman with stringy black hair. Her brown eyes were wide with surprise, and her bubble gum popped in her face.

"Sorry, ma'am, I was taking a screenshot and forgot the sound was on."

"It's okay," Claire said, turning back to the shelves. She glanced at the woman out of the corner of her eye but resumed her shopping. Surely a liquor store employee didn't moonlight as a reporter for *Channel Eight News*.

Claire walked carefully to the register, gingerly setting four bottles on the counter.

"Are you that girl? The one who escaped the Widowmaker?" The faded name tag on her brown smock read Monica.

Damn it. "I am," Claire admitted.

"I'm sorry for what happened to you. I think you're real brave."

"Thank you. Bravery had nothing to do with it though. It was fight or die."

"Would you sign this for me?" Monica dragged a pack of menthol cigarettes out of her back pocket.

Claire cringed. "Oh, I don't think that would be appropriate. Tobacco is responsible for preventable deaths of over like eight million people a year."

"Please? It's really for my daughter, Emma. She's four. Every time your picture comes on the TV she runs to watch."

"Ah. Okay. Let me see if I have something else in here." Claire dug through her purse. For a moment she wished for Luke, who always carried a tiny notebook in his pocket in case inspiration struck. She fished out an old receipt and a permanent marker. Claire scrawled "For Emma—always stand up for yourself" and her name on the back and handed it over. Her cheeks burned again. What was she doing? She wasn't a celebrity. As Monica took the receipt, the handwritten, itemized list on the front side materialized.

- 1 Penis Cake Pan
- 12 Light Up Pecker Necklaces
- 12 Bags Gummy Dicks
- 1 Pack Metallic Dick Glitter

Claire's mouth gaped open in horror, and she almost reached across the counter to snatch it back. The list was for Nicole's upcoming bachelorette party. Did a four-year-old have the reading comprehension necessary to understand traditional bachelorette party décor? Before she could demand it back, the clerk folded the paper and slid it in the back pocket of her jeans.

"Thank you. That'll be $51.07," Monica said, tapping at the register.

Apparently, there was no attempted-murder-victim discount on wine. Claire dug her credit card out and handed it over, already mentally cataloging the routes of the other liquor store in the area. She couldn't come back to this one after autographing such a penis-heavy shopping list.

The bottles rattled in the back seat of her car as she drove over one of West Haven's infamous potholes. A glass of wine, a pair of leggings, maybe a pint of ice cream. Those were the only items in her arsenal that could turn this day around. Thanks to the Rachel snafu, she didn't even get Chinese.

As Claire turned onto Beaumont Street and slapped her turn signal on for the parking garage, her heart jumped. Ever since Barney had held her in the underground parking garage of his new hotel, the sight of one sent her into an emotional tailspin. Her heart rate climbed as she pulled into her parking spot and opened the door. A light overhead flickered. Something felt wrong. The walls were too close, the air too dense. Her footsteps echoed in the emptiness. She rubbed the healing marks on her wrist from the cords that had bitten into her skin.

The unease lingered as she let Rosie out to pee. She peered into the face of each passing stranger. Barney wasn't eligible for bail. There was no reason for her to be nervous.

So why couldn't she shake the feeling that she was being watched? A tingle ran up her spine as she ushered Rosie back inside and half-ran into the stairwell. They climbed the stairs to the fourth floor, where Claire unhooked Rosie's leash so she could sniff each neighbor's beige, unremarkable door.

Were her eyes playing tricks on her, or was her front door ajar? She narrowed her eyes. Oh, shit. The front door to her apartment hung open.

Her stomach clenched like she was hurtling along in a car that had just slammed to a stop. She had definitely locked the door before she left that morning. One of her least-endearing qualities was performing a dance move every time she did something important, like locking a door or turning off the stove. Her right elbow was still tender where she had banged it into the doorframe while performing a step-ball-change on the way to the office. So, who was in her apartment?

In an instant, she was beneath the Heirloom Hotel, hands bound behind her as a dark shadow approached. She fell against the wall, scrabbling for her Taser and fighting to take a breath. Her pulse beat behind her eyes. Did she call the police? Luke?

Rosie wandered into the apartment, completely unperturbed.

Claire found her voice at last.

"*Rosie!*" she shouted, dropping everything she held and diving headfirst into the apartment. Bottles rattled in the hallway. She landed hard on her elbow as she fell next to Rosie and rolled to cover her body with her own.

"Miss Hartley?" came a vaguely familiar voice from her kitchen.

A man stood next to the island. Scratch that—a mountain of a man. He was easily the tallest person she had ever seen. A ton of electronic equipment was scattered in front of him. His face was half in shadow.

Claire leapt to her feet, holding Rosie on her hip like a baby. She reached for her Taser, but she had dropped her purse in the hallway. She grabbed a wooden croquet ball from a basket on her bookshelf and threw it as hard as she could at the intruder's face.

He caught it with one hand, as easy as breathing.

"Who the hell are you?" she demanded, backing away.

The man stepped into the slender beam of fluorescent light. "It's okay, Claire. I'm not surprised you don't remember me. You were a little indisposed when we met last week. I'm Sawyer." He held a hand the size of a dinner plate to his chest. "I run a security company, and I'm here to install a system for you—Luke said you wouldn't be home, so he gave me your spare key. Sorry for startling you. Is your dog okay?"

He was talking fast, clearly embarrassed. He wore a black polo with Sanctum Security stitched into the left breast...make that gigantic pec. Bulging arm muscles threatened to rip through the hem of his shirt sleeves. His eyes were a warm amber color, and they crinkled kindly in the corners. A no-nonsense crew cut topped off his look. He stepped between the island and the bar and closed the gap between them. One hand that was bigger than her torso extended, and she shook it reluctantly.

Claire glanced down. The dog was wiggling and whining, fighting to get down, but seemed unhurt. "She's fine. Sawyer? The one who found me—"

"Outside the hotel, yes." He held onto her hand a beat longer than was necessary.

A memory struck her like lightning—staggering down a

dirt road in her wedding dress, trying to stay conscious as a wounded, panty-stealing psychopath had chased after her. Pine needles had bitten into her palms when she'd fallen. Her dress, drenched with blood, had weighed a thousand pounds as she'd half crawled down the driveway. A sedan had roared down the road, nearly running her over. Sawyer had jumped out and incapacitated Barney with his stun gun. Claire's only words of thanks to Sawyer that evening had been a plea for extra guacamole when she mistook his 911 call for a taco order.

Her chest wound ached as she pulled her hand back and clutched it to her heart. "I never had the chance to say thank you. If you hadn't found me, I would almost certainly be dead."

"You did. I got the gift basket yesterday. The beef jerky was fantastic. And I never had the chance to apologize. I can't believe I was working for a serial killer."

She flinched as though she had been slapped. That was right—Sanctum had been contracted to provide security around the hotel as construction was being finished.

"Sorry," he said, taking a step back. He tapped his head with a knuckle. "Don't always think before I speak. You were handling yourself really well before I got there, if that makes it any better. Most people wouldn't have gotten that far. I'm sorry for what happened to you, and I'm sorry I didn't get there sooner."

His gaze drifted to her gray scoop neck T-shirt and the exposed bandage. Shit, she hadn't changed it today, and she had totally gotten it wet when she plunged into the pool. Luke would have a fit. Not that she cared what he thought. He couldn't even manage to tell his own mother than he was seeing someone. Sort of.

She shrugged and tugged the neckline of her shirt to

cover the bandage and the other, more shallow mark on her neck. As if the stabbing wasn't bad enough, Barney had also thoughtfully traced a mark of some sort into her neck.

"Do you mind if I install the system while you're here?" He picked up his toolbox, as though certain she was about to banish him from the premises.

"That's fine," Claire said slowly. How was it possible that she was so frequently surprised by strange men letting themselves into her apartment?

Sawyer picked up a complicated-looking LED screen the size of a sandwich and began tinkering with it. "I'm also one of Kyle's groomsmen. We played lacrosse together in high school."

Ah. So this was the towering Samoan who had accidentally broken another player's jaw with a lacrosse ball in eleventh grade. The legend suddenly seemed more credible.

"I'm the maid of honor. It's good to formally meet you," she said, smiling a bit. Sawyer exuded warmth, and he had a gentle demeanor despite his gigantic stature. "You said Luke gave you a key? Did he authorize this system installation?"

He glanced down at a work order. "Yep. Already paid in full."

Claire swore. If she wanted a security system, she would have bought one herself.

"You're free to refuse the service, of course. But considering your unique circumstances, I think you would feel safer with it."

"Let's hope I never need it." She was confident that she had paid her dues in the crime victim world. One traumatic kidnapping should surely earn her a couple of crime-free years. She was a proposal planner, not a detective, despite the murder binder she had put together on the West Haven Widowmaker. It was currently collecting dust in her living room. The mystery was solved, the case closed. She was ready to take off her investigator hat and return to the world of happily ever afters. If she could just kick the crippling anxiety that seemed to have cropped up in the last week, she would be unstoppable. Oh, and the sleepwalking. What was the deal with that?

Rosie wiggled and Claire set her on the floor. Ever the guard dog, she immediately ran over and sniffed the hem of Sawyer's pants. She sat on her hindquarters and looked up at him happily, tongue flopping out of the space where she was missing a few teeth.

"Who's this little princess?" Sawyer's head disappeared behind the bar.

Claire cocked her head. She walked around the corner of the bar to find Sawyer splayed out on his back next to the kitchen island, hugging Rosie to his chest and scratching her behind the ears.

Rosie barked and licked his face, rolling around on his barrel of a chest.

"Rosie," Claire scolded. "Sorry," she said. "She loves meeting new people." She opened her junk drawer, fondly known as her Drunk Drawer because it was the one place in her apartment that she allowed to be completely disorganized, and handed Sawyer a lint roller.

"The best part of this job is meeting all the dogs," he said, rolling over and standing back up. He brushed half-heartedly at the dog hair spread over his chest, then shrugged and set the roller down.

She laughed. "That is an unexpected perk." She walked back to the hallway and brought her purse and bottles of wine inside. Fortunately, none of the bottles had shattered during her dramatic game of hallway hot potato.

"Are you having a party?" Sawyer asked, gesturing to the

four bottles of wine. "I can come back at a more convenient time."

Claire sighed. "No, just me, my assistant, and our inability to cope with life."

She hadn't noticed the night before, but the apartment smelled stale. She sat her purse down on the table and swiped her finger across the wooden surface. Her finger left a trail through a thin layer of dust. This was her safe heaven, her second office. Or at least it had been before Barney Freakin' Windsor had broken into it and stolen her wedding dress.

She crossed to the window by her kitchen table and slid it open, pulling at the screen out of habit. It didn't budge. The sun had dropped low on the horizon. Families flocked down the sidewalks, ducking into the pub on the corner. A full moon had already risen, out of place against the blue sky. Her mom, the self-proclaimed psychic, would surely blame the moon for the chaos that was unfolding. Or maybe Mercury was in retrograde.

Claire opened her refrigerator and unloaded the wine. An old, wrinkled lemon sat by itself in her produce drawer. After pulling it out, she sliced it quickly on a wooden cutting board and dropped it in her sink. She ran the water and turned on the garbage disposal. Old lemon smell was better than stale apartment smell.

Rosie, who was completely incapable of handling any appliances that made noise, stopped sitting on Sawyer's foot and scrambled into the kitchen. Her ears bent backward as she bared her teeth, barking at the disposal until it was turned off.

"Drama queen," Claire muttered, shaking her head and scrubbing the sink with a sponge. Luke shouldn't have scheduled work on her apartment without giving her a heads up to clean.

She turned the water off and surveyed the rest of her kitchen. Her grandmother's simple white vase, which had been shattered when Barney broke into her apartment, had been clumsily glued back together by Mindy. It now served as a bookend for a binder of Claire's favorite recipes, which she kept on the counter.

"You must have had a shitty day. There's a lot of tension in your shoulders," Sawyer observed.

Huh. She hadn't even noticed, but he was right. She rolled her shoulders and neck. "You're not wrong."

"Want to talk about it? I'm happy to listen, free of charge," he said as he opened a laptop. Golden eyes framed by thick, dark lashes peered over the top. The best eyelashes were always wasted on men.

"Not really," Claire said. Certainly not with a stranger who had last seen her looking like an extra in a horror movie. She pawed through her cutlery drawer. Where the hell was her backup corkscrew? Her good one was at Luke's, and all she had left was a novelty one shaped like a mustache.

Sawyer nodded and looked down at his screen. There was silence except for the tapping of large fingers on keys.

But then again, he was an impartial third party. He had been there that night, saw what no one else had witnessed. No need to hide her crazy from him.

"It's just," she began, stabbing the corkscrew into the first bottle. "I thought I was done with shitty things happening to me. I was stalked, kidnapped, and almost murdered. You would think that would be enough bad things for a decade at least, if not a lifetime. But no. My wacko nemesis is suing me because I punched her in the face after she showed up uninvited to Nicole and Kyle's engagement dinner and insulted the bride."

Claire yanked on the cork, but it wouldn't budge. Her phone vibrated. Luke was calling. There was no way in hell she was about to answer. All the thoughts she had been keeping deep down were suddenly rushing to the surface, ready to explode all over this man she barely knew.

"And then," she continued, letting her voice raise with her frustration, "she decided my ex-fiancé, whom she is currently sleeping with, was the perfect person to serve the summons to me in the middle of a meeting with a client. Then I got chased by the paparazzi, wound up at my sort-of boyfriend's house where his extremely stern and terrifying mother showed up out of the blue and startled me so much that I almost drowned. Then some girl asked me to sign a pack of menthols for her four-year-old like I'm a Kardashian. Oh, and let's not forget the minor fact that today was supposed to be my wedding day."

Sawyer gently closed a hand over Claire's. He tugged her fingers off the corkscrew and took the bottle from her. He tugged on it once and the cork slid out smoothly with a satisfying *pop.*

"And now I can't even open my own damn wine." She buried her hands in her hair. All that dumping and she hadn't even mentioned the sleepwalking and possible dumpster taco. What a freakin' day.

He poured a glass and set it in front of her. He then crossed to the corner of the dining area where she had abandoned her rolled-up yoga mat after a class. He handed it to her and she looked at it. Was he telling her she needed to clean up despite everything she had just said? If so, he was going to be leaving without his testicles.

"You do yoga? I think you need this."

Ah. So he wasn't telling her to clean up. Good. "I think you're right," she said, clutching the roll of foam. "Thank you."

"I won't be too loud," he said, moving some complicated-looking electronics to the bar so they were closer to the front door. "Take your time."

Claire wandered into the living room and took the strap off her mat. She shot a glance over her shoulder at Sawyer, who had pulled out a measuring tape and a stud finder. She unfurled the mat in one swift motion. A small cloud of dust soared into the air. Between proposal season and the abduction, it had been awhile since her last class.

"Gross," Claire said, immediately sneezing.

Before she could center herself with yoga, there was still work to be done.

She walked to her bedroom and popped the door open with her foot. Keeping her back to the wall, she crossed to the far side of the room and took down the sword that was mounted between the two windows facing the street. It had arrived in a care package from her mother and stepfather a couple days after the abduction. Even though Barney was behind bars, her home hadn't felt secure since he broke in a month ago. Sawyer probably would have noticed if there was an intruder in her apartment, but it didn't hurt to double-check.

Gripping the weapon tightly, she dropped to the carpeted floor and flipped her bed skirt up. She stuck the sword under the bed and waved it around for a moment before ducking to inspect. There weren't any murderers lurking under the box springs, but she had accidentally stabbed the emergency escape ladder her mother had sent her despite Claire having a functioning fire escape outside her bedroom window. The closet was clear too. She crossed to the window and dragged the blinds down with one finger, peeking through the hole.

The rusty, rickety fire escape swayed in a sudden gust of wind, and no murderers clung to it. She breathed a sigh of relief and mounted her sword then rifled through her drawers. She hadn't done laundry since getting out of the hospital, so it was slim pickings. Leggings with a hole in the knee were stuffed all the way in the back.

Claire returned to the living room and stepped onto her mat. Sawyer tapped at a small console he had installed on her wall. She wasn't about to let a strange man fiddle around in her kitchen unsupervised. The muscles behind her knees burned as she bent forward, craning her neck to keep him in her eyeline. What were the odds that she could escape if Sawyer turned out to also be a homicidal maniac? Slim to none.

Her phone vibrated in the pocket of her leggings. Luke again. She ignored the call.

The edge of Aaron's proposal binder stuck out of her purse. A knot twisted her stomach. Aaron was by all accounts a normal, non-murderous person. His background check had come up clean, he wasn't on any dating websites, and his date with Jane that Claire and Mindy had spied on had been nothing short of endearing. But Barney had been equally unsuspicious. What if Claire was wrong again?

She dipped lower until her fingers touched her ankles, then her toes, then the mat. There would be time to worry about her clients later. She bent and breathed, relaxing into the pose. The fabric of her bandage scraped against her holey leggings.

Even though she was getting sued by a venomous demon disguised as a proposal planner and she had just had whatever was the opposite of a meet-cute with Luke's mom, there was so much to be grateful for. Her friends, family, and dog were safe. The West Haven Widowmaker was behind bars, and she had put an end to his killing spree. Despite the psychological damage and feelings of panic she had every time she encountered a parking garage, it was over. Life could return to normal.

She stretched, reached, and breathed through several rounds of sun salutation, feeling calmer after each repetition. She blocked out everything that was wrong with her life and instead focused on the rhythm of her breath. In, out. Easy, controllable. There was no Wendy, no Jason, no stab wound burning with each breath.

She promptly lost any sense of Zen when someone knocked on her front door. Her heart staggered. But she was being an idiot; she was expecting company.

By the time she made her way to the front door, Sawyer had already opened it. Mindy entered, raven hair piled into a messy bun on top of her head. A lavender-colored sweatshirt with a coffee-colored stain on the arm hung off one tanned shoulder. Her green eyes locked on to Sawyer as she crossed the threshold. A flush crept over her cheeks, and she tugged at her sleeve.

"Hey, Min," Claire said, unable to keep a hint of amusement out of her tone.

"Hey, boss," Mindy said, offering a large paper bag that had a wet spot in one corner.

"Thanks." Claire took it from her and set it down on the kitchen island, withdrawing two pints of ice cream.

Mindy gave Sawyer one last look and followed Claire around the bar and into the kitchen. Mindy backed up to the kitchen sink, which was out of view from the front door.

"I didn't realize Sawyer was going to be here," she whispered furiously, so quietly Claire almost didn't hear her. "He puts the *moan* in Samoan."

Mindy grabbed a spoon from the dish drying rack and looked into it. She tugged the elastic from her bun and let her hair fall to the small of her back. After running her hands through it, she tugged her top down an inch.

Claire smiled. Her mother's persistent etiquette lessons resurfaced. An introduction was necessary. "Oh, Mindy, I don't know if you've met Sawyer. He's one of Kyle's groomsmen. Luke apparently commissioned him to install a security system. I was not expecting it."

"She almost decapitated me with a croquet ball," Sawyer called from the front door.

"Yes, we met...uh, last week," Mindy said, tactfully skirting around the exact circumstances of their encounter. "Thank you for saving my best friend's life. I owe you one," she added, crossing back to the front door and firmly shaking Sawyer's hand.

"Any time," he said, smiling as he turned back to the security system. If he noticed that she had suddenly taken her hair down, he didn't say anything.

"Speaking of lifesaving," Mindy said, digging through her purse. "Put this on." She handed Claire a smart watch.

"Ooh, I love it! But my birthday's not for another two months. You didn't need to get me anything." Claire slid the watch on her left wrist and admired it.

"It's not really for you. It's for us. It has GPS, so if you ever get abducted again, we'll be able to find you."

"You are a lifesaver," she said to Mindy. "Let's hope I never need it. So, about this impending lawsuit."

"Oh, Claire. We're going to ruin that bitch's day." Mindy drew Claire in for a tight hug. The smell of honeysuckle engulfed them.

Mindy took a step back. "I hope you don't mind, but I called in some reinforcements."

As if on cue, there was a knock at the front door. Sawyer glanced through the peep hole and opened it again. Nicole and Kyle entered, smiling sympathetically.

"Dude." Kyle, lawyer extraordinaire and Nicole's boyfriend since their college days, greeted Sawyer with an overly enthusiastic back slap, then pulled him into a bro hug.

"I thought you were working on your flowers," Claire said. Her friends had just dropped everything on their very busy schedules to help her at a moment's notice. The weight of the day lifted off her.

"Screw the flowers. Roses, lilies, they all die the next day," Nicole said, elbowing her way into the foyer and dropping a bag of junk food on the counter.

"Actually, you can donate your flowers to nursing homes after the—oof," Claire said as Nicole swooped in and hugged her tightly.

"Plus, we all wanted to be with you, considering what today could have been." Nicole pulled back and held Claire at arm's length, looking her up and down as though she were searching for physical scars from the trauma of her cancelled wedding.

"I heard you could use some legal advice," Kyle interrupted, reaching for the manila envelope Claire had tossed onto her table. His words slurred slightly. All the papers promptly fell out onto the floor.

Nicole laughed as she ducked and gathered them into a neat pile. Kyle settled into a chair at the dining room table and pored over the documents.

"Sorry—Kyle had a rough day between work and not giving a shit about flowers, so I made him a mega margarita before we came. He's a little tipsy," she whispered in Claire's ear.

Sawyer had retreated to her dining room window, where he was setting up a small, complicated-looking device. As her friends bustled around making snacks and pulling glasses from her cabinet, warmth filled her from head to toe. When so much of her world was changing, it was a relief to be surrounded by friends. Mindy gripped the neck of a bottle of sparkling wine, wiggling the cork with her thumbs and grunting. A vein stood out on her otherwise flawless forehead.

The cork rocketed out of the bottle and smacked off the ceiling. Whoops. Hopefully, her landlord wouldn't notice the dent at his next visit.

Mindy poured the champagne into four glasses and handed them out. The crisp bubbles hit Claire's tongue like Pop Rocks. Kyle drank his in one gulp and banged the glass onto the table. He walked over to Sawyer, who had moved back to the front door, and started a conversation about football. Apparently, his sage legal advice would have to wait.

"So, what else is going on? I can tell it's not just the lawsuit that's bothering you." Nicole mopped up Kyle's splattered champagne and rinsed the rag in the sink.

Claire frowned and leaned against the kitchen island. "I met Luke's mom today."

Nicole whirled. Water dribbled onto the hardwood floor. "Today? I thought she was coming tomorrow?"

Claire retold the harrowing tale of her encounter with Rachel. "And that's not even the worst part."

Nicole's eyes were wide. "What could possibly be worse than assaulting your potential future mother-in-law with a pool skimmer while topless?"

It was definitely too early to label Rachel a possible future mother-in-law. Yikes, what a nightmare that would be. "He didn't tell her that we're...whatever we are. She didn't know who I was."

Nicole's mouth fell open. "Oh my god. He didn't tell her anything about you? Not even the part where he knew the girl who got kidnapped and almost murdered? Sorry," she apologized quickly at the look Claire gave her.

"I guess not. I didn't stick around long enough to figure out. He's called me like fifteen times since I left," Claire said, sliding her phone across the island. "I guess I should be glad I'm not the only person he withholds information from."

Nicole flipped the phone over and twisted a strand of her thick brown hair between her fingers, her signature stressed-out move.

"Kyle always said Luke's family was never very touchy-feely," she said in a hushed tone. "Maybe he just didn't know how to bring it up to her. What was she like?"

"Like a dildo made out of ice. She was stamping her Prada shoes on the concrete when I woke up and then she proceeded to judge me."

"To be fair, you were topless."

"It was an accident," Claire said, picking up her glass of wine and downing half of it in one swallow. First impressions were so important. When she'd first met Jason's mom, she'd worn a perfectly pressed blouse and had a hostess gift in one hand and a homemade dessert in the other. How had her first encounter with Luke's mom gone so horribly wrong?

Nicole stopped twisting her hair. "What are you going to do about dinner tomorrow?"

"Drink a lot of wine and say as little as possible." What were the odds that a combination of carefully selected wine and an overly elaborate dinner menu would erase the memory from Rachel's mind? Maybe the situation was still salvageable.

There was another knock at Claire's front door, and everyone froze. Kyle held a karate pose. Sawyer glanced through the peephole and turned to Claire.

"It's Luke," he said to her with a question in his eyes.

Ugh. "It's fine. Let him in."

It would be easier to yell at him if they were in the same room. Sawyer cracked the door open.

Luke, looking slightly disheveled and alarmed, burst through the front door, carrying pizza boxes. "Claire," he said, zeroing in on her. "We need to talk."

Nicole picked up her champagne flute and walked straight out of the kitchen into the living room. She started a loud conversation with Kyle and Mindy about cloth napkins. Sawyer walked back into the hallway and fiddled with the window between the bedroom and bathroom. Hopefully, he was planting a motion sensor and not rigging it so he could sneak in and murder her later.

"I don't really feel like talking, Luke," she said, leaning against her refrigerator. She wanted nothing more than to collapse into bed and sleep for a year. "This has been the worst day since... well, since last week."

He crossed over to her and put his keys and the boxes on the kitchen island. He slipped his hand over her cheek, caressing with his thumb. "Look, I'm sorry I didn't tell my mom about you. But to be fair, we don't talk about anything but work and the stock market. It's the Islestorm way."

Claire bit her lip. She had been known to conceal things from her mother. Maybe she had reacted too harshly. The back of her neck prickled. Someone was watching her.

Sawyer's golden eyes shone from the end of the hallway, half in shadow.

She dropped her voice. "You're still in trouble. She saw my boobs. My *boobs*, Luke. Painfully white as a freshly sliced bagel."

"You were really topless?" he asked, cocking an eyebrow.

"Due to an unfortunate near-drowning incident, yes, your mother was the lucky fifteenth person to accidentally see my breasts this month." Policemen, friends, paramedics—a literal parade of people had witnessed her blood-drenched bosom. She should probably never go out in public again.

"You are the sexiest woman alive." Luke lowered his mouth to hers and pulled her roughly toward him. He dipped her right in the middle of the kitchen.

Claire balled her hands at her sides and went as rigid as a board. Luke kissed her harder and eventually she wrapped her arms around his neck, laughing in spite of herself. The longer she knew Luke, the harder it was to stay mad at him. Strength rippled in his neck and shoulders as he held her, and desire stirred deep in her belly. Surely her stab wound had healed enough to take a ride on the Luke Express.

When he brought her back up, she took a step back and crossed her arms. "I'm still eighty percent mad at you."

"But I brought your favorite pizza," he said, gesturing at a pair of cardboard boxes on the island.

"Fifty percent mad at you," she corrected.

"And a cannoli."

"Damn it. Okay, fine." She leaned forward and gave him a tiny peck on the cheek. It was getting too late in the day to murder him anyway.

"So what's going on? You said something terrible happened today."

"Oh," she said, picking up her wineglass and immediately downing what was left. She shuddered and made a face.

"This can't be good."

"It's not good. It's awful. Do you remember Wendy?"

"Your psychopath stalker?" He crossed his arms, clearly bracing for the worst.

"One of many. She's suing me."

"You're joking."

"Nope. Jason served me the papers this morning."

Luke's face reddened, and his eyes narrowed. "She got Jason involved?"

"Yep. Just what I needed."

"What did he say to you?" There was danger in Luke's eyes.

"Whoa, calm down there, alpha male." She laid a hand on his chest. "Just the usual. He was sorry I got kidnapped, et cetera. Not sorry enough to decline serving me papers, though, I guess."

His frown deepened. "What's she suing you for?"

"Assault and battery," Kyle chimed in from the other room. "It's a pretty clear-cut case, unfortunately. You did kind of beat the shit out of her. But don't worry, we'll figure something out." Apparently, he had sobered up enough not only to provide legal counsel but also to eavesdrop.

Claire grimaced. "I still maintain that she deserved it."

"She did," Luke said, drawing her into his arms again.

She breathed in his familiar scent and relaxed, smiling in spite of her shitty day. They picked up the pizza boxes and made their way into the living room.

Halfway through her second slice, a hand landed on Claire's shoulder. She nearly jumped out of her skin.

"Sorry." Sawyer withdrew his hand. "I'm pretty much

finished installing your system. Can I show you a few things?"

"Of course. Thank you."

He brought her to the front door and showed her how to operate the video doorbell and alarm. Luke's eyes burned into her as she connected the system to an app on her phone. What was the deal with all the staring? He was the one who had hired Sawyer to install the stupid system in the first place.

Sawyer stepped into the hallway and closed the front door to demonstrate how the camera worked.

"What's the password?" Claire called through the door. Only the bottom of his chin was visible on the monitor.

"Shiraz?" he guessed.

She opened the door and welcomed him back inside. "I'm entirely too predictable if you guessed it on the first try," she joked.

Sawyer smiled, revealing shockingly white teeth. "Do you have any questions?"

"I think you covered it all," she said.

He reached into his back pocket and pulled out a business card. "If you think of anything, here's my work number. Or," he said, shooting a glance across the room at Luke, "if you're interested in learning some self-defense techniques, I teach classes. After seeing your reflexes earlier, I think you would do great. The foundation is there, all you need is practice. It might bring you some peace of mind."

"Thank you, Sawyer," she said, smiling warmly. "I may have to take you up on that."

She held out a hand, and he clasped it in his own, completely engulfing hers.

"See you later, guys," Sawyer said as he stepped out the door. "Kyle, see you on Sunday for the game?"

"You know it," Kyle said over a mouthful of pizza as Sawyer disappeared.

Luke stood and walked over to Claire. "What's the verdict?" He gestured toward the control panel.

"It's nice, I think. You didn't have to do it, but thank you." She looped her pinky through his.

"Welcome," he said, pulling her to him. His hand burrowed in her hair as he lowered his mouth to hers. Tingles shot from her fingers to her toes. As far as apologies went, this one was right on the money.

Kyle cleared his throat loudly. Claire and Luke broke apart, laughing. Luke swatted her on the butt as they sat back down on her overstuffed couch and spent the evening with their friends. Today had been a far cry from the perfect wedding day Claire had imagined, but even flashing her (maybe) boyfriend's mother and getting sued by her arch-nemesis was better than marrying an adulterous douchebag.

CHAPTER FIVE

To Do:
- Call the VA clinic to confirm leg delivery
- Research firework companies

"Today's the big day, Tyler!" Claire exclaimed as her client opened his front door. "Are you excited?"

Jerry, one of Claire's camera crew, stood behind her on the porch, video camera in hand.

"You have no idea," Tyler said with a grin and rolled his wheelchair onto the front porch, then spun around to lock the door. A frayed T-shirt with the word "Army" written in capital letters stretched across his broad chest. His left arm had a full sleeve of tattoos, featuring a flaming eagle and album art from a metal band that Claire had listened to in college.

She gripped his hand. "It's going to be great. Let's get this show on the road."

Tyler tossed her a set of keys, and she managed to catch them. He led the way down a ramp and along the pathway to a handicap-accessible van.

The cameraman continued to film as Claire started up the van. The side door opened automatically, and a ramp unfolded itself. Tyler, clearly used to the boarding process, rolled onto it smoothly and entered the car.

Today was going to be a much better day. She hadn't woken up in the middle of the street with a dumpster taco. The paparazzi must have had a bigger story to chase, because she hadn't seen anyone all day. She hadn't even assaulted anyone with a pool skimmer. And she got to work on one of her most romantic and heart-wrenching proposals to date. She was in her element.

"So, Tyler, why don't you tell the camera why today is such a big deal," she encouraged from the driver's seat. Jerry turned around to film.

"Today is a big deal because I am getting new legs," he said, patting his thighs. Both his legs stopped a few inches below the knee, and he wore compression socks over the healing skin.

"And thanks to some help from the VA and Moon Prosthetics, I'll be able to kneel and propose to my girlfriend, Ericka, when she comes home from her deployment next week. She has no idea."

"And what else is part of Ericka's homecoming surprise?"

"I bought us a house!" He smiled proudly.

Claire smiled and wiped a stray tear away with her thumb.

"I saw that. You're already breaking your promise," Tyler teased from the back of the van.

"I'm sorry," she said, sniffling. "It's just so romantic. War hero is injured while fighting for his country, falls in love with his nurse, and welcomes her home from her deployment by proposing to her in the home he bought for them. It's just beautiful."

"I couldn't have done any of this without you," he said. "I didn't even know about the down payment program until you found it. And you organized those volunteers to paint the house and move everything in for free."

She shrugged, sniffling and trying to collect herself as they pulled into the prosthetic office's parking lot. "It's nothing. You meet a lot of people in my line of work. I'm honored to help."

They had barely taken their seats in the waiting room when a physician assistant in blue scrubs popped open a door in the corner of the room. "Tyler Roberts?"

Claire and Jerry followed as Tyler wheeled his way back down a long hallway, passing several exam rooms. She made eye contact with the receptionist just before passing through the door. Claire nodded, and the receptionist left her chair.

The physician assistant pressed a button, and a set of double doors opened to reveal the physical therapy room. The fluorescent lighting was harsh, and everything smelled like disinfectant. A set of steel parallel bars stood in the middle of the room.

It wasn't the most romantic setting for this portion of the proposal story. It was too bad the parallel bars weren't in an emerald-green meadow dotted with wildflowers, or maybe on a white sand beach next to turquoise waters. But not every part of a proposal could be romanticized. Unless she could get Jerry to film a sunset workout montage of Tyler getting used to his new legs. *Hmmm.* Philadelphia wasn't that far away; she could totally envision Tyler running up the Rocky steps.

She flipped open her binder and scribbled a quick note.

Moments later, a doctor knocked on the door and then entered, carrying a large box.

At a nod from Tyler, Jerry began filming. Within minutes, the doctor had secured new prosthetics to Tyler's legs. She made several adjustments and wheeled him over to the parallel bars.

Tyler's mouth was set, face hardened in concentration. Jerry filmed from the opposite end of the bars.

"Okay," the doctor said, stepping back from the table. "Now take it easy, but I want you to try to get to your feet and hold on to these bars." She gripped Tyler's left arm firmly, and Claire leapt up and supported his right.

Together they lifted him out of his chair. Tyler gripped the bars on either side and straightened his back. He wobbled for a moment and then stood strong.

"How does it feel?" the doctor asked.

"This is incredible," he said, looking down at his feet. "I'm standing for the first time in over a year." He took a wobbly step forward.

Tears pricked at Claire's eyes again, but she blinked them away. Tyler was amazing. He easily could have given up after his injury and subsequent discharge. Instead, he persevered. Through rehab and his transition to civilian life, he had never let his injury hold him back. He had a job, a home, a ton of hobbies, and a steadfast devotion to his girlfriend. The earth-shattering trauma he had endured did not define him. How did he do it?

"Be careful," his doctor cautioned. "Don't do too much too fast. Get comfortable with them."

Tyler gripped the bars for a moment as he wobbled, but then he took another step. And another. Then he let go of the railing all together. His steps were clumsy, like a baby learning to walk for the first time.

He made it all the way to the end of the parallel bars, turned around, and kept going. He pushed his wheelchair out of the way with one foot and took his hands off the bars.

"Maybe you'd like to take them for a spin out in the hall-way?" the doctor asked, holding the door open. "Carefully," she added.

Tyler straightened his spine and took careful, measured steps across the room. He crossed the threshold, showing no signs of slowing down. Jerry stepped out in front of him to keep filming. Claire and the doctor followed immediately behind, pushing a physical therapy chair in case he lost his footing.

Dozens of workers lined the hallway, dressed in red, white, and blue scrubs. They clapped and cheered as he made his way slowly down the hallway. It was only here, surrounded by a crowd of supporters dressed in the colors of the country he had defended and sacrificed for, that Tyler broke down. Tears streamed down his face, and he slowly made his way, nodding at the doctors and nurses.

All four of Tyler and Ericka's parents waited at the end of the hallway. Tyler nearly stumbled into his dad's arms. There wasn't a dry eye in the bunch.

***

AN HOUR LATER, CLAIRE PULLED INTO TYLER'S DRIVEWAY with a joyful heart. Every cell in her body shimmered with energy and light as she pulled the door open so Tyler could exit. Tyler had reluctantly transitioned back to his wheel-chair, as the doctor had firmly instructed him to ease into using his prosthetics. She walked him to the front door, a prosthetic leg in each hand. It was going to be a stunningly beautiful proposal for two wonderful people.

She deposited his new legs in the bedroom. A flash of light from the window revealed the red marks on her wrists where she had rubbed her skin raw trying to escape. The joy evaporated. A knot grew in her stomach.

"Hey, Tyler?" she asked as she turned to leave.

He spun around to face her. "Yeah?"

"Sorry if this is a weird time to ask. How did you…" she paused, searching for the words. "Overcome everything that happened to you?"

Tyler pressed his hands together. "It was tough. Really tough. I was angry for a long time." He trained his eyes on the bay window in the living room, and he looked a little older than he had in the car.

"I don't think I would have been able to dig myself out if it wasn't for my therapist," He added.

Therapy. It figured.

"He helped me figure out how to let go of the anger, how to move forward," Tyler continued. "He reminded me that I'm so much more than my limitations. And then there was Ericka, of course. She was my rock, my legs, my wings. She gave me something to fight for. I knew she deserved the man I could be, not the angry, bitter shell that was left behind."

Claire bit her lip. The feelings were back. Another tear threatened to leak out. "Hey, save that for your proposal speech, okay?"

Tyler's gaze swung back to her. His brow furrowed. "Are you doing okay? I know you said you didn't want to talk about it—"

"I'm fine," Claire interrupted with a smile. "I just think you're amazing. And I'm really glad you're in a better place." She leaned over and gave him a hug.

"If you ever want to talk about it—"

"Thank you, Tyler. Really." She straightened back up. "Seven more days. Oh, here." She pulled a laminated sheet from her purse and handed it to him. "The master timeline for the next week. I'll see you soon."

She stepped down the ramp and got back into her car. Tyler waved from the window, looking slightly less happy than he had earlier. Damn it. She should have just kept her questions to herself.

"Why don't you just ask your clients about the most traumatic event of their lives, dumbass?" She muttered to herself as she waved back.

As she backed up, she caught a glimpse of herself in the mirror. With her streaky mascara, she now bore an undeniable resemblance to Marilyn Manson. Awesome. That would definitely help repair her relationship with Rachel.

She pulled into a parking spot at the grocery store and refocused on the next task—dinner with Luke's velociraptor of a mother. She had completely and utterly blown her first impression. Was it even possible to recover from a faux pas of that magnitude? And what would it be like to dine with a frigid, machete-up-the-ass defense attorney like Rachel? Claire had a sinking suspicion that even if she secretly hired a team of three-star Michelin chefs, the dinner would not be up to Rachel's standards.

Claire stepped inside the store and dialed Nicole's number.

"Hey, Claire. What's up?"

"Just trying to mentally prepare for my dinner with the Antichrist." She inspected a hunk of romaine lettuce and set it back down.

"Oh, god. I forgot that was tonight. What are you going to make?"

"Five courses. Bacon-wrapped scallops, crab bisque, garden salad, chicken marsala, and banoffee pie."

"That's ambitious," Nicole said. There was a shuffling sound on her end. "If that doesn't convince her that you're awesome, nothing will."

"She's probably a vegetarian." Luke had declined to offer any details about his mother's dietary habits. It was not his most helpful moment.

"Then that bitch can have salad and pie."

Claire snort laughed and clapped a hand over her mouth. "I love you. How's your day going?"

"Excellent. I'm prepping a shoot for Venor's alumni event tomorrow." Nicole was an up-and-coming photographer with her own studio and gallery downtown.

"An alumni event? Why weren't we invited?"

"We were. You said it was 'a thinly veiled excuse to squeeze every last penny from our pockets.'"

"Oh, that's right. And still true." She tossed a pack of bacon into her cart. "How's Kyle feeling today?"

"Bit of a headache, but he'll make it. He spent his lunch looking over the charges against you. He said he has a good feeling about it."

"A good feeling about me being sued?"

"No, a good feeling that he has grounds to countersue." Nicole laughed.

"I don't know what that means. But I trust him. Talk later?"

"Of course. Let me know how everything goes tonight. You've got this. Have you been thinking about tomorrow? Are you nervous?" Nicole's voice was softer now, more hesitant.

Claire's heart tripped. Barney's preliminary hearing. She had been so successful in blocking out all thoughts of him that she had almost penciled in a meeting at the same time as the hearing. As if this week wasn't shitty enough, now she had to go to court and possibly come face-to-face with the man who stabbed her a week ago. Kyle said she would probably be sequestered and wouldn't even need to come to the courtroom, but what if he was wrong? And she needed to pick her mother up from the airport in the morning. That was always an ordeal.

She took a deep breath. "I don't want to talk about tomorrow. One crisis at a time."

"It'll be okay. We'll be there for you. All of us," Nicole said in a soothing tone.

"Thanks, Coli."

Claire hung up and checked out with a cart full of groceries and a beautiful bunch of gerbera daisies. Maybe a five-course dinner would be enough to redeem her. Mothers always liked her—she was polite, gave thoughtful gifts. Rachel would change her opinion of her, and the pool incident would be a mere footnote in their successful relationship.

When she slammed her car door, she glanced in the rearview mirror. Well, shit. She hadn't fixed her Marilyn Manson makeup before going into the store. Maybe that's why the toddler twins in front of her screamed bloody murder when they saw her. Their mother didn't even ask for a signed copy of a bachelorette party shopping list. Rude.

CHAPTER SIX

"Luke?" Claire called out as she unlocked his front door. "Could you help me with the groceries?"

Rosie ran inside, her stump of a tail wiggling so hard it was in danger of dislodging. She beelined through the foyer and into the kitchen where Luke stood with a cup of coffee.

"Hi, sweetheart," he said, reaching down to rub Rosie's furry body. She leaned against his leg, panting happily as Claire set two reusable grocery bags on the kitchen island.

"Are you talking to me or the dog?" Claire asked.

"Both." He walked over and gave her a chaste kiss on the cheek.

Rachel cleared her throat noisily at the breakfast nook.

Her cup of coffee was still steaming, and her expression suggested she had just watched someone vomit.

Oh, good. Her attitude clearly hadn't improved since the day before. Why had she insisted on cooking for this dragon of a woman? They could have just gone out to a nice dinner at Mario's, but no. When Luke dropped the bomb that his mom was staying for a couple of days, Claire had latched on to the opportunity to impress her. What an idiot.

"Nice to see you again, Rachel," Claire said. She pulled the bouquet of gerbera daisies out of a bag and handed them to her.

Rachel handed them back. "I'm allergic to daisies."

"Oh, I'm sorry," Claire said. Of course she was. "Let me just put these outside."

She scurried out the front door and closed it behind her, breathing deeply. Strike one. She laid the flowers on the railing of the porch and crossed the yard to her car. In true Pennsylvania fashion, a warm early summer afternoon had taken a sharp turn, the temperature inexplicably dipping down into the fifties. She shivered as she popped open her trunk.

Luke followed her, wrapping an arm around her waist.

"Hey," he said, spinning her around. "Just breathe. It's only my mom."

"Only your mother who thinks I'm a gold-digging topless pool girl."

"She doesn't think that. She just doesn't know you." He brushed a curl out of Claire's face. "Don't let her intimidate you. She's been like this since the divorce. Dove into work and never came up for air."

The knot in her stomach did not relax. As he helped her carry the rest of the groceries inside, she forced a cheerful smile and decided she was going to remain positive no matter how many times Rachel rolled her eyes. And maybe she'd hide a bottle of wine in the dishwasher for emergency top-ups.

"How can I help?" Luke asked, rolling up his sleeves and revealing some swoon-worthy forearms.

"You should spend some time with your mom," she said as she tied on an apron. "I can get things started in here."

Plus, it would prevent her from flinging a frying pan full of bacon-wrapped scallops into Rachel's smug face.

"I would love a walk," Rachel added, standing.

"Okay. We'll take Rosie," Luke said, grabbing her leash from its peg by the front door. "Call me if you need anything."

Rachel puckered her withered lips together as though she was smiling, but it didn't reach her eyes.

Claire shuddered as she turned back to the kitchen island. The second the front door slammed, she piped some metal music through the kitchen's built-in speaker system and set her mind to preparing dinner.

***

FOOTSTEPS FELL ON THE FRONT PORCH TWENTY MINUTES later, and she quickly flipped her phone to a classical music station. She could only imagine what Rachel would have to say about Claire's favorite band, Nightsmear. She straightened her apron as Rachel and Luke walked inside.

"Oh, I love Prokofiev," Rachel said as she removed her cashmere scarf, adopting a thick Russian inflection on the last word.

Claire froze with a spatula in her hand. What or who was Prokofiev? Her gaze darted from the mushrooms in her frying pan to the bottle of vodka on top of Luke's wet bar.

"Remember how you used to play the third piano concerto for me after a bad day? So dynamic," Rachel said, removing her coat with a flourish and handing it to Luke.

Who spoke and acted like this? Was she a villain on a telenovela?

Luke laughed. "My fingers would cramp up, but it was worth it."

Claire smiled in spite of the icy presence in the room. The thought of a lanky teenage Luke bent over a piano softened her heart.

"It smells great in here." He stepped around the kitchen island and inspected the contents of the pan.

"Excuse me," Rachel said, disappearing down the hallway.

"How was your walk?" Claire asked, setting a wooden bowl of tossed salad onto the island.

"It went well. The ice queen routine is part of my mother's enduring charm. You shouldn't take it personally."

"Lovely," she said, fighting the urge to roll her eyes. "Did you tell her about the thing?"

"I did."

"And you made it clear to her that I'm not a gold-digging tramp?"

"Well, I wasn't going to lie to her."

She rammed her elbow into his side.

He laughed and spun her around, pressing her against the countertop. He buried one hand in her hair and planted a sensual kiss on her neck. Claire closed her eyes, body warming at his touch. Her limp hand barely held onto the spatula.

"Ahem," said a small voice from the foyer.

Luke sprang back, taking a few strands of hair with him.

"Ouch." Claire pressed a hand to her skull.

"So, Chloe. I hear you were kidnapped by one of your clients." Rachel clutched her phone in her raptor-like fist.

Clang. The spatula wobbled on the tile. Particles of sauce and bacon streaked across the white cabinets.

What in the actual hell?

Luke opened his mouth to speak, eyebrows already drawn together, but Claire grabbed his wrist. He picked up a dish towel and wiped at the sauce on the cabinets.

"It's Claire, actually. I'm sure Luke mentioned that," Claire said coolly, picking up the spatula and washing it in the sink. The shock was starting to recede, but she still felt as though she had been blindsided by an avalanche. Was this how she treated all of Luke's girlfriends?

"Right. Claire. Such an old-fashioned name. Must have slipped my mind," Rachel said, but she didn't sound sorry. It sounded like a calculated move, but Claire wasn't about to bite.

"I would love a glass of wine, by the way," Rachel continued smoothly, as though she hadn't just brought up the taboo topic of the evening. She sat carefully on one of the bar stools and neatly crossed her ankles. Her nude pumps didn't have a single scuff mark. "Just the one, though. I have a lot of preparing to do for the work week after dinner. What's the first course?"

Of course she would assume there were multiple courses. Good thing Claire had gone the extra mile. "Bacon-wrapped scallops," Luke said. Claire had emailed him the menu the day before.

Claire took a deep breath and tried to calm down. Maybe Rachel just wanted to address the elephant in the room and get it out of the way. "I recommend the Sancerre," she said, parroting what she had studiously read on the internet earlier. She drew a bottle from the wine fridge and handed it to Luke.

"Hmm. Sancerre. Is that your favorite wine, Claire? Maybe the kind you were drinking the night of your alleged kidnapping?" Rachel pried, drumming her manicured nails on the countertop.

"Mom, what the hell?" Luke slammed the bottle on the counter.

Claire stared at her blankly. Apparently, this interrogation was not going away. "You know, I don't remember what wine there was at the party. It probably has something to do with me getting chloroformed halfway through."

"Regardless," Rachel said, sliding her empty wine glass toward Luke, "with the addition of bacon, I should think a dry rosé would be more appropriate. Do you have anything like that, Lucas?"

Claire's hands went numb.

"I think I have a bottle of rosé in the wine cellar. Let me look." He slid the Sancerre back into the wine fridge. He disappeared down the basement stairs, closely followed by Rosie. Great, he had left her alone with the enemy.

Claire turned back to face the oven so Rachel couldn't see her rolling her eyes. Not only did she mention the kidnapping twice, she second-guessed her hostess on the wine selection. What a contemptible, tactless twatwaffle. Rachel's gaze penetrated the back of her neck, but she wasn't about to turn around.

Luke came back with a bottle of rosé and, for some reason, his toolbox. He poured three glasses of wine, passing one to his mother and one to Claire. He left his on the counter and flipped open the top of the toolbox. He pulled out a screwdriver and began tinkering with the basement doorknob.

"Delightful," Rachel said, sampling the rosé. "So, Claire. We were discussing your abduction."

"Mom," Luke said with a warning in his voice.

Claire, who had begun plating the bacon-wrapped scallops, dropped the frying pan onto a trivet with a bang. Her hands shook. Emotions she had been unwilling to acknowledge for the past week were bubbling to the surface. An eruption was coming, and it wasn't going to be pretty.

She slammed an appetizer plate and a fork in front of their guest. If she was irredeemable in Rachel's eyes, there was no reason to hold back. She pressed both of her hands to the granite countertop and made direct eye contact with Rachel.

"You know, Rachel, you didn't strike me as the type to play the pretend-to-accidentally-forget-your-son's-girlfriend's-name-in-order-to-undermine-and-demean-her card. I definitely didn't have you pegged as someone to play the ask-your-son's-girlfriend-about-the-most-traumatic-thing-to-ever-happen-to-her-while-she's-making-me-a-five-course-dinner card. I understand that you caught me in an awkward situation yesterday, and maybe you're upset with Luke for not telling you he was seeing someone."

She gestured at Luke. He was frozen, holding the latch assembly for the door in one hand.

"Maybe you even think I'm a worthless idiot because my career is devoted to making people happy. The truth is, I don't care what you think of me. I was stalked and hunted, abducted and tortured. I stared into the eyes of the West Haven Widowmaker as he carved into my flesh with a hunting knife." She dragged her blouse to the side, revealing the bandage.

There was a flicker of something in Rachel's eyes. Was it

sympathy? No, she was probably suppressing a fart. Ice Queens didn't audibly fart.

"This whole mean girl routine has probably served you well in the courtroom over the years," Claire continued, waving her hand in a circle, "but let me assure you, I am not afraid of you. So, I would appreciate if you could cut the bullshit. Now please eat your scallops, they're getting cold."

There was a ringing silence, like the aftermath of an explosion. Claire maintained steady eye contact until Rachel picked up her fork and nodded.

"Fair enough," Rachel said, and speared a scallop. She popped it into her mouth. "These are adequate."

"Thank you," Claire said, pulling bowls from the cabinet with more force than was necessary. Alice would have been horrified at her outbursts. It was a good thing her mother was in Florida and wouldn't be arriving until tomorrow morning. Crap, she needed to leave early enough to pick her up from the airport. She made a mental note and moved on.

Luke came to stand by Claire's side. He put one hand on the small of her back. Maybe she was imagining it, but his breath seemed shaky. "Claire's been through more than most people go through in their entire life. If you can't find another topic of conversation and show her some basic respect, you need you to leave now."

Rachel set her fork down. "Now, Lucas—"

Luke silenced her with a steely glare.

"Perhaps I've been a bit...unkind." Rachel slowly pushed her appetizer plate away and folded her hands in front of her. "I'm a curious person, and that wasn't appropriate. I apologize."

"Great," Claire said, snatching her plate. Surely smashing it over Rachel's head would be more satisfying than dumping it in the dishwasher.

"I'm going to get more wine," Luke announced, stomping back down the basement stairs.

Claire prickled. He had defended her, which was nice. But he had just left her alone with the enemy. Again. And now the basement door didn't have a doorknob. What if she needed to storm down there in the middle of dinner? You couldn't slam a door with no knob.

"So, Claire," Rachel began. Oh, boy. Ice Queen wasn't done with her questions. At least she had gotten the correct name this time. "What are your intentions with my son?"

"Excuse me?" Claire asked, spinning around. She had been immersed in her plans to crack a sleeping pill into Rachel's wine glass.

Rachel leaned forward, and her green eyes bored into Claire's. It was almost like an evil, female Luke staring back at her. Had she and Luke ever tried the face swap app? "Your intentions."

"Oh, I'm just using him for his pool." Claire pulled a potato peeler out of the cutlery drawer. She wasn't going to win any brownie points with this one. Her beloved-by-mothers streak was one hundred percent broken. Just like her business's reputation for happily ever afters. She might as well lean into the slide.

"Clever. Are you seeing each other exclusively?"

"I—yes." Claire hesitated. Luke had said a couple weeks ago that there wasn't anyone else after she had not-so-subtly interrogated him about his reputation of being a ladies' man.

"And you are living here?" Rachel asked.

Where had he gone to get more wine, Siberia? Claire slid the garbage can out and viciously peeled a potato. Rosie stood next to the can, on high alert for scraps. "No. I have my own apartment in the city. But I do stay here sometimes due to needing constant bandage changes from the stabbing that you enjoy bringing up so much."

"I see. What do your parents do for a living?" Rachel continued her cross-examination. There was no denying her occupation.

"My mother is...an entrepreneur." Better to gloss over her mother's psychic television career. Why was she answering this evil woman's questions? Their conversation was hardly less awkward than silence. Maybe she was making an effort to get to know Claire? "My stepfather is a mechanic and handyman."

"And your biological father?"

Luke walked into the room and paused mid-step, dangling a bottle of Riesling precariously by its neck. He had never heard the answer to this question either.

Claire bristled. For a prickly curmudgeon who couldn't manage to get her name right, Rachel sure had a lot of personal questions. She didn't owe her any more details. But maybe Luke had a right to know. "He hasn't been in the picture for twenty years. I have no idea what he does for a living."

"Hmm," Rachel said noncommittally as Luke refreshed her glass of wine. Rachel didn't protest, so she apparently didn't plan to stick to her one-glass rule. Hopefully, some booze would lubricate her enough to remove the ten-foot pole from her ass.

Luke gave Claire's hand a reassuring squeeze as he passed her and returned to tinkering with the doorknob. He eventually reattached it, twisting it several times, then came hesitantly back into the kitchen as though expecting a bomb to go off. He picked up a knife and began dicing the potatoes Claire had just peeled.

She took the opportunity to turn her back to Rachel and

toss some scallops into her mouth. Screw Rachel—they were better than adequate. She set a plate with the rest of the scallops next to Luke and washed the frying pan.

"You said you had a sister?" Rachel asked, smoothly transitioning to a new topic.

"I didn't say that, actually." How did she know that? Luke must have told her more than he admitted to on their walk. "But yes, Charlie. She lives in Los Angeles." She opened the oven to glance at the chicken marsala, refusing to make eye contact.

"Any nieces or nephews?"

"Enough with the questions," Luke half-shouted. "Leave her alone. Why don't you tell us about the case you're in town for?"

"There isn't much to tell," Rachel said. She drummed her manicured nails on the countertop.

"Really?" Luke raised his eyebrows. "Earlier you said it was one of the riskiest cases you've ever worked on."

"Yes, well, that's neither here nor there," she said evasively. "How's your latest project coming, Lucas?"

He threw the potatoes into a pot and emptied the bagged salad into bowls. He launched into the story of his scheduled interview with Jennifer Heiser's mother.

By the time the main course was ready, Rachel had picked through her salad, drunk a third glass of wine, and not-so-subtly commented on the lack of cloth napkins. In the meantime, Luke had applied lubricant to a squeaky cabinet door, fixed a wobbly chair in the dining room that was never used, and aggressively mashed the potatoes.

Rachel and Luke discussed work, and the hostility in the house downgraded by a centimeter. In fact, Rachel seemed to have forgotten that Claire was there at all, and instead turned her full attention to Luke. She barely looked at her chicken marsala and garlic mashed potatoes as she raised a bite to her lips. They discussed Luke's work and then Rachel's most recent case, in which she had gotten a corporate embezzler off with just a fine.

"I had a lovely dinner at George and Stella's last week," Rachel said, setting her fork down. "Stella made a croquembouche. I adore being her dessert guinea pig."

Luke stiffened, and Claire couldn't tell if he was offended by the mention of the couple or the dessert. The names didn't ring a bell.

"I don't want to talk about George, Mom." He abruptly stood up from the island and carried his plate to the dishwasher.

Claire paused with a mushroom on her fork. She looked back and forth from Luke to his mother as if they were in the middle of a tennis match. Claire's phone buzzed on the counter, signaling an incoming call, but she didn't reach for it.

"You don't care about your only brother?" Rachel asked.

"You have a brother?" Claire reeled as though she had been slapped across the face. Luke had outright said he didn't have a brother several times in the brief period that she had known him.

"You never told her about George?" Rachel asked incredulously.

Claire's mouth dropped open. Was there no end to the infantry of skeletons in Luke's closet? What else was he hiding?

"George isn't part of my life anymore." He grabbed a butter knife. His knuckles were as pale as the glob of potatoes on his plate.

For the umpteenth time that evening, Claire seethed. She set her fork down before she stabbed it into someone's neck. Of course there were more secrets, more lies. She had had enough of those for a lifetime.

"Sophia will be five soon," Rachel said softly. She didn't seem to notice Claire's quiet rage. "She hasn't seen you since her second birthday."

There was a niece too? If George and Stella had a dog, Claire was going to lose her shit.

"I have some work to do," Luke said, throwing his chair back. "Good night."

Luke stomped down the long hallway and closed his office door with a snap. The door popped back open a second later, and he stomped back to the kitchen, taking the cleared plates and putting them in the dishwasher.

"Thank you for dinner. It was delicious. I'll clean this up tomorrow, and I'll pick you up in the morning," he said rigidly, kissing Claire on the cheek before disappearing again.

A ringing silence was left in his wake. Rachel's pencil-thin eyebrows knitted together.

Claire's phone buzzed again, and she excused herself, happy to get out of the kitchen.

"Hello?"

"Claire, it's Kyle."

"Oh, hey. What's up?"

"I know you don't want to talk about it, but we need to discuss the hearing. Just to prepare you for what might happen. Any chance you could come over?"

Dread snaked through her like hot lead. After Rachel's hostilities, she had almost forgotten that Barney's preliminary hearing trial was happening tomorrow.

"Oh. Yeah, I could do that." She clutched a wall for support.

"Breathe, Claire. Remember, this is just the hearing. It'll

be short, and you may not even be called into the courtroom. We have more physical evidence for your case than most prosecutors could get in a year's worth of cases. This is going to be a slam dunk."

She exhaled noisily. "Okay. I can do this. I'll be there in like fifteen minutes," she said. "Oh, wait," she said, bringing her phone back up to her face so quickly she nearly dropped it.

Claire tiptoed through the living room to the rarely used dining room, hiding from Rachel.

"What do you know about Luke's brother, George?"

"Ah," Kyle said, sighing deeply. "Haven't heard his name in a while. I think that's a story that Luke had better tell you himself."

Disappointing, but... "Okay. Bros before hoes, I get it. See you in a minute."

She hung up and walked back to the kitchen. Rachel was examining her reflection in her wineglass.

"I'm sorry, Rachel. I'm needed at work. There's banoffee pie and coffee if you're interested."

Claire whistled for Rosie and bolted from the house, leaving her lying boyfriend locked in his office and his wretched old mop of a mother slumped at the island. That was enough Islestorm interaction for one day.

CHAPTER SEVEN

"MOM, YOU COULD HAVE KILLED US," CLAIRE SPUTTERED AS she frantically stabbed the button to roll down the heavily tinted window of Luke's new black sedan. Thick white smoke billowed out into the warm morning air. The imposing structure of the West Haven Courthouse was barely visible through the smoke. It looked more like a museum than a courthouse, with wide, sweeping stairs and dramatic brick arches. "You can't just fill a moving car with smoke."

All she wanted to do was get through the hearing without any shenanigans. And here she was, rolling up to the courthouse like she had just left a Grateful Dead concert.

Beside her, Luke put his window down too, wafting the smoke out into the balmy summer morning. He looked amused despite the fact that he clearly hadn't slept. She wasn't speaking to him after the George incident—they had tabled their discussion regarding his surprise secret brother until after the hearing.

"Claire Aurora Hartley, I can't believe you got in a brand new car without saging it first," Alice Alejo said sternly. Claire's mother had arrived that morning, fresh off a plane from Florida, the way a hurricane does—infrequently but with dramatic flair and potentially catastrophic fallout.

"Did you not get the kit that I sent you? The energy is so stale in here it's like an abandoned law library," Alice continued. She unbuckled her seatbelt and thrust her smoldering bundle of sage into the front seat, leaning as far as possible toward the windshield.

Claire was engulfed in the earthy smell of angelica root, which her mother swore by for protection. She and Luke made eye contact over her mother's mass of perfectly coiffed blonde hair. He shrugged.

Claire bit her lip. Luke had sprung for a new car with tinted windows before Claire had even made it home from the hospital. He still had his dad's old, beat-up truck, but any time they went somewhere together, they took the new car. But all the tinted windows in the world wouldn't save her from the microscope she was about to be under.

Alice swung her arm counterclockwise in a half circle. She likely would have fallen into Luke's lap if her gargantuan breasts hadn't been lodged between the driver and passenger seat. Apparently satisfied, she returned to the back seat. Flinging her curly blonde tresses over one shoulder of her hot pink pantsuit, she dug one well-manicured hand through her designer purse. "It's no wonder you keep getting followed by the paparazzi."

"Mom, I'm being followed by the paparazzi because I was almost murdered, not because I didn't smudge Luke's car. What are you doing? Put the spray bottle down."

"We have to follow the smudging with rose water for protection and warmth."

"It's eighty degrees, Mom. We don't need more warmth." Claire clutched the door handle. She wasn't ready to face the horde of reporters who were frantically approaching the car, but the smoke was giving her a headache. Luke reached over and stopped her. He got out first, leaving Claire to stew in the suffocating smell of rose water and sage.

He opened Alice's door first and helped her out. Alice extinguished the smoldering bundle with a bottle of water and hid it a sandwich bag in her purse. With any luck, it would be confiscated by courthouse security.

Detective Smith trotted down the stairs in front of the courthouse, having apparently spotted Claire and the small circus she had brought along. His shrewd blue eyes swept over the crowd before zeroing in on her. He wasn't tall or particularly big-boned, but he had a quietly commanding presence, and the people clustered around the courthouse stepped aside as he approached.

"Wait," Alice said to Luke as he reached for Claire's door. She reached into her purse once more and withdrew a small quartz stone. She tossed it into the back seat of the car before opening Claire's door.

Claire shook her head as she stepped out into the harsh sunlight. As soon as she exited, dozens of reporters converged on the car. Shouted questions didn't even register. Luke and Alice flanked her and shoved a path through the crowd. Alice had almost certainly just delivered a sound elbow to the abdomen of a reporter who tried to thrust his microphone in Claire's face. Luke's jaw was clenched, and there was a tic in his right eye.

Detective Smith met them halfway, calling a couple of cops over to help control the crowd. Other than his unusually large ears, he was an unassuming man, which was probably ideal for a detective. He shook her hand briefly before turning back to the throng. He turned his head to speak to her over the shoulder of his neatly pressed charcoal suit.

"Miss Hartley. I know this will be a challenging day for you," Detective Smith said as he strong-armed a particularly aggressive reporter.

Claire followed behind him, ducking her head as they made their way to the steps. "You could say that."

The detective's badge glinted in the sunlight as he led the way. A low-hanging boom microphone mussed his neatly parted salt-and-pepper hair.

Tension radiated from Luke. He stepped half in front of her as they walked, shielding her as much as possible from the desperate horde screaming questions at her.

"Miss Hartley, how do you feel about being in the same building as the West Haven Widowmaker?" one woman shouted.

"Widowermaker," Claire muttered under her breath. Was that the same toothy reporter who had accosted her outside her warehouse a few days earlier?

"What do you say to the families of the other victims?" a woman with startling blue eyes yelled at her.

"Has your business suffered after planning a proposal for a serial killer?" another called.

"Back off," Luke commanded, jabbing a finger into the breastbone of a short man with a sprinkling of freckles across his milky-white skin.

Finally, after a blur of desperate faces, microphones, and shouted questions, the courthouse doors swung shut behind them. The silence was deafening. After a minor incident at the metal detectors where security confiscated what appeared to be a voodoo doll from Alice's purse, they approached the courtroom.

Claire's heart pounded erratically. Just on the other side of those imposing double doors was the man who had fooled her, abducted her, and tried to kill her. The stab wound on her chest burned. Her hands balled into fists at her side. Some days, the anger burned so bright and hot that she wanted to drive to the prison and punch Barney right in the testicles. But the testicle punch would have to wait for another day. She probably wouldn't even see him.

"Miss Hartley." Detective Smith stepped in front of the courtroom doors, blocking her path. "This is Ada Washington, a crime victim advocate."

Ada stepped forward and shook Claire's hand with both of hers. Barely noticeable wrinkles hugged the corner of her mouth. Her natural hair had been straightened, and her shoulder-length bob shone under the overhead lights. Caramel-colored eyes stared out of cat eye glasses.

"I'm sorry to meet you under these circumstances," Ada said tactfully, releasing her grip on Claire's hand. "I've seen your work. Your proposals are wonderful."

"Thank you," Claire said.

"Your family is welcome to proceed into the courtroom," Ada said with a nod toward Luke and Alice. Luke looked worried, and Alice was rooting through her purse again. "However, because you are a witness, you'll have to remain outside. Standard procedure," she said. "If you'll follow me, I'll show you to a lounge you can wait in for the duration of the hearing."

Alice thrust her purse into Luke's arms and hugged Claire so ferociously that something in her body cracked. Was that a rib?

"Mom, I'll be fine."

Alice pulled back and gripped her arms. The worry line between her eyes stuck out more than it used to. She looked back at Luke.

"I know you will, sweetie. I love you." There was one last suffocating hug, and then she whirled away in a cloud of angelica root and lemon grass.

Luke hugged her more gently, and he pressed his lips to Claire's ear.

"You can do this." He gave her a quick kiss on the cheek, and then he, too, was gone.

Claire followed Ada a few yards down the hallway. A small, open lounge with a view of the courtyard was littered with outdated wooden benches and tables. Ada provided Claire with a bottle of water and then left.

The rigid wooden chair was as uncomfortable as it looked. A clock on the wall ticked incessantly. Wood polish and cheap, lemon-scented cleaning products perfumed the air. It was going to be a long day.

"There she is!"

Claire glanced up at the loud whisper. Nicole and Mindy, both dressed in power suits, strode down the hallway looking over their shoulders every couple of steps, as though they were expecting to be yelled at.

"You guys," Claire said, standing as they engulfed her in hugs. "What are you doing here? I told you that you didn't have to come."

"Please, like we were going to miss this. You're not allowed inside?" Nicole asked Claire, laying a hand on her shoulder.

"No. They don't want the witnesses hearing the testimonies or something," Claire said.

"Then you're going to need this," Mindy said, reaching into her bag and drawing out a gossip magazine and a large thermos.

"Coffee?" Claire asked appreciatively, hefting the thermos.

"Sure," Mindy said, swooping in for one last hug. "We'll tell you everything. I'm going to take such detailed notes that the court stenographer will be forced to retire in shame."

"Love you." Nicole engulfed Claire in her coconut-scented shampoo briefly before the pair made their way to the courtroom.

Claire surveyed the lounge again. If she leaned to the right, the entrance to the courtroom was just barely visible. She took a notebook with proposal notes out of her purse and stared at it for a moment, willing it to distract her. A diagram of a marching band spread out before her, but she idly tapped her pen against the drum major, unable to focus. People were still filing in to the courtroom, so the proceedings probably hadn't started yet. How long would this take?

Stilettos snapped across the linoleum. They sounded expensive. Claire glanced up. Rachel. What the hell? Claire stiffened and slid her chair to the left. A loud screech split the air. Hopefully, Rachel hadn't seen her.

What was the ice queen doing here? Shouldn't she be sharpening a pitchfork or sacrificing a virgin in a volcano somewhere? Maybe Luke had asked her to come to provide insight.

After a quick glance around the corner to make sure Rachel was indeed gone, Claire took a sip from the thermos, expecting a steaming shot of caffeine. She choked and sprayed a fine mist over her notebook and the table. A hand clapped her on the back, and she nearly knocked the thermos over.

"You okay?" a familiar voice asked.

"Sawyer," she choked out. The table and chairs looked like dollhouse furniture as he sat down across from her, dressed in a navy suit and surfboard-sized black dress shoes. He looked like a bodyguard, or maybe a professional wrestler.

"Sorry, my friends brought me this. I was expecting coffee and instead got a very strong hit of vodka," she whispered, sliding the mug across the table to Sawyer.

He sniffed it and shuddered, then slid it back to her. His nose was broad and flat, as though he slept with his face smashed into a pillow and it had gotten stuck that way.

Claire shrugged and took a big sip before moving it off to the side. "I didn't realize you'd be here. Makes sense, though."

He nodded. "I did tase the bastard. How have you been?"

"Fine. No one's broken into my apartment since the system was installed, so thank you for that."

Sawyer smiled. His lips were large and velvety-looking, and his teeth were perfectly white against his tanned skin. His shoulders rippled as he took his phone out of his pocket.

"Have you given any more thought to self-defense classes?"

She smacked the table with one hand. "I have, actually. I'm sick of feeling powerless. I needed three people just to get me through the crowd and into the building today. I was going to call you next week to schedule a lesson."

"Sounds great. It'll be good for you. Help you feel a little more in control."

"I do love to be in control," she said, smiling wryly. She abandoned her notebook in her bag and picked up the gossip magazine. For once, her mind refused to focus on work.

"Care package from Mindy and Nicole." She gestured to the magazine. "I don't usually read these things."

"Mindless garbage can be a great distraction. I watched two full seasons of *Stepwives of Secaucus* a couple years ago," Sawyer said, gesturing to the picture of a brunette woman who was apparently sporting a new nose job on the cover of the magazine.

"My sister and I watch that show all the time. I didn't have you pegged as a reality TV guy." Claire raised an eyebrow. A loud yawn caught her off guard, and she wiped a hand at the corner of her eye, trying not to smudge her makeup. She had barely slept the night before and had woken in the middle of four different nightmares about Barney. But at least she hadn't sleepwalked. That was a problem for another day.

"I'm not. It was a weird time. You look exhausted."

She frowned. Apparently, her special green-tinted undereye primer hadn't gotten rid of the bags.

"I don't mean you look bad," he corrected quickly. "You look great. You were just yawning and I figured with today coming up you probably didn't sleep. I'm going to stop talking now." He folded his hands and placed them on the table.

Claire laughed. He was so nice. An open book, really. It was a far cry from interacting with the perpetually grumpy and mysterious Luke. "It's fine. I am tired."

Tired of a lot of things.

"If you want to close your eyes and rest a little bit, I'll keep an eye out," he said.

A protest was on the tip of her tongue, but she yawned again, so violently that she shuddered. The swig of vodka was dragging her eyelids down. The sun filtering through the window distinctly reminded her of sitting in the Burger King sunroom as a child.

"I might do that. Thank you, Sawyer," she said, promptly laying her head down on her magazine. Just a brief power nap.

"Unhand me!"

The shout startled Claire awake. She sat upright as though she had been electrocuted. Her cheek was damp, and the magazine clung to her face, swinging like a pendulum for a moment before dropping back onto the table. She wiped at the dampness on her cheek and glanced across the table, relieved to see that Sawyer had disappeared. Drooling on a gossip magazine outside a courtroom probably didn't do much for her public image.

She stood, walked into the hallway, and took a step toward the courtroom.

The heavy wooden double doors burst open. A bailiff the size of a redwood stepped into the hallway, carrying a hot pink bundle over his shoulder.

"Put me down, you oaf! I'm not finished with her." The hot pink bundle was Claire's mom, screaming obscenities and flailing. One of her bubblegum-pink high heels flew off and knocked a personal item bin off the security table.

Sawyer, who had been approaching the doors looking ready for a fight, caught the bin before it hit the ground.

"Ma'am, you are not permitted to verbally assault the litigators." The bailiff deposited her on a chair in the atrium.

Alice tried to rise, but he held his nightstick in her direction.

"Mom? What the hell is going on?" Claire asked. So much for making it through the trial with no unnecessary shenanigans.

More shouts came from inside the courtroom. A gavel banged in the background.

"I can't believe you would take this case," Luke said as the door flew open again. Even from this distance, his eyes were stormy and dangerous. "How in the hell is this not a conflict of interest? You're defending the man who tried to kill my girlfriend."

Oh, he said the g-word. Did that make them official? But he had lied about George. And didn't tell Rachel she existed. Wait, who was he talking to?

Rachel strode out just behind him. Her cheeks were flushed, and her eyes were even sharper and more unforgiving than they had been the night before.

"Lucas, I would hardly consider this minor dalliance your 'girlfriend.' She doesn't even know the difference between a salad bowl and a soup bowl."

Claire's mouth dropped open. Who the hell cared what kind of bowl was being used if someone served you a free meal in it? That was it, she was going to kill her. Luke started to speak, but he was cut off.

"You dried-up old hag!" Alice leapt up from the chair and charged toward Rachel.

The bailiff, moving surprisingly quickly for a man of his size, scooped his arms underneath Alice's and held her back. Deprived of arm movements, Alice instead began jumping, kicking her legs out in Rachel's general direction.

Sawyer moved toward Alice but turned to look back at Claire. She shook her head, and he stopped.

"How dare you speak of my daughter that way?" Alice spat at Rachel. "She is a beautiful, smart, independent businesswoman who has suffered unspeakable horrors at the hand of your *client*." She emphasized the last word as if it was profane.

Claire gasped. That fossilized twat was representing Barney. No wonder she had been grilling her the night before. Was she even allowed to do that?

"Mrs. Alejo, I'm just doing my job. And my job entails uncovering the truth, and the truth is that your daughter isn't as innocent as she likes to pretend. She assaulted someone in front of a hundred people shortly before she was 'abducted,'" Rachel said with air quotes.

A hand flew to Claire's chest. She was frozen in place like an ice sculpture. Every time she thought Rachel couldn't possibly be more heinous, she proved her wrong. The Islestorms were quicksand, sucking people in and suffocating them with lies and subterfuge.

Alice wriggled even harder, like a bull caught in a pen. The bailiff cleared his throat loudly, and the cop who had been sitting behind the metal detector with earbuds in suddenly jumped up.

"What seems to be the problem here?" he asked, sounding awfully official for someone who had been blatantly ignoring his job.

"Little help here, Steve?" The bailiff looked pointedly at the middle-aged psychic who was doing her best to escape his grasp.

"What kind of a mother could defend a man like Barney Windsor? You're the real monster here. Your heart is as black as your aura" Alice hissed as she was transferred back to the chair. Fighting words from the television psychic. The cop pulled her arms behind her and snapped on a pair of handcuffs, threading them through the slats of the chair. Alice shot daggers at Rachel, who ignored her.

Sawyer was trying to catch Claire's eye, and when he succeeded, he scrubbed his hand against his cheek. She shrugged at him, confused. Did she still have drool on her face? Her cheek didn't feel wet.

"You seriously went through our recycling?" Luke said to his mother, hands balled into fists at his side.

"I have an obligation to my client—" she began but stopped when the courtroom doors opened again.

Mindy and Nicole slid out, looking alarmed. They spotted Claire and hurried down the hallway, flanking her and snaking their arms through hers.

"You used your relationship with me to get information on Claire. I'm going to tell the judge about the conflict of interest," Luke said, whirling around and heading for the courtroom.

"Maybe you should let me handle that," Kyle, who had just exited, said. He was grinning despite the chaos.

"Lucas, the jury has a right to know about Claire's violent history," Rachel continued, softer this time. "And you never told me you were dating her until last night."

Luke turned to her, rage flaming in his eyes. "Shut the hell up. And get your things out of my guest room. You're not welcome in my home anymore."

Claire gasped. Rachel's face fell. The doors slammed open again, and the judge appeared in her billowing black robes.

"Counselors," the judge said. "This is a courtroom, not a circus tent. As riveting as this family drama is, it won't be tolerated. And you," the judge said, turning to Alice. "You are dangerously close to being held in contempt."

Alice took a deep breath and trained her baby blue eyes

on the judge. "Your honor, do you have any idea what it's like to get a call in the middle of the night telling you that your daughter has been stabbed? And you're six states away and she's bleeding out under a retrograde Mercury? Claire almost died at the hands of that man, and this woman's trying to make it seem like she's some underdeveloped, gin-guzzling middle schooler with a violent streak. That's not my daughter."

The judge dropped into the chair next to Alice. She leaned in and whispered something too low for Claire to hear. The judge patted Alice on the hand before standing back up.

"I have a courtroom to run. I expect everyone except Alice—and the witnesses," she said with a stern glance at Claire and Sawyer, "to be back inside and ready to proceed with the hearing in five minutes." She spoke with no room for argument and disappeared through a side door.

"I'm going to have to ask you folks to return to the lounge area," the cop said to Claire and Sawyer.

"I'm just going to make a quick pit stop," Sawyer said as he headed to the restroom.

Mindy released Claire and gave her another hug. When she pulled back, her mouth formed an O of surprise.

"Claire, your face—"

"What about it?"

"Mindy, we have to go in," Nicole hissed, waving at her friend.

"Scrub it," Mindy whispered, mimicking Sawyer's hand motion from earlier.

"Why the hell is everyone telling me to scrub my face?" Claire muttered to herself, shaking her head. She cast one more glance at Alice, who was still handcuffed to the chair and staring daggers at the courtroom doors.

Her footsteps echoed in the hallway as she made her way back to her table. She was certain she had applied her foundation earlier. Maybe her bronzer was uneven? She dug through her purse until she found the small, striped compact Nicole had given her for her last birthday. She flipped it open and gasped in horror.

The word "vagina" was stamped in yellow across her cheek. She glanced at the magazine on the table. The glossy paper was warped over an article titled "Is my vagina normal?"

"Oh my god." She desperately scrubbed at her cheek. It wasn't going away.

"Here," Sawyer said as he reappeared. He handed her a damp paper towel.

"Thank you," she said, slapping it onto her skin and rubbing. She pulled the paper towel away to check her progress. So much for painstakingly blended foundation. She was going to look like a red-faced teenager when the press swarmed her after the hearing. No wait, it was worse than that. "It's still there," she groaned. Was she going to have to walk around for the rest of her life with a stab wound and the word "vagina" staining her cheek?

"Let me," Sawyer said, taking the chair next to hers.

Claire wondered briefly if he would accidentally crush her head but handed him the paper towel.

He gently gripped her chin and tilted her face toward him. He smelled like summer, bright citrus mixed with sunshine. His rough hands were gentle as he rubbed at her cheek. It was oddly erotic. She leaned the rest of her body away from him. How awkward. She barely knew him, and she had a boyfriend (didn't she?). Even if he was a grumpy, pathological liar.

"Much better." He balled up the paper towel and tossed it ten feet away into a trashcan.

"I'm no longer a walking billboard for reproductive organs?"

"Not for that one, anyway," he said apparently without thinking, because a millisecond later, his face was as red as the traffic light outside. "I mean, there's only so much you can do about—uh, you know what? Never mind." He cleared his throat and stood, walked over to the window. He clasped his hands behind his back, as though the tiny courtyard he was surveying was his kingdom.

Claire suppressed a snort laugh and went back to her slightly warped magazine. Her eyes were fixed on an article about celebrity beach bodies, but her mind was racing. Her anxiety, which had already been at heart-palpitation level the entire morning, inched up another notch. Kyle had said the preliminary trial would be a slam dunk, and that there was more than enough evidence for Barney's case to go to trial. But what if the universe was gearing up to smite her? Why the hell was Rachel representing Barney? What did Rachel say that set Luke off so much? Something about the recycling? And how long would it be until Alice made a voodoo doll of Rachel?

After a small eternity, the courtroom doors opened again. She and Sawyer both stood, uncertain if they were allowed to approach. Nicole and Mindy shoved their way to the front and half jogged to Claire.

"It's going to trial," Nicole blurted out, wrapping Claire in another rib-cracking hug.

Claire audibly exhaled, a breath that felt like she had held it the entire morning.

The girls began talking over top of each other. "Rachel tried to make you seem like an alcoholic," Mindy began.

"*What*?" Claire interrupted. An alcoholic? Sure, she had indulged in more wine this week than she normally did. But if getting abducted and being grilled by Rachel didn't excuse a couple extra glasses of wine, what did?

"Totally victim-blaming, very tone deaf in this political climate and—" Nicole interrupted. She talked with her hands when she was upset. Her princess-cut diamond nearly slashed Claire's cheek.

"Also, I need you to find out where Luke's mom lives," Mindy interjected. "On an unrelated note, I need to go to the grocery store and buy six dozen eggs, a blow-up sex doll, aerosol hairspray, and a crème brûlée torch," Mindy said.

"That bad, huh?" A ball of lead had formed in Claire's stomach. She picked up the thermos that was on the table and took a big sip. If she was already an alleged alcoholic, she might as well embrace it.

Nicole squeezed her hand. "You weren't exaggerating when you said she was a hybrid of a shark and a velociraptor with a clump of broken hypodermic needles for a heart. But Kyle can and will beat her. The evidence is insurmountable, no matter how much she tries to drag your name through the mud. It's honestly stupid of them to let it go to trial."

"Let's hope. I better go see if they've un-handcuffed my mother." Claire linked arms with Nicole and Mindy and started to walk down the corridor.

"Hang on." Claire stopped suddenly and was almost knocked down by the other two. She unwound her arms and turned to look behind her. "Sawyer?"

Sawyer, who had slung his jacket over one shoulder and seemed to be engrossed in his phone, looked up.

"Thank you. Again. For everything, especially from saving me from gracing the cover of the *West Haven Times* with the word 'vagina' on my face," she said, covering the short distance between them in a few steps. She stood on her tippy toes and wrapped her arms around him as best as she could. It was like hugging a stone pillar. She wasn't entirely sure he had passed her not-a-serial-killer test, but he had gone above and beyond to help her out today. Not to mention saving her life the week before.

He hesitated, then leaned down to hug her back. They broke apart after a few seconds.

"I'll call you next week. About the lesson, I mean," she said.

"I look forward to it." He clapped her on the shoulder. Her knees almost buckled under the weight of his hand.

When Claire turned around, Luke stood behind her, arms crossed over his chest and mouth set in a hard line. Had the trial and his mother's betrayal set him off, or was it Claire's embrace of the man who saved her life? If Sawyer hadn't responded to the security call and tased Barney, Claire would almost certainly be dead. Although Luke had solved the mystery and rolled up with the police a minute later, it wouldn't have been enough. In fact, two men in the past two weeks had prevented her untimely demise— Sawyer and Jamarcus—and neither one of them had been Luke. Did that bother him?

Claire opened her mouth to speak even though she had no idea what to say, but she was cut off by her mother's voice.

"Finally!" Alice rubbed her wrists where the handcuffs had been. Her wayward stiletto and purse had been returned.

"Clairebear," she said simply, wrapping her daughter in her arms.

"Can we go? I'm starting to feel like a zoo animal."

Rubberneckers exiting the courtroom swiveled to stare at her.

"Hang on." Mindy gripped Claire's arm and turned her away from the crowd. From her bag, she produced a makeup sponge and a travel-size bottle of Claire's shade of foundation. She had taken to carrying it after Claire's abduction to help her cover up bruises between client appointments. "I see you got the vagina off your face," she said as she dabbed at the spot where the makeup had rubbed off.

"Sawyer helped," Claire said.

Mindy paused and looked directly into Claire's eyes. She was lovely, like a barely contained wildfire.

"You should be careful."

"With what?" Claire asked. Could Mindy tell Claire had hit her head off a cabinet that morning?

"Sawyer," Mindy said, barely above a whisper. "Don't pretend you haven't noticed how he looks at you."

Claire frowned.

"Don't frown. Now I have to even this side out," Mindy sighed, returning to dabbing.

"If he's looking at me, it's probably just because he's shocked to see me in any state other than topless and covered in blood. He saved my life and he's Kyle's grooms-man. Are you proposing that I ignore him?"

Mindy closed the bottle of foundation and tucked it back in her purse. "Just be careful."

"Oh, thank you for reminding me. Luke lied about having a brother, so I have to go address that now. Thanks for the hooch." Claire handed the mostly full thermos back to Mindy.

"*What*?" Mindy said, but Claire ignored her. They would have time to talk about the George situation after she had words with Luke.

She turned back to her mother, who was chatting with Nicole.

"Claire, darling. I don't have to be at the airport until later this evening. I thought we could go back to your apartment and I'll make lunch for everyone. I was thinking Grandma Alejo's empanada recipe."

Claire hesitated. After the craziness of the morning, she was torn between her love of Mexican food and her deep desire to be alone and process the day.

"Let's do lunch at Luke's," she suggested. "He has more room. And a wine cellar." Not to mention his house was more conducive to a post-lunch screaming match.

CHAPTER EIGHT

To Do:
- Marching band practice
- Forward Aaron the updated quotes

"The high priestess." Alice tapped a hot pink fingernail against a black and gold card. "You're about to begin a journey where you will be tested. You should trust your intuition. Follow it."

Claire sighed and propped her head in her hand, elbow planted on Luke's breakfast nook table. The bay window behind her let in plenty of late afternoon sun, illuminating the row of cards in front of her. After several less-than-subtle hints from her mother, she had erroneously agreed to a tarot reading. Dull pain throbbed behind her temples. Rosie whined and laid her head on Claire's lap. Claire patted her absentmindedly.

Rachel had shown up halfway through lunch to collect

the bags that Luke had tossed unceremoniously onto the porch. Mindy had farted into her toiletries bag, claiming that it would give Rachel pinkeye, and Claire could have sworn she saw her mother take a sock from the laundry bag.

Nicole, Kyle, and Mindy had gone home shortly after, bellies full of empanadas and homemade tortilla chips. Now she and Luke were slowly passing the time until Alice left for the airport. Their argument hovered on the horizon like storm clouds.

"The queen of cups." Alice glanced at Luke, who was wandering around the kitchen with a video camera, clearly amused by the proceedings. A beautiful flower arrangement stood behind him. It had been waiting on the porch for them when they arrived at his home—a thank you from Kayley Herrold's family for telling their daughter's story and putting the Widowmaker behind bars.

"Wait. I can interpret this one." Claire put her hand on the queen and wiggled her around on the table. "Drink more wine, Claire. Thou cannot pour from an empty cup," she said in a British accent.

"Thank you, queen of cups," she said in her normal voice, reaching for an almost-empty bottle of pinot noir. Alice slapped her hand.

"No. This generally means you are lovely and caring, deeply empathetic, with an open heart. Maybe too open."

Claire grunted.

"The moon," Alice said, gesturing to a card of a dog howling at the moon. "How has your anxiety been, Claire?"

"You mean since I was stabbed last week? Oh, great. It's been super manageable."

"Sweetheart." Her mom reached across the table to hold her hand. "Did you call any of those therapists I sent you?"

Again with the therapists. They sure hadn't worked for

Alice and Bio-dad when they had tried couples counseling as a last-ditch effort to save their marriage. The last thing Claire needed right now was someone delving into her childhood and blaming her deadbeat dad for all her current problems. That was a can of worms she was more than happy to leave firmly sealed.

"I don't need a therapist. I'm fine," she said, withdrawing her hand. "People get stabbed every day. What's the next card?"

"The tower." Alice frowned at the image of a woman falling from a flaming tower.

"Seems about right." Claire shot daggers at Luke, who snorted audibly from across the room. "Should I petition the city to install trampolines outside my apartment?"

"I don't think so, sweetie. The tower means change, possibly chaos. Sometimes destruction."

"Fabulous, I haven't hit my 'destruction' quota yet this month."

"And..." Alice glanced at the last card.

"Who's the old guy holding the stick?" Claire asked.

"The emperor. He usually means something to do with structure or authority. Sometimes he represents a father figure."

"Maybe Roy was supposed to come here with you," Claire said pointedly. She missed her stepdad and his kind, quiet ways.

"He was going to, sweetie. Someone's water heater exploded right before we were going to leave for the airport." Alice scooped up the cards and shuffled them back into the deck.

"You're sure it had nothing to do with his pathological fear of planes?"

"He doesn't have that anymore. I took him to a hypnotist." She handed the deck to Claire.

"Of course you did. Well, thank you, Mom. Oh look, your cab is here." Claire turned at the sound of gravel crunching on the driveway.

She was relieved for a millisecond, but then remembered that she had no idea when she'd see her mother again.

"We would have happily driven you to the airport, you know," Claire said, collecting her mother's carry-on bag from the foyer. A proponent of always being prepared, Alice always carried a fully stocked carry-on with extra outfits even for same-day trips.

"I can feel that you two have some things to talk about," Alice said, leaning in and hugging Claire tightly. "Best not to delay, darling. Hurt feelings hurt the body."

In a flash, Alice crossed the room and drew Luke into a smothering hug. He gingerly put the camera down on the kitchen island and returned her embrace.

While Alice knelt and scratched Rosie behind the ears, cooing over her "granddog," Luke picked up the suitcase and opened the front door. Claire helped Alice up from the floor, and they walked arm-in-arm to the cab.

The wall of pine trees that lined the driveway cast long shadows over the neatly trimmed grass. The sun was setting. Dinner and the card reading had taken longer than Claire thought. She really should have devoted some more time to reviewing Tyler's proposal.

"Take care, sweetheart." Alice's worry line was back.

"I'll miss you. Let me know when you land?"

"Of course. I love you."

"Love you more," Claire said, welcoming one last hug.

Her mother slid into the back seat of the cab, waving as the car reversed and disappeared down the lane.

Luke had rested his arm around Claire's shoulders, and he was unfairly distracting her by rubbing his thumb into the base of her neck.

"Hey, Luke?"

"Hmm?"

"Remember that time I told you that if you ever, ever lied to me again, then we were done?" she said quietly.

"I don't remember that."

"Do you remember that time you told me twice that you didn't have a brother? And it turns out you do in fact have a brother?"

Luke sighed. His hand dropped from her shoulders.

"You don't know the whole story."

She turned to face him. She wouldn't be surprised if steam was pouring out of her ears. "So, tell me the whole story."

He averted his gaze and put his hands in his pockets. "It's hard to explain."

Her face screwed up like she had just eaten a sour candy. "Are you kidding me right now? How hard can it possibly be to tell me the truth? Do you have any idea what I've been through in the past two days? In the past month? If I can survive being targeted by a serial killer, you can muster up some strength in that dangly little sack of yours and find the courage to tell me the truth."

"Claire, it's—" He paused, but she shushed him.

If she had to stand in his presence for even one more minute, she was going to explode like an atomic bomb.

"Let me guess. It's complicated. You know what? Save it. You're wasting my time. I don't want to hear any more lies today. I have things to deal with. Take me home." She never should have let him drive this morning.

"Come on." He reached for her, and she slapped his hand away. If he touched her, all of this resolve was in danger of crumbling.

He buried the hand she had slapped into his hair. He opened his mouth to speak, but she stopped him.

"You know what? I don't care. I don't care about your brother. I sure as hell don't care about your psychotic, victim-blaming attorney of a mother." Claire turned on her heel and stomped back toward the house, stabbing at her phone to bring up her ride sharing app.

There was another crunch of gravel on the driveway, and Claire whirled around. The taxi was back. It pulled to a stop, and the back door opened. Her mother smiled kindly from inside and extended one manicured hand.

Claire opened the front door, snapped a leash on Rosie, grabbed her purse and shoes, and stormed across the yard past Luke.

"Claire, come on. Can we talk about this?"

"I tried to talk, Luke. Remember that." She helped Rosie into the cab and slammed the door behind her. She turned to her mother, willing herself not to cry.

"How did you know?"

"I had an intuition, sweetie. Oh, my sweet Queen of Cups," Alice said, pulling Claire into her. She stroked her hair, the same way she did after Claire had gotten a B on a spelling test as a child. Rosie jumped up from the floor and settled on both of their laps, sending a cloud of dog hair flying.

"Go easy on him if you can," Alice continued. "There's something very deep and very painful there. He's not ready to talk about it. Trust takes time to grow."

Claire closed her eyes and breathed in the rich spice of her mother's perfume. Though Alice was absolutely bonkers most of the time, she was still a pretty great mom.

CHAPTER NINE

To Do:
- Pencil in hot yoga
- Persuade Barney to murder Luke

CLAIRE THREW HER PURSE ONTO THE COUCH AND KICKED OFF her shoes, utterly exhausted from the trial and fighting with Luke. Not even a long walk with Rosie had been able to lift the crushing weight of this day from her shoulders. Moonlight streamed through her kitchen window, casting a pale glow on the murder binder she had abandoned shortly after returning home from the hospital. It still felt strange to walk into her apartment alone. Prior to her abduction and Barney's subsequent arrest, her friends had rotated through her apartment, barely leaving her alone long enough to pee in solitude.

She trudged to the bathroom and glanced in the mirror. Her eyes were hollow, her skin paler than usual. But at least she wasn't a vagina billboard anymore. She washed her face furiously in the sink, eager to rinse off the day.

Her phone vibrated, and she picked it up to see a text.

Luke: *Can we talk?*

Her shoulders hunched up around her neck. She decided a middle finger emoji was a sufficient response and opened her bedroom door, tossing her phone onto the bed where she wouldn't have to see it.

She started for the shower but remembered the bottle of pinot grigio that Past Claire had very thoughtfully left in her refrigerator. She padded down the hallway on bare feet, and then yanked the refrigerator door open as if it had personally wronged her. With her fingers inches away from the bottle, Rachel's allegations crept into her mind. *An alcoholic?!* She snatched her hand back.

"I don't have a problem," she shouted at the bottle, slamming the fridge door and filling up her water thermos instead.

Though a shower water was substantially less fun than a shower wine, Claire needed one either way. She closed her bathroom door to prevent Rosie from gnawing on her bathmat, lit the aromatherapy candle on her sink, and dimmed the lights. After she removed her courtroom outfit, it puddled on the floor. She ducked under the steaming head of her shower, welcoming the warm spray on her exhausted body.

She scrubbed at her mascara and lathered shampoo into her mass of curls, still fuming over Luke's lie and his mother's surprise betrayal.

"Is that the kind of wine you were drinking the night of your alleged abduction?" she mimicked to herself, angrily gripping her bodywash. No wonder Rachel had interrogated her so heavily. She was using her, preparing more information for Barney's case.

Suddenly, a loud, pulsating wail sounded from the hallway outside her apartment. Claire flinched. *Crash.* The bodywash dropped to the floor, narrowly missing her big toe. Rosie barked furiously. *Shit.*

Claire shut the water off, stumbling out onto the wet tile of her bathroom floor. She wrapped a towel around herself and threw open the door.

The flashing light of the fire alarm system illuminated the gap beneath her front door. Groaning, she hesitated between her bedroom and bathroom. Should she try to fight her way back into the button-down shirt or risk having no clean laundry besides her Camp Susquehanna T-shirt from eighth grade?

"EMERGENCY. ALL RESIDENTS MUST IMMEDI-ATELY VACATE THE PREMISES," a prerecorded voice announced in her hallway.

"Ugh!" Claire scuttled down the hallway with wet feet. There was no time for dillydallying about clothes. On the off chance that this was real, she had to save the essentials. She shrugged into a bathrobe and flung open the hallway closet. A pink backpack hung on a hook inside, and she yanked it off the wall. Darting from room to room, she tossed in a picture of her and her mom, her wallet, phone, Rosie's favorite stuffed toy, her laptop, and Tyler and Aaron's proposal binders. Between those essentials and the water filtering straw and emergency flashlights, the backpack was at capacity. With a wistful look at her row of designer shoes, she closed the closet door and padded back to the front door.

"Damn you, Mrs. Kline, and your burnt popcorn," she

said. The third-floor resident had set off the fire alarm twice last year.

Claire threw her front door open, tightening the sash of her robe with one hand while the other clutched Rosie's leash. The backpack dug so deeply into her shoulders it might as well have been filled with bricks. Maybe she needed to switch to virtual binders.

Claire joined the shuffle of sleepy residents heading toward the staircase. She didn't smell smoke or burnt popcorn, but she didn't like to take chances.

"Oh, Mrs. Dodge, you really shouldn't take the elevator." She rushed over and gripped the arm of her kind and elderly neighbor.

"Nonsense. If I lived through World War II, I can live through this damn fire alarm," Mrs. Dodge said, stubbornly pressing the down button. The elevator was a dimly lit, outdated nightmare at the best of times. In a fire, it would be a death trap.

"How about you come with me," Claire suggested in her best customer service voice, trying to banish the mental image of the elderly woman trapped in an elevator as the world burned around her.

"All right, fine. At least let me walk your dog," Mrs. Dodge said, extending a hand for Rosie's leash.

Claire happily released the leash to Mrs. Dodge and helped her down the remaining three flights of stairs and then outside.

A handful of stars were scattered across the inky black of the night sky. The temperature had once again dived sharply into the fifties. A breeze bit at Claire's calves, still coated in small beads of water. She retreated to the far end of the walkway in front of her building, shivering and drawing the robe more tightly around her. A crowd of neighbors grew, most of them retirees with bifocals and fuzzy slippers.

A fire truck pulled up to the curb, siren blaring and lights flashing. A handful of firefighters leapt off the truck and entered the building. Claire blushed as one glanced at her. She hadn't even had a chance to wash the shampoo out of her hair. She sat on the low brick wall that lined the entrance to the apartment building, crossing her legs at the ankle and sitting erect, as though someone was going to come by with a ruler and judge her posture.

Doozer, a neighborhood English Mastiff who weighed more than Claire, lumbered up to her and Rosie. His owner, Chuck, was infamous for never leashing him. Rosie recognized her friend and play bowed, tiny stub of a tail wiggling. The dogs circled repeatedly, bounding after each other and barking. Rosie gently nipped at Doozer's ankles.

"Rosie—don't." Claire sighed. She eased the backpack off and set it on the wall next to her. If this leash broke, Doozer's owner certainly wasn't going to be any help tracking the dogs down. Chuck was thirty yards down the sidewalk, smoking a cigarette under a streetlight.

Doozer had somehow looped a leg through Rosie's leash. Claire stood and bent at the waist. A gust of wind descended, and her robe flapped in the wind. Doozer grabbed the end of her robe and tugged.

"Doozer, no! That's not a toy!" Claire cried, but it was too late. He ripped at the robe, tearing it from her body and darting off across the front lawn. Claire shrieked and lunged for it, but she had forgotten about the low wall. While Doozer and her robe cleared it easily, Claire slammed her shins into it and tumbled, completely naked, through the frigid night air. She landed in a holly bush, sticks jabbing her in a number of unmentionable places.

"Ow," she said breathlessly, stunned by the impact. For a moment, she simply looked at the night sky. What had she had done to piss off the big guy upstairs? She had just wanted to get through the hearing without any issues. Instead, Luke's mother had publicly slandered her, her mother had nearly been arrested, and she had screamed at her lying boyfriend in the front yard like she was auditioning for an episode of Jerry Springer. Now she was lying naked in a bush while her apartment building might be on fire. Where could she go from here?

There wasn't time for more introspection. Claire flailed her way out of the bush, cheeks hot. Rosie's leash was still wrapped around her wrist. At least she hadn't escaped and started a colony of feral, cheese-loving Corgis. Claire ripped her backpack from the wall and slung it over her front, covering what she could and crouching behind the wall.

"Claire, dear, are you all right?" Mrs. Dodge asked, clearly holding back laughter. "That damn dog. Here, take my dressing gown." She struggled to untie her sash.

A black SUV with a Sanctum Security logo pulled up behind the fire truck, and Sawyer Goulding emerged. Oh, good. Another person to witness her humiliation. He slammed his door shut and strode toward the building like he was preparing for battle.

Oh, hell. Claire tried to duck behind the wall again. But Sawyer, a good foot taller than the other nosey nellies who had gathered, spotted her easily.

"Claire, are you okay? Why are you hiding behind—oh," he said, visibly doing a double take. He stepped in front of her, obscuring everyone else's view. He shrugged off his jacket and held it out in front of her, craning his neck to look behind him rather than at her naked body. Should she be grateful or insulted? Sure, she hadn't made it to her hot yoga or core crusher class this week, but she hadn't completely dissolved into a shapeless puddle of wine and pizza. He waited for her to drop her backpack and crawl into the jacket. He zipped it up for her, thumb accidentally grazing the side of her right breast.

"Sorry," he said before quickly patting Rosie on the head and leaping back over the wall.

"Thank you so—" Claire began, but Sawyer had already disappeared into the building.

The sleeves of the jacket dangled almost to her knees. It smelled like Sawyer, citrusy and bright. She zipped Rosie into it with her, allowing her furry face to poke out the top. She had a feeling Sawyer wouldn't mind.

After what felt like hours, the firefighters filed out of the building, signaling an all clear to the residents. Claire rolled her eyes, accepting that she was correct in her burnt popcorn assessment.

She ran into Sawyer as he was leaving the lobby.

"Oh, Sawyer," she said, gently dropping Rosie to the floor. "Thank you so much for this. Tonight wasn't exactly an opportune time for burnt popcorn. If you don't mind, uh, following me back to my apartment, I can give you your jacket back." Her robe, which Doozer's owner had finally returned, was slung over her shoulder, now dirty and frayed from the dog's wayward adventure.

Sawyer looked around for a moment and leaned down to pet Rosie.

"Sanctum manages the fire alarms in this building. It wasn't burnt popcorn. Someone pulled an alarm on the second floor," he said quietly as they walked to the staircase. He held the door open for her.

"Oh," she said, eyes widening in surprise. "Is everything okay?"

"Everything's fine. They didn't find a fire. It could have just been a punk kid pulling the alarm," he said as they climbed.

Claire tilted her head. She hadn't seen any children outside. "I don't think many young families live here."

"My thoughts exactly."

"I didn't know Sanctum was in the fire alarm business," she remarked as they climbed the stairs.

"These are not ordinary fire alarms." Sawyer gestured to one on the stairwell wall. "They're Bluetooth and Wi-Fi enabled and can be monitored from anywhere with the Sanctum app. They also have a pinhole camera that records for ten seconds after the alarm is pulled. My own design. We're strictly business-to-business right now, but someday I hope we'll be able to sell home systems for consumers."

"That's amazing. So there should be footage of who pulled the alarm?"

He frowned. "Someone covered it with a piece of electrical tape."

"That is one dedicated and suspiciously informed prankster," she said as he held the door to the fourth floor open for her.

They walked down the hallway, passing several unremarkable still life paintings of the West Haven area. Rosie darted from side to side, sniffing each doorstep.

Claire approached her door and slapped her forehead.

"Shit. I didn't do a dance."

"What?" Sawyer asked.

She twisted the doorknob and found it unlocked. She pushed it open. *Whoops.*

"You know, your new security system is only as good as the door that's keeping people out," he hinted.

"I forgot in all the kerfuffle," she said, shrugging. "I'll be right back," she said sheepishly, running into her bedroom and throwing on her Camp Susquehanna shirt and a pair of paint-stained athletic shorts she found in the back of a drawer. She really needed to do some laundry.

"That looks bad," Sawyer said when she got back to the living room.

She looked down at her T-shirt. Her nipples had hardened in the frigid air and were definitely poking through the shirt. She crossed her arms over her chest. "Well, I wasn't planning on hitting the runway in it."

"Not your shirt. Your shins."

She glanced down at her battered shins. "Oh. That does explain the searing pain." The jacket was heavy in her hand as she passed it back to him. "Thank you so much. You saved me. Again. At least this time I was only likely to die from embarrassment and hypothermia and not from a homicidal maniac."

"You were significantly easier to rescue this time. I'll see you later. Lock the door behind me." He waved as he left.

Claire let Rosie off her leash and rinsed her hair in the sink. She towel dried it as best as she could and collapsed into bed, a halo of wet hair surrounding her. The news of the fire alarm clouded her mind. Who had pulled it? And why?

After plugging her phone in, she briefly ran through her schedule for the next day. It was time to put this catastrophically crappy day behind her. She stretched, thoroughly exhausted, reaching one hand under her pillow to support her head. Her fingers brushed against something, and she shot up like she had been electrocuted. An envelope slid out from under her pillow.

What the hell was this? She hadn't been sleep-hiding her mail, had she?

There was no name or address on the outside. This hadn't come from the postal service. Her stomach dropped, and she tore the envelope open. Inside was a plain white sheet of paper. Spiky, slanted handwriting covered the sheet.

You won't escape next time.

Claire froze. Her pulse skyrocketed. The note fell from her hand and fluttered onto the duvet. Static buzzed incessantly in her ears as she tumbled out of bed and onto her hardwood floor.

It couldn't be happening again. Barney was in prison. Had he paid someone to harass her? Even though he was imprisoned, he had vast reserves of cash.

Were the walls closing in? That must be why her vision was darkening at the edges. Her heart thudded erratically. She climbed to her knees. Pain shot through her chest. Oh god, was she having a heart attack on top of everything?

Rosie leapt down from her side of the bed and whined, pressing her front legs onto Claire's chest and licking her face.

Summoning every ounce of strength she had left, Claire crawled out of the room and away from the note. Short gasps racked her body. What was wrong with her? Her anxiety had been through the roof since the abduction, but this was something worse. Was she dying? Some latent injury from her stab wound?

She needed to go check the security camera and look for footage. Or call for help. But her limbs weren't cooperating, and she had just abandoned her phone in the room with the threatening note. Could the note-leaver still be here?

The thought drove her to her feet. She stumbled to the

front door and smashed the panic button on her security alarm. An LED on the console blinked.

Brrrrrr. That was the sound of Claire's phone vibrating on the bed. But she wasn't about to go fetch it. The intruder could still be in the apartment. She hadn't even checked the bedroom closet. A prickle of fear ran up her spine.

Acting on instinct, she grabbed the console table in the hallway and dragged it in front of the bedroom door. There. That would at least slow him down. Now what? She crossed to the living room and pulled a Taser out of her purse. It settled in her pocket, but it didn't feel like enough.

A sword on her drying rack caught her eye. Kyle had used it to dramatically open a bottle of sparkling wine on pizza night. She darted into the kitchen and picked it up. It swung in front of her as she moved into the hallway.

Rosie followed hot on Claire's heels, still whining. The sword trembled in her hand while her breath came in sharp jabs. She approached the hallway closet, stepping silently across the floor.

"HA!" she screamed, flinging the doors open with one hand and stabbing into the closet with the sword.

Shit. RIP winter coat.

She shoved her clothes aside and thoroughly inspected the closet. Apart from a handful of coats and some cleaning supplies, the closet was empty. She slunk back into the living room. Someone could be hiding underneath her couch. She dropped to her knees and slashed the sword underneath the couch. It clanged off a leg, and Claire jerked her arm so hard that the sword ricocheted and sliced across her left forearm.

Fuckity fuck. That would be a tough one to explain to her doctor.

Blood oozed from her wound, running off her arm and

spattering onto the hardwood floor. She toddled over to the hallway closet and yanked her least-favorite scarf from its hanger. The wound burned as she wrapped it repeatedly around the wound, tightening the knot with her teeth.

She picked up the (now-bloody) sword. Ignoring the stabbing pain in her chest and the blood-soaked fall accessory on her arm, she yanked open her bathroom door. The shower was next—no intruder in there either.

She strode systematically through the house, peeking behind curtains and checking every nook and cranny. No one was hiding behind the bottle of creamer that had the whole refrigerator to itself. There wasn't an unusually small intruder curled up in the kitchen sink. Rosie followed every step of the way, licking frantically at Claire's bare legs. Not her most helpful moment.

Finally, she came to rest against the refrigerator. The stainless steel cooled the back of her neck. Her heart no longer galloped, but her limbs shook like leaves in the wind. Should she brave the bedroom and snatch her phone? There was no telling how long it would take Sanctum to respond to the panic button.

A thudding came from her front door. Thank god. Backup.

"Come in," Claire croaked. Her voice was like someone who had smoked five packs a day for a decade.

The knob rattled, then the door flew open. A large, dark shape ninja rolled into her apartment. Rosie immediately barked and growled. Her lip curled as she approached the figure with bared teeth. Claire gripped the handle of her sword.

Sawyer leapt to his feet, holding his stun gun out in front of him.

"Is someone in the apartment?" he barked, spotting her frozen at the refrigerator.

"I'm not sure. I haven't checked the bedroom." Her voice wavered again. *Get it together, Claire.*

Sawyer strode down the hallway like he was about to storm a castle. He thrust the table out of the way and threw the bedroom door open. He disappeared inside.

Claire's knees gave out. She slid slowly down the refrigerator until she puddled on the floor. She was safe. So why was her vision going dark again?

Painful, shallow breaths stole past her lips. The chest pain was back. Maybe she really was having a heart attack.

"All clear." Sawyer stepped into the hallway. He looked around for a moment before spotting her on the floor. The entire kitchen shook as he dropped to his knees.

She turned to him. Tears leaked out, spilling down cheeks that twitched on their own. Was she going to die?

"Woah, hey. Are you having a panic attack? Here." He gathered her into his arms and pressed her into his chest.

Oh, a panic attack. Not death, then. That was good.

"Breathe with me, Claire. Feel my heartbeat." He said, gently tugging her palm upward and onto his broad chest.

In for seven, out for eleven. Was it possible to breathe away a panic attack? Her body still trembled, but as he held her, the panic edged away. There was no one in her apartment. She was safe. Rosie was safe.

"You're safe," he said, as if reading her mind.

Thank god it had been Sawyer who responded. He had such a calming presence. She wasn't sure how many surveillance techs worked at Sanctum, but Sawyer had already seen her blood-drenched and inches from death. Explaining her circumstances to a newbie would have been even more painful.

Minute by minute, her breathing slowed and got deeper. The sense of dread was still there, but it began to fade and blur at the edges like an inky watercolor.

Was she going to have to tell Luke about this? Even though they weren't officially together, it felt strange to be held by another man. As much as she didn't want to admit it, she would have given her last bottle of wine to be in his arms right now. She pulled back and leaned against the fridge again.

"Could you check the rest of the apartment too? In case I missed anything."

"Absolutely." Sawyer set to work re-investigating the spots she had already checked. "Can I ask what happened?"

"I found a note under my pillow."

He swiveled and stared at her. "Are you serious?"

"It's on the bed."

He walked toward the bedroom, boots thumping heavily on her wooden floors. He pulled a pair of gloves from the utility belt he wore. A moment later, he reappeared with the letter and envelope in hand.

"Jesus. Do you still have Detective Smith's phone number?"

"In my wallet," Claire said, pointing with a shaky finger to a hook by the front door. She hadn't bothered to take it out of her backpack.

Sawyer pulled out a bottle of water, bag of dog treats, travel umbrella, emergency thermal sleeping bag, and a plastic pouch with twelve pens in different colors before successfully finding her wallet. He fished Detective Smith's card out and dialed, quickly relaying the information. Then he made sure the door was bolted tight before coming to sit with Claire again.

"The apartment's clear. Detective Smith is on his way.

Are you feeling any better? And what the hell happened to your arm?" he asked, spotting the ugly beige scarf that was now largely saturated with blood.

"I may have impaled myself while checking the apartment for intruders."

He shook his head. "Self-defense class. This week. No arguments. Do you have a first aid kit?"

"It's at Luke's," Claire said, marveling at how wildly unprepared she was. How unlike her. Barney had really messed with her equilibrium. "It's fine." She gestured weakly with her bloody arm.

"I think I have one in my car. Let me just—"

"Stay. Please," she said, heart rate escalating at the thought of being in the apartment alone.

"Okay. Why don't we at least wash the wound and find something a little better than a scarf to dress it?" He took her hand to help her to her feet.

"I can do it." She took her hand back and straightened her shoulders, standing tall as she walked to the sink. She didn't need a man to tend her wounds. She was a grown-ass woman. A grown-ass woman who had just dissolved into a panic attack and who may have been targeted by someone yet again, but a woman nonetheless.

In a refreshing change of pace, Sawyer didn't follow her and micromanage every aspect of her wound care. Luke flat-out refused to let Claire dress her stab wound. Or at least he had before she decided she wasn't speaking to him.

Sawyer tapped at her security system as she flicked on the light above her sink. Blood swirled down her drain as she rinsed her arm. When the dish soap made contact with the cut, she flinched.

Sawyer swore, and her eyes snapped up.

"What?" she asked, wrapping a layer of paper towels

around her arm. She shoved her hand into an oven mitt to keep them in place. Close enough.

"I'm not sure if you want to see this," he said, standing in front of the touchscreen mounted on the wall.

"Show me." She crossed her arms over her chest. Enough with men trying to protect her feelings.

He stepped away from the screen. Footage rolled of the empty hallway outside her front door. The alarm blared in the background as a figure dressed all in black approached, darting its head from side to side repeatedly before it came to a stop in front of the door. The figure was tall and lanky but had broad shoulders and a visible Adam's apple. A black ski mask covered all but the person's eyes, which were so dark that they appeared black. The doorknob rattled, and the figure disappeared from the screen as he entered her apartment. The video captured the man leaving a few minutes later.

Claire backed away from the screen, gripping the countertop to keep herself steady. A stranger had been in her apartment. Again. The four walls that were supposed to be home suddenly felt like a prison.

"Couldn't he have at least worn a less stereotypical outfit to break into my apartment? He looks like a cat burglar from the 80s," she joked in spite of the lump that was lodged in her throat.

"Here," Sawyer said, laying her cell phone on the countertop. "Thought you might want this. I texted Luke from my phone and let him know what was going on."

She groaned and turned away.

"Should I not have done that?"

"We're not in the best place at the moment," she said,

"I'm sorry to hear that. Do you want to talk about—"

He was cut off by a sharp knock at the door. "West Haven Police Department," Detective Smith announced.

Claire crossed to her front door and unbolted it, peeking through the crack before removing the chain.

Detective Smith asked what felt like a million questions, especially about the bloody sword on Claire's countertop. He was accompanied by two other cops, one of whom was kneeling at her front door, dusting for fingerprints. At their request, Rosie had been barricaded in the bathroom because she kept rolling over next to them, demanding belly rubs.

"Can you think of anyone who would do something like this? Maybe as a practical joke?" the detective asked, nub of a pencil poised above a miniature spiral-bound notebook.

"Wendy Flutter is suing me," Claire said wearily, resting her head in her hand. She had collapsed into a chair at her dining room table, an untouched glass of water next to her.

Detective Smith's eyebrows knit together, and he glanced again at the note.

"It doesn't look like her handwriting," she admitted. Wendy had a looping, flowing script and dotted her I's with hearts. The intruder on the video didn't look like her either. If it was Wendy, the figure surely would have been wearing a designer catsuit and ski mask. "She could have written it with her nondominant hand, I guess. It doesn't look like Barney's handwriting either, for what it's worth."

"We'll get this to a handwriting expert," the detective said, sliding the paper and envelope carefully into an evidence bag.

Great, a handwriting expert. That would surely result in all kinds of leads.

"I can't believe it's happening again," she said to Sawyer as the cops reviewed the footage from the security system, which Claire had downloaded and emailed to Detective Smith.

Sawyer laid a hand on her shoulder. "Nothing is going to happen to you. It's probably just some copycat asshole playing a joke."

"An asshole who knows where I live?" she asked, eyebrows raised.

"Yeah." He didn't sound convinced. "I'm going to go re-calibrate your motion sensors again," he said, sliding his chair back from the table and disappearing down the hallway.

Claire's phone buzzed in her hand. She turned it over, expecting more empty apologies from Luke, and instead found a series of texts from her downstairs neighbor, Kara, and her mother. She opened the text from Kara first.

Kara: *Is there a herd of elephants in your apartment or are you having extremely passionate sex that's measurable on the Richter scale? My chandelier is swaying.*

Claire smiled in spite of the circumstances. Kara had moved in the month before, and she and Claire had instantly bonded over their love of dogs. Kara had an Australian shepherd named Sammy, who tried to herd Rosie at their first meeting.

Claire: *Rosie has taken up CrossFit.*

By some miracle, Kara had no idea who Claire was, or at least pretended not to. It was nice having an acquaintance who didn't walk on eggshells around her.

She switched to the message from her mother. Should she tell her about the note?

Alice: *Are you okay, Clairebear? I'm sitting on the tarmac and I felt a disturbance.*

Suddenly, her front door banged open. All three cops whirled with blinding speed and pointed their guns at the intruder. Claire kicked her chair behind her and dove under the dining room table, slamming her elbow off a leg as she went down. She flipped onto her back and ripped away the duct tape securing the aluminum baseball bat to the underside of the table.

"*Hands in the air,*" Detective Smith barked.

"*Get down now,*" the female cop closest to the door yelled.

"Shit," the visitor said.

Were those worn high-top sneakers? She would have recognized them anywhere.

Luke dropped to his knees and raised his hands.

"It's okay," Claire said to Detective Smith as she crawled halfway out from under the table, still clutching the bat. "It's just my... Luke."

"Is this your first visit to the apartment tonight?" Detective Smith apparently recognized Luke from the hospital, because he didn't bother asking for identification.

"Yes. I got a text from Sawyer that said there was another break-in." Luke's eyes zeroed in on Claire's makeshift oven mitt bandage.

"Where were you between the hours of 6:30 and 8:00 p.m.?" Detective Smith continued.

"I was at home."

"Can anyone corroborate that?"

"I have a security system that records when I leave the house," Luke offered.

"You'll send me the footage," Detective Smith said, lowering his gun.

"Of course," Luke said, still on his knees.

Detective Smith nodded to the other cops, who lowered their weapons and went back to canvassing Claire's apartment.

Luke stood and walked over to where Claire sat on the floor, half under the table. He crouched next to her and pulled her into a tight hug.

She was still beyond furious at him, but their argument suddenly seemed less devastating than it had a couple of hours ago. While the identity of Luke's mysterious brother remained a burning question, the note had shifted her perspective. The nightmare she thought had ended appeared to be ramping up again. There was time to argue about mystery brothers later. She melted into the hug, taking comfort in the familiar shape of Luke's torso.

"Are you okay? Why the hell are you wearing an oven mitt?"

"There was a minor sword incident," she admitted.

He tugged the mitt off and began unwinding her paper towel bandage. "I leave you alone for three hours and your apartment gets broken into and you, what, stab yourself with a sword?"

"I also fell over a wall and into a holly bush completely naked." She flinched as he examined her forearm.

"What?"

"Never mind." She was still mad at him. He hadn't earned all the details.

"You need more pressure on this." He shook his head. "Where's your first aid kit?"

"At your house."

"Shit. This is pretty bad." He straightened up and tugged his T-shirt off.

"Luke, you don't need to—"

Luke ignored her and twirled his T-shirt between his fingers until it resembled a rope. He wrapped it tightly around her forearm and tied the ends together. The wound smarted.

"Ouch." Claire flinched.

"You're coming home with me." As was often the case with Luke, it wasn't a question.

"No," she said firmly, thrusting the end of the bat in Luke's direction.

"You can't stay here. It's a crime scene. Again," he added, gesturing at the female cop, who was inspecting the floorboards with a black light. Claire hadn't vacuumed since coming home from the hospital. The cop would be able to collect enough dog hair to knit a winter sweater.

"Then I'll get a hotel room." He and his tantalizing gray sweatpants weren't about to cloud her judgment.

"You know the hotels around here aren't dog-friendly."

"Then I'll stay at the warehouse," she said stubbornly.

Luke lowered his voice. "If this creep knows where you live, he sure as hell knows where you work. And if the press hear about this, they're going to swarm you even more. Do you really want to put Rosie in danger?"

Claire bristled. "It's not like your house is any safer. Do I need to remind you what happened to Rosie at your house?"

"I've completely upgraded the security system since then. We have a gate to keep the press out. It's much safer than the warehouse."

She refused to respond.

"Half your clothes are there. I won't even talk to you. And I have wine." He extended a hand to her.

Claire sighed and accepted his hand. She *loathed* having to rely on other people. Luke helped her to her feet. She brushed against his bare chest as she stood and stubbornly ignored the butterflies that had suddenly taken up residence in her stomach.

Stupid, bossy, pathological liar with abs she could bounce a quarter off.

Detective Smith came over, apparently unconcerned by Luke's new shirtlessness, and assured her that he would call if they found anything. He gave her permission to leave. Sawyer said he would make sure the place was locked up tight. As strange as it was to leave four people alone in her apartment, she didn't have much of a choice. She looped Rosie's leash around her wrist and followed Luke downstairs. For once, he didn't try to coerce her into using the spooky death trap elevator.

"I'm driving," Luke said.

"Whatever." The day was catching up with her, and she could barely keep her eyes open as she climbed into Luke's car.

Rosie refused to sit in the back seat and insisted on perching on Claire's lap. She hugged the dog to her chest and scratched her behind the ears as the city flashed by.

Luke's eyebrows were knit together. Something was clearly bothering him, and the quiet hung heavy between them.

"Your nipples are looking particularly brown this evening," Claire said as they paused at a red light, bathed in the unflattering yellow neon from a bar sign.

"Why did you call Sawyer?" he asked.

"What do you mean?"

"You called him instead of me."

"I didn't call him. I hit the panic button on the security system."

"Oh."

There was silence for several more minutes as Luke drove. A club passed by the window, thumping with electronic dance music. The streets were mostly empty at this time of night, but a group of teenagers perched on a bench.

"But you still didn't call me," he said as they passed the city limits. His hands tightened on the leather steering wheel.

She stared at him. "Do you not remember three hours ago when you refused to tell me the truth about your brother?"

He looked back at her. "Why didn't you ever tell me about your dad?"

She glanced at the speedometer. How many injuries would she sustain if she jumped out of the car? What were a few more bangs and bruises? She was already covered from head to toe. "You met Roy at the hospital."

"Your bio-dad," Luke corrected.

"Because he's a piece of human garbage who isn't worth the breath it would take to explain him."

Luke sighed and tapped his thumb on the steering wheel. "So is my brother. It's not easy for me to talk about."

"That doesn't mean you should keep it bottled up forever and lie to me about his existence," she chastised.

"I'll tell you what happened. But not tonight. This day has already been enough of a shitshow."

"You're not kidding."

Finally, they turned onto Luke's road. At least she could hide in one of the fifty-seven rooms in his house and process what had just happened. Luke hit the button to open his gate. It rose slowly in front of them.

"I thought maybe you called him because he was there for you. During the Barney incident. He saved you."

Apparently, they were still talking about the Sawyer thing. Claire tilted her head. "Is this why you've been acting like a grumpasaurus every time he's around?"

He shrugged. "I was too late. Sawyer wasn't. It would make sense for you to feel like you can rely on him."

She rubbed at her temples. "Sawyer was only 'there for me' because he happened to be the closest Sanctum personnel to both crime scenes."

"Conveniently," Luke muttered to himself.

CHAPTER TEN

To Do:
- Figure out better sleepwalking prevention solution
- Linens for A's proposal

Caw.

It was dark. Everything was dark. Crickets chirped in every direction. The snap of a twig sounded like a gunshot in the darkness.

Ouch. Something stabbed into the arch of her foot. Claire's eyes flew open.

Shadowy trees surrounded her. She was barefoot again. Oh, hell. She had sleepwalked right into the woods. The hair on the back of her neck stood up, and her pulse skyrocketed. The last time she'd been in the woods, she'd been staggering down the gravel driveway outside the Heirloom Hotel. Fighting for her life in the blood-soaked remains of the wedding dress she was supposed to wear yesterday. There was no knife-wielding serial killer chasing her this time—at least as far as she knew—but the wound on her chest throbbed.

Leaves rustled in the wind. Another twig snapped somewhere close. A shiver ran down her spine. Was someone else out there? Could it be the person who left her the note?

She shuddered at the memory of the envelope under her pillow. Her home, her safe place, had been violated again. Who would have gone to such great lengths to leave her the note? What were they trying to accomplish? They could have dropped it in the mail like Barney did. But there was something personal here—they wanted to scare her. They wanted her to know they could find her.

It could have been Wendy. She certainly hated Claire enough to torture her legally and illegally. But somehow Claire couldn't reconcile the image of the nasty, conniving woman who slept with her fiancé with a clever invader pulling a fire alarm and breaking into her apartment. Unless she had help.

Caw.

Something moved on her arm. She bit back a scream. A small black bird perched on her forearm, pecking at a handful of something wet and cold clutched in her left fist.

What. The. Fuck.

She jostled the bird off and opened her hand. A meatball squelched and dropped to the ground along with a handful of noodles. Great, unconscious Claire had decided to take another midnight stroll accompanied by a fistful of carbs.

Get it together, Claire.

She flailed her hand and wiped it against a nearby tree trunk. Hang on, her right hand was full too. A slice of moonlight penetrated the thick canopy of trees overhead. It glanced off an eight-inch chef's knife. What the hell was her unconscious doing? Knives and spaghetti hands? At least if she was attacked by a bear or a mountain lion, she could defend herself.

She made a mental note to research sleep restraints and set her mind to getting out of the forest before Luke woke up and found her missing. Again. There was no need to panic. She couldn't have gotten that far from the house while barefoot. Could she?

She tipped her head and glanced above her. The tree canopy was so thick she could barely see any stars. So that navigation method was out. Not that she knew how to use them anyway. She used her non-spaghetti hand to pat her legs and chest. No pants again. This was starting to become a real problem.

No phone either, but what was in her bra? Oh, good. A slice of garlic bread. As if hand spaghetti wasn't enough, she could now top off her meal with bra bread. She flung it into the woods like a Frisbee.

Okay, no phone and no stars. She could do this. She had spent most of her adult life in West Haven. The creepy, barely moonlit woods didn't scare her. Squinting her eyes in the dim lighting, she scanned her surroundings.

Aha! About five feet behind her, a noodle rested on a bush. She must have come from that direction. She stepped toward it carefully. A blanket of dead leaves carpeted most of the ground, but her feet seemed to find every stray acorn and pinecone.

Okay, so she had made it five feet. Better than nothing. She took another look around. Was it her imagination, or did the trunk of that tree have something red and wet on it? She stepped carefully around a stump and inhaled deeply. Yep, that was Luke's homemade pasta sauce.

She walked hesitantly past the tree, eyes peeled for signs of unconscious Claire's path. Another noodle trembled on a fern ten feet away. Thank god she had picked such a messy snack for the road. Five feet beyond, she found a branch that had snapped in half. Not definitive proof of her passage, but close enough. She followed that direction for another few yards.

Something was moving behind the trees in front of her. Her gut clenched. Was it a bear? A mountain lion? Some other wild animal who loved spaghetti? Or worse—the person who had left the note under her pillow?

She held the knife out in front of her, tip facing down like Roy had taught her. Claire's high school hadn't been the safest institution in the state. Something sharp on the forest floor jabbed into her foot.

"Mother fu—" She clutched her foot. Whatever jabbed her didn't feel natural. She knelt and dragged a hand through the carpet of dead leaves. Her fingertips brushed a small, metallic cylinder. She held it up to the snatches of moonlight filtering through the trees.

It was a pen. An expensive-looking pen. What the hell was this bougie-ass pen doing in the middle of the woods? Had Luke flung it out here in a fit of rage? But he usually wrote in pencil. Hmmm.

She shrugged and pocketed it. No sense in wasting a nice pen. The shape moved again in the darkness, and Claire's breath hitched. She had almost forgotten about it. Should she move toward the shape, or away?

Screw it. She charged through the woods, completely disregarding her footing. A low-hanging branch scratched at her cheek as she ran.

"Ha!" she shouted as she approached the figure. She burst out of the tree line, knife drawn and at the ready.

Oh, thank god. It was Luke's pool. The mysterious moving figure was Rosie's unicorn float skimming across the surface.

Claire dropped the knife to her side and bent at the waist, willing her breath to slow. She had made it out of the woods completely on her own. No compass, no pants, no problem. And she had found a cool free pen. Adrenaline coursed through her veins, and she felt strangely invigorated, as though the sleepwalking escapade had made her invincible. Maybe this was just her subconscious's way of preparing her for the unexpected. It wasn't really a problem, just a safety drill. Everything was fine.

CHAPTER ELEVEN

To Do:
- Update dog sitting binder- corn allergy!
- Figure out who's stalking me

Mindy threw a suitcase into Claire's arms.

Claire staggered and dropped the heavy case onto the warehouse floor. It had only been twenty-four hours since the hearing, but it felt like much longer.

"I'll be watching Rosie while you're gone," Mindy said, hurling Claire's purse onto the mahogany conference table and rooting through it. She withdrew four packs of gum, a baggie full of dog treats, a stack of multicolored sticky notes, and a Taser before finding a leash.

"Absolutely not. You don't even know her bedtime song," Claire protested.

Mindy looked up from the binder she was struggling to heave out of Claire's bag.

Sweet dreams, little Rosie
A kiss for every toesie
Unicorns will greet you
In a magical canoe

Mindy took a breath to continue in her off-key voice, but Claire held up a hand to stop her. "Okay, fine, you know the song. But I can't leave. Tyler's proposal is next week. It's crunch time."

"And we already have everything ready for it. The decorations are going in on Wednesday, the firework technician is ready to go, the marching band has been practicing for two weeks. Tyler's PT is going well. You need to escape for a few days. It's just a long weekend, Claire," Mindy said, plopping a heavy backpack down on top of the suitcase. "I packed all the essentials for you."

"I am not leaving," Claire said stubbornly, crossing her arms over her chest. "What if the police need me?" She stomped up to the table and shoved the dog treats and sticky notes back into her bag. She sure as hell wasn't leaving.

"Detective Smith is the one who suggested you go!" Mindy sighed. She grabbed one strap of Claire's purse and pulled.

Claire grabbed onto the other one and tugged it toward her.

"Get out of town for a few days, let them sort this out," Mindy said sternly. "Besides, fall proposal season is coming up. *Farmer's Almanac* is predicting that the foliage is going to be more vibrant than it has been in years. Think of all the hiking and pumpkin-themed proposals, Claire. This may be the last chance you get to take a trip for months."

Fall proposals! She loved fall proposals. The crisp chill

in the air, the plaid, the pumpkins. It might only be June, but it was never too early to start planning some fall ideas. Maybe they could offer mini proposal packages? Still romantic and beautiful, but more cost-effective for clients and less time-consuming for the business. But that would take away from the impact of the uniquely tailored proposal for each person. And Happily Ever Afters was not about cookie cutter proposals.

Wait, what were they arguing about again?

Claire's grip must have loosened on the strap, because Mindy heaved it away from her. Damn it.

"I'm not going to let some note-leaving creep run my life. I don't need to take a trip. I need to be here for my clients." Claire walked over to her massive whiteboard (which had recently been de-murdered after their Widowmaker investigation) and picked up a marker. She studied the color-coded To Do lists and crossed off "silence-breaking blog post." She had posted a story from her backlog of proposals in anticipation of Pride Month, featuring a sweet couple who had met when Kelly took Jade's pottery class. Jade had proposed to Kelly with a beautiful ceramic ring she had crafted herself.

Claire had had to turn comments off on her blog following the incident. Some were sympathetic, others cruelly questioned her judgment and professionalism. She had considered posting something about Barney and her experience, but the heinous crime didn't have a place among the joyful and romantic posts on her blog. Frankly, he wasn't worth the time it would take to write about him.

"We still need to set up a supervised date with Zayne and Alex. I'm still not fully convinced that she's not sleeping with his brother," Claire said.

Mindy slapped the marker out of her hand. *"No more*

work. Stop being a child and sit your ass in that chair. Luke should be here any minute."

Claire bristled. "Why the hell is Luke coming?"

"You didn't seriously think I was going to send you to an undisclosed location alone, did you? You would have turned around immediately and come right back to work."

Well, there went that plan.

"You're killing me." Claire collapsed into the chair at the head of the conference table. She didn't want to go on a trip. She definitely didn't want to go on a trip with the infuriatingly egotistical man who repeatedly lied to her.

What truths would she uncover on a weekend trip with Luke? Did he have a hoard of children with different mothers? Maybe some problems with recreational drugs? Sure, they were on slightly better terms after the break-in. But the more time she spent with Luke, the more she realized she didn't really know him at all. And what was the deal with the secret brother?

"Where are we going?" she huffed.

"I understand you're emotionally fragile right now," Mindy said, "and some asshole is leaving notes under your pillow, but you're being a bit of a bitch. Your smokin' hot boyfriend is whisking you away to a romantic location for a long weekend. Suck. It. Up." She jabbed Claire's arm with freshly manicured fingers.

"Fine." Claire pulled out her phone. "But it's not Africa or the Caribbean, right? I may want to start a family within three-to-five years, and nobody knows how long Zika stays in your system."

"There's mosquito repellant in your luggage."

"You thought of everything."

"I always do." Mindy, apparently satisfied that Claire was not going to barricade herself in the office, opened her laptop and sat down at the conference table. She kicked her kitten heels off, dropping them to the floor as she sat cross-legged in her chair.

Claire ran a hand over the cover of Tyler's proposal binder. "Tyler and Ericka are good together, right?"

Mindy lifted her eyes from the screen. "Of course they are. Remember that Skype date we recorded? She adores him."

"And Tyler. You think his feelings are genuine?"

Mindy snapped her laptop shut and placed her hands on either side of her, leaning forward to stare at Claire. "Don't do that."

"Do what?"

"Doubt yourself. Do not give Barney that control."

Claire's voice wavered. "Mindy, I helped a serial killer propose to his girlfriend."

Her friend's expression softened. "He had everyone fooled, even his fiancée. She *lived* with him and had no idea."

Sure, that much was true. Barney was an elite-level con man. But how could Claire have spent hours just steps away from a serial killer and never felt even a hint of danger? Her inability to recognize evil had cost them dearly. They had upgraded their client screening process to include criminal background checks, which were not cheap.

She gripped the back of a chair. "Our whole brand revolves around our success rate. And he absolutely destroyed it. I'm obviously not as good at reading people as I thought. All our clients are probably destined for divorce. I obviously have no idea how to have a functional relationship if my fiancé left me for my archnemesis and my boyfriend withholds every detail of his life from me."

Mindy whipped a spray bottle out of Rosie's overnight bag and blasted Claire in the face with a stream of water.

"Stop it," she ordered as Claire sputtered and wiped at her face. "You are a wonderful human being, a great boss, and smart as hell. You are wound so tightly right now that I am slightly concerned about a complete mental breakdown, and I really think you need to get laid, but that doesn't change the fact that you are the best."

Claire smiled, but she didn't feel it inside. She was putting all her energy into a losing battle. "Thank you for saying that. Strangely enough, I feel almost comfortable leaving you in control." She reached across the lacquered surface of the table and squeezed Mindy's hand.

Mindy raised her eyebrows and drew her dark braid over her shoulder. "After three years, you should be."

"We are a pretty kick-ass team," Claire mused aloud. She squared her shoulders and tried to push the lingering feeling of doubt out of her mind. Tyler wasn't a murderer.

She jumped when the side door by the end of the industrial shelving flew open. She reached for her Taser, but it was on the other side of the conference table. Damn it, Mindy.

Luke sauntered in, leather jacket tossed over one shoulder. Every part of him appeared to be casual, but even Claire's extremely nearsighted sister Charlie could have picked up on the stress in his shoulders and the way his eyes continuously darted around the room, probing corners and shadows. Why did he insist on opening doors in such a dramatic fashion?

"You ready?" He picked up Claire's suitcase and dropped it almost immediately. "What the hell is in here?"

"Mindy packed it. It's probably full of vodka and romance novels," Claire said.

"She's not wrong," Mindy said as she typed furiously on her laptop.

"You'll remember to sing her the song?" Claire asked Mindy as she turned to her dog. She dropped to her knees in the middle of the warehouse floor and opened her arms.

"Of course," Mindy commented as a fawn-colored rocket sprinted toward Claire and into her arms, nearly knocking her over. Claire's black outfit was now covered with a cloud of ginger fur, but it was worth it.

"Maybe she can come with us." Claire buried her face in Rosie's wiggling body. How could she go three days without seeing Rosie? What if something happened to her?

"Put the dog down, Claire," Mindy instructed, picking up the spray bottle again and shaking it. Rosie backed away, ears drawn back.

"Dogs come on airplanes all the time," Claire said, reaching for her retreating dog.

"Rosie hates flying. They'll put her in a crate all by herself under the plane," Mindy said tactfully.

Claire straightened up. "They wouldn't dare."

"Come on. We'll miss our flight." Luke gripped Claire's elbow.

Claire stood and began rifling through her purse. "No. I could get her registered as an emotional support animal. What'll that take, ten minutes at the courthouse? I'll just call my doctor real quick and—"

Suddenly, the world was upside down. Claire dangled over Luke's shoulder like a rag doll.

"Help with the bags, Min?" Luke said nonchalantly, carrying Claire to the side door.

Rosie barked and jumped at Luke's legs, and Claire stretched out a hand.

"Roro, who wants a treat?" Mindy crinkled a treat bag.

Rosie about-faced in a millisecond and sprinted to the conference table. Mindy handed her a small bone, and Rosie retreated to her dog bed in the corner, crunching noisily.

"Traitor!" Claire called out as Luke pushed open the door. It snapped shut behind them.

"We can't go," Claire said, still upside down. "Those flower beds are atrocious. Someone needs to weed them."

"The weeds will be here when we get back."

"What if the press starts an exposé on the business and airs footage of the flower beds?"

Luke set her down by the passenger door without comment. Claire crossed her arms and frowned at him, but he ignored her and opened the trunk for Mindy, who was struggling out with Claire's bags. The morning sun was creeping up in the sky even as heavy clouds rolled in.

"I want a picture every hour," Claire said as Luke hefted the suitcase into the car.

Mindy wrapped Claire in one of her signature suffocating hugs. "I'll send two. Don't worry about a thing, okay? I know that's impossible for you, but try. Everything will be fine."

"And you'll be safe?" Claire almost whispered.

"Always," Mindy said, smiling soothingly at her.

"Love you," Claire said as she opened her car door and got in.

"Love you more." Mindy slammed the door.

Claire instinctively reached into the back seat to buckle Rosie into her seatbelt. But Rosie wasn't coming. A pang of regret hit. She had rarely spent more than a night away from Rosie since she had rescued her after her breakup with Jason.

The car lurched into reverse, startling her from her

reverie. Now she was going on a trip to an undisclosed location with someone she was barely speaking to. Awesome.

Rain pummeled the windshield as they drove. The car jerked when they splashed into one of West Haven's famous potholes. Luke's stormy eyes flashed to the rearview mirror every couple of seconds.

"So," Claire said as they began to leave the city behind. "What did your mother have to say for herself? You said she texted this morning as I was leaving."

He had miraculously remained unconscious while she was on her midnight jaunt through the woods. She even had time to clean the marinara stains off the wall and door before crawling back into bed.

Luke's grip tightened on the wheel. "She said she was just doing her job."

"Ah, yes. When I'm doing my job, I, too, like to accuse my family's significant others of being lying, violent alcoholics. She knew who I was." Claire shook her head.

"Let's not talk about my mother. We're not really on speaking terms right now," he said as he laid a hand on Claire's thigh.

She was still angry—about so, so many things—but his touch sent a tingle up her spine. She pulled out her phone and opened her calendar.

"You better not be doing work." He swatted at her phone. "Mindy made me promise I wouldn't allow it."

"Just emailing Charlie an updated copy of my last will and testament," Claire said, attaching a PDF to her email to her sister. "I do it before every flight, so you can save your judgmental looks."

"How's life in the PR world?" Luke asked.

"Very scandalous. One of her clients impregnated his

maid and then tried to convince his wife to formally adopt the baby."

He whistled. "Sounds almost as stressful as planning proposals."

She hit him on the arm. "If you would tell me where we were going, I could stress about that instead." Though truthfully, anywhere was better than her twice-broken-into apartment. At least her getting on a plane would be inconvenient for whatever creep was stalking her.

"Trust me, you'll love it. The food, the culture, the people—well, maybe not the people. They don't love tourists. But the food and the culture for sure. We used to vacation there in the spring sometimes when I was a kid."

"Okay, fine. I'm relinquishing control and preparing to be dazzled." She leaned back into the beige leather of Luke's sedan.

The rain tapered off as they pulled into the airport and parked the car. Claire locked the doors and ignored the handful of people in the lot as she hip-thrusted and disco-pointed across two parking spots. It was better to be humiliated in public than to have a panic attack over the Atlantic because of an unlocked car.

Luke shook his head, but he didn't say anything. They boarded a shuttle to the terminal, and he wrapped his arm around her shoulders.

Claire breathed in his woodsy smell and closed her eyes. In her mind, she conjured a large cardboard box—a solid one, like the boxes from the book fairs of her youth—and consciously deposited all of her worries about her clients and her safety into it. She taped that bitch shut and shoved it into a corner of her mind. When she opened her eyes, Luke was smiling at her. She was still totally mad at him. But they were going on an adventure.

They arrived at the terminal and began the tedious process of catching a flight. Once their luggage was successfully tagged, they joined a surprisingly short security line.

"Miss," a TSA agent interrupted, "please step forward."

Claire submitted herself to the general humiliation of the TSA screening.

"Excuse me, ma'am. Do you have some electronic devices in your carry-on?"

Claire froze. She had done a cursory glance through the bag and had only seen her favorite book, a change of clothes, and some miscellaneous toiletries.

"I don't think so. My assistant packed my luggage for me, though, so maybe I missed something."

"Your luggage was buzzing as it came through the X-ray machine," the TSA agent said loudly as she slapped on a pair of latex gloves and began unzipping pockets.

Claire blushed, instantly mortified. "Oh, my goodness. I can't imagine why it would be buzzing. I'm so sorry," she said, taking a respectful step back. Luke's eyes burned into her. "Please take all the time you need."

"I intend to," the worker said. Her nametag read Dinkle, and she was built like a tank—short legs, wide hips, and arms that looked like they could crush someone. She shined a flashlight through the contents of the backpack and unfolded Claire's clothes, dropping her spare underwear onto the dirty airport floor.

This is how I die. Dead from embarrassment in the airport security line. Wendy will win Planner of the Year after all. Or maybe they could award it to Claire posthumously?

"Aha!" Agent Dinkle said triumphantly. "What the hell is this?"

A hot pink cylinder in a Ziplock bag buzzed noisily in her hand, and she stared pointedly at Claire.

Oh my god, I am going to kill Mindy.

"A vibrator," Claire mumbled. A crowd of people still struggling to put on their shoes stopped to stare.

Luke stepped forward and blocked their view. "We're going to Paris," he explained.

"*What? Paris?*" Claire shouted. "Oh my god, oh my god," she said, jumping around and holding onto Luke's arm. "I've wanted to go since I was a little girl."

"I know, your bathroom is covered in French art."

"The croissants! The patisseries! Oh my god, can we see the Eiffel Tower?"

Agent Dinkle sighed deeply, clearly irritated at Claire's joy. "Ma'am, I need you to open this and take out the batteries."

Claire took the bag and opened it clumsily, only half paying attention and peppering Luke with questions as she twisted the cylinder.

"Where are we staying? Left bank? Right bank? Where will we have dinner? Can we see the Champs-Élysées? Nicole is going to be so jealous," she continued as the screw top finally popped off. The batteries sprang out of the vibrator and escaped from the lip of the bag. They rolled across the floor.

"Gerald! Watch out, there are some vibrator batteries on the floor behind you," Agent Dinkle called to her teammate.

At this point, everyone in line had turned to watch, barely concealing their laughter.

"Huh?" A lumbering man turned around from his conveyor belt and stepped right on one of the free-rolling batteries. His foot slid out from under him, and he went crashing to the floor, sending a bag of Cheerios and a sippy cup flying out of the bag he was checking. The cereal exploded onto the floor, scattering across airport security.

Claire gasped and tried to run over to help, but Luke grabbed her arm.

"Stay here. As much fun as it would be to see you in handcuffs, they will tackle and arrest you."

"Oh, god. I'm so sorry, sir!" she called after the man who was now lying prone on his back and probably questioning his career.

Gerald snorted like an angry bull as he rolled himself from his back to his front and then clambered up.

"Ma'am, I'm going to ask you to keep control of your belongings before you seriously injure someone," he said, plodding over and handing her the remaining battery.

"I'm sorry. We're going to Paris," she explained. She was too excited to worry about some grumpy TSA agents.

Gerald rolled his eyes and turned away from them, walking back toward his line. Halfway there, he slipped on a stray Cheerio and crashed into the conveyor belt.

"Okay, time to go." Luke stuffed the now-silent cylinder and batteries into her backpack. He grabbed Claire by the arm and dragged her away from security.

Several people behind them applauded. The mother who had lost the Cheerios glared. Claire turned toward them and thrust her shoes, which were still in her hands, dramatically into the air.

"We're going to Paris!"

CHAPTER TWELVE

THE SUN WAS RISING OVER THE CITY AS CLAIRE AND LUKE stepped onto French soil. Nearby buildings were bathed in gold light, adding to the inherent charm of the City of Love. Cars, Vespas, and taxis honked and fought for a position along the road in front of the airport, even at this early hour.

Claire blinked, trying to clear the sleep from her eyes. She followed Luke blindly, stumbling as they joined the taxi line.

"You good?" he asked with a smile.

She squinted in the morning light, yawning as he tucked her into his side. Even thousands of miles away from home, he still smelled like freshly mowed grass and musky warmth. He pressed a tender kiss to her forehead, and she smiled.

"I can't believe you're not brushing up on some conversational French or digging through a map right now. It's very uncharacteristic of you," he said, regarding her with fake surprise.

"My clients are asleep. And that's what Google Translate is for." She stifled another yawn as she snuggled in closer to him.

People of all ethnicities bustled by them, speaking a myriad of languages. Drivers honked impatiently as the sun crept higher into the sky.

"You gave up control. You know what this means, don't you?"

"It means you owe me a generously buttered croissant and a brief nap before we start this adventure," she said.

"Yes, but that's not all. This means that you trust me."

"I wouldn't go that far." She cracked one eye open to stare up at Luke.

"It does, though. You, Claire the Great, independent, and sassy, have handed me the reins. This might be the first time it has happened." He looked around as if this was new territory for him.

"I have merely accepted the fact that you know more about this city than I do, and I don't want to step on your male ego by suggesting your planned activities aren't a good enough use of our time." She peeled herself away from him and attempted to smooth her hair, which had gone all wonky during the flight.

"You *did* plan activities, didn't you?" she asked, regarding him sternly. "We're not just going to wing it like backpacking college students taking a gap year, are we?"

"Please. It's going to be a great day." He leaned down and kissed her full on the mouth.

She flushed in pleasure, then drew back. Did she have red-eye breath? But his warmth and presence filled and energized her. Maybe, just this once, red-eye breath didn't matter.

"You know, you can't just take me to Paris every time we have an argument," she said, adjusting her backpack.

"Of course not. This is just stop number one on our apology world tour."

"I believe what you meant to say was 'Claire, I understand how important honesty is to you. I will not lie to you ever again, and I will make you a PowerPoint with a complete list of my family tree going back at least three generations, including footnotes that denote whether or not I am estranged from them.'"

"Honesty, got it. I'll add it to my to do list," he said as a taxi finally pulled up. "By the way, what did you tell your mom about the note?"

Claire frowned in silence. She had only told Alice that she was taking a trip and had omitted the reason why.

"That's what I thought. I am sorry, though, you know. For not telling you about George. I'll do better."

"Family is tough," she conceded as Luke took her bag. "I'm sorry for not being more up front about my bio-dad."

"You're forgiven." He kissed her hard and fast on the mouth and tugged her into the taxi.

Claire perked up as they wound through the city. She plastered herself to the window, pointing every few moments when she saw something she recognized.

"Luke! There's the Louvre." She gestured at the glass pyramid. "Are we going to go there? I've always wanted to see the Mona Lisa."

He smiled mysteriously. "Maybe."

Endless storefronts flashed by, windows full of colorful macarons and fashionable clothing. Her stomach audibly growled.

Minutes later, they pulled up in front of their hotel.

"Holy shit," she whispered as she stepped onto the cobblestone street. The tip of the Eiffel Tower was visible behind Hotel Lemont.

"I love it," she said. Maybe it was just the little pink cylinder in her luggage, but she was practically vibrating from head to toe.

Luke tipped the taxi driver and carried their suitcases inside. She listened in wonder as he checked them in, French pouring from his mouth as naturally as English.

God, that's sexy.

"Where did you learn to speak French?" Claire inquired as they loaded into an elevator.

It was rickety at best, and it lurched upward inch by inch. Just like the nightmare shaft in her apartment building. She instinctively tightened her wrist to draw Rosie close before remembering that she wasn't here.

"I had a buddy in the Navy whose family had emigrated from France. We had a lot of boring, late nights together in the hospital."

Luke put his arm around her again. His eyelashes were thick and dark, and he looked insanely sexy in his black leather jacket and jeans. Something in Claire stirred despite her near-starvation and jet lag.

"What floor is our room on?"

"Fourteen." He glanced at the old-school arrow that currently pointed at the number 3.

"Good." She dropped her backpack on the floor and grabbed Luke by the jacket, yanking him roughly to her. Her suitcase toppled to the floor as her hands fisted his collar. It was hard to tell if it was the charm of Paris or her body betraying her with hormones, but she wanted—needed—Luke.

His tongue explored the inside of her mouth, and he gripped her so tightly that she nearly cried out. He reached down and cupped her ass, clad in her skintight jeans, lifting her up so that her legs wrapped around his waist. He pressed her into the corner of the elevator. She wondered briefly if there was a security camera in the shaft.

Ha—*shaft.*

It felt like the first time again—their first kiss in Luke's library. Her stomach somersaulted. His hands were magic. She threw her head back with a moan of pleasure, and Luke greedily sampled her neck, softly nibbling and kissing in equal measure. One hand moved from her back to her front and began a slow ascent, burrowing under her lace balconette.

She arched against him, desperate to be close. Between her former fiancé sleeping with her nemesis and the recent stabbing, Claire's trauma had prevented her from opening herself—emotionally or physically—for months. But suddenly, she was open. She wanted Luke now.

The elevator dinged softly, jerking to a stop. *Shit.* Claire flailed, trying to withdraw her legs from around Luke. He set her down and her knees buckled. She landed hard on the faux marble floor of the elevator.

"Ahem." A soft-spoken protest preceded the entrance of a smartly dressed woman, clad in black from head to toe.

Claire sheepishly righted her suitcase. What did she care if a French stranger caught her in a compromising position on an elevator? She would never see this stern Rachel-lookalike again. Luke grabbed Claire by one arm and pulled her to a standing position. She crammed herself into the corner of the elevator and tried to smooth her hair back down. Her tailbone ached from the impact.

Luke couldn't hide his smile as Claire shifted uncomfortably. He checked his watch while they climbed another three floors before mercifully reaching the fourteenth.

"Well, that was embarrassing," she said as she rolled her suitcase into the hallway. The hotel was more modern than the exterior and elevator suggested. Black and white were the predominant colors, with bold geographic designs claiming much of the wall space.

"Are you hurt?" Luke laid a gentle hand on her rear end.

"Just a mildly broken tailbone. Nothing that'll get in the way." She smiled as he unlocked the door to their room.

The black-and-white theme continued in their room. Heavy curtains decorated in fleur-de-lis covered the windows, and a thick white rug cushioned her feet.

Claire threw her backpack on the floor and shoved Luke backward onto the bed. She leaped on top of him and continued what they had started in the elevator.

He flipped her onto her back and planted a trail of kisses from her neck to the button of her jeans. When he arrived at her stomach, it growled like a feral cat.

"Ignore it," she said, reaching to pull him back to her.

He laughed and dropped a kiss on her hand. "I believe I owe you a croissant."

"But sex!" She wriggled and tried to pull her T-shirt over her head.

Luke stopped her. "I can't concentrate with your stomach rumbling like a volcano. I need you to be in fighting shape. Croissant now. Sex later."

Claire frowned and shoved him off her. Fighting shape? Was he going to ask her to run some type of obstacle course beforehand? "Fine. And some ground rules for when this does happen. Are you up-to-date on your STI screenings?"

He nodded. "Clean as a whistle."

"Good. Same. I'm on birth control, but we'll use backup

protection regardless because a baby is *not* in my two-year plan. Understood?"

He nodded again and smiled. "Are you going to make me sign a contract? A non-disclosure agreement, maybe?"

"Shut up. I'm going to shower before we go. I'm still sticky from the ginger ale and Xanax cocktail that helicopter mom dumped on me on the flight."

"Go ahead." He set his toiletries bag on the dresser. "I have to make a call."

She fought with the shower for a moment before figuring out how to adjust the temperature. For once, she didn't think about her clients or the mysterious note as the warm water washed over her. Her attention remained on the fact that this was her first shower in France, which made it all the more enjoyable.

She opened the door a short time later in nothing but her towel. Surely Luke couldn't turn her down if she was already naked. A sliding door she hadn't previously noticed was open, leading to a tiny balcony with a table and chairs.

He stood at the railing, speaking on his phone.

She paused for a moment, simply admiring him. He was bathed in the golden light of the early morning, his button-down shirt rolled up to expose his devastating forearms. His jeans hung low on his hips, weighed down by the keys he carried even though his car was thousands of miles away. His shoulders were tense, and his knuckles were white as he gripped the railing.

She came up behind him and planted a soft kiss on his neck, right on top of the long, thin scar that disappeared below his collar. How did he get that scar? Even if she asked, he probably wouldn't tell her the truth. But good lord, it was intriguing.

"I have to go, Pete. I'll send you the final details on

Sunday. Yes, I understand. Bye." Luke ended the call and tucked his phone back into his pocket.

"Trouble with work?" she asked.

Pete was a producer for both of Luke's documentaries. He was an odious man, but he allowed Luke free creative control of all his projects.

"Pete's just hardballing me on the documentary. Toying with my funding. Nothing unusual," Luke said, turning to face her. He looked tense and distracted.

Great. Sex was definitely off the table now.

"I'm sorry." Claire pulled him into a hug and rested against his chest. His heart was beating faster than usual. Pete was ruining her chill Paris vibe. And she still wanted that croissant. "What did he want?"

"They want me to come to California for a few weeks."

Her heart skipped a beat, and she drew back. The note under her pillow surfaced in her mind as if dredged up from the bottom of a well. Luke had entered her life barely two months ago and had been a grumpy, judgmental annoyance from their first interaction. He had also concealed his theory that she was the next target of the Widowmaker and interfered with her painstakingly crafted proposals. They were polar opposites on the romance scale, and he repeatedly rolled his eyes at her life's work. So why was the idea of this cocky nuisance leaving so unsettling?

She had never truly felt like she needed anyone before. Jason was more of a semi-mobile pile of potatoes who occasionally burned frozen pizzas than a life partner. But Luke was something else entirely. And she could never ask him to jeopardize his career to stay behind for her.

Oh, right. She needed to say something. "For what?"

"There's been a lot of interest in the documentary, and there are some people I need to meet with. Other producers, financial backers. Animation, photography, narration, all kinds of things. They're getting impatient. But I'm not going. Not while you're in danger."

Her insides squirmed, and guilt settled over her like a gravity blanket. She crossed her arms over her chest and took a deep, shaky breath.

"You have to go. No one knows more about the story than you. I'm going to be fine. The person who left the note was probably just a bored asshole. I'm not in danger. Besides, I have a small army of people in West Haven who are borderline as obsessed with my safety as my mother."

He cupped her chin in his hand. His eyes were soft, like a Caribbean cove on a cloudless day. "You could come visit. Think about it. Long weekends in wine country, toes in the Pacific." A worry line creased his brow.

"You know I can't. Between proposal season and my multitude of trials and lawsuits, I can't leave. I wish I could. But you have to go. I'll miss you, though." The words tumbled out of her mouth before she had even given the feeling a name. *Yikes*. She was going to miss Luke. When Jason had gone on week-long hunting trips with his dad, she never missed him. She had relished the extra space in the bed.

Luke raised his eyebrows. He looked amused.

"Shut up. I'll be fine. I'll be so busy with work that I'll barely even notice you're gone. End of discussion. Now can we go get a croissant? And then sex?" She took a step back and thrust the door open. It banged off the frame, but for once he didn't comment.

He followed her and smiled, and the mood in the room lifted. "Sounds like a plan."

Claire opened her suitcase and, for a moment, thought it was empty. Then she realized everything Mindy had packed for her was black. Black shoes, black tops, black skirts and pants. The funeral-chic attire really should have clued her in to their destination, but she had been too distracted to analyze the clothing choices.

"I hope she packed you enough shoes," Luke said, peering over her shoulder.

"There are four pairs in here," Claire said, drawing out a pair of knee-length boots. "I really wish she would have left me a few more options, though. I just ordered these perfect strappy sandals—"

"Enough shoe talk. Breakfast now."

"Fine, fine." She disappeared into the bathroom with an armful of clothing.

CHAPTER THIRTEEN

To Do:
- Brush up on conversational French
- Send donuts to the West Haven PD

EQSA

"It's smaller than I thought." Claire stood in the shadow of Notre Dame. She shaded her eyes with one hand and stared up at the space where the spire once stood, grasping an espresso in the other hand like a lifeline. Scaffolding disguised the front of the cathedral, and tarps covered holes in the roof. The fire that had ravaged the cathedral had certainly done some damage, but much of the original beauty remained. The bell towers emerged from the scaffolding, standing tall and unchanged. It felt like the stained-glass windows could see her, recognize her. Two damaged but resilient souls, calmly regarding each other across the courtyard.

"You know how you build things up in your mind sometimes, but when you actually finally experience them, they're not what you expected at all?" she asked Luke.

He cleared his throat. "You are talking about the cathedral, right?"

She smiled. "Yes, the cathedral."

"It only looks small from this view. Here." He took her hand and led her around the side of the church.

The sunshine was bright and warm. Although the air smelled distinctly like stagnant water and mud, courtesy of the adjacent Seine River, nothing could spoil the view.

"Oh," she said. The cathedral, deceptively narrow from the front, seemed to stretch to infinity. "I take back everything I said."

"Isn't it beautiful?"

"This spot would be perfect for a proposal." She whipped around. "Closer to sunset, maybe in the spring. They could start on a river tour of the Seine and cross the bridge, stand here under the belfry."

She waved her hands vigorously, sloshing some espresso out of her cup and onto her hand.

"Friends and family members could stand over there holding candles, lining a path littered with white rose petals. Maybe a violinist or a string quartet. More private than the Eiffel Tower. Just imagine the pictures." She clasped a hand to her heart. It was so freakin' romantic.

"You could actually make that happen," Luke said quietly, coming to stand beside her. He pulled a napkin from his pocket and dabbed at the spilled coffee. "How many requests for international proposals have you gotten in the last few weeks alone?"

She slumped a little. "I don't know that it would be worth the effort. I have no connections here. I'd have no control. I don't speak the language. How would I even begin to overcome that?"

"Hire a business consultant. Open another branch, find a couple of locals to run the day-to-day. You could be writing happily ever afters for the whole world."

"Great, then we could service serial killers worldwide. What a fabulous idea. Besides, you think proposals are stupid." She turned to stare him down. A stiff wind blew her hair across her face. A strand stuck stubbornly to her lip gloss.

Luke grasped her hand and pulled her along. "Not all of them are stupid. You've shown me that there's value in making a big gesture. I don't necessarily understand why that requires a Jet Ski, but people express love differently I guess."

She whistled. "Luke Islestorm, you're a changed man."

"I wouldn't go that far."

She shoved him playfully. "What's next on our adventure?"

"You'll see."

HOURS LATER, CLAIRE THREW OPEN THE DOOR TO THEIR black-and-white hotel room and tossed half a dozen shopping bags onto the floor.

"I love the Champs-Élysées," she said, collapsing onto the bed. "Do you think they would let me live there?"

Luke appeared in the doorway, laden with more bags. "I don't know how we're going to get all this crap home."

"I'll buy another suitcase."

"Did you really need six pairs of shoes when there's already four in your suitcase?"

"Luke," she said, very seriously. "Fall is right around the corner. And I'm a master packer."

She rolled off the bed and inspected her suitcase. "Where are we going for dinner?"

"It's a surprise."

She sighed. Being along for the ride was getting old. "At least tell me how I should dress. Dressy, casual? Not that it really matters since it'll be black regardless."

"Dressy, I think. You'd better hurry or we'll be late," he said, tapping his watch.

She headed toward the bathroom.

"Wait," he said. "Give me your phone. No working, remember?"

Claire sighed and pulled out the phone that she had stuffed in her bra not a moment before. She was only going to check a few emails. The high school marching band was supposed to send her a video of their song and formation. She threw it at him before slamming the bathroom door.

Claire opened the bag Mindy had packed for her. She lingered for a moment on a lacy black bra. What the hell. She pulled it on and paired it with a tiny pair of black cheekies. The underwear might mean a permanent wedgie for the evening, but if Luke was finally going to take a peek under the hood, it would be worth it. A cocktail-length little black dress clung to her curves. Pearls her mother had given her for her sixteenth birthday curled around her neck, matching studs adorning her ears.

She twisted her wild hair up into an elegant topknot and transitioned to her evening makeup with a quick smoky eye and false eyelashes. For once they adhered without gluing her eyelids shut, and she said a small prayer that they would not wind up falling off in the middle of an amorous escapade. The large, flesh-colored bandage that covered her accidental stab wound didn't really go with the dress, but there wasn't much she could do about it.

She emerged from the bathroom moments later, and Luke lit up when he saw her.

"You look incredible," he said, grabbing her hand and twirling her around.

She giggled and tried not to trip in her black stilettos. A rare compliment from the Grumpmeister. "Thank you. Shall we?"

He led the way to the restaurant, occasionally pausing to point out a historical landmark or location of a childhood memory. Claire's feet ached by the time they reached the restaurant, and her underwear was indeed burrowing into her butt crack. She shifted uncomfortably as Luke checked them in. Maybe she could dislodge the wedgie by shifting her weight. No such luck. The only thing she managed to accomplish was getting a bizarre look from the *maître d'*.

A waiter led them to a table by the window. They passed a dozen couples dressed in black, hunched around their candlelit tables. Would it kill them to add some color to their wardrobes?

A glass ceiling stretched above them, revealing the Eiffel Tower in all of its lit-up glory. Even at a considerable distance, it was shockingly tall.

Claire sat, unable to stop gawking. "Oh, Luke. It's beautiful."

"I thought you'd like it here. Red or white?"

"What? Oh, cabernet sauvignon, *s'il vous plaît*," she said, seeing the waiter standing politely next to them. He made a small bow and then disappeared.

"So." She scooted closer to the table. "Tell me more about your progress on the documentary. And when do I get to see it?"

Luke was always careful to talk about his documentary in abstract terms or from the perspective of the victims.

"Not until it's perfect. I have so much information, so many stories to tell. At this point, I think a miniseries is going to be the best way to really tell them all, maybe even a separate forty-five-minute segment for each victim. But the producers are still after me to add a few things." He spread his napkin over his lap and drummed his fingers on the table.

"Like what?" she asked, taking a sip of the wine that had been promptly delivered at her elbow. Pleasantly earthy and full-bodied. She glanced at the menu, but it was all in French. It would be incredibly rude to pull out her phone to translate while Luke talked about his project. It looked like Luke was going to be ordering for her.

"A couple more interviews, maybe people who knew Barney at school, that kind of thing."

"You're doing something incredible, you know."

"I know," he said, also staring at his menu. He put it down abruptly. "Wait, what specifically?"

Claire laughed. "Telling their stories. The girls—they had whole lives. They loved, they laughed, they may have smoked a fair bit of marijuana and experimented a little too much in the bedroom if my roommate Courtney was any indication. But they lived."

"Exactly," he said, fidgeting with the corner of his menu. "To most people, these women are just a list of names in the news. But they were so much more. Did you know that Ariel Pullizi volunteered at her local animal shelter every week? Or that Jennifer Heiser was fluent in Portuguese?"

Claire shook her head.

"That's because the media doesn't treat them like people —like individuals. They're all lumped together as a set, practically anonymous. Not if I can help it," he muttered, turning back to his menu.

She reached across the table and squeezed his hand. He was so cute when he talked about work. He returned her squeeze, then took a sip of wine.

"What are you ordering?"

"I don't know. I can't read any of it," she whispered. She wasn't sure if the wine was stronger than what she was used to or she was getting tipsy on the atmosphere of France, but her head was beginning to swim pleasantly. She took another sip of wine.

He smiled. "I'll take care of it."

Claire took another glance around the restaurant. Wine glasses and carefully polished silverware gleamed. Candle-light flickered softly. Warmth flowed from the tips of her toes to her ears. She was safe here, surrounded by tanta-lizing smells and free-flowing wine, a fierce and grumpy protector at her side. Whoever threatened her was thou-sands of miles away. And tonight, she was finally going to break her sex embargo.

When the waiter passed by again, Luke ordered for them both. She didn't bother to ask what she was getting.

"Tell me something I don't know about you." She stared dreamily up at the Tower.

Preferably about his mystery brother. Or why his mom was such a raging bitch. Maybe he would be more open if he had more wine.

He leaned back in his chair, looking utterly at ease in a foreign country. "All right. I once played Peter Pan in a school play."

"Shut up," she said, a bit louder than she intended. She leaned forward and bumped the table, sloshing the wine in her glass. A couple at the next table turned to stare at them.

Claire paid them no attention. "Please tell me there were green tights involved."

Luke smiled mischievously. "There may have been. Now you return the favor."

"But I want to hear more about the play. What grade was this? Did you have to kiss anyone? Did you wear pants or was your package just snugly supported for all to see? Are there pictures?"

It would almost be worth opening up a line of communication with Rachel to score some pictures of Luke in green tights.

He crossed his arms. "Your turn."

"Fine, let me think." She propped her chin in her hand. Her glass had magically refilled itself, and she took another sip. "Okay, this is going to sound silly. Even though my mother is clearly unhinged and I think most of what she says is either completely made up or derived from just paying attention and making educated guesses, there have been times where she has inexplicably known things that she couldn't have known."

He raised an eyebrow. "Like what?"

Claire shook her head. "Countless things. Where a departed family member of someone we never met buried a collection of gold coins. The combination to a safe in some inherited mansion in Tennessee. The location of a secret will from someone's grandfather who had almost certainly been murdered by a family member." She ticked the encounters off on her fingers. "I started a blog for her side quests—that's what we called them—when I was in middle school. That's how she ended up getting her TV show."

Luke narrowed his eyes. "There has to be some kind of logical explanation."

She shrugged. "She claims the 'veil' is thin around her."

"I bet." He clearly was not convinced. "To be fair, there have been zero ghosts in my car since the sage incident. Claire Hartley, paranormal enthusiast," Luke said, smiling to himself. "You learn something new every day. What about your dad? Is he paranormally inclined as well?"

She thunked her glass onto the table. "Roy grew up in Guatemala before moving to Miami as a teenager, so he has some pretty unique superstitions. He swears that he saved a middle school girlfriend from a *sisemité*."

"A what?"

She shrugged. "It's like a big murder gorilla or something."

"Interesting. And your biological father?"

"He might as well be a murder gorilla," she muttered, spreading her napkin on her lap and digging into the basket of bread. Shopping had left her starving. And she didn't want to talk about her bio-dad.

"How did he feel about your mom's—uh—abilities?"

"Oh, he loved them. That's why they're still together to this day," she said through a mouthful of bread. He was totally prying. But maybe if she opened up a little, he would reciprocate.

He buttered his roll and stared out the window.

Screw it. It was worth a shot. "He left when I was five. A few days before my sixth birthday. I barely remember him, but I doubt he put much stock in my mom's career."

"You must have been devastated."

Claire shrugged. "Charlie hates him to this day, but she was sixteen when he left. It was different for her. Like I said, I only remember snippets of him. But I *do* remember what happened after he left. My mom couldn't afford the mortgage on her own, so we had to sell our house on the lake and move into this tiny apartment full of spiders. Charlie had to take two part-time jobs to help out. Our front door didn't even have a real lock. We used to move the couch in front of the door every night before bed."

"That does explain some of her obsession with personal safety." Luke reached across the table and held Claire's hand. She was eighty percent sure that hand had some butter on it. "Did you ever hear from your dad?"

She shook her head. "Years later, my aunt ran into him at the grocery store with his new family. He married a cashier from a health food store, and his daughter—my half sister, I guess—is almost exactly six years younger than me," she said, withdrawing her butter hand. She had spent so much time and effort suppressing all thoughts and memories of her biological father that she had almost forgotten she had a half sister wandering the earth. It wasn't her fault that their shared father was a skeevy adulterer. What was she like? Maybe that was a question that didn't need an answer.

"He sounds like a dirtbag."

The waiter arrived and set two plates in front of them. It smelled amazing, but the meal was still a mystery. Screw it, the time for subtlety was over.

"Yep. Well, now that I've told you my deep dark family secret, spill. What's the deal with your brother? Did he steal your girlfriend? Crash your first car? Give you a wedgie at school?"

"That wasn't part of the agreement." Luke cut into the meat on his plate more aggressively than was necessary for such a tender-looking cut.

"Luke. Come on." She stared at him earnestly until he met her eyes.

"Fine, but only because I know you won't let this go. My dad's dead. My brother killed him."

"*What*?" she practically shouted. The fork fell from her

hand and thudded to the floor. Another one appeared at her side as if by magic.

"I'm so sorry, Luke. What the hell happened?" She clutched her new fork like a lifeline. People at the restaurant were staring at them, but she didn't care. She had found an obituary for Luke's dad when she'd internet stalked him before agreeing to work with him for Nicole's proposal. But that obituary sure as hell didn't mention anything about George Islestorm II getting murdered by his son.

Luke set his fork down and turned to the window. He grimaced as if he was passing a kidney stone. "It happened while I was deployed. I was in Afghanistan and I got a call from my brother. He said my dad had been in a car accident. They weren't sure he was going to make it. Meanwhile, I'm half a world away, suturing people and administering fucking flu shots. I applied for emergency leave, but the day it got approved I got another call. This time from my mother. That phone call was one of the only times in my adult life I've heard her show any kind of emotion. They were already divorced at that point, but I think she always loved him."

He took a deep breath and rubbed his eyes, leaning back in his chair. He didn't meet Claire's gaze.

"She and my dad had set my brother up as medical power of attorney when they made their will. My brother made the decision to pull the plug on my dad. He knew I was trying to get home. He took away my last chance to see my dad alive."

This may have been the longest string of sentences Luke had ever said to her.

"You never got to say goodbye," she said softly.

"No. I came home for the funeral. We almost got into a fistfight. Never spoke to him since."

"I am so sorry about your dad. Did your brother—" she hesitated, not wanting to push the subject. "Did he say why he did it?"

"Some bullshit about not wanting to keep dad 'in limbo.'"

Her shoulders slumped. She stabbed her fork into the mystery dinner. Now she was the asshole for grilling him on a dark family secret. "That's awful. You must miss him so much. I'm sorry for asking you to talk about it."

Luke picked up his fork and resumed eating. "It's okay. I should learn to talk about it. It almost felt kind of good."

Wow. Mystery solved. No wonder he hated his brother. If god forbid something ever happened to Alice, Claire would never shut off her life support without Charlie. And yet, it sounded like his brother hadn't had sinister intentions. It had been three years since his father's death. Three years of his niece's life missed. Time he would never get back. But she surely wasn't going to bring that up to him. It wasn't her place. Was it?

They chewed together in silence for a minute. Whatever he'd ordered for her was delicious. Duck, maybe?

"Have you ever considered reconnecting with your brother?" Claire asked quietly in between bites. She couldn't help herself.

He shook his head. "He was a douche even at the best of times."

Must take after Rachel.

"He sent me a few emails over the years, but I never responded," Luke continued. "Every time I see a picture of him, all I can think about is my dad."

"But he's family," she said, taking a sip of water. "And your niece—"

"Have you ever tried reconnecting with your dad?" he asked, eyebrows raised.

"Fair enough. Not my place. Sorry."

They finished their meal in silence. A pall had been cast of the magic of Paris. It served her right for snooping, but at least now she knew the truth. He had been honest with her, even when it hurt. It was time to shake off the family trauma and recapture the magic of Paris while they were still here. Maybe the night could still be salvaged.

"How are you feeling?" Luke asked as they exited the restaurant and stepped under the stars. He took her arm.

"Great." Claire rolled her shoulders back. For the first time in weeks, she wasn't tense. Luke had finally been honest with her. She was an ocean away from paparazzi, from her attempted killer, from whomever had tucked the message under her pillow. Surely that was just someone playing a prank. Wendy was probably bored. There was no way Barney could be pulling strings from prison, right?

Did Paris have binder stores? Maybe she should start a list of suspects, just in case. With Luke in California, she would have an easier time doling out vigilante justice. "And you?"

"Good. I think the company helps." He lifted her hand to his lips and brushed a kiss over her knuckles.

Her toes curled in her shoes. The note-leaver could wait.

"It's amazing that you can see so many stars in the middle of the city." She paused in the middle of a busy crosswalk and twirled around. The streetlights of Paris blurred around her like a strand of Christmas lights. She stopped mid-twirl and gasped.

"Luke, let's go to the Eiffel Tower. Please? It's nighttime now. You promised."

"To be honest, it's a little overrated." He grabbed her

hand and hustled her to the sidewalk. "But everyone should see it once."

"Mister hipster not impressed by what was once the tallest building on earth." She smiled. The wine danced through her system and lifted her spirits. She was in freakin' Paris. Her heels no longer bothered her. She could probably twirl the entire way to the Tower.

They passed more trees and fewer buildings. The smell of urine was undeniable, but it was at least partially masked by the delicate smells floating out of nearby patisseries.

"This bun is too tight." One by one, she plucked bobby pins from her hair and allowed the curls to fall, wild and unbridled, down to her mid-back. Her flying elbow nearly made contact with a stranger's chin, and Luke pulled her into his side, laying his arm around her shoulders.

"Whoops." She giggled. "Luke, your phone is ringing."

He pulled it out of his pocket and glanced at the screen. "Just work again," he said, silencing it and tucking it away.

"It's okay for you to answer it. I know how important it is."

"No need. Nothing is more important than what's going on right here, right now." He planted a kiss on the top of her head.

Warmth rushed from the tips of her fingers and toes directly to her lady parts. "What does Pete expect you to accomplish from Paris?"

A crack in the sidewalk nearly sent her sprawling.

Luke pulled her in tighter. "I'm not sure. He probably just wants to confirm my arrival date."

"Holy crap." Claire jolted to a halt. They had rounded a corner and entered the Trocadero Gardens. Fountains danced all around them, splashing rhythmically. The Eiffel Tower rose magnificently in front of them.

"Pete can suck it." She grasped his arm as they walked slowly down the sidewalk, growing ever closer to the mammoth structure.

A gentleman on a park bench nearby was playing a soulful melody on a saxophone. The notes bounced off the nearby trees and benches, filling the gardens with sound.

Luke stopped and she turned to face him. One calloused hand extended to her, and she took it. He pulled her close and snaked his other hand around to the small of her back, leading her through the same dance they had practiced countless times for Nicole's proposal in his ballroom at home. It wasn't a perfect fit with the saxophone's rhythm, but it was close enough.

People on the sidewalks gave them a wide berth, stepping onto the grass to avoid the dancing couple and clearly muttering *Americans* under their breath.

Claire laughed as Luke spun her out. She thrust her hand out to the side. He stood still for a moment, and she strutted around him, sliding her hands over his lapel and coming within a hair's breadth of a kiss.

He pulled her in again and dipped her low, raising her back up tantalizingly slow. They widened their steps, covering the entire sidewalk. The saxophone player picked up his speed. Claire leaned into Luke with one leg cocked, and he dragged her several feet. Had she scuffed her shoes? Oh, well. She had just bought a half dozen more pairs.

Luke spun her again, gripping both her hands and locking them over her head, bringing his hands slowly, sensually, from her wrists, to her elbows, thumbs spreading to cup the sides of her body, desperately close to the curve of her breasts.

She locked eyes with him as he tugged her close. Heat

radiated from him, and a longing she had never known burned in her belly.

He leaned in, tantalizingly close like the first time they'd kissed. Claire's lips parted, begging for sweet release. This time, there wasn't a battered copy of *War and Peace* waiting to smash into her skull and send her to the hospital. There were only stars above them, and if one of them plummeted to the earth, they would have a whole different problem.

Abruptly, the song ended. The saxophone hung loosely by its neck strap as the gentleman opened his instrument case. Rude.

A man with a handlebar mustache cleared his throat uncomfortably as he passed. Claire and Luke pulled apart. The spell was broken.

They were standing in grass, and one of Claire's heels had sunk into the ground after their last dance move.

"So," she said, attempting to wipe the dirt from her heel. "The Eiffel Tower."

"Yeah." He turned to look at it, buttoning the front of his suit jacket. Hopefully, he was concealing something interesting in his pants.

"These people are judging us so hard," Claire whispered loudly to him as they continued to walk along.

"Definitely. Maybe we should really give them something to talk about."

"Right here?" Her gaze wandered to the flash of his belt buckle. "We might get arrested."

"No, not that. I think we should go star spinning."

"Star spinning?" What the hell was that? She was not in any condition to be launched into space.

"Surely you've heard of it," Luke said, eyebrows raised. Maybe it was a rich person thing.

"Is that some kind of euphemism for recreational drug use?" she probed.

He laughed. "No, it's something I used to do when I was a kid. My brother and I did it a couple of times when we were here on vacation. I had almost forgotten about that."

He led her out into a patch of grass and bent down on one knee.

Claire's heart leapt into her throat. Her mind raced a mile a minute. There was no way Luke was proposing. They had only known each other for two months. This wasn't the Middle Ages. But they were in Paris. In front of the Eiffel Tower. After sharing a borderline sexual dance. And they had already been through more than some couples go through in a lifetime together.

Was this seriously happening?

"Don't get excited." He threw up his hands as if to proclaim he was innocent.

Her heart dropped a centimeter. So, he wasn't proposing. Of course he wasn't. That would have been insane. Wouldn't it?

"Here." He slid his hands down the length of her shin to the buckle of her shoes.

She bit her lip. If he got any closer, the heat emanating from her neither regions was going to scorch his eyebrows off. Could he tell she was half an inch away from tackling him? She gripped his shoulders for stability. God, they were solid. What would the buttons on his shirt sound like if they were ripped from the cloth?

He fought with her shoe for a moment before tugging it free. He removed the other one and stood. Claire had shrunk several inches.

"So, how do we do this?" She tucked her shoes into her oversized purse.

"Pick a star. Any star."

She turned her gaze upward. "Got one," she said, zeroing in on one that was twinkling. Or was that a helicopter?

Luke walked several feet away from her, also looking up. "When I say go, keep your eyes fixed on that star. You have to spin in place for fifteen seconds, and then we're going to try to run the rest of the way to the Eiffel Tower."

"You want me to spin around and then run to the Eiffel Tower? What if there's broken glass or rusty nails or cigarette butts—"

"Claire Aurora Hartley. Where is your sense of adventure?"

A thrill ran through her at the sound of her full name on his lips. She bit her tongue. He was right. She needed this.

"Okay. Ready when you are."

"*Go!*" Luke yelled. He spun clockwise like a well-dressed top.

Claire kept her eyes fixed on her star and started rotating, taking tiny steps. The hem of her dress lifted as she twirled, skirt flaring out in a wide circle. She raised her arms out to her sides, too, spinning for the sake of spinning. Her world blurred gently at the edges, trapped in a kaleidoscope of stars.

Somewhere around the count of eight, she stumbled. Her foot fell more heavily behind her, and suddenly she was staggering more than spinning.

"Luke—"

"Keep going, just a few more seconds! Aaaand run!"

Luke stopped mid-spin and took off in the direction of the Eiffel Tower.

"Oh no," Claire said. She had stopped spinning, but the world hadn't. She ran forward at a drunken tilt, arms flailing out to either side of her. All she had to do was aim for the giant, glowing steel structure. But one side of her body seemed heavier than the other, and it was dragging her straight for a fountain.

"Luke!"

She tripped over something in the grass and came down hard onto her knees. She rolled over and lay still, staring up at the stars that had betrayed her. They spun stubbornly above her. The fountain tinkled pleasantly in the background. Partially dead grass poked at her legs.

"That was harder than I remembered," Luke's voice said at her side.

Claire reached out one hand and felt an expensive leather jacket next to her. Luke's clean, comforting smell engulfed her. She ran a hand down his chest, and he leaned over so that he was nearly on top of her. He plucked a blade of grass from her hair and tossed it to the side. For a moment, he just looked at her.

The moon had risen above his head, creating a halo. His five-o'clock shadow stood out in the half-light. She ached to feel it against her skin. She grabbed a fist full of his shirt and tugged him to her.

Luke crushed his mouth eagerly to hers, and she released the sigh that had been pent up all evening. She tugged at his shirt, sliding her hands underneath so she could feel every hard inch of his chiseled abs.

His hands traveled from her hair down to her chin, gently forcing her lips from his so he could feast on her tender, exposed neck. His hand hesitated at the hem of her dress before slowly, carefully, sliding its way up.

When his wandering mouth hit her collarbone, her hands fisted at her sides, tearing up clumps of grass. She pressed her hips into his. Who cared if they were in public? She wanted him, and she didn't care who saw.

"Ahem," someone said nearby.

They broke apart. The end of a nightstick thrust into her face. Not the nightstick she had hoped to see.

Luke hastily apologized in French and tugged Claire to her feet. She straightened her dress and curtsied at the policeman, smiling sheepishly as they took off in the opposite direction.

"Oh my god, so embarrassing." She hid her face as they half-ran down the sidewalk. Her bare feet slapped the sidewalk. She was totally going to get tetanus. And thrown out of the country. Why hadn't she checked that she was up-to-date on her immunizations before traveling internationally? So irresponsible. "Did I just curtsy at a policeman?"

"You did." Luke laughed deeply. He paused in a brick alleyway. A black cat ran out of its hiding space when they approached, bolting for the opposite side of the street. The crowd had thinned out.

"Here, let's get your shoes back on." He tugged her down the alleyway until they were mostly concealed between a dumpster and a large stack of wooden crates. What was that smell—old brie? Yikes. She was definitely sober now.

He pulled the shoes out of her purse and bent to put them on her feet.

She leaned against the wall for support, grateful to have something solid to lean on. Luke was like quicksand.

"That's better," he said, buckling the last clasp. He was suspiciously adept at buckling women's shoes. What if he had a foot fetish? He rose, staring at her with stormy eyes, and laid one hand on her waist while the other cupped her cheek.

"Do you have any idea how beautiful you are?"

"Stop it." Heat crept into her cheeks. Her blood boiled with need. "I have a stab wound and grass stains on my knees." Not to mention the cut from the sword incident, and some bruises on her shins where she had tumbled over a wall.

"I'm serious. Seeing you here, so carefree and relaxed. It's a whole new Claire I never knew existed." He leaned in and kissed her neck again. Her elbow knocked against the side of the dumpster.

"It's easier to relax when you're an ocean away from people who want you to die," she whispered, but the words didn't hold the same weight they did at home. Luke's mouth was a glorious distraction. The smell of old bread and rancid sauce emanating from the trash was barely noticeable.

His head snapped back to hers. "I will always keep you safe." His hand slid underneath her dress again, sliding up her thigh.

But, historically speaking, he hadn't. He hadn't even divulged that he suspected she was being targeted by the Widowmaker until she brought it up herself. And, as he pointed out earlier, Sawyer had saved her when it really mattered. Not that she could hold that against him. It wasn't his job to make sure she wasn't murdered. And then there was the fact that he was leaving for California for an unknown number of weeks.

"I can keep myself safe," she began to argue, but he silenced her with his mouth. Her legs were jelly. Her lips parted graciously.

Luke's hand reached the apex of her thighs, and he cupped her gently.

She gasped. The heat washed over her like an inferno. She hadn't been touched like this in eons.

He reached down and grabbed her leg, wrapping it around his waist. His normally rough hands glided gently over the lacy fabric of her underwear (which had mercifully removed itself from her butt crack), caressing and teasing. Claire moaned softly, arching into him, aching for more.

She trailed one hand down his torso to his belt buckle. She tugged one way, then the other. It wouldn't budge. Who had made this belt, abstinence activists? Annoyed, she simply ran her hand over the front of his pants, eliciting a moan from him.

He tugged her panties to the side and began to stroke her again, this time skin-to-skin. Tingles exploded down her arms and legs. Was she finally going to figure out what was underneath Luke's pants next to a dumpster in Paris? Could they get arrested for this?

He broke away. "Maybe we should go to the hotel."

"No." She dragged him back to her. "Here."

He tugged her neckline down, put his mouth on her skin. Her knees buckled, and she almost fell. Then he was lifting her, pressing her against the brick wall. Could he hear her heart thudding in her chest?

He hitched her dress up, wrapped both of her legs around him. Claire blindly wrestled her arms around his neck, pressing herself as close as she could to his glorious, solid frame. She wanted—needed—to be as close as possible. With one hand on the wall and one hand firmly on her ass, he swiped her underwear to the side and filled her at last.

She gasped at the impact. How long had it been? Were there cobwebs down there? There was a hint of pain in her pleasure.

Why was it always the grumpy jerks who had the best dicks? Was there some kind of scientific correlation between dick size and ego size?

All thoughts promptly spilled out of her head as Luke

rocked rhythmically. A mountain was building beneath her, forcing her higher and higher. Her head thumped against the brick wall and her legs burned with the impact of holding herself up, but she barely felt it. Her fingernails raked down his back.

His breath was ragged in her ear.

"Luke," she barely managed to say. Her fingers and toes curled.

Together, they burst over the peak. Claire bit her lip to keep from crying out as the waves of pleasure thundered over her. Luke gripped her so firmly that she was certain she would have bruises tomorrow.

His eyes had never been as green as they were in the alleyway, like the broken glass that crunched under his feet.

"Wow," he said simply, leaning Claire against the wall.

"Wow," she agreed through heaving breaths.

A trash can at the end of the alleyway tipped over.

Claire screamed and pushed Luke away from her. He stumbled backward, and she fell butt-first into the pile of wooden crates.

Luke picked a broken beer bottle from the ground as Claire gasped, splayed between a pile of knocked-over crates with her dress hiked up. Her tailbone ached at the impact. Her elbow had gone completely through one of the boxes and her arm was now stuck. She stared into the darkness as she struggled to stand.

Luke shouted something in French, defensively holding the broken bottle. A black shadow moved toward them, and Claire screamed again. She ripped her elbow from the box and leapt onto one of the crates. A family of rats scurried past. Bared yellow teeth glinted in the moonlight as the black mass scuttled by.

Luke charged down the alley toward them, hissing and

stomping his feet. The rats scattered, scrambling for the street.

"Are you hurt?" He bent to look into her eyes.

She glanced down at her body. Her elbow had sustained some alarming new scratches and her tailbone smarted like she had been walloped, but it could have been worse.

"I think I'm okay." She tried to stand and winced, rubbing the knee that had smashed into the cobblestone. She was a mess from head to toe. But that was nothing new.

"Come on." He picked her up.

"Don't forget my purse," she said. He grabbed it and slung it over his shoulder. Her knees and elbow stung, and her months-long dry spell had ended next to a dumpster in an alleyway with an army of rats for an audience. Paris wasn't exactly turning out to be what she expected. At least she had gotten some new boots out of it.

CHAPTER FOURTEEN

To Do:
- Buy another suitcase for boots and purses
- Check on Rosie

A KNOCK AT THE DOOR DREW CLAIRE FROM SLEEP. WHY WAS she so exhausted? The sheets puddled around her waist, and the bed next to her was empty. Where the hell had Luke gone now? If he had ditched her in France after finally getting laid, she would burn his house to the ground.

Wait, she hadn't sleepwalked in the middle of the night and crawled into someone else's room, had she? But no, those were her shoes by the bathroom door. Thank god.

She rolled out of bed and tugged on the terrycloth robe. Why did her tailbone hurt so much? Oh, right, the Great Rat Crisis. She reached instinctively for Rosie's leash, but her furry best friend was three thousand miles away. Her shoulders dropped, and she made a mental note to demand a picture. Mindy better have sung her the bedtime song. Rosie couldn't sleep without it.

Another knock sounded, and Claire tied the sash of the robe before cracking the door open. A hotel employee offered a tray of something that smelled delicious. Luke must have ordered breakfast in bed. She stepped back and allowed the employee to arrange the dishes and a beautiful vase of flowers at the tiny table in the room before departing.

Claire crossed the room and twitched the curtain aside. Luke was standing shirtless on the balcony, phone pressed to his ear. Freakin' Pete, the night owl workaholic.

She had time to brush her teeth and put on a coat of mascara before Luke slid the balcony door open.

"Morning, beautiful." He ducked his head and planted a kiss on her cheek. "Sleep well?"

"Too well," she said. She hadn't even sleepwalked. The city of Paris should really thank her. Who knew what kind of damage she could have done? "You?"

"Not bad." He sat across from her. "I hope you don't mind I ordered breakfast."

"It smells amazing. What's wrong? You look tense." She took a sip of the café au lait. Delicious.

"Nothing, just work stuff." He removed the silver lid to reveal a croissant with jam and a *pain au chocolat*. How did the French stay so skinny while eating nothing but carbs? Smoking, probably.

"Pete again?"

"Yeah, listen. I—" He glanced at the flowers on the table. The knife fell from his hand and clattered on the table. "I didn't ask for flowers."

"It's probably part of the room service deal," she said, spreading fig jam on her baguette.

"There's a card."

The bottom fell out of her stomach. The pastry thunked onto her plate. "What?"

Luke reached out and pulled a small, square card from the flowers. He ripped the envelope open and pulled out a sheet of cardstock.

"What does it say?" The room was starting to blur at the edges and shadows danced across her visual field.

"Get your phone. We need to call Detective Smith."

Claire slid sideways out of her chair, and the darkness claimed her.

The smell of ammonia hit her like a meteor. She gasped and sat up, nearly smashing her head on the breakfast table. She was still in the hotel room, thank god, and not in a French hospital. Her health insurance definitely wouldn't cover an international fainting spell. Luke knelt next to her, a small packet open in his hand.

"How's your head?" he asked.

"I'm fine. Are the police coming?"

Someone knocked at the door. Luke squeezed her shoulder and got up.

"Don't get up yet. Take it slow."

The door opened, and a team of people walked inside. They immediately canvassed the room.

How could this have happened? Who could have found out where she was staying? Had someone followed them to Paris? How dedicated was this psycho, anyway?

Luke stood in the corner of the room with his phone on speaker and appeared to be translating for the French cop next to him. A lady with a camera took pictures of the breakfast table, where the note still sat.

Claire climbed shakily to her feet. She rounded the table and peered over the cop's shoulder at the typed note.

"You can run, but you can't hide," she whispered. Chills exploded down her spine despite the fact that her stalker had invoked the most overused bad guy line in the history of time. She collapsed onto the bed and hugged her knees to her chest, but she couldn't catch her breath.

There were so many people jammed into this room. It was suffocating. She grabbed her hotel key off the bedside table and rushed barefoot out the front door. A frenzy of French exclamations followed her, but she headed straight for the stairs.

She half-sprinted down thirteen flights and burst into the lobby. She heaved the front doors open and stepped out into the sunshine. The robe hung around her. Shit, she didn't have any clothes on underneath. Now she looked like a crazy person wandering around Paris barefoot in a robe. Thank god Doozer, the robe-stealer, was a seven-hour flight away.

To her right, a small garden sat back from the bustling street. She hurried through the archway of climbing roses and followed a concrete path to a bench. A small fountain tinkled pleasantly, masking some of the noise from the street. She staggered to the bench, barely sitting before her knees collapsed.

Roses perfumed the sharp breaths she was able to steal. Whoever had sent the note surely wasn't winning any points for creativity. They couldn't have used a more generic threatening phrase. But how the hell had they found her? She was in a different friggen country. Were they tracking her phone? Was it Barney? How could he possibly know where she was from inside the prison? He had to be working with someone. The Widowmaker was behind bars, but he wasn't done with her.

"Claire?" Luke's voice came from the archway.

"Here." She sat up straight and ran a hand through her hair.

Luke slid onto the bench next to her and pulled her close. "It's going to be okay."

"Is it?"

He eased back from her and held her at arm's length. "Like I said last night, I won't let anything happen to you."

"You can't promise that. And besides, you're going to be in California soon anyway." Anger flared inside her. Why was the idea of him leaving so upsetting? She had never needed anyone before. Not even her ex-fiancé.

"I'm not going."

She shrugged his arm off. "Luke, you have to. This is your career, your livelihood. I won't keep you from it. I'll be fine. In case you forgot, I was all alone when Barney kidnapped me. He stabbed me and tortured me, and I still lived. Whatever this copycat weirdo throws at me, I can handle it. I don't need a keeper. Just...don't tell my mom."

He was silent for a long minute. "I should have been there." He wasn't talking about breakfast.

She reached for his hand. The anger fizzled. "You were."

"No. I was too late. You would be dead if Sawyer hadn't shown up, and I'm going to have to live with that for the rest of my life."

"Hey, I was handling myself just fine. Sawyer even said so. Sure, he tased him. But I was like fifty yards from the highway. I could have made it." She had also passed out from blood loss and hallucinated a taco order, but still. "Are they finished up there?"

"Almost. Want to day drink and look at some fine art?"

Claire stood and offered one shaky hand to Luke. The smell of ammonia still burned in her nostrils, and her stomach churned like she was on a ship at sea. But this was

Paris. This international creep would *not* ruin the first vacation she'd taken in years. She needed to compartmentalize what just happened and get on with the trip. There was a partially stale baguette to eat and activities to cross off the To Do list.

THE NOTE HAD UNDENIABLY STOLEN SOME OF HER ENJOYMENT of Paris. It seemed to have affected Luke too. Even as they viewed some of the most precious works of art in the world, there was a pallor over the day. The rich brush strokes of Gustav Klimt seemed less remarkable after the threat. The Mona Lisa smiled mockingly at them. At least the wine was still good.

Claire shivered and drew her shawl around her as they stepped onto the gangway of a dinner cruise boat, one of Luke's last surprises for the weekend. As much as she appreciated the change of scenery, she was ready to be back home and in control of her life and her daily activities again. Her ankle wobbled on the slick surface, and he steadied her. Candlelight flickered through a long row of glass windows. The stars were out again, though not as clear as the night before.

A waiter led them to a small candlelit table. Champagne bubbled in glasses. The boat hadn't even left the dock before they both downed their first glass.

"Your phone's ringing again." Claire plonked her empty glass onto the table. She bristled. It must have been the fifteenth time today. Something was up, but getting information from Luke was like beating a stone wall with a dandelion.

"Sorry. Let me just turn it off."

"Are you sure you don't need to talk to him?" He was definitely hiding something. Again.

"It can wait." He lifted their glasses as a waiter passed by. The dinner was already shaping up to be their second-most tense. Right after the Rachel incident.

"Really? He's called like a thousand times." A backlit monument slid by them, but she missed what the tour guide had named the structure.

A waiter passed by with hot hors d'oeuvres. She had no idea what she grabbed—a crab puff maybe?—but it melted in her mouth.

They sat in silence as the boat passed half a dozen landmarks. Tension radiated between them like a collapsing star. They ate their salad course wordlessly.

"Okay, this is ridiculous." Claire slammed her fork down on the table as they approached Notre Dame. "Tell me what's going on. I know it's not just the note that has you so uptight."

Luke rubbed his eyes and leaned back in his chair. "I have to ask you something."

It was about freaking time. "Okay, shoot."

"I hate to ask you this."

Uh-oh. What could it be? Was he going to work with Wendy on a project? Was his mother moving in with him? "We're not having a threesome with Pete. I don't care what he promised you."

"It's not that. The reason why I've been getting so many calls from the producers is because they want me to have one more interview before they'll approve the funding for production, advertising, soundtrack, everything that will make a difference in how many people this will reach. It's a big interview. You."

The bottom dropped out of her stomach. She gripped her butter knife so tightly that her knuckle cracked.

"Me?" she croaked.

"You're the only survivor of the West Haven Widowmaker."

"You can't be serious." The shock began to ebb, but her heart still pounded as though she was being chased. Was she really hearing him correctly?

"He's right. It would really help the documentary." He looked at her with soft eyes. "It's not a complete story without you."

"Is this why you brought me to Paris?" Claire whispered incredulously. "You wanted to butter me up so you could make me relive the worst night in my entire life for your personal gain?"

"No, I wanted to keep you—"

"Safe." She cut him off. "Yeah, sure. I know I joke about this a lot to try to cope with the trauma, but do you see this bandage?" She pointed at the mark on her chest. "This is a daily reminder of the night I was stabbed by a psychotic serial killer. I was drugged, bound, gagged, and violated, mentally and physically. I was *inches* from death that night, Luke. If Sawyer hadn't shown up, Rosie probably would have been an orphan. My mother would have lost a child."

Luke bristled. "It might be good for you to talk about it. You won't go to therapy. You haven't come to terms with what happened." He reached for her.

She slapped his hand away. Considered flipping the entire table over. "It's been two weeks. If you think for one second that I'll find some remarkable catharsis by describing all the gory details of my almost murder to your audience of mouth-breathing couch potatoes, you never knew me at all."

She leapt up. Her chair fell, but she didn't pause to straighten it.

"Don't you dare come near me." She held her arm out, one finger pointing accusingly at Luke as he attempted to stand. "I can't believe that I gave myself to you, and all you wanted was a fucking interview. That's what it's been about from the beginning, isn't it?"

Rage was settling back in, hot and fierce like a coiled dragon.

"Should we review your track record?" she continued. "You knew I was a potential target for murder, but you never told me. Then I almost died, and you're asking me to relive the experience on camera *for your profit*. You never cared about me. You only care about yourself, your career, your life."

"You know that's not true." He reached for her hand, but she snatched it back.

People were staring, but she didn't care. She'd never see them again.

"You don't understand," Luke said. "I already told him I couldn't get the interview, but he knows about my relationship with you and he insisted. He says some of the backers will pull out if I can't get it. I had to try."

"Then find another backer. Jesus, Luke." If Hollywood wasn't full of rich, opportunistic middle-aged men, then everything she had ever seen on TV was a lie.

"It's not that easy." He rubbed a hand over the back of his neck.

Unbelievable.

"You know what? This is over. Don't fucking follow me. I am not your pawn. I am worth more than this. I owe you nothing. I am going home, and I don't care if I ever hear from you again. Enjoy California, you narcissistic fuckbag."

Every tendon in her body screamed at her to plunge her fist into that arrogant face, but by some miracle she refrained. She didn't need another lawsuit. Armed with her clutch and her dignity, she stormed out of the dining room and onto the deck of the ship. When had it started raining? That was just fucking perfect.

"Claire, wait—" Luke said from inside. He was trapped by a waiter with a huge serving tray, but not for long.

She needed to get as far away as possible. The deck was slick underfoot as she hurried down the length, tears blurring her eyes. How could he do this to her? Was every moment together just a grand scheme to get her on the documentary? Her cheeks burned. Nobody was going to take advantage of her. Not ever again.

As she rounded the stern of the ship, she hit another slippery patch. Her heel skidded, and she crashed into the metal railing. Her entire world went upside down for a moment. Rivets on the boat flashed past before she plummeted into the cold, murky water of the Seine.

She spluttered and coughed. River water went up her nose. *Holy shit.* She'd really done it now. Damn it, her phone! It couldn't get wet. What if a client needed her?

Her clutch trembled above her head as she treaded water with one arm. With any luck her phone would have survived her brief aquatic touchdown. The boat puttered away from her. No one had even noticed that she had fallen overboard. At least Luke was getting farther away by the second. His betrayal had hit her like an uppercut.

Shit, speaking of wounds. Dirty river water probably wasn't great for hers. She swam one-armed as best as she could to the bank. Thankfully, she had fallen out right at Notre Dame. She hoisted herself up a rock ledge and onto the walking path that lined the river. Her carefully chosen little black dress clung to her thighs and dripped torrents of river water onto the sidewalk. She stumbled up the stairs to the street and shivered in the chill night air. Trembling fingers unzipped her clutch and dragged her phone out. It was still dry and turned on. Thank god.

She paused under a streetlight, catching her breath. So this was it. Rock bottom. Almost murdered. Twice betrayed by the first person she had opened her heart to after breaking off her engagement. Never again.

She couldn't call a cab in this state. There was no choice but to walk the eight blocks back to the hotel. Her shoes squelched as she walked, and if she had a dollar for every time someone gave her a funny look, she could have covered her return plane ticket by the time she pushed open the hotel door.

Half an hour later, she ran down the hallway, dragging two suitcases behind her. She had commandeered Luke's to hold her new shoes. And when she got home, she would burn the suitcase and anything that was left of him.

She collapsed into a cab. Ugh, she didn't speak French.

"Airport, airport," she said over and over. Eventually the cab driver seemed to get the idea and headed off in the right direction.

As they passed through the shadow of the Eiffel Tower, Claire laid her head against the window and closed her eyes.

# CHAPTER FIFTEEN

To Do:
- Burn Luke's house down
- Screen new applicants

"Un-fucking-believable." Claire stared at herself in the dingy airport bathroom mirror. A man spoke over the loudspeaker in French. She tossed the bandage saturated with river water into the trashcan and inspected her wound. It didn't look infected, at least. Which was good, because her first aid kit was back at the hotel with the lying, selfish, soul-sucking demon. A small bottle of rubbing alcohol and box of bandages from the airport drug store sat on the counter next to her.

She pulled paper towels out of the dispenser and splashed the alcohol onto them. She pressed the mass to her skin.

"Mother fu—" It might as well have been a poultice

made out of murder hornets. A woman came out of one of the stalls and shot a panicked look at Claire, leaving without even washing her hands. Great, now she was scaring people away from practicing basic hygiene.

How had it come to this? A few weeks ago, she was on top of the world. She had pulled off the biggest proposal of her career and had a blossoming new romance with a sexy filmmaker. Today she was sitting alone in a dirty airport bathroom waiting six more hours to board her flight back to the United States. Betrayed by the first man she had opened her heart to after Jason had cheated on her. Kidnapped and stabbed by a client. And now, stalked by a new, faceless enemy.

What had she done to deserve this vicious retaliation from the universe? Her entire job revolved around making people happy. She rescued animals, donated to charities. Sure, she had had some unkind thoughts about people in the past—Wendy and Jason in particular. But why was she being punished?

And why *wasn't* Luke being punished? He had openly admitted to wanting to exploit her for his new project. Maybe she should sue him so she could afford to pay for Wendy's lawsuit. Surely a judge would be sympathetic to a betrayal of this magnitude. One thing was for sure, though. Luke Islestorm was dead to her.

Claire was startled out of her reverie by the sudden vibration of her phone. Alice was calling. She answered the video call and propped the phone on the sink while she peeled open a new bandage. Hopefully, the airport Wi-Fi would be enough to hold the conversation. She could really use some sage wisdom from her mom.

"Hey, Mom. Did I tell you I'm in Paris?" Claire said sheepishly.

Alice sniffled. Claire glanced at the screen. Her eyes and nose were red. Uh-oh. This was not good.

"What's wrong?" She slapped a new bandage on and picked up the phone.

Alice took a deep breath, then sighed. "Claire. Why didn't you tell me what happened?"

"What do you mean?"

"About the break-in and the note." Alice ticked them off on her fingers like she had a long-running list of grievances against her. She turned her watery blue eyes back to the camera. "I had to find out from your sister that you're in mortal peril. Again. And that you fled the country. You didn't think your own mother should be aware?"

Dammit, Charlie. Her stomach sank like a bag of bricks. "I'm really sorry, Mom. I didn't say anything because I didn't want to worry you. We don't know that it was anything sinister. It could have just been a bored teenager who lives in my building."

There weren't any teenagers in Claire's building as far as she knew, but Alice didn't need to know that.

"Wouldn't you have wanted to know if something like this happened to me?" Alice asked quietly. "Wouldn't you be furious if I didn't tell you and you had to find out from someone else?" She took a deep breath, like she was preparing to drop a bombshell. "I'm disappointed in you, Claire."

The words were like getting slapped in the face with a hand covered in tacky costume jewelry. Claire's mouth fell open, and she gaped at her phone like a goldfish. Alice had been her personal cheerleader for her entire life. Not once had her mother ever said those words to her. Not when she got a B on a term paper, not when she punched a girl in the mouth for bullying her friend in kindergarten. Claire's penchant for withholding information in order to protect her mother had dramatically backfired. Shame crept in, hot and suffocating.

"I—I'm sorry. You're right. I should have told you."

"I hope you get home safely," Alice said coolly. "I expect you to tell me if anything else happens. Good night, Claire." She hung up before Claire could respond.

Claire collapsed with her back to a stall. She slid down it until she was puddled on the floor. She buried her face in her hands.

Disappointed. The word still stung. Her eyes filled with tears, but she blinked them back. Just when she thought things couldn't possibly get worse. Now she had pissed off Alice, the only person on the planet who was supposed to love her unconditionally. Was this even deeper than rock bottom? Because it sure felt like it.

She hadn't told her mother about the Paris flowers. To be fair, Alice hadn't really given her a chance to tell her. But she should probably send a text to the group message just in case. She stared at the empty message bubble.

Claire: *Hi, I'm coming home from Paris early. Luke and I broke up and also I got more creepy stalker flowers. Hope the weather's nice at home.*

She started to erase the message, then sent it anyway. Messages full of exclamations from Charlie poured in. Alice's contact showed three blinking dots, but then they disappeared. Her own mother was so disappointed in her that she couldn't even react to a personal safety crisis.

Claire took a deep breath and got to her feet. She tucked her phone back in her carry-on and surveyed the bathroom for any items she left behind. Seeing nothing, she squared her shoulders and strolled back out into the airport. There was no choice but to move on.

"I JUST HAVE ONE STOP BEFORE HOME." CLAIRE RATTLED OFF Nicole's address to the cab driver. She had taken over Rosie-watching duty for the day while Mindy went camping with Gavin.

Claire ran a hand over her neck. All the tension in the world seemed to have settled on her during the transatlantic flight.

The driver nodded wordlessly and put on his turn signal, pulling out of the airport.

She texted Nicole. She was definitely going to be surprised when she showed up a full twelve hours early—and without Luke. Claire leaned back in her seat. A sparrow flitted past her window.

Luke's betrayal burned like a bee sting. Her cheeks were dry and tight where her tears had dried over the Atlantic. She had oscillated between pissed off and humiliated a dozen times during the trip.

She had felt so full and so safe just twenty-four hours ago. How had her life become such a mess? Again?

Nicole: *Everything okay?*

Claire: *Yeah, just caught an earlier flight.*

Nicole: *Good. Can't wait to hear about Paris :)*

Her phone pinged with a series of texts from Luke, but

she couldn't bring herself to open any of them. Nothing he had to say was going to be worth her time.

When Claire pulled up in front of Nicole and Kyle's apartment, the steps seemed as insurmountable as Mount Everest. But her furry best friend was waiting for her. "Keep it together, Claire," she muttered to herself, then told the driver, "I'll be just a second."

He nodded and pulled a folded newspaper off the passenger seat, meter still running.

Claire knocked on the door, more than ready for her fur baby to leap into her arms.

"Hey, Coli—oh!" she exclaimed when Nicole opened the door and she saw their kitchen. Candles were arranged on the table, and a bottle of champagne was chilling.

Nicole was wearing a red mini dress, and her hair was carefully gathered into an elaborate knot. Kyle, who had a spatula in his hand, was dressed in a sports coat but wasn't wearing any pants. The apartment smelled like marinara sauce and excess garlic.

A sudden realization dawned on Claire. "Oh crap, it's the second, isn't it? Your dating anniversary! I'm so sorry for intruding."

Nicole smiled. "Stop it. You're the reason why we started dating. It would be weird if you weren't here. Oh, maybe you should tell that story for your maid of honor speech."

"Please. It's already in there." She had written the six-page document the day after Nicole and Kyle's engagement.

A streak of fur came sprinting out of the bathroom, part of a roll of toilet paper dangling from her mouth.

"Roro!" Claire dropped to her knees. Rosie launched herself at Claire like a shedding, ginger missile. She licked Claire's face furiously, and Claire hugged her tightly. Rosie was the only living creature who could never disappoint her —no matter how many shoes she ate.

"I see you weren't being a good girl." She laughed and tugged the toilet paper roll out of the dog's mouth.

"Don't worry about it. She was great," Kyle said. "Only tried to knock the garbage can over seven or eight times."

Claire laughed in spite of herself. "We're working on that, but she's been resistant to the training. Thank you so much for watching her. I'll get out of your hair—the meter's running." She leaned over and picked up Rosie's overnight bag.

"The meter?" Nicole paused as she tied an apron around her waist. "You took a cab? Was something wrong with Luke's car?"

Claire straightened and gripped Rosie's leash. "It's no big deal, we can talk about it later."

"Are you sure? There's something you're not telling me." Nicole came closer and grabbed Claire's hand. Her brown eyes probed Claire's.

She should have known. Nicole was like a drama-sniffing bloodhound. "Everything's fine. We'll talk tomorrow. Enjoy your dinner. It smells amazing. And thanks again for watching this little terror," she said, leaning in and giving Nicole a hug. There was no way she was ruining their romantic night with her stupid boy problems.

Get it together, Claire. She sniffed loudly, choking back the tears that were threatening to leak out.

"Wait. You're not going home alone, are you? It's not safe, Claire," Nicole said, squeezing her hand.

"The note was a dumb prank. Barney's in prison, and he has no friends because he's a psychopath."

"I don't think you should—"

"Trust me, it's fine," she said firmly, snapping Rosie's

leash on. "But don't tell Mindy, please. You know how she gets. She only just stopped sleeping on a cot in front of my door."

"Fine. Call me if you need anything. And I mean anything. Love you," Nicole said, giving Claire another squeeze.

Claire climbed into the cab with Rosie, bolstered by the presence of her furry companion.

"Where to, miss?"

She relayed her home address and sent a quick email to Mindy to let her know that she was home early and would be available for a meeting tomorrow to talk about screening their new applicants.

As they rounded the corner of Claire's street, dozens of cars and news vans came into view. They surrounded the apartment building like an encroaching battalion. An icy fist gripped her throat, and she could barely choke out the words, "Just drive. Keep going. Anywhere but here."

The mustachioed cab driver glanced at her in the rearview mirror but obliged.

The reporters perked up when they saw the cab going past the building, and six or seven people rushed into the street with cameras, peeking into the window.

"It's her!" Claire heard a muffled voice say. "Miss Hartley, are the rumors true? Have you received contact from a Widowmaker copycat?"

What the shit? Who the hell had told them? Only her family, close friends, and the police knew about the note. They would rather stand in the Black Friday line outside Target in subzero temperatures for a week than betray her. So, who was it? Could there be a mole in the police station? Or did Luke leak the information after their fight?

She hid her face in Rosie's fur, blocking out the press's frantic shouts.

"Jesus," the cab driver said, inching along as reporters practically scrambled on top of the car, shutters clicking from every direction.

She glanced behind her as they rounded the corner of the street. Several reporters climbed into their news vans, camera crew winding up their cables as quick as they could.

They hit a red light, and the invisible fist around Claire's stomach tightened.

"Where do you want me to go? Where will you be safe?" The cab driver said, speaking in complete sentences for the first time. He wrapped his arm around the passenger's head rest and glanced over his shoulder at her.

Claire paused, Mindy's address on the tip of her tongue. But she and Gavin had gone glamping overnight and wouldn't have cell service.

"Let me call someone," she said, bringing up her phone. She would rather set herself on fire than go to Luke's. Nicole and Kyle were celebrating. Who was left?

She scrolled aimlessly through her contacts. If she wasn't safe in her own apartment, she probably wouldn't be safe by herself in a hotel. She had no one, and reporters could be at her warehouse, too, for all she knew.

Her thumb paused over Sawyer-Sanctum in her contact list. He was almost certainly tired of rescuing her. But he might be her last hope.

"They're getting out of their cars. They're crazy," the cab driver said.

Claire glanced behind her. A reporter from *Channel Eight News* and another man hoisting an expensive-looking camera climbed out of a van several car lengths behind them.

She clicked on Sawyer's contact. The phone rang twice.

"Hey, I need your help."

CHAPTER SIXTEEN

To Do:
- Find a way to lose the press's interest—plug a
different charity every time they harass me?
- Send applicant acceptance letters
- Check in with Aaron

THE CAB WOUND ITS WAY DEEPER INTO THE WOODS THAT surrounded West Haven, the opposite end of town from Luke's house. Every time Claire glanced behind her, headlights still followed them into the darkness. At this point, she wasn't sure whether they were reporters or locals.

"Almost there," the cab driver reported, slowing down. They hadn't passed a mailbox in a mile or two.

"Are we near the lake?" Claire asked.

"'Bout a half mile off this road. Good kayaking in the summer."

"Good to know."

The cab turned at a barely noticeable driveway with a Private—No Trespassing sign planted firmly in the ground. The mailbox leaned slightly on its post.

As they left the paved road, the cars behind them slowed and then stopped. Bastards. The cab pulled up outside a charming Cape Cod home. The house, though unassuming, was surrounded by beautiful landscaping. A mechanically edged flower bed contained a handful of hostas. A rock-lined pathway led the way to the wraparound porch. Crimson geraniums flanked the front door in squat pots.

Claire paid the driver and opened her door, ready to drag her bag out of the trunk. Her heart stopped.

Wait. Her friends and the cops weren't the only people who knew about the note. Sawyer was the first one to respond to the scene. How could she have forgotten? Could he have told the press? And now she was stranded at his house in the middle of the woods with no neighbors for a good mile. Not to mention he was gigantic and could probably subdue her using only his nondominant pinkie. How could she be such an idiot?

The ground trembled beneath her, and a low *boof* came from somewhere behind her. She whirled around. All her tasers were at home, the warehouse, or Luke's car. Damn TSA. She was ready to hurl her bag when a Rottweiler with a big, goofy smile approached the cab.

"Well, hello, handsome." Claire held out her hand.

Rosie hid behind Claire's legs, sniffing fearfully at the newcomer. She generally preferred pugs and other verti-cally challenged dogs.

The giant sniffed her hand for a moment before licking it and letting out another boof. He disappeared around the corner of the house.

Claire's heart thudded uncomfortably. Surely Sawyer

hadn't leaked the information to the press. He had saved her life. And he was one of Kyle's best friends. But how well did she know him really? She needed to be sure. Maybe it was best to come right out and ask while she still had a witness present.

Sawyer emerged from a side door, tugging his customary black T-shirt over an impressive set of abs. Though she was emotionally distraught and slightly concerned that he was a rat, she wasn't blind.

"Are you okay?" he asked as soon as he approached. He reached toward her but seemed to think better of it.

"I'm fine. Hey, any chance you leaked the story about the note in my apartment to the press?"

Sawyer did a double take. "Leaked what? The note?"

The cabbie got out of the car and pulled her luggage from the trunk. He paused, also looking at Sawyer.

Claire crossed her arms and stared him down. "Did you tell the press about the note?" Each word was as sharp in her mouth as a dagger.

"God, no." There was shock in his eyes. "I would never do that to you. To anyone."

All the signs of genuine surprise were there—wide eyes, expression of disbelief. But she had been fooled before.

"Okay." He passed for now. But she was going to keep her wits about her.

Sawyer raised his eyebrows but took her bags from the cabbie and thanked him before ushering her inside. Her heart thudded again as she crossed the threshold. There wasn't any sinister energy emanating from the house. On the contrary, it was well-worn and comfortable, if a bit crowded.

While Luke's house was one you'd find in a magazine, Sawyer's was one you'd find if you went to visit your grandma. A hand-me-down oak table and mismatched pair of kitchen chairs stood to her right. The living room, in which every flat surface was crowded with picture frames, was on the left.

"Will you stay here for a minute? I want to make sure the paparazzi clears off the property," he said, strolling over to a cabinet and entering a code on a small keypad.

"Sure," she said as the cabinet door popped open.

Sawyer consulted the contents for a moment before drawing out a shotgun.

Her breath hitched. Was "clearing off the paparazzi" just code? Was he going to shoot her in cold blood?

"Make yourself at home," he said, gesturing to the mismatched navy blue couch and plaid-patterned armchair. "I'll be right back."

"Thanks." Claire set her bag on the floor. Sawyer left through the side door, and she stuffed her phone into her bra. It might not save her, but it would certainly take him longer to find it.

She pushed a plaid curtain to the side. He *was* walking toward the driveway, so maybe murder wasn't on the agenda after all. Unless he was just lulling her into a false sense of security. Her fingers shook as she typed a quick message to Mindy. She probably wouldn't have service in the woods, but at least if she disappeared someone would know.

Claire: *Long story. If I go missing, I'm at Sawyer's house. I'm wearing black shorts, those Vera Wang sandals you tried to steal last Friendsgiving, and a white button-down top. You know my laptop password. All my account passwords are stored in the "Grocery List" Excel file. Track my phone.*

She sent her location for good measure and tucked her

phone away. What kind of home did a security professional keep? Were there nanny cams and motion sensors everywhere? She peered at a one-eyed teddy bear on a shelf next to a comic book. Dozens of framed pictures cluttered Sawyer's furniture. In one picture, two women hung from his biceps as he held them off the ground. In another, a beautiful redhead in a park ranger uniform thrust her hands toward the sky.

There was time to worry about the enigma of Sawyer later. For now, she needed an emergency weapon. How hard could that be to find in a security guy's house? She hustled into the kitchen. Perfect. A butcher block. She pulled a small paring knife out, wrapped it in a tea towel, and tucked it in her bra underneath the other boob. Hopefully, that would be enough to prevent her from impaling herself. Then she crossed back to the living room to casually study more of the photos.

The front door banged open.

Claire screamed and leapt backward. It was time. He was coming for her. Her shin crashed into the coffee table, and she fell backward and hit the ground hard. Her already bruised tailbone smarted. She splayed with one leg trapped under the couch and one hand stuffed into her bra, reaching for the knife.

Sawyer's head hovered over the couch. "Sorry, the door sticks. All clear out front. Am I—uh—interrupting?"

She snatched her hand out of her bra. Her ears went hot. "No, I'm just—"

"Hiding weapons in your bra in case I'm a murderer? Not a bad move." He rounded the couch and bent down. He reached out a hand.

She took it, and he pulled her up to standing as easily as if he was picking up an empty laundry bag.

"You're right." Claire fished in her bra and drew out the paring knife. She handed it to him. The jig was up. If he did decide to attack her, he knew exactly where to look. Damn it. "Sorry. I'm finding it difficult to trust people these days."

"Understandable." He smiled as he unrolled the knife. He handed it back to her.

"Got some strawberries you need me to hull?"

"Nah. If it makes you feel safer, you should keep it."

"Thank you." Her guard came down a millimeter. But she would still stab a bitch if she needed to.

"You look like you could use a shower and maybe a cup of tea."

She frowned and smoothed a hand over her hair. It wasn't damp anymore, but it probably still had Seine filth on it.

"Not because you look bad or anything, just because you just got off a flight. I always feel gross when I fly," he rambled. "I'm not trying to be creepy, just thought maybe you'd want to feel clean after—you know what, I'm going to stop talking now."

She smiled. "A shower would be great, if you don't mind."

"Sure. Don't forget your knife."

Sawyer led her down a narrow, wood-paneled hallway to the bathroom. He hadn't even asked her anything else. How could that be? He didn't even know her that well, but he had opened his home to her as readily as if she were his closest friend. Either he was gathering intel or he really was a decent human being.

"I don't really have any girly soap or anything." He rubbed the back of his neck. "Help yourself to anything in here, though."

"Thanks, Sawyer. Listen, I—"

He put a gentle hand on her wrist to stop her. "You don't need to explain."

"Thank you," she said again, weariness settling into her bones.

He shut the door and left her to her thoughts.

THE STEAMING SHOWER IN THE 50S-STYLE BLUE BATHTUB HAD brought with it some clarity and acceptance. This wasn't the first time someone had stomped on her heart with a pair of cleats. She could handle a little heartbreak. Give a girl a fresh pair of leggings and she could do anything.

She wiped a spot clean in the steamy bathroom mirror. You couldn't even tell she had crawled out of a river and been publicly humiliated in a foreign country. *Ha.* She twisted her hair up into a towel and zipped her suitcase shut. The paring knife glinted on the bathroom sink. She shrugged, then wrapped it in a clean sock and shoved it back into her bra. Maybe if he did attack her, he wouldn't expect her to use the same hiding place she had already exposed. She paused with her hand on the doorknob and triple-checked that she was wearing pants. There would be no repeats of the Luke Incident.

Stop thinking about Luke.

The seductive scent of warm bread greeted her when she emerged from the bathroom.

"Wow, that smells amazing." She stepped into the kitchen and sniffed appreciatively.

Rosie was in the living room, playing tug with the Rottweiler. Crap, she hadn't even asked his name. Or brought a host gift. Alice would have been even more disappointed in her.

"Oh, thanks," Sawyer said as he pulled a loaf of home-made bread from the oven. "Gentle, Diesel," he said over his shoulder. The Rottweiler released the rope and sat on his butt.

Sawyer shut the oven and turned back to Claire. "I just happened to have a stew in the crockpot that's almost done. Are you hungry?"

"Starving. Thank you so much. I really am sorry to just show up like this. I didn't know who else to call."

"You can always call me."

"Thanks." She stepped behind the bar to keep some distance between them. Sawyer seemed like a genuine, warm person. And he had quite literally saved her life. But she had planned a proposal for a serial killer. Her judgment was garbage. She couldn't afford to misjudge someone else. "How can I help?"

He shrugged. "You could set those bowls out if you want." He gestured to a mismatched pair that looked like he had been toting around since college. She should send him a matching set from Crate and Barrel to say thank you. Assuming he didn't murder her.

She placed the bowls on the table along with silverware and napkins and curled up in a chair, hugging her knees to her chest. How did these spindly wooden chairs support Sawyer's weight?

Her phone beeped, and she glanced at it. It was a confirmation text from a florist in Miami. Alice's apology flowers and chocolate assortment had just been delivered. Hopefully, it would soften her mom's heart.

"Feel better after your shower?"

"So much better." There had been something comforting about the modest, outdated charm of Sawyer's bathroom. It reminded her of the first house she had lived in with Roy.

"So, the paparazzi were waiting for you when you got home?"

Claire nodded.

"Are you sure your driver didn't call them?"

Of course he didn't. But… "You know, I actually have no idea. But I wasn't even supposed to come home until tomorrow morning. As you probably guessed from my interrogation earlier, somebody leaked the news about the note. One of them screamed it at me through the windshield. Luckily they only know about one."

It was time to deploy the plan she had formulated in the shower. As of that moment, only she, Luke, Charlie, Alice, and the police knew about the Paris note. If she told Sawyer and it ended up in the news the next day, she would know he was untrustworthy.

Sawyer looked at her earnestly as he sawed off a piece of homemade bread and offered it to her.

"Did you say they only know about one note? As in there was another one?"

She nodded and took the bread from him. "Buckle up. It's story time."

Sawyer spoke little during her recounting of the Paris trip. She left out the part about Luke's betrayal. And the sex. What was it about Sawyer that made her want to spill her guts? She still didn't feel totally at ease, but he was like a blank sheet. She could hurl any thoughts in her head at him and he would let them stick without judgment. He listened carefully, maintaining eye contact and occasionally interjecting with a supportive comment.

After dinner, he led her to the living room. She felt lighter as she sank into the overstuffed couch. He hadn't told her she was being crazy or irrational. He hadn't handcuffed her to a radiator and refused to let her be on her own. And she had told the whole story start to finish without crying. Who needed a therapist now, Luke?

Stop thinking about that idiot.

Diesel and Rosie lay together on a massive plaid dog bed, snoring in tandem.

"Sawyer?" she asked, turning to find him.

"Hmm?" he asked, returning with two glasses of wine. "Thought you could use this after today." He placed a glass in her hand.

"More than you know." She sniffed the glass hesitantly. What was she expecting to smell? Roofies? Did roofies even have a smell?

"It's safe." Sawyer nodded at the glass. He sat in the plaid armchair opposite her.

Her heart thudded in her chest. The sickly sweet smell of chloroform had floated to the surface of her memory again. "Oh, I wasn't—"

"I would respect you less if you hadn't." His thousand-watt smile lit up his entire face.

"I trust you. I think." The knife sock jabbed into her ribcage. She shuffled it out of the way and took a sip. The wine—an earthy Bordeaux, if she had to guess—tasted ordinary. Who knew Sawyer had good taste in wine? "Just know that if you plan to murder me, Rosie will be an orphan. You don't want that on your conscience."

"If I murdered you, I would one hundred percent dognap Rosie and take her across the country under an assumed name."

Claire frowned. "That's comforting."

"Sorry, bad joke." The glass looked comically small and spindly in Sawyer's meaty fist. He swirled it expertly before taking a sip. "You were about to say something? Before the roofies incident."

"Oh, right. I know I've said it before, but I never really thanked you properly for saving my life." Suspicious or not, she wouldn't be here if he hadn't intervened.

His glass clattered when it hit the dog-shaped coaster on the worn coffee table. "You did. At least twice now. Besides, you don't owe me any thanks. Any decent human being would have done the same thing."

"I'm not sure that's true. You literally put yourself between me and a maniac. And here I am treating you like a criminal."

Sawyer smiled. "You're right to be suspicious. You went through a terrible trauma. I still think you would've been fine without me, though. You're resourceful. Scrappy, even."

"I don't think I would have. But I appreciate your confidence." She leaned back again, tugging a flannel blanket around her. It smelled like the woods.

He was silent for a moment.

"Have you ever talked to anyone about what happened that night? Like really talked?" The armchair squeaked as he leaned back.

She bit her bottom lip. "Kind of. Just bits and pieces. Every time I try to tell the whole story, it's like a wall goes up and my mind just shuts down. They—my family and friends —know the important parts."

He nodded. "That's pretty common after a trauma, according to my mom anyway. She's a psychologist. You know, a few sessions with a therapist would probably be really helpful for you."

Ugh, again with the therapy. She didn't need someone poking around in her brain.

"That's what everyone's saying." She shook her head and fixed her gaze on her sleeping dog.

"You can talk to me too. If you're not ready for therapy."

Claire smiled. "Thanks. It's hard to talk to my friends about it. They're been treating me like I'm made out of glass. Nicole cries every time I bring it up, and Mindy starts swearing and plotting revenge. And my mother—don't even get me started."

And Luke? He only wanted her to talk to his camera.

"Did you want to talk about why you're here? And not at Mindy's or Nicole's? Or Luke's?" Sawyer asked. Curiosity must have finally won out.

"Searching for more information to sell to the press?"

His eyebrows knit together.

"Sorry, that wasn't fair." Maybe he would have some valuable insight about the Luke situation. Her only other close male friend was Kyle, and she wasn't about to discuss her relationship—or lack thereof—with Luke's best friend.

She stood and walked behind the couch. This didn't seem like a story to tell sitting down. "Mindy and Nicole were busy. And Luke and I kind of...imploded."

Claire rehashed the story. Sawyer listened patiently as she paced around the room. Did all of this sound juvenile? When she finished, she turned to him hesitantly.

"I'm not in any position to comment on your relationship. But that was a shitty thing to do."

"Thank you. It really was." She leaned against the back of the overstuffed couch, vindicated. A yawn escaped that was so large, her entire body shuddered.

"You look exhausted. Want to hit the hay?"

"That would probably be best," she said, an ocean of weariness seeming to weigh her to the spot.

Tomorrow would be a better day. It had to be.

"You can have my room," he said, standing up. He rounded the couch and stood next to her. "I'm in the middle of re-painting the guest bedroom, and I don't want you inhaling all those fumes."

"Oh, no. You took me in. The couch is more than fine." She stood up straight. Something fell at her feet. The paring knife, wrapped in one of her socks, had fallen out of her bra.

"Oops," she said, and bent down to get it at the same time as Sawyer. They cracked heads like billiard balls and Claire crumpled to the floor.

"Oh, god, are you okay?" He leaned over her, one hand pressed over his face and the other planted on the floor by her head.

Her right eyebrow smarted where it had smacked off Sawyer's broad forehead. The popcorn ceiling above her was begging to be scraped off. Sawyer's biceps bulged above her. A tattoo she had never noticed snaked underneath the seam of his T-shirt. It was hard to tell from this angle, but it looked like the corner of a map.

"I'm fine." She rose to her elbows and skittered backward like a crab. There was no reason for her to be eyeing Sawyer's biceps. He was a friend. An acquaintance, even. "Sorry."

Sawyer sat back on his haunches and pushed the knife sock closer to her.

"It's yours, seriously. I just changed the sheets," he said, gesturing back the hallway.

There was no point in arguing. "Thank you, Sawyer. You helped me even though you barely know me. I really hope you're not a shady murderer because I feel like we could be really good friends." She laid the paring knife down on an end table and took a step back.

He smiled. "You're welcome. I hope you're not a

murderer either. The last time I had one in my bed things got out of hand."

Claire laughed, the first time since the ill-fated dinner cruise.

"Good night," she said, dragging her carry-on bag down the hall.

Sawyer's room was the same as the rest of the house, a little bit crowded with knickknacks, but cozy as could be and unusually clean for a bachelor. A collection of vintage comic books lined a bookshelf, and a quick Google search revealed that the series of framed geographic prints on the wall were from a Samoan artist. Wood carvings in abstract shapes littered the flat surfaces in the room. It must have been a bitch to dust. She climbed into the massive bed, and her elbow knocked against yet another framed picture—the redhead from the living room. Who was she?

She crawled under the sheets—surprisingly high thread count for a guy—and sank into their coziness. For the first time since Luke's betrayal, she felt safe. She stayed conscious long enough to plug her phone into the charger, and then sank into the blissful oblivion of sleep.

CHAPTER SEVENTEEN

To Do:
- Doublecheck Ericka's flight info
- Send care package to T&E's neighbors

Holy shit, had she peed in Sawyer's bed? Claire hadn't
wet the bed since second grade. Everything from her waist
down was soaking wet and cold against her skin. How was
she going to explain this? Trauma-induced bladder failure?
Jet lag?

Please, please have a washer and dryer. She opened her
eyes, already plotting a million different excuses in case he
caught her.

She wasn't in bed. She wasn't even lying down—she was
standing.

Ah, hell.

She glanced down at her feet. Dark water sloshed rhythmically against her shins. For a moment, she was back in

Paris, staggering through the stagnant Seine, trying to escape Luke. But this was a lake. And it didn't smell like sewage and betrayal. So, where the hell was she?

She turned and stepped on something sharp.

"Goddammit," she said, instinctively lifting her foot from the water and grabbing it. The motion set her balance awry, and she staggered. Her world tilted, and she came down hard. She gasped. The knee-high water hit her like an icy fist and stole her breath. Rocks jutted into her shins.

"Whoa, let me help." Sawyer's voice came from behind her. A large shadow sloshed through the dark toward her.

"Sawyer?"

"You're a sleepwalker, huh?" He hoisted her out of the water like a soaked rag doll.

"Only recently." Claire wrung her T-shirt out. Oh, good, the paring knife was back in her hand. God, it was cold. Her nipples were probably visible from outer space.

"Since the Barney thing?" He put his arm out, and she latched onto it as they crossed the stony bottom of the lake back to the shore.

"Yeah. I woke up in the middle of the street last week, and once in the woods at Luke's. Before he utterly betrayed me, anyway. Unconscious Claire usually brings a snack along, but I don't see any spaghetti this time."

"Maybe not, but I did witness you stuff an entire block of sharp cheddar down your pants before you went out the back door."

So, that was what the lump on her left hip was. Nocturnal pants cheese.

"I'm so sorry." She tripped on something tall and hard in the lake and stumbled forward. Could this weekend get any worse?

"It's just cheese." Sawyer laughed and steadied her.

"Why didn't you wake me?"

"I thought maybe you were working something out subconsciously. You walked half a mile barefoot with a knife in your hand before plunging into the lake."

She groaned. This was not good. "Maybe I need to start zip-tying myself to the bed frame at night."

"My mom has treated several sleepwalkers. A therapist can teach you some techniques to prevent it from happening."

"Yeah, yeah." A shiver racked her. She didn't have time for a therapist. And the sleepwalking wasn't a problem. It was just some unconscious exercise. Hitting her step goal early in the day. It was responsible, really.

***

"Are you sure you're okay?" Mindy asked, glancing at Claire as she gripped the wheel exactly at ten o'clock and two o'clock. Rain pelted the windshield of her SUV.

Claire sighed. "I don't know." She sipped the raspberry mocha iced coffee Mindy had brought her as Sawyer's house shrank into the distance. He hadn't tried to murder her in her sleep. They had even nailed down a date for Claire to come in for a self-defense class that week. "I feel... violated. Used. Lied to. Take your pick."

Mindy sighed. "I mean, of course he would want you for the documentary. Professionally speaking, he would be crazy not to. You are the only surviving victim. But I can't believe that he actually crossed the line and asked. Especially after taking you to Paris and dropping your panties in an alleyway."

Claire groaned. "Don't remind me. I just want to rewind to six months ago when I didn't know Luke existed." And before she was hunted by a psychopath and sued by the Bride of Satan. And before she started taking nocturnal adventures. She wasn't going to mention the sleepwalking to Mindy or Nicole. There was enough going on.

Claire gripped the armrest as Mindy rounded one of the many hairpin turns on Sawyer's road. A mysterious aqua-colored scrap of fabric clung to the arm of her jacket. Claire flailed her arm until it dropped onto her lap. *Yikes, a thong.* She shrieked and promptly dropped it on the floor.

"Oops, sorry. I forgot those up here when Gavin and I were at the drive-in movies last weekend. There's hand sanitizer in the glove box."

Claire shuddered and pulled on the glove box handle. A United Kingdom guidebook fell out.

"Planning a trip?" she asked, holding up the guide.

"Maybe," Mindy said. "Gavin's been a bit distant lately, so I've been tapping into my inner anglophile."

Claire leafed through the book. A couple of pages were dog-eared. "Do you think he's homesick?"

"That's what I thought. I tried to make him 'bangers and mash,' as he calls it, but I burned the sausages."

Claire smiled. "Maybe he could use a night out. I haven't seen him since trivia night at Ringers."

"I have something in the works. Hopefully it helps." Mindy drummed the steering wheel in time with the pop song on the radio.

"He probably misses his family. I'm surprised he didn't go home for the summer."

"He couldn't with the internship. You know Pierogi Drive is basically the Wall Street of West Haven. Anyway, enough about my relationship trouble."

Mindy put on her turn signal. They sat at the traffic light outside Claire's apartment. There must have been more exciting breaking news in West Haven, because the news trucks were finally gone.

Claire frowned at the droopy, neglected plant in her fourth-floor window. "Thanks for picking me up, Min."

"Any time. I'm sorry about what happened with Luke. We will fix it with drinks and dancing and a nice trip to Sephora. Want to do a run-through of Tyler's proposal after you have a nap? I can't believe it's just four days away."

"Let's do it now. I don't need sleep. I need to work." Claire pulled her phone out of her purse, ignoring the eight missed calls from Luke and opening her notes on Tyler's proposal. "Almost everything is done. We just need to pick up the fireworks tomorrow, make sure the handyman finished installing all those safety railings in the house, double-check the flower arrangement, and make sure her flight time hasn't changed."

"Perfect. I'll verify that today. Oh, Claire, I almost forgot," Mindy said as she pulled into a spot on the street. Her voice was gentler now, less businesslike. "Coli's field day thing for the bridal party is this Saturday. And then the awards are the following Friday."

Claire groaned as she exited the car and slammed the door. Nicole, arguably the most competitive and adventurous person she had ever met, had planned a field day full of events for the bridal party to bond. She had arranged it before Luke and Claire's relationship had imploded. Now Claire would be playing flag football with the man who karate chopped her heart. Maybe Coli would switch it to tackle football so she could at least ram her head into his gut.

At least the Chamber of Commerce Award for Event Planner of the Year was all but guaranteed to be hers. Nicole's May proposal had been a masterpiece, even with the carriage tampering. But the ceremony meant sitting in the same room with her ex-fiancé and the twatwaffle who was suing her. And now that Luke was dead to her, she would be arriving dateless.

"Want to be my date? I don't think I can face Wendy and Jason alone. I'm going to need some backup." She pushed open the door to the stairwell and began to climb, Rosie trotting after her.

"I would, but I had to pencil in a meeting at the gallery with Nicole and Aaron. We're going to show him the gallery while his girlfriend is visiting her parents. I could see if we could change the time but—"

"Don't worry about it. It's okay. Ask him about the progress on his sketch, will you? I know he's sheepish about it, but Jane is going to love it." Claire clasped her hands to her heart. With the private room set up at the gallery and custom uplighting, it was going to be stunning.

Rosie tugged her down the hall toward the apartment door. Before the trip, Claire had forgotten to pack Rosie's second favorite toy, a one-eyed monkey named Sam. He probably needed a quick tumble in the washing machine. She added it to her To Do list as she pulled out her keys and slid them in the door. She pushed her front door open and faced her friend to mention the lighting she wanted for Aaron.

"*Ahhhhhh,*" Mindy screamed.

"What? What?" Claire turned around in time to see an expensive purse go flying across the room.

A shadowy figure turned away from the window at the last second and caught it by one strap.

Claire hammered the panic button on her wall unit as Mindy picked up a bar stool. Mindy ran across the room, holding the chair in front of her like a battering ram.

Claire sprinted into the living room and yanked Taser #5 from its hiding place under the coffee table. She swung it like a gun and pointed it at the intruder. Rosie sat on her butt and tipped her head.

This was it. It was happening. Whoever the new stalker was had broken into her apartment. And he was going to pay.

"That is quite enough," the shadowy figure said, relieving Mindy of her chair and artfully using her momentum against her, twirling her and dropping her into the chair as easy as breathing. He stepped in front of the window and revealed his face. A face she hadn't seen for two decades, but there was no mistaking him.

Claire stopped, mouth gaping open. She couldn't think. She couldn't breathe.

"Dad?"

CHAPTER EIGHTEEN

JACK HARTLEY STOOD IN CLAIRE'S KITCHEN, DRESSED IN overshined dress shoes and a black suit and tie. His salt-and-pepper hair was combed perfectly into place, and a clear earpiece nestled in his right ear. His footsteps were completely silent as he stepped closer to her. He was tall, but not so tall that he would stand out in a crowd. A distorted, male version of herself stared back at her. The slope of her nose. Her earlobes. Her own brown eyes peered out from an unfamiliar face, and she didn't know whether to scream or run or cry.

The bottom fell out of her stomach, and her head spun like she had climbed onto a Tilt-A-Whirl. What could he possibly want with her after two decades of silence? And how had he gotten past her security system?

Had she stumbled into some kind of alternate universe? One where she had a caring father who made sure she arrived home safely and who would offer to sit on the front porch cleaning a shotgun in case that good-for-nothing Luke ever came back?

But no. Jack Hartley wasn't that kind of father. He wasn't a father at all. At least not to her.

Mindy cleared her throat, still sitting in the kitchen chair. "So. What the hell are you doing here? Did Claire's sudden media appearance remind you that you had a daughter you abandoned twenty years ago?"

Claire's phone vibrated in her pocket, but she couldn't catch her breath. Her eyes flicked between Jack and Mindy, and she was unable to find her voice.

"Claire," Jack said, digging in his pocket. "Forgive the intrusion. When we heard you were out of the country, we had to catch you as soon as you came back. Local law enforcement really should have informed us of your whereabouts but—"

"We?"

He withdrew a badge from his wallet and flashed it at her briefly. "FBI. We need your help."

For fuck's sake.

She stared at him, then threw her purse onto one of the barstools. She slapped the Taser on the counter then marched up to Jack. "Did I stumble onto the set of a bad movie? You come back into my life after two decades of absolute silence, claiming to be with the FBI, and you suddenly think I owe you something?"

He flushed, and his brows knit together.

"I understand you have some qualms with our shared

history, but this is all trivial in the light of what we're facing."

Trivial?

Claire turned away from him and pressed her hands to her face. Her nostrils flared. Had she not suffered enough? Would this hellish nightmare of a summer ever end?

"Let me see your credentials," she said flatly. No way she was going to take his words at face value.

"Fair enough." He flipped open a small black wallet and handed it over.

"Jack Hartley, special agent. That's just...great." She folded it back up and fought the urge to fling it at his head. Her hands shook as she handed it back. "So, twenty missed birthdays and an unanswered invitation to my wedding is trivial?"

"I'd like to talk to you about all that sometime. I really would. But right now, I need your help. The country is facing an imminent threat."

"Unless there's an emergency overstock of tacos in a bunker in Waco that is about to expire, I'm not interested in helping you."

"Claire. This is serious."

She closed her eyes and took a deep breath. Clearly he wasn't going to go away. "Do you mean Barney? He's in prison."

"Barney?" Jack scoffed. He paced up and down the hallway, checking the door frames and feeling underneath side tables. Was he trying to find her emergency pizza money? "You got a note before you left, yes?"

"That's really none of your business. Detective Smith is handling it," she said, crossing her arms in front of her.

"I'm afraid this is out of Detective Smith's jurisdiction." He opened then closed the blinds on her kitchen window. "We don't believe that note came from someone looking to get a rise out of you. We believe Barney was a minor cog in a much bigger, much deadlier machine."

Her blood ran cold. More Barneys? Could it even be possible? "I don't understand."

"Most of this is confidential," he said as he ran his hand over the top of Claire's windowsill and peered into the bottom of a vase. "But I'll tell you what I can. We don't think Barney was working alone."

Claire's breath caught in her chest. So, her note-leaver wasn't just a punk kid playing a horrible joke? "But the Widowmaker victims—he knew them all. What motivation would someone else have—"

"Yes, Mr. Windsor knew all his victims. But there are over forty thousand missing women in the United States at any given time. We've received some intelligence that suggests that some of these disappearances are connected in ways that we never dreamed."

"What, like the A-A-S-K? The American Association of Serial Killers?" Claire shook her head.

"That may not be far off."

Claire's stomach fell into her butt.

The wooden chair creaked. Mindy gripped the arms with wide eyes.

Claire's hands shook, and she curled them into fists. "What kind of intelligence?"

Jack resumed his pacing, over-polished shoes barely making a sound on the hardwood floor.

"Over the past several decades, numerous bodies of missing women have been recovered across the country. Over one hundred of these women had a symbol etched into their skin. And those were just the ones who hadn't decayed beyond recognition. There's no telling how many more there were."

"How old were these women? Where did you find them? What's the commonality?"

Jack turned to look at her. Did he look...impressed? No, that was definitely wishful thinking. "That's the thing. The commonality isn't clear. They were found as near as Philadelphia and as far as Anchorage. The only common thread that links the victims is that they're all women. All different ages. Most were young and beautiful, but some were older. Many were career-driven, powerful women."

Oh, for fuck's sake. Would this nightmare never end? As if things weren't bad enough when there was just one Barney. Now there was a *legion* of Barneys across the country? And they wanted revenge on Claire? Absolutely not. Time to move to Canada.

Something about his explanation didn't sit right. "That doesn't make sense," she said slowly. "None of Barney's victims were particularly powerful. Ariel was a waitress. Courtney was a perpetually intoxicated architect."

"Regardless, we believe they're connected. We never saw the symbol on a live person. Until we saw you on TV."

"Symbol? What symbol?" She looked down at herself.

Jack reached for her, and Claire flinched. Something flashed in his eyes, but the shadow had passed before she could interpret it.

He brushed her hair aside, revealing her shoulders and collarbone.

"That's not a symbol, it's a stab wound." Idiot.

"Not that one." He gripped her shoulders and marched her over to the mirror next to the front door. "That one."

She squinted in the half-light. A one-inch strip of skin that was normally covered up by a bra strap shone bare. Ah, of course. The shallow mystery scratch Barney had thoughtfully left her. It didn't look like much at first. Claire had simply written it off as another ghastly physical reminder of the horror she had gone through. But, as she leaned into the mirror, she made out some minute details.

She gasped, immediately transported back to the dingy parking garage where the fluorescent lights hummed like a swarm of wasps. The air smelled like the basement of a new house, but the acoustics didn't match. Her hands were bound behind her back, and Barney had taken his knife and carved something into her skin. At the time, she had thought it was his initials. But this didn't look like initials. What the hell was it? A person?

She touched the mark on her neck. "Barney's other victims. Did they—?" How did she finish this sentence? Did he brand them too? Were they also gifted with temporary tattoos?

"We don't know, but we suspect they will if we can find them before they're decomposed beyond recognition."

Jack pulled a manila folder out of his nondescript black briefcase, which he had stashed on the bar. He laid a stack of pictures down. Claire approached hesitantly.

"These are some of the victims that have been recovered across the country," he said, flashing through photo after photo. Claire's stomach lurched. Even though the pictures were mostly close-ups of the symbol, the blood-spattered flesh and first-hand knowledge of the horror these women had faced in their last hours weighed on her like an anvil. The symbol was large in some, and barely decipherable in others. There were minor differences in each, but the general shape was undeniable. Vaguely humanoid with a strange protrusion. What was it?

Claire shuddered and covered the mark with her hair,

willing it to disappear. If her sleepwalking was stress-induced, as she was beginning to suspect, she definitely needed to zip-tie herself to the bed frame tonight. It was that or end up pants-less on a roof with an emergency churro clenched between her butt cheeks.

Mindy had moved to the couch in the living room, staring warily at Claire's father and yammering away on her cell phone. She had called Sawyer and cancelled the emergency call when Claire had calmed down.

"There are two reasons why I'm here, Claire." Jack sat down on the very edge of one of the barstools, leaning forward and staring intently into her eyes.

Great. The guy left for twenty years and then only reappeared to ask *her* for something. Classic deadbeat dad. Was he going to ask for money next? "You said you needed my help. With what?"

He shuffled the pictures back into a neat stack and tucked the envelope in his briefcase.

"First, the locations of Barney's missing victims. Their families deserve closure."

Claire crossed her arms. A headache was forming. "I already told the police everything Barney said to me that night. He didn't tell me where the bodies were."

Jack nodded. "We also need information on this group, organization, cult, whatever it is they're calling it."

"How do you expect me to get all this information?" And why was this her responsibility? Surely an agent could torture the information out of him just as easily.

He pressed the tips of his fingers together. "Our agents have visited Barney in prison, tried to interrogate him. He refuses to speak to us. We even asked his ex-fiancée to go on local TV and make an appeal to him directly, but it didn't work."

Aha! So that was why Victoria looked so shifty during her interview with Marnie.

"He says he'll only speak to you," he said slowly. "We need you to go to the prison and talk to Barney. And while you're there, we're hoping you can get some information on this group."

"No."

The word had been on the tip of her tongue, but Claire wasn't the one who said it. She turned. Mindy stood in the living room with her fists clenched at her sides, manicured nails biting into her palms.

"This is your daughter, Mr. Hartley. Your little girl. Of course, that doesn't mean anything to you now because it certainly didn't mean anything to you when you walked out on her and Alice and Charlie twenty years ago."

Jack was pale again, except for his ears, which had started to burn red. "Claire, I would be happy to talk to you—"

Mindy held up a single finger.

"But now we know, you left because you were scum. You ran out on your family when you accidentally started a new one with the cashier from the health food store. You have no idea what horrors Claire faced that night, and what's even worse is the fact that you obviously don't care. You're only here because of what Claire could do for you. Like so many others, you want to use her."

Mindy walked closer to him and jabbed him in the lapel.

"You don't know anything about her. You don't know that she still eats strawberry shortcake every year on her birthday because that was the last birthday cake you made her before you left. You don't know that young Claire would run out and check the mail every day, hoping for a card or some sign that her dad was still alive. Claire is a survivor.

She has survived something no one should ever have to witness, and she has flourished for two decades without you."

"Mindy—" Claire found her voice. "Calm down. It's okay. But you," she said, swiveling to point at Jack. "Get out of my house. I don't care who you work for. You don't have the right to come into my home without permission."

Jack frowned. "Claire, I—"

"Mindy. Get my mother on the phone." Alice was the only thing in her arsenal enough to scare an FBI agent out of her home.

"Okay, okay." He backed toward the door. "Take my card."

Claire stared him down. He might as well have been holding a live snake.

He put the business card on the bar and backed up another step. "I'll give you some time to process, but I'm afraid we're on a time limit. There's no knowing when the next victim will be taken. I'll be in touch."

CHAPTER NINETEEN

To Do:
- Move to a new city under an assumed name
- Stretch for Field Day

CLAIRE HIT "PUBLISH" ON HER BLOG POST AND SNAPPED HER laptop shut. How was she supposed to focus on engagement party etiquette when her deadbeat dad had just shown up out of the blue with a wild conspiracy theory?

She glanced at her bookshelf. A picture of her, Charlie, and Alice in matching Christmas sweaters stood in front of a row of romance novels. They would both be pissed if they knew Jack had shown up out of the blue. Her first instinct was to hide it from them, to preserve the peace. But maybe there was something to what her mom had said. Both of them would want to know if he had reappeared in their lives.

Claire picked up her phone and started a group video

chat with her mother and sister before she could change her mind.

"Clairebear? Is everything all right? Are you in jail?" Only Alice's nose and lips were visible. She sounded less upset than she had the previous day, which was something. Maybe the flowers had helped.

"Why do you always assume I'm in jail? I'm not in jail. Back up some, Mom. Oh, there's Charlie."

Charlotte, Claire's older sister by ten years, appeared onscreen. "Hi, bug," she said to Claire. "Mom. You need to back up, we can barely see you."

Alice sighed and took a step back from her camera. In the background, Roy was installing new hardware on their kitchen cabinets.

"Hi, Roy," Charlotte and Claire said together.

"Hola, niñas." He waved a drill at them.

"What's going on?" Charlie was sitting in her home office, twiddling a pencil between her long, slender fingers. Her voluminous hair was twisted back into a bun. A row of abandoned coffee mugs stood behind her. Unlike Claire, she had inherited Alice's baby blue eyes. Loud music thumped in the background. Her husband, Bill, who was a lawyer by day and drummer by night, must have been practicing again.

"So, I'm trying to be more honest. I just needed to tell you both something." Claire took a deep breath.

"You're pregnant!" Charlie screeched.

"God, no." Claire took her birth control as religiously as many people caught their favorite TV show. A surprise pregnancy would probably be a less painful revelation to make in this moment, though. "Jack is in town. He came to see me."

There was a ringing silence. Charlie's mouth fell open. Alice's eyes bulged.

"Jack? You don't mean your father?" Alice nearly whispered.

Claire nodded.

"That son of a bitch," Charlie swore. The pencil in her hand snapped.

Alice collapsed into a kitchen chair. Roy knelt next to her and rubbed her back, muttering comforting words in Spanish.

"What did he want?" Charlie's mood had shifted on a dime.

If Claire had asked her, Charlie would have caught the very next plane to West Haven to help her strangle their father.

"He wants me to go the prison and talk to Barney. They want body locations of his previous victims." Was she even allowed to tell them the other part? Jack hadn't explicitly said, but he had mentioned it was confidential.

Alice cried out as though someone had just stuck her with a white-hot poker. "Absolutely not. How could he expect you to face that despicable man again? Claire, I need you to get me a lock of Jack's hair. I don't care how you do it."

Claire sighed. "Mom, you can't keep making voodoo dolls every time someone upsets you. It's not ethical."

"Isn't it? Why don't you ask Rachel how her bowels have been treating her?"

Hell hath no fury like Alice Alejo with a box of pins and a grudge. Maybe she'd make one for Luke too.

"Ah, shit." Charlie clapped a hand to her forehead.

"Language, darling," Alice interrupted.

"Sorry. Big Z just got busted for coke *again*. I have to go.

Claire, don't do anything Jack tells you to do. Love you both." Charlie signed off.

Big Z was Mindy's favorite rapper and one of Charlie's most problematic clients. He was constantly embroiled in media scandals that threatened the sales of his rap albums. Charlie had pulled him out of more binds than Claire could count.

"I don't care what Jack says, you're not going to that prison." Alice looked as scandalized as if Claire had just suggested she was going to go skinny dipping in a baby pool full of pissed-off scorpions.

Claire bit her lip. Something Jack had said had been gnawing at her. "You don't think it might help the families of the victims get some closure? If I did get Barney to tell me the body locations?"

"Clairebear. That is not your responsibility. You suffered at his hands. They have no right to ask you to do that. Tell him no, okay, sweetheart? And tell him if he bothers you again, he'll be hearing from me. I love you. And thank you for the flowers. But please don't hide things from me again."

"I won't. Love you too, Mom." Claire hung up. The conversation hadn't left her with the peace she was hoping for.

A text from Luke popped up. She ignored it, but her stomach clenched all the same. What would Luke have to say about her bio-dad returning? It was almost as if talking about Jack in Paris had summoned him. But there was no sense in wondering what Luke would think. He was dead to her.

"CAN WE MOVE THAT BIG PIECE TO THE FAR WALL?" CLAIRE asked.

It had been less than forty-eight hours since Jack's revelation. No matter how hard she tried, she couldn't compartmentalize and bury the news. Not even throwing herself into Aaron and Jane's gallery proposal could prevent images of the victims from popping into her mind as she lay awake in bed at night. If she was truly the only person Barney would speak to, didn't she owe it to them to try? Didn't she have a moral obligation to help? But trying meant facing her attempted killer. The thought made her blood run like ice in her veins.

Nicole and Kyle, each gripping one end of an eight-foot oil painting, carefully shuffled across the hardwood floors of the gallery. They secured it to the wall with picture wire and stood back, revealing a watercolor of a little girl on a swing made of a tangle of flowers.

"Perfect." Claire pointed to another painting. "Coli, what do you think about this one?"

She hadn't had the heart to tell Nicole about her father's visit. She was lady-balls-deep in wedding plans, and Claire refused to take the spotlight off her for even a moment. Nicole, wearing an old Venor University T-shirt and paint-splattered shorts, considered a charcoal portrait of a liver-spotted grandmother with kind eyes.

"I love this. It shows her mastery of the human form. Plus, it's super hard to nail liver spots. Let's put it with some of the other portraits on this side." Nicole carried the frame off into a different room.

Rosie sat in the middle of the floor in a strip of sunlight, forcing everyone to walk around her.

Sweat glistened on Kyle's forehead, highlighting the

beginnings of a receding hairline. He took a swig from an aluminum water bottle and sat heavily on the floor, shaking the gallery. It had been barely five years since he had worn a Viking beer helmet and stolen a golf cart from campus security. They were getting older, and the crazy days of their youth had been replaced by careers, marriage, and nightmares.

She really needed a night out.

"Luke's been asking about you," Kyle said pointedly. Probably lashing out because she had asked him to move a particular painting six different times.

Claire sighed and turned her back to him. "I don't care."

"He's really sorry, Claire. The whole documentary is at stake. And he's right, you know. An interview with you would really take it to a whole new level. You know what a perfectionist he is when it comes to his work."

She whirled around, a hammer in one hand. "Kyle, I love you. But make no mistake, if you try to talk about Luke again in front of me, or try to justify his decision to make me re-experience the worst thing that ever happened to me so that he can sell this documentary, I will pack you into one of those shipping crates and send your ass to Madagascar."

He cleared his throat uncomfortably. "Need help moving your stuff back into your place?"

"That would be great. I'll text you."

He disappeared into the back room, clearly too uncomfortable to keep occupying space with her.

"Do you want me to tell Luke not to come this weekend?" Nicole asked softly, touching Claire's arms with unnaturally cold fingertips. "It's kind of crazy to expect him to come all the way from California for a field day anyway."

Great. The field day. She had almost forgotten. In

keeping with their grand tradition of over-the-top dates and action-packed adventures, Nicole and Kyle had decided to have a "bonding exercise" for the bridal party. And what better way to bond than try to kill each other at sports? Claire's broad jump could use some work, but she was fairly confident in her flag football skills.

She sighed. It was all for Nicole's love story. She wouldn't be responsible for making it anything less than perfect.

"No, he's the best man. He should be there. I appreciate the offer, though." She pulled Nicole in for a tight hug.

Nicole walked off with another frame as Claire checked her phone. Four more missed calls and two voicemails from Luke, and one missed call and voicemail from an unknown number. A knot grew in Claire's stomach. Had her stalker progressed to threatening her via phone calls?

She spun around to face the gallery storefront, peering out the windows. None of the passersby appeared to be taking an inordinate interest in the gallery, but she hid behind an Asian-themed folding screen as she played the voicemail.

"Claire, it's Jack. Just wanted you to have a number to reach me by when you change your mind. Think about it."

She exhaled noisily. At least it was her deadbeat dad and not her stalker. She had to take good news where she could get it these days.

Her finger hovered over the delete buttons next to Luke's voicemails, but she thought better of it and tucked her phone into her pocket.

"Are you okay? I haven't seen you make such a serious concentration face since that Spanish final sophomore year." Nicole peeked around the corner of the folding screen.

Claire jumped. For a moment, she considered telling her

about Jack's visit, about the organization, about everything. But it wasn't fair to burden her. "Yes, sorry. Just double checking a few things for Tyler's proposal. It's going to be great." She forced a smile.

Nicole sighed and sat down in a black director's chair. "You're sure this doesn't have anything to do with Luke?"

For once, it did not.

"You mean the person who is dead to me? I'm sure."

Nicole bit her lip, seemingly choosing her next words carefully. "You know you'll have to talk to him eventually. He'll be there on Saturday." It wasn't a question.

Claire whistled for Rosie. "I can't talk about this right now. I have a class with Sawyer. See you later?"

"Of course. Let me know how class goes." Nicole drew Claire into another tight hug. "Love you."

The summer sun burned oppressively outside the gallery. Claire tied her hair up into a ponytail, half wishing she was still speaking to Luke just so she could use his pool. But there were other pools that didn't come with a douchebag clause. She slipped her headphones into her ears to block out the street noise and tugged Rosie along. Rosie trotted along beside her, chasing a bug.

"Heel," she said, wrapping the nylon leash around her wrist.

Rosie ignored her and barked threats at a Pomeranian across the street.

Claire sighed and continued walking, half-dragging the easily distracted dog behind her. Sanctum Security head-quarters was only three blocks away, but that didn't stop Rosie from sniffing four streetlights, chasing two squirrels, and attempting to steal a cheeseburger from a toddler.

Fighting Rosie's chaotic walking pattern, Claire checked her appointments. Mindy had forwarded a confirmation email from their fireworks technician. As long as Tyler—or Ericka, for that matter—didn't turn out to be a serial killer, the proposal would be stunning. She switched from email to the West Haven News homepage and scanned for mentions of missing women. None had been reported. Maybe Jack was completely wrong about the network of killers. She wasn't putting anyone in jeopardy by refusing to go see Barney. Was she?

As she approached the front doors of Sanctum Security, she found Sawyer already leaning against them.

"Fourteen," he said.

She could barely hear him over her headphones. She popped them out and tucked them back into their case. "Sorry, fourteen what?"

"That's the number of mistakes you made in your three-block walk from Nicole's gallery."

Mistakes? Claire made a face, and her inner perfectionist shuddered. "What do you mean? What kind of mistakes?" She glanced down. Her shoes matched today, so it wasn't that.

"Come inside. Rosie can come too." He pulled the glass doors open.

Claire strong-armed Rosie into the office, still reeling from Sawyer's accusation. Sanctum was the exact opposite of Sawyer's house. Everything was stainless steel and glass. The receptionist had a pixie haircut and a neck tattoo of a lotus flower.

"Any updates since I was out, Candace?"

The receptionist shook her head. "Not really, Mr. Goulding. Just an AFA at Giuseppe's restaurant. Brad's on it." A fork rested in a half-eaten carton of what appeared to be roasted broccoli and brussels sprouts. Either she had a gut of steel, or she wasn't shy about fumigating the office with cruciferous-vegetable-induced flatulence. She offered Claire a bottle of water as Sawyer filled out a security badge.

"Wow, this is very official," Claire said as she hung the visitor badge around her neck.

"We are in the business of security." Sawyer pushed open a set of double doors.

They walked into a training room, complete with wrestling mats, weight equipment, and punching bags. Claire bounced on her toes, beyond ready to start punching things.

"Ooh. Where do we start first? I would love to hit something." Her purse hit the floor.

He scooped it back up and handed it to her. "You're not ready for that yet. Especially after what I saw this morning." He led her to a side door, which opened into a classroom with about twenty desks.

She shot him a dirty look and sat in the front row. "What do you mean?"

Rosie leapt onto a seat at the desk beside her, panting happily and looking quite pleased with her newfound height.

Sawyer leaned against the large wooden desk at the front of the classroom. "The best defense you can possibly have is simply being aware of your surroundings. First lesson: try not to wear your hair in a ponytail when you're walking alone."

"But why—*ow!*" Claire screeched as his hand whipped out and gripped her hair, dragging her head down onto her desk.

Rosie jumped out of her chair and growled at Sawyer with bared teeth.

"Rosie, hush," Claire said, face smashed against the spiral of her notebook.

"It's okay," Sawyer said, releasing her. "I wanted to see her reaction. Good girl." He pulled a dog treat out of his pocket and tossed it to her.

She sniffed it suspiciously for a moment and looked at Claire before taking it and retreating into a corner. She kept her eyes on Sawyer.

"Ponytails are easy for bad people to grab," he continued, walking back to the front of the classroom. "Do yourself a favor and make it harder for them."

"Point taken," Claire said, rubbing her neck.

"Did I hurt you?" he asked sheepishly.

She shook her head.

"Good," he said in a much louder voice. "Second lesson: do not wear headphones, earbuds, or anything else in your ears that will compromise your awareness. Do you know why so many women get abducted when they're jogging?"

"They're usually listening to music?" she guessed. Running without music sounded almost as bad as getting abducted.

"Exactly. And if you're listening to music, you can't hear footsteps or cars approaching. Third problem. Your eyes are glued to your phone."

"I get it—I should be watching my surroundings," Claire grumbled, skin prickling.

He smiled. "For someone who is so controlled and disciplined, you certainly have a lackadaisical approach to personal safety."

"Sawyer, this is central Pennsylvania. It's not like I'm walking through downtown Detroit wearing a suit made of hundred-dollar bills. I'm more in danger from being trampled by a rogue cow or runaway cheesesteak cart."

"An interesting take. And yet, remind me. Were you in Detroit when you were abducted?"

She sighed. "No."

"Where were you?"

"Here," she said in a mopey voice.

"Exactly. Over eighty-five percent of sexual assault victims know their attacker. It doesn't matter where you live if someone has set their sights on you."

"I'm glad we're not mincing words. What else am I doing wrong?" She opened her notebook to a new page and pulled a pen out of her purse. It was fatter than usual. She rolled it in her hand to study it. The mystery pen from the woods! She had nearly forgotten.

She brought it closer to her face. There were initials on it. *ESA* Who the hell was ESA? Edward? Edgar? Ellen? She didn't know anyone with those initials. Maybe it was the previous owner of Luke's property. He had told her who they were, but she couldn't quite remember the name. Something to do with fancy toilets.

She shrugged and jotted down over a dozen additional tips from Sawyer, ranging in topics from vehicle safety to doorbell etiquette.

"Now we're going to head out for some practice in the field," Sawyer said.

Claire closed her notebook. Rosie came to her side, dragging her leash.

"Oh, sure. Now you come," she said, looping the leash around her wrist. "Where are we going?"

"Just a few blocks down," He led her back out onto the street. Claire reached for her phone, then immediately snatched her hand back. Emails and appointments could wait. She would show him. She would be so self-aware that even her FBI bio-dad would be impressed. Damn it. She wasn't thinking about him either.

"What are we missing?" Sawyer asked, raising his eyebrows.

"Oh, right," Claire said, reaching up and tugging the elastic band away from her scalp. Her hair tumbled down in an unmitigated disaster of curls.

"That's perfect," he said, smiling at her. "Your technique, I mean," he said, clearing his throat. "You are far less susceptible to attacks now."

"Thank you for the advice. Oh, before I forget, how much do I owe you?" she asked, searching for her wallet. "I can go back." He had walked her straight past the receptionist with no mention of payment.

He laid a gentle hand on her arm. "There's no charge for this. I just ask that you listen, take me seriously, and inform your friends. Especially that wild, dark-haired one. What's her name again?"

Claire's heart warmed, and she smiled. "Mindy," she said, stifling a laugh. "I don't think she needs any help, but I owe my life to you. I'll do whatever you ask."

He exhaled. "You don't owe me anything. You're a fighter. With a little instruction, it'll be very difficult for anyone to hurt you again. Well, physically anyway."

He stopped outside a frozen yogurt store and held the door open for Claire.

"Is this part of the test?" she asked, tying Rosie's leash to a heavy metal table and stepping inside. She swept the interior. Six flavors of yogurt. Thirty-two toppings. The teenage cashier had braces and a *Seventeen* magazine sticking out of her purse.

"No, I just feel bad for grabbing your ponytail." He handed her a bowl.

"Oh, it's okay." It may have been overly theatrical, but it was necessary.

"How have things been since the other night? Mindy said your dad was the reason you pressed the panic button."

Claire swirled some chocolate yogurt into her container and began mindlessly adding toppings. "Oh, things are great. My biological father showed up for the first time in over twenty years, but only because he wants me to go to prison and interrogate the man who tried to kill me. He looks like me. Same eyes and everything. Oh," she said, lowering her voice and scanning the room. They were alone except for the cashier. "There's also allegedly a secret society of men murdering women all across the country for unknown reasons, and I have accidentally been implicated as the only living victim."

In the three days since she told Sawyer about the second note, there had been no mentions in the local news. Maybe he really was trustworthy. Was that why she felt so relaxed around him? She hadn't even paused to consider if she should tell him the whole truth. It had just tumbled out. She barely knew him, but she had word vomit drama dumped on him every couple of days. He probably thought she was nuts.

He stood frozen with a bottle of chocolate syrup in his hand. A plop of syrup fell, viscous and dense, onto the counter.

She hurriedly wiped it away with a napkin before turning back to him. He still hadn't moved.

"Yeah, you're gonna need to unpack that for me," he said, setting his yogurt on the scale.

Claire added hers as well and quickly slid the cashier a bill before Sawyer could protest.

"Stop," she said when his mouth opened, one hand clearly reaching for his wallet. "You are giving me free lessons. I buy you as much froyo as I want."

He gave her a disapproving look but thanked her. They sat outside despite the clouds that had begun to gather. Rosie curled comfortably at Claire's feet. Sawyer pivoted so his back was to the storefront.

At his request, Claire re-told the story of her father's sudden appearance and the horrors he unveiled.

Every so often, Sawyer's eyes darted in every direction, undoubtedly keeping track of potential threats and watching for danger. It seemed unconscious, even natural for him. Claire felt a sense of peace sitting next to him, even with pedestrian traffic on both sides of the street. Her stalker wasn't likely to threaten her when she was sitting next to a six-foot-eight security expert with pecs the size of cantaloupes.

"So, he wants you to go to the prison and interrogate the man who tried to murder you." His thick brows furrowed.

"Yes, my father's paternal instincts are off the charts," Claire said glumly, stirring the melted remains of her yogurt.

"How did you feel when you saw him?"

"Terrified at first. I thought it was my stalker. I hit the panic button right away."

"That's good." He reached across the table and took her hand.

Claire froze at the contact and pulled her hand back, feigning a cough.

"Sorry," Sawyer apologized, crossing his arms over his chest. "I had four sisters growing up. I sympathize and comfort with physical contact. It gets me in trouble sometimes."

She smiled. "I bet it does." She wondered briefly what else those enormous hands could do, but it instantly felt like a betrayal. Even though Luke was dead to her. She scooted her chair back an inch and continued her story.

He sighed. "You don't deserve this."

"I didn't think that I did. But this is all just too much. The universe has to be punishing me for something."

"Maybe it's leading you to something. In a really dickish way."

"Another murder attempt, probably," she said, shuddering. She glanced around. "There must be some cosmic punch card I have yet to fulfill."

"Speaking of murder, it's time for our out-of-classroom exercise. What was the cashier's name?"

"Amanda," Claire fired back. *Ha.* She had repeated the name in her mind several times in case he had asked.

"Good. How many froyo flavors?"

"Six, but one dispenser was broken. So five."

"Not bad, Hartley. How long has the guy with the briefcase been sitting on that bench?"

"Uh." She looked across the street in the direction he pointed. Damn it. She hadn't noticed him at all. "Three minutes?" she guessed.

Sawyer shook his head. "I'm not saying you to have make a mental catalog of absolutely everything you see everywhere you go. But it is important for you to pay attention to people. Especially anyone who looks suspicious, who feels a little off. Trust your instincts."

"My instincts and I aren't on very good terms. They led me to plan a proposal for a man who killed five people. Six, if you count his dad."

"He fooled everyone. Don't be so hard on yourself." He started to reach across the table again, but pulled his hand back and tapped the metal surface instead. "You're alive. Focus on that."

She sighed and leaned back in her chair. A raindrop landed on the top of her head. At least she hoped it was a raindrop. The way her year was going, it was probably bird poop.

"I wanted to tell you, I looked up the video of the proposal you did for Kyle and Nicole. It was amazing."

The plastic spoon fell from her hand. She was so used to Luke disparaging proposals at every turn that any unsolicited compliment from a man about her profession made her immediately suspicious. "Oh—thanks. A lot of work went into it."

"I bet. The archery, the obstacle course. Every part of it was so well thought out. How do you do it?"

Okay, it didn't sound like he was being sarcastic. "It's a combination of interrogation, internet stalking, and borderline obsessive planning. If you're ever in the need for proposal planning services someday, I'm your girl."

"I wouldn't consider anyone else. It's one of the biggest questions you'll ever ask in your life. Everything should be perfect."

"Thank you. I'm so glad you get it. A lot of people think elaborate proposals are stupid." Luke, for example.

Sawyer raised his eyebrows. "Then they're stupid." Damn straight.

"So, how long have you been in the security business?" She took a visual sweep of the area as she asked the question. The man with the briefcase was still sitting on the bench. What was his deal, anyway?

"About six years now. I got a degree in engineering and my first idea was the fire alarms, like the ones in your building. That went over so well that we were able to expand into complete security systems. That's what I'm really passionate about. Safety, preventing crimes. I design all our systems." Rain pinged steadily off the table.

"That's amazing. But you own Sanctum, don't you? How do you have time to run the day-to-day?"

"I have a business manager, Jill. She handles all that stuff." He glanced up at the sky and wiped something off his cheek. "I think we're about to get rained on. If you're up for it, I think we should have another class next week and start moving to physical defense."

He gathered their empty bowls and tossed them in a nearby trash can.

"Oh, I am beyond ready to kick some ass," Claire said, slinging her purse over her shoulder and detangling Rosie from the table.

"Let's get you back to your car."

Claire shielded her electronic devices in her purse, and they began to walk back, their pace more leisurely than a couple caught in the rain should be. A quarter mile from the Sanctum building, the rain turned from a minor shower to a downpour.

She dug through the purse with one hand as they ran. Where the hell was her travel umbrella? Pre-abduction Claire would have checked the forecast three times already today and been prepared for any kind of weather. Barney had taken so much from her. She wouldn't stand for it. Just as soon as she got in the car and made sure the rain didn't fry her phone.

Dozens of people ran off the streets into the safety of shops and vehicles.

They both ran, sprinting for shelter. It felt good to run. She was strong, she was fast, and she was capable.

Or at least she was until she tripped on a crack in the

sidewalk and fell magnificently, landing on her hands and knees.

"Oh, God, ow. No, go on without me. You can still make it!" She swiped a hand across her forehead, where her hair was matted to her face. Of course she hadn't thought to apply her waterproof mascara today. Another strike against the woefully unprepared, current-day Claire.

Sawyer ignored her pleas and scooped her up into his arms. His neck was slippery, and she fought to hold on. He gripped Rosie's leash in his other hand and ran them under the awning of the Sanctum building.

"You can put me down." Claire laughed, squirming slightly in his arms. His breaths were even and slow, not like the ragged ones that racked her lungs. She really needed to start running again. Stalkers be damned.

He set her down, and Claire limped over to a pillar to catch her breath. Her hands and knees stung where they had hit the pavement.

Sawyer's shirt now clung to his impressive physique.

"Let me see your hands," he asked, gently turning them palms-up. He stroked his thumbs over her palms in a confusingly tender gesture. Her heart beat anxiously in her chest.

Sawyer was the polar opposite of Luke. It wasn't just that he was kind and respectful, or that he had saved her life. His eyes distinctly reminded her of her childhood cat's, and they crinkled kindly around the edges. He was truthful, straight-forward, and tender. He even complimented her work. She could tell in her bones that when it came to Sawyer, what you saw was what you got. What a refreshing change of pace.

"Are you hurt?" he asked, moving his hands from her wrists to her cheek.

"No," she said, even as her palms stung. The heat from his hand warmed her.

They stood there for a moment. The rain beat a staccato rhythm on the awning. Why was this awkward? It shouldn't be awkward. They were just two friends—acquaintances, really—with a scheduled appointment.

Sawyer swiped a thumb under her eye. "Mascara," he explained, wiping it off on his jeans.

Her shoulders relaxed when he took a step back. "Forgot to go waterproof today. This storm came out of nowhere," she said, crossing her arms over her chest.

"Right?" he said, scanning the street again. "That's June for you."

Great, now they were awkwardly small-talking. Why was it so hard to be friends with a member of the opposite sex?

Rosie chose that moment to rid her fur of excess water, shaking the entire length of her body.

Claire squealed and squeezed more water from her shirt. It spattered onto the ground. "I had better get her home," she said, laughing nervously and gesturing to the dog. "She hates being wet."

"No problem. So, see you same time next week?"

"Definitely." Claire turned to go, but only got a step or two down the road when she turned back. "Sawyer?" She called from the downpour. There was no point in running. She was already soaked.

"Yeah?" He paused with one hand on the door.

"You're coming to the field day thing this weekend, right?"

"For Kyle and Nicole? Yeah, I'll be there. Fair warning, I played a lot of flag football in my day."

"That doesn't scare me," she teased. "I'll see you there. Also, there's this thing that I have to go to next Friday."

With Luke dead to her and Nicole and Mindy in a meeting, she had no date for the awards. Maybe it would be nice to have a friendly face along. And, as a bonus, he could strictly enforce a perimeter around Claire if the alleged serial killer ring decided to act up at the ceremony. Or if Wendy came over to gloat about the lawsuit.

"It's an awards ceremony for entrepreneurs in the valley," she continued. "I am currently dateless, and my nemesis—the one who's suing me—will be there with my ex-fiancé. Any chance you'd want to come along as a friend?" she asked, putting perhaps a little too much emphasis on the f word. "Maybe tackle anyone who tries to murder me?"

"I will be your personal security detail," he said, winking as he went inside.

By the time she had made it back to her car, she and Rosie were drenched from head to toe and her stomach was in knots. She popped her trunk open and pulled out a towel. At least she hadn't neglected her emergency towel. She flung it into the back seat before buckling Rosie into her seatbelt.

The windshield was hopelessly fogged up from the volume of wet hair in the car. Claire cleared a circle on the inside of the windshield and saw a small plastic bag tucked under her wiper blade. A paper was barely visible inside.

"Seriously, a ticket? Thanks, universe," she muttered to herself about unclear street cleaning schedules as she opened her door, welcoming another wave of water into her already hopeless hair.

She snatched the bag from her windshield and shut the door behind her.

Her blood ran cold at the sight of her name scrawled across the front of the paper. This was no parking ticket.

She engaged her automatic locks. Sawyer had been very clear on the importance of vehicle safety. Should she run back to Sanctum? Sawyer would open it. Or Kyle and Nicole. But she had burdened them enough this week.

With shaking hands, she opened the bag and carefully unfolded the note.

Welcome back. We are always watching. Stop digging for the truth, or we start digging your grave.

CHAPTER TWENTY

To Do:
- Order some furry handcuffs
- Update social media release form

CLAIRE'S ARMS WERE ASLEEP WHEN SHE AWOKE THE MORNING of Tyler's proposal.

"*Ha!*" She shouted to the ceiling. She may have invisible pins and needles stabbing along the lengths of her arms, but she hadn't woken up standing in the middle of Market Street at midnight eating a bowl of pot pie. Hopefully, this would be the first of many wins today.

Rosie leapt onto the bed and licked her face. Claire wiggled against the scarves that anchored her to her headboard. Maybe she hadn't thought this through.

Ten minutes later, after extricating herself from her restraints and barricaded bedroom door, she sipped her first cup of coffee and peeked out her hallway window to the ground below.

"Oh, shit. Not again."

News trucks lined the sidewalk in front of her apartment building. The landlord had closed the rear entrance to repaint. And her dog very much had to pee. She was trapped. What had suddenly piqued their interest? She had done a quick internet search that morning and there was no mention of a second (or third) note. Sawyer hadn't told anyone.

Rosie whined and licked her ankle. How was she going to get downstairs without being spotted? She glanced at her watch. Tyler's proposal wasn't taking place until dark, but there were so many details to check up on. Everything had to be perfect. She needed to take care of this now.

Claire opened her hallway closet and pulled out a backpack. "Come on, Ro. You know the drill."

Rosie climbed obediently (for once) into the backpack. Claire slung it over her back and threw on a pair of sunglasses and a wide-brimmed straw hat. She shut off the motion sensor and opened her bedroom window. Distant car horns and the smell of freshly baked bagels greeted her as she swung one leg over the sill. Her stomach lurched at the smell. The buttery croissants she and Luke had shared on their way to the Champs-Élysées had smelled almost the same. But that was a lifetime ago.

With one leg hanging out the window, she stopped and glanced at the news vans. Two anchors from separate channels were speaking on camera thirty yards from her window, but they didn't seem to notice her.

She shuffled out onto the fire escape and quickly descended the three rickety flights to the sidewalk. She nipped around the corner of the building and hustled to

Buchanan Park before letting Rosie out to pee and scrambling back up the fire escape.

She stopped when she hit her floor. She had just openly left her bedroom window ajar in a city of 300,000 people, at least one of whom was taking an inordinate amount of personal time to threaten her. Detective Smith had told her when she'd turned in the latest note that they were waiting for approval to place Officer Schiccitano as her full-time guardian angel, but it hadn't been approved yet. Sure, she had only been gone for ten minutes. But what if they were watching her? Were they inside her apartment right now? She didn't have time for this.

She stuffed her phone in her bra and slid the window open wider. She swung the backpack off and let Rosie out. Rosie ran happily to the bedroom door, panting. Surely she would have noticed if there was a stranger in the house. But Claire wasn't in the business of taking chances. She scuttled across the apartment to her purse, which hung next to the front door. She dug her Taser out and held it out in front of her.

"Hello? Murderers?" she called out to the quiet apartment. "It's me, Claire. I have a crazy day planned, and I would really appreciate it if you could pick another day to kidnap me."

Only silence greeted her.

She combed methodically through her apartment, checking every nook and cranny. The apartment was empty. She heaved a sigh of relief as she put her weapon back and leapt into preparations for the big day.

"OH, I'M SO EXCITED!" CLAIRE BOUNCED ON HER TOES AND straightened a picture frame. The marching band was tuned and hiding in the backyard. The fireworks technicians were ready. Family hid behind the van in the garage. All they needed was their future bride and groom.

"I know I say this a lot, but this proposal is perfection," Mindy mumbled over a mouthful of safety pins. Part of the red, white, and blue bunting they had draped on the safety handrails was threatening to droop, but everything else was in place.

"I just hope they're happy. And that Ericka isn't secretly a serial killer. That would really bum me out."

"I think we're good," Mindy said, gesturing to a picture of Ericka giving an Afghan child a cup of water.

Headlights turned into the driveway. Claire slapped Mindy on the arm. "They're here! Drop the pins and get out there. Remember, give him a minute to explain about the house, then distract Ericka with her parents so Tyler can slip away and get his legs on. Then you're in charge of the photographers."

"Got it." Mindy flung the container of pins across the room and disappeared out the front door.

"I can't believe it's finally happening," Claire squealed to herself as she took one last look at the hallway. Candles flickered softly on the floor. Photographs of the couples were hung throughout the cozy little house. Magic was truly in the air.

She stepped into the living room and twitched the curtain aside just in time to see Ericka throw herself into Tyler's arms. Claire's heart soared. There was no mistaking the look in Ericka's eyes. She and Tyler were crazy in love.

The doubt that had haunted Claire since the abduction lifted ever so slightly. Yes, she had made an unbelievable error in judgment by working with Barney. She had already learned from her mistakes. Criminal background checks and stricter screening processes were now even more essential to protect her clients. She would never again plan a proposal for a serial killer. But this moment—the reunion of lovers, the promise of a single, perfect, life-changing event—was everything she believed in. Her joy, her passion. Her life's work. Barney was an anomaly. She could do this.

She stepped out the back door and took one last cursory glance over everything—the marching band, currently in a kneeling position, firework technicians barely visible a hundred yards out. Jerry, Claire's primary camera person when Luke was busy and/or dead to her, had set up a tripod slightly off to one side. The grass had just been mowed, and Ericka's favorite flowers were planted in neat rows in the flowerbeds. A couple peeked out of a second-story window in the house next door, waving at Claire and gesturing to the earplugs she had hand delivered to them. They waved small American flags. She waved back.

"Wildcats to your station," Claire hissed to the drum major, who stood in place and gave everyone a hand motion.

The band stood and tiptoed silently into formation in the backyard. Tyler, now on his crutches, hustled around the side of the house and disappeared behind the band, where a heart-shaped collection of flower petals waited to surround him. It was a windy evening, so at the last minute, Claire had to hot glue individual weights to the petals to prevent them from scattering. It was worth every burnt fingertip. Family and friends lined the path, holding small American flags. The smell of Korean barbecue—Ericka's favorite—emanated from two grill tables manned by local chefs.

"Where did Tyler go?" A voice came from inside the

house. Through the window, Ericka touched an arched doorway, running a hand over the fabric-draped security railings in the mid-century ranch.

"I think he's in the backyard, sweetie. He said he had something to show you." Ericka's mother beamed behind her. "Maybe you should try the back door."

Claire stood and signaled to the drum major and her lights guy. They both stood ready, looking to her for guidance. As soon as she heard the knob turn, she cued them. Floodlights came on in ten-foot intervals, lining their massive back yard. An American flag unfurled behind the groom, who was hidden by the tuba section. The drumline played a brief cadence and started a patriotic march.

Ericka stopped in her tracks, blinking in the sudden light. She was a commanding presence in her army uniform and combat boots, even though she couldn't have been more than 5'2".

Shutters clicked from her camera crew, and the bride-to-be cracked a giant smile.

Ericka walked down the back porch stairs slowly, in time to the march. The marching band parted down the middle as she walked forward, splitting section by section. As they neared the end of the song, the last row parted, revealing Tyler, standing tall and unassisted.

Ericka clapped her hand to her mouth and ran to him, closing the last few yards between them in seconds. She folded herself into his embrace.

"But I don't understand. How are you standing?"

Tyler lifted the hem of his pant leg, revealing his new titanium addition.

Tears filled Ericka's eyes.

Tyler gripped Ericka's hand firmly. Claire's breath

hitched. Had the doctor really cleared him to kneel, or had Tyler just insisted on it? Damned HIPAA laws.

He turned one prosthetic foot onto its toe, and slowly slid it backward until he was kneeling.

"Ericka, from the moment I saw you at my bedside after the worst day in my entire life, I knew that one day you would be my wife. I have never seen anyone assemble a rifle as fast as you or cook spaghetti better than you. Sorry, Mom," he said, glancing over his shoulder.

"You have been the great love of my life, and my inspiration to keep trying after my injury. You are the kindest, bravest, most incredible woman I know. I bought this home for you. For us, to start a lifetime of happiness together. Would you do me the great honor of being my wife?"

Ericka nodded forcefully, tears now dropping freely. "Yes!" She pulled Tyler to his feet to hug him properly. Her hat fell to the ground as he pulled her in for a celebratory kiss.

Claire brushed a tear from under her eye. It was even better than she had imagined.

There was thunderous applause, and the marching band broke into song. The neighbors in the upstairs window lit sparklers. Claire cued the fireworks technician, who sent a burst of red, white, and blue sparks into the sky. Ericka's parents clapped and wept behind them.

Ericka jumped when the fireworks started, and the bottom dropped out of Claire's stomach for a split second. Tyler had suggested them, since the Fourth of July was the first holiday they had celebrated together. Could fireworks trigger PTSD? Ericka and Tyler both had combat experience. How could Claire have been so careless?

But in a millisecond, they were back together again,

hugging and celebrating. Claire breathed a sigh of relief. Neither seemed any worse for the wear.

As the fireworks fizzled out, the marching band filed out around either side of the house. Servers passed hors d'oeuvres while the chefs prepared the Korean barbecue. Champagne flutes were making the rounds. Family had descended on the couple.

Claire took a last look around to make sure unattended candles had been extinguished, and that the final handrails had been securely attached to the wall in the kitchen.

She turned to sneak out and let the happy couple celebrate, but Tyler's voice called out to her.

"Claire!"

She spun back around, smiling.

"Ericka, this is Claire. She made it all happen."

"It was nothing," she said, shaking Ericka's hand.

Ericka had a very firm grip, and the emerald-cut diamond on her ring finger sparkled when she smoothed a hair back into her tight bun.

She pulled Claire aggressively into a half hug. "Thank you. You've given us so much."

"You deserve it. Thank you both for your service. Now go, enjoy your new home and each other."

Claire turned and walked away, feeling lighter and yet heavier than she had in weeks. She pulled her phone out of her pocket. For the first time since Paris, there weren't any messages from Luke. It had been less than a week since her escape from the Seine, and he had grown tired of her already. Why did that make her feel so strange? She shouldn't have been surprised. He had a reputation for being a ladies' man. When he couldn't get her to do the interview, he cut ties. Simple as that.

The bridal party field day loomed on the horizon. In

fourteen short hours, she would be face-to-face with Luke, and there was nothing she could do about it. It was going to take every ounce of strength she had not to nail him in the nuts with a perfect football spiral. But it was for Kyle and Nicole, and Claire couldn't ruin their day. No matter how asinine Luke was.

She collected Rosie from her helper, Emily, and crawled into her car a block away. Her back seat and trunk were free of murderers. There weren't even any threatening notes stuffed under her wipers. The serial killers must have had a more pressing engagement that evening.

Jack's words about future victims popped into her head again. A tingle ran down her spine. There was no guarantee that he was correct. People went missing every day. Her stalker could just be a bored high school kid copying a killer.

Maybe she should make that binder. Just in case.

CHAPTER TWENTY-ONE

To Do:
- Don't stab Luke at field day
- Email Torrance for T & E engagement pic
sneak peek

CLAIRE WAVED TO OFFICER SCHICCITANO AS SHE LOCKED HER car door and stepped onto the park path. He had finally been put back on full-time Claire watching duty, and his girthy mustache hadn't changed a bit. As nice as it was to have a dedicated guardian angel, his presence was a constant reminder of the unseen danger that followed her.

Other than the police, she hadn't told anyone about the latest threat. She had shoved it to the back of her mind while she was putting together Tyler's proposal, but now it was starting to resurface. Now was as good a time as any to practice her situational awareness. Any one of these creeps could be the note-leaver. She tightened her grip on Rosie's leash and ignored her compulsion to pull out her phone and check her emails. Instead, she focused on surveying the other people in the park.

"Lady in a red bandana. Gentleman in a bowler hat carrying a tan briefcase. Creepy twin girls with pigtails screaming about ice cream. Guy with cute butt reading woodworking magazine," she whispered to herself.

The sun beat down even though it was barely ten a.m. It was going to be a scorcher. She really should have used her heavy-duty primer and setting spray. The metal playground slide on her right looked like it would sear the flesh off the legs of anyone brave enough to get on it. The city should really do something about it.

Nicole had refused Claire's offer to help with the field day. She was going in blind and about to come face-to-face with Luke for the first time since their blowout. And she needed to fight her natural clumsiness and mercilessly beat him at whatever sporting events Nicole had cooked up. It was sure to be a disaster. But at least she wouldn't have to speak to him for long.

She crossed the baseball field, searching for her friends and keeping a wary eye on the other people in the park. Officer Shiccitano stayed fifty yards behind her. She really should have brought him a breakfast sandwich. If her memory served her, he had a penchant for pastrami and fried egg.

Oh shit. Was that Luke's car by the football field? Nausea twisted her stomach,

and her hands shook.

Nope. It was some other douche in a black sedan with tinted windows. For all she knew, it could be her stalker.

"Good luck snatching me with fifty thousand protective men in my wake," she muttered to the sedan. It was true—

between Luke, Kyle, Sawyer, and Officer Shiccitano, no one stood a chance of kidnapping her today. Of course, the last time she had been abducted, she had been twenty feet from a room full of seventy-five people. But this was different.

Finally. There was Nicole. She was bent at the waist, setting up a series of orange cones on the football practice field.

"Do you need help?" Claire called as she approached.

"Nah, I have pretty much everything we need," Nicole said, kicking a tote at her feet. Brightly colored flag football belts, a coiled rope, and a Frisbee were visible.

Claire looped Rosie's lead around a nearby tree and secured it with enough slack to allow her beloved furry friend to lay in the sunshine. She pulled a bowl out of her purse and filled it from her water bottle.

"Are you okay?" Nicole asked in a quieter voice. "He's not here yet."

Claire shrugged and occupied herself by bending forward, curling her fingers underneath her toes until she felt the tug in her hamstrings. A hot yoga and core crusher class this week had left her primed and ready to kick some ass.

It *was* weird that Luke wasn't here yet. A stickler for punctuality, he had been known to berate anyone who was less than ten minutes early. With any luck, his flight would have been cancelled. But luck hadn't been on her side in some time.

"I'm fine. I'll have to see him again eventually. I'm just not sure what I'll say to him. Where's Mindy?"

"Under that tree," Nicole said, gesturing to a prone figure in a shady patch of grass.

"Hangover?"

Nicole nodded.

"I hope she's not on our team." Claire bent over and reached into her tote bag, digging until she found some ibuprofen, a packet of sugar-free blue Kool-Aid, and a bottle of water. She walked over to the shady spot and plopped down beside Mindy. "Good morning, sunshine."

Mindy groaned. Her long, wavy black hair was gathered into a messy ponytail,

looped through the snap back of her navy baseball cap. Heavily mirrored sunglasses shielded her eyes.

"Thank you. Why do we have to do this?"

"Because we love Nicole and want her wedding day and every wedding-related event building up to it to be exactly as she imagined," Claire said, deadpan. She handed the bottle to Mindy, who sat up to guzzle it before returning to the ground, groaning.

"So many shots. Why am I dating a college boy again?"

"Because you like him, and he's a suspiciously good baker. I'll see you when it's time for the first event," Claire said, patting her on the knee before standing back up.

She hesitated as she crossed the empty stretch of field. Was the ground shaking? An earthquake would be a great excuse to miss this cursed field day. Damn, those safety tips she had looked up while entertaining the idea of a visit to California only covered what to do indoors. Maybe the ground would be merciful and swallow her up before she saw Luke's stupid face.

A shadow crossed her visual field. Her heart leapt into her throat. Was that a fist swinging out of nowhere? The kickboxing lessons she had taken with her mom in high school came flooding back.

She ducked and spun like a dancer, almost graceful (for once) as she faced her attacker. Her hands automatically came up, one clenched in a fist protecting her jaw, and the other in an attack-ready stance. It was a good thing she had read all those articles on personal safety tips in preparation for her next class with Sawyer. No one would get the jump on her today. An abduction would really put a damper on Nicole's day.

Sawyer's massive silhouette blocked out the sunlight. He clapped slowly.

"Excellent work. You were paying attention to your surroundings, and I didn't even manage to get a hand on you. You're learning."

She reached over and slapped him lightly on the arm. "I almost punched you in the face."

He shrugged. "Generally your attackers aren't going to send a courtesy note letting you know when they'll be attacking. You responded well today, but we still have a lot of work to do."

She checked her watch. Field Day officially started in ten minutes. She cast another glance at the parking lot. No Luke. Maybe a distraction would take the edge off. "Want to go over a couple of things while we wait?"

"That's a good idea. Okay, so when you were attacked the night of the abduction—"

Claire flinched.

"Sorry. The night of the incident, you were attacked from behind, weren't you?"

"Yes, from behind."

"The favorite attack method of cowards. Okay." He held her shoulders and stood behind her. "Depending on how someone grabs you, there are several different ways to defend yourself. Let's say someone comes up behind you and—because you are so small, no offense—puts you in a chokehold."

He hunched down so he was more at Claire's level. In

one swift motion, his right arm whipped out and squeezed tight around her neck. His biceps bulged into her cheek, squashing her jaw. She fought the urge to dig her nails into his skin and scratch furiously. As the panic rose, she flashed back to the dark hotel hallway, where she had walked, unaware and with mashed potatoes still staining her dress, directly into Barney's waiting arms. While Barney hadn't had Sawyer's strength, he did have chloroform.

Claire glanced across the field. Officer Schiccitano had set up a folding chair at the edge of the baseball diamond. He licked his thumb and turned a page on the paperback he was reading. Mindy had sat up underneath her tree and had slid her sunglasses down her nose, watching their encounter intently.

"Now this feels pretty terrible and effective, doesn't it?" Sawyer asked.

Claire found that she couldn't speak easily, so she tried nodding instead.

His arm relaxed and drew away from her neck.

She rubbed her neck and took several deep breaths.

"When you feel someone coming in for a chokehold, the best possible thing you can do to defend yourself is to tuck your chin. When you tuck your chin, you prevent the attacker from getting a firm hold around your windpipe."

She tucked her chin obediently. Oh good, a double chin. She would hate to look her best when her ex-boyfriend showed up. Was her foundation rubbing off too? Not that she cared. She wasn't trying to impress Luke. If he even showed up.

"Now grab my wrist and take a step to the side."

"Which hand?"

"Whichever is closest. Good," Sawyer said. "By stepping to the side, you've thrown me slightly off balance. Next you're going to take the hand that was grabbing my wrist, and smash it right into my groin. But please don't actually do that."

Claire giggled in spite of herself as she brought her arm down in a slashing motion, stopping just before she made contact with his gym shorts.

"Great, now, assuming that your attacker is a male, this is going to hurt like hell and cause him to crumple a little bit. When that happens, take that same elbow and smash it up into my face like you're pulling the cord on a lawn mower. You should feel it in your shoulder blade. Perfect. Step-groin-nose. Now do it quickly. Your attacker isn't going to allow you to take your time. Good."

A sense of calm grew within her even though a 250-pound man held her in a choke hold. She was capable. "But what if my feet don't touch the ground? What if someone like you who can throw me around like a sack of potatoes attacks me? I can't take a step if I can't reach the ground."

"I'm glad you asked. I'm going to lift you, but just tap my arm twice if anything feels wrong or too uncomfortable."

When her feet left the ground, dangling uselessly, her anxiety spiked. Her hands tightened around Sawyer's arm. So much for being strong and capable.

"Move one leg like you're going to take a step, then swing it back and kick backward as hard as you can. Again, please do not actually kick me in the groin."

"What the hell?" a very familiar voice asked.

The bottom dropped out of Claire's stomach. That was Luke's irritated voice. She had last heard it when he had nearly flipped a table while putting together a one-thou-sand-piece puzzle of the Grand Canyon.

Sawyer swung around, still holding Claire off the

ground. "Oh, hey, Luke. I was just showing Claire some self-defense moves."

She squirmed and tapped his arm twice.

"Oh, sorry," he said, quickly releasing her. Her knees nearly crumpled when she hit the ground. Sawyer and Luke both reached out to steady her, then stepped back and stared at each other. The tension in the air was palpable.

"Thanks for showing me that, Sawyer. So basically, always aim for the groin."

"Congratulations, you have just mastered ninety percent of self-defense." He laughed and crossed his arms and planted his feet wide, as though he was planning to stake a claim on that particular patch of grass.

She laughed nervously and turned around. The macho energy was exhausting. "Oh, it looks like the bride-to-be needs my help," she said loudly, taking a step toward the table Nicole had set up.

"No, I don't," Nicole called out firmly.

Claire glared at her.

Luke came up beside her and grasped her arm. A rush of heat hit her at his touch. Her skin tingled. He was more tan than he had been in Paris, but the tan couldn't hide the dark circles under his eyes. He looked as though he hadn't had a decent sleep—or meal—in a week.

"Can we talk?" he asked.

"Now isn't a good time. This is Nicole and Kyle's day." She tugged her elbow from his grip. The sun was too bright, but irritated as she was, she wouldn't have put sunglasses on for anything. She couldn't stop pouring over every inch of his face, like a comforting book she had read a hundred times. If the book was about a stupid megalomaniac with an affinity for sadism.

Rosie yipped from her tree tether, standing on her back legs and fighting to get to Luke.

"Sawyer, my man!" Kyle called from next to Nicole. "How crazy was that game last night?"

"Hey, Kyle," Sawyer said, lumbering over to where he stood. He kept his eyes on Claire even as they talked.

"You haven't called," Luke said quietly. There was sadness in his sea-green eyes.

Claire raised her eyebrows. She didn't have time for this. "I've been busy. And I don't want to talk to you."

He nodded and shoved his hands in his pockets. "Did you at least play Rosie my bedtime voicemail?"

"I didn't listen to any of them. I couldn't." Her face was hot.

Rosie was fighting her leash, running in half circles and barking to get Luke's attention.

"Claire, I'm sorry," he said, turning to face her and holding both of her hands in his. "I'm sorry I asked you to relive that night. You have every right to be upset with me. You are more important to me than any project. But don't throw away everything we have on one act of stupidity."

She bit her tongue, holding in the flood of words that she had pent up since she ran away in Paris. Tears pricked in her eyes, but she was not about to waste any more bodily fluids over this idiot. "This really isn't the time or place to discuss this. I refuse to overshadow Nicole's gathering with our relationship troubles. We can talk later."

When Luke withdrew his hands, relief and dismay hit at the same time. He nodded and walked toward the table, greeting Kyle.

Okay, so maybe he hadn't forgotten about her. There was no evidence of a new girlfriend along with him either. What was she supposed to make of that? And why wouldn't her stomach come back up to its normal position?

"What happened?" Mindy asked, from behind her.

Claire jumped. Replacing her customary heels with sneakers had rendered Mindy a ninja.

"We're going to talk later. Maybe."

Mindy grunted and stared in Luke's direction. "Do you need me to put some bees in his car? Because I'll do it. He would never know."

"I have no doubt. But I'm good, thanks." Who knew what the universe would do to her next if she put bees in her ex's car?

CLAIRE CROUCHED NEXT TO NICOLE, HEAD DOWN AND ONE hand pressed into the grass. Luke's eyes burned into her, but she refused to look. If Nicole wanted to play football, she wasn't going to let anything distract her.

Nicole bent over, resting the football on the ground. The red plastic flags attached to her waist danced in the wind.

She snapped the ball back to Mindy, who caught it and sprinted forward like she had been shot out of a cannon. She ran almost to the sideline at full speed, twirling to evade Kyle's grasp. All the vigorous lovemaking must have kept Mindy in tip-top shape, because she didn't even look winded when she hit the end zone unimpeded. She took a bow, and Nicole and Claire clapped.

"Impressive," Kyle said, rolling up the sleeves of his T-shirt. "Our turn."

Kyle bent over, looking to each side as he formulated his play. He glanced behind him to where Luke waited, hands outstretched. "Kamikaze?"

"Kamikaze." Luke confirmed.

Kyle tossed the ball backward to Luke, who let out a terrifying yell and stormed straight through the middle of the field. The girls were so startled by the yelling that they didn't even reach for him until he was five yards beyond them.

Claire slowed down, allowing Nicole to reach Luke's belt and yank a flag off. She didn't need to be that close to his quicksand crotch.

"Damn it. First down, though." He tossed the ball back to Kyle to repeat the process.

In spite of the awkwardness of playing against her ex-boyfriend and the man who saved her life, Claire's competitive spirit began to emerge. This was something she had control over. She couldn't keep strangers from trying to kill her, but she could sure as hell run fast enough to rip off some flags and take Luke down a peg.

Kyle snapped the ball to Luke again, who hesitated for a moment, seeking an opening.

"Luke, I'm open!" Sawyer said from Claire's right.

She edged sideways to cover him, but Luke seemed to be pretending that he hadn't heard. Sawyer's jaw hardened as he jogged down the field.

"It's cute that you think you can cover me," Sawyer said nonchalantly.

"Whatever," she said, eyes still on the ball.

Kyle sprinted past her at full speed, and Luke released a perfect spiral.

She sprang into action, sneakers pounding into the grass as she moved to cover the space between them. Sawyer's footsteps fell behind her. She pivoted and turned into the path of the ball, stretching her hands above her head. The ball slammed into her hands, and Claire winced as it nearly left her fingertips. She managed to snatch it from the air and tuck it into her side, exactly like Roy had taught her.

Just as she secured the ball, something smashed into her right hip, sending her sprawling to the ground. She fell with a heavy thump onto the grass and groaned. Sawyer's weight abruptly collapsed on top of her, knocking the wind out of her.

"Oof," she whispered. Were those her ribs cracking or had she accidentally brought a carton of eggs to the field day?

"Shit. Sorry, Claire. I couldn't stop," Sawyer said. He rolled away and leaned over her, crouching down and blocking the sun with his head. He reached down and swept away some of the hair that had been loosed from her ponytail. "Are you okay?"

Claire had just opened her mouth to respond when an angry voice interrupted.

"Last time I checked, this was no-tackle football."

Oh, boy. The testosterone fest that had been simmering all morning was about to come to a boil.

A familiar hand reached out and shoved Sawyer. Sawyer stood with impressive speed for someone of his size and whirled to face Luke. "It was an accident. I apologized. Sorry again, Claire."

She waved faintly from the ground.

"You could have seriously hurt her." Luke's eyes narrowed. His face was flushed, and a vein was visible in his forehead. This was not good. A groomsman fight was *not* on the agenda for field day.

"Really? Because I'm pretty sure the expert on hurting Claire is standing in front of me," Sawyer said, danger in his toffee eyes.

If she clutched the football any harder, there was an excellent chance it would pop.

"You son of a bitch." Luke took a step toward Sawyer. His hand was already clenched in a fist.

A shrill whistle blew.

"*Gentlemen*," Nicole said loudly, coming to stand between them. "This is a friendly game of flag football. If you two can't cooperate, you will be removed from the game. And I don't think you want Kyle to face all three of us by himself."

Luke swore under his breath and turned around, striding off to the sidelines.

"Wow, he is super threatened by Sawyer," Mindy said quietly as she lifted Claire to her feet.

"No kidding." Jealousy was not a good color on Luke.

The rest of the game was uncomfortable at best. The tension between Sawyer and Luke was palpable. The joyful banter and wisecracking had ceased, and the girls won without difficulty since the groomsmen were too busy infighting.

"Well, that was a disaster," Nicole said as she packed the last of the flag football belts into the tote.

"I'm so sorry, Coli," Claire said, putting away the remaining orange slices she had brought. Her cheeks burned. She had ruined a bridal event, something she swore she would never do. And worse, it was for her best friend. "I never thought Luke would act like that."

"Men," Nicole said, tutting in disgust. "Oh, shit. We have bigger problems," she said, staring off into the distance.

"What?" Claire asked, immediately scoping out Rosie. Her furry best friend was still lying in a patch of grass, furiously licking peanut butter out of a treat ball.

"Who's that guy by your car? That isn't your cop detail, right? Should we call the detective?"

Claire sighed. "No, that's not my cop. It's fine. I'll explain later."

Jack Hartley leaned against the hood of Claire's Audi. Luke stood by his car, staring suspiciously at Jack, and Sawyer hovered two cars down. To a passerby, it probably looked like a strange photo shoot for an album cover.

"You better not be putting yourself in danger again," Nicole said darkly.

"I'm not. Can I help you take that back to your car?" Claire picked up Nicole's tote, desperate to delay her departure for another few minutes. Maybe she could just walk home. It was probably only four or five miles. Anything would be better than confronting what waited for her in the parking lot.

"I think you have enough to deal with," Nicole said. She took the tote from Claire. "But thanks. See you on Wednesday for the final approval of the staging?"

"I'll be there. How are the pieces looking?"

"Great. The gallery is almost done. We're having a six-by-four frame brought in for the print of Aaron's drawing."

"Perfect." Claire reached for her notebook. She jotted down a quick note and tossed it back into her bag. "Have you seen the work in progress?"

"I saw it on Friday. He took some lessons. It's so good," Nicole said, smiling in the same dreamy way Claire did when she was imagining a happy ending. "He took such care with the details—the wrinkles in his jeans, the curls in her hair."

"I can't wait to see it." A thrill ran through Claire. It was going to be nothing short of magic. "And you're sure blowing it up isn't going to make it look all pixely and terrible?"

"Relax, I know a guy. It'll be perfect."

"Did you get the box of twinkle lights I sent over?"

"Yes, I was thinking of putting them—hey, knock it off. I know what you're doing. Stop dillydallying and go deal with that shitshow." Nicole gestured toward the parking lot. "And text me later."

"Damn it." Claire slung her bag over one shoulder. "Fine."

She took her time crossing the field and untying Rosie, uncomfortably aware of the three sets of eyes on her. Though slightly out of breath by the time she trudged up the hill, she would rather be kidnapped by Barney again than admit it.

"Jack," she said.

"Afternoon, Claire," he said formally. A gust of wind shot through the parking lot, but not a single hair moved on his moussed head. Was wind-proof hair maintenance something they taught at the FBI?

He bent and extended a hand to Rosie, who sniffed it suspiciously. She didn't bark, but she hid behind Claire's legs.

"I was wondering if you had given any thought to what we discussed earlier," he said, standing back up and crossing his arms.

"I'll do it," Claire said. Survivor's guilt had settled heavy on her heart after days of staring at the bright faces of the Widowmaker victims. Five women before her died because they didn't have a Sawyer to leap in and tase Barney. If she had the ability to get some closure for the families, she would squeeze every last bit of information from that chloroform-toting maniac. The new murder binder in her purse contained notes about what Jack had told her and pictures of the mark on her neck.

"Really?" he asked, eyebrows raised above the rim of his mirrored sunglasses. "You'll go see him in prison?"

She nodded. It was sure to be the worst thing she'd done since getting abducted, but this time Barney would be in chains. The control was hers.

"Come by the precinct tomorrow," Jack said. "We'll discuss your tactics."

"Tomorrow doesn't work. I'll come on Tuesday," she said firmly, staring him down.

"Very well." He walked around the front of his car and opened his door. "Oh, and Claire?"

"Yes?" If he was going to ask her for some other exorbitant favor, she was going to give him a colossal wedgie and roll him down the grassy hill into that children's soccer game.

"Nice form down there," Jack said, gesturing to the football field.

"Roy taught me a lot," she said over her shoulder as she buckled Rosie into her seatbelt.

"I'm sure he did." His smile faded, and he ducked back into his car.

As soon as Jack's car door closed, Luke and Sawyer both moved toward her at the same time.

Claire held up a hand. "Sawyer first," she said. That was likely to be the far less messy conversation.

The vein in Luke's forehead started to bulge out again, but he stood silently by his car.

"Did he come to ask you about the thing?" Sawyer asked in a loud whisper, crossing his arms and frowning.

Luke's eyes narrowed.

"He did," she said, barely above a whisper. "I'm going to

do it. I feel like I have a duty. I don't want anyone else to go through what I did. Don't get me wrong, I don't want to see him ever again, and I don't know if I'll be able to get him to talk, but those families need closure. And if there really are more homicidal incels like him out there, they need to be brought down."

"I'll help you." Sawyer reached out and touched her arm gently.

"Thank you. I may need it." The hood of her car was hot beneath her back as she leaned against it. Perfect, more back sweat before she spoke to Luke. "See you for class on Wednesday?"

"Sounds good. And wear a dress this time, or an outfit you would normally wear when walking around downtown. Don't forget to take this out before you go home." He tugged on her ponytail.

"I won't." She smiled and reached up. The elastic snapped as she tugged it from her hair. Curls fell down her back, engulfing her in the smell of rose hips and jojoba.

"See you later." He gave a small wave and climbed into his black pickup truck.

"Who was that?" Luke asked, already leaning against the hood of her car.

"That was my biological father, Jack." Claire fidgeted with her keys. She would have rather thrown herself face-first into a cauldron of discarded bacon grease than chat with her ex about her deadbeat dad. What was it, National Asshole Day?

"Your bio-dad?" Luke stared off into the distance as though he meant to get a second look. "As in the one who abandoned you almost twenty years ago?"

"The one and only."

"What the hell is he doing back now?" He reached

through the back window to pet Rosie, who rolled onto her back and wriggled in her car seat.

Claire took a deep breath. "There's a lot of stuff going on right now that I'm trying to deal with. He's one of those things."

"I hate not knowing what's going on in your life. Why didn't you tell me?"

"I didn't want to talk to you after Paris." Her cheeks were hot and tight from sweat. She just wanted a nice shower and maybe some light murder research. Was that so much to ask for?

"Why was he here?" he probed.

"He works for the FBI. Long story short, I'm going to see Barney in prison."

Luke blinked. "Why the hell would you do that?"

She paused. Luke didn't know about the existence of Barney's mysterious group. If it even existed. She didn't owe him an explanation. He practically had a full-time job in keeping things from her. Why shouldn't he be in the dark for once?

"For...closure," she decided. Ha. Screw him.

"Are you sure that's going to help? Facing him?" he asked softly, reaching out and rubbing her arm, which was covered in goosebumps despite the sticky humidity. His touch only elicited more. *Ugh*.

"I'm certain that it will help more than hashing it out on camera for an audience of thousands," Claire said coolly, wrenching her arm out of his grasp and getting into her car.

She drove away without a backward glance.

CHAPTER TWENTY-TWO

BIRDS TWEETED NOISILY OUTSIDE THE WEST HAVEN POLICE Department. A suspiciously cheery sound for such a grim setting. It must have been Claire's lucky morning, because the media that had camped out in front of her apartment building for the last three days had vacated the premises. Claire stuffed her phone back into her purse, mind still buzzing with ideas for the escape room-themed proposal that had passed their final test that morning. Sawyer probably would have had a fit if he saw her walk from the car to the station with her head buried in her phone. But surely no one would abduct her at a police station.

She pushed her way through the heavy double doors. What was she getting herself into?

"Claire Hartley," she said to the cop behind the desk. He glanced at the calendar on his desk, and then at Rosie, who was panting happily, tongue lolling out of her mouth on one side. She wasn't about to leave her alone in her apartment with a stalker on the loose.

"Special Agent Hartley is expecting me," she added. Anything to move this trash heap of a day along. She pointed to Rosie. "She's with me."

"Sure. Follow me," the officer said, leading her back through a row of cubicles to an interrogation room. "Coffee? Tea?"

"Coffee, please. One cream, two sugars."

She shivered as she slid into one of the unforgiving stainless-steel chairs. The door remained open, but the walls seemed to be closing in. She inhaled deeply and pulled out her newly revamped notebook.

She ran a finger over the Self-Defense and Interrogation Tactics label she had printed the night before. The flowery writing was definitely leaning slightly down to the right. And one of the rhinestones was a millimeter off. She'd have to do it all again.

Rosie, on the other hand, wasn't bothered at all by the interrogation room. After sniffing every corner of the room, she wound herself around Claire's chair twice and settled at her feet.

Claire checked her phone again, but there was no service in the interrogation room. Mindy was covering the client calls, but what if there was an emergency?

"Sorry to keep you waiting," Jack said brusquely as he rushed into the room, wheeling a large whiteboard.

"It's fine." Claire didn't look up. She carefully put her phone away and folded her hands on the desk before facing him.

Her father took the seat opposite her, fluorescent lights shining on his salt-and-pepper hair.

"The FBI extends their thanks for your cooperation."

Claire bit the inside of her lip. If one more phony statement came out of his mouth, there would be a record-shattering eye roll.

"Our purpose here today is to teach you some techniques you can use when you visit Mr. Windsor at the penitentiary." He cleared his throat. "Please stop me if you have any questions. Thank you, Officer Jordan."

The front desk officer dropped off two steaming mugs of coffee, both the same beige color.

Claire and Jack both took their spoons, stirred counterclockwise, and tapped twice against the rim of the cup before taking the first sip. *Ugh*. If Jack noticed, he didn't say anything.

"Sorry about this, by the way." Jack waved a hand at the room. "They're having a meeting in the conference room."

"It's fine." Claire glanced at her reflection in the two-way mirror. She shuddered. How many times was she going to reassure her absent father that things were "fine?" Things hadn't been fine for months. Years, really, if she wanted to count her daddy issues.

He cleared his throat. "The first thing we wanted to ask was if we could photograph your neck wound."

"Oh. Sure." She took off her blazer and scrunched her sleeveless top to the side.

Jack waved to a cop in the hallway, who came in with a digital camera.

Claire craned her neck, trying to get her face as far as possible from the mark in the photograph.

When the man with the camera left, she put her blazer back on. There was a darkness in Jack's eyes. He seemed more determined as he flipped to a new page in his own (poorly decorated) notebook, all business.

"The first thing I want to talk about are some interrogation tactics." His chair screeched on the tile floor as he slid it back from the table. He rose and walked to the corner of the room, where he had parked the whiteboard. At least he knew the value of a good whiteboard.

He wrote DECEPTION on the board in capital letters. Claire copied the word down.

Jack clasped his hands behind his back and paced. "We have an advantage over Mr. Windsor. He is trapped in a cell for twenty-three hours a day. His news sources are limited, and his connection to the outside world has been largely fragmented since the prison reports only his lawyer and his mother have visited him."

Shit. She had nearly forgotten about the treacherous, pinch-faced litigator that her mother had nearly assaulted. Damned Rachel. Was she going to be even crueler to Claire in court now that she and Luke had broken up? Maybe she would double down on her hatred for Claire and become Wendy's lawyer too.

Jack was still talking. "He doesn't know what we know or what we don't know. When you speak to him, I recommend you suggest that we know more than we actually do."

He paused mid-pace and gestured at the word on the board. "Deception may be our best tactic here. When you speak to him, you want to deceive him. Trick him into giving something away. He doesn't know that you're aware of the group's existence. He won't know for sure that we sent you. My suggestion is that you come right out and tell him you already know about his group because someone from it has already implicated him on a larger scale in exchange for immunity. Get him to turn on them."

Her head was already spinning. She scribbled down another note. Her stomach had twisted into one of those metal brain teaser puzzles Jack had left behind when he'd abandoned the family. Barney had evaded capture for so long. The FBI couldn't crack him in person. Would he really be undone simply by a bit of deceit from one of his victims?

"And here's what we know about this group so far," Jack said, erasing his first word and scribbling more down.

"We know that this particular group targets women." He wrote WOMEN on the board and underlined it. "All the known victims with this mark have been women. All different ages, different stages of life. Several were powerful executives or business owners, stockbrokers or lawmakers," Jack said, ticking them off on his fingers. "This suggests some kind of—"

"Fear of powerful women? Of women in control?" Claire interrupted.

"Yes, exactly. We can't be sure, of course. Some of the marked victims, like Ariel, were waitresses or retail employees. We suspect the outliers are victims of personal vendettas, potentially unrelated to the group's mission."

"When he—that night." She still couldn't say the words. "He did make it seem like it was purely a personal vendetta. All because I shot him down in college. Same with the other girls."

"You took the control from him," Jack suggested and wrote CONTROL on the board. "And you bruised his ego, which is probably worse to him."

Claire exhaled deeply and buried one hand in her hair. This was such a bullshit reason to end someone's life. If she killed everyone she couldn't control, Wendy and Jason's corpses would be sprawled on the sidewalk outside her apartment right now. Luke's too.

Jack capped the marker and returned to the table. He leaned toward her, both elbows on the table.

"I know what you're thinking. This is bullshit. And it is." He tapped his thumb against the stainless-steel table. "Control is a huge motivating factor in many serial killer cases."

"Fabulous," she said flatly. "Is there anything else you can tell me about the group?"

"We—well, *I*, technically, believe that we're dealing with some sort of cult. The geographic disparity, the symbol, the similarity in victims all point toward a wide-scale organization with a disciplined rule set and mission. Ordinary people with ordinary troubles who are fed up and swept up in hating the world that hated them. There must be a leader, and they must have some way to communicate."

"So, what do you need me to find out?" She flipped to a fresh page in her notebook, pen poised at the ready. What she wouldn't give to be writing out a list of décor for that escape room proposal. Every time she thought her detective days were over, some homicidal maniac decided to ruin everything.

"We don't know what he'll give you, or if he'll give you anything at all. But we want to know the name of the organization, who is the leader, what is their end goal, how many members there are, whether this is a domestic or international organization, how they find and recruit members, how they select their victims. Everything."

"I wouldn't be surprised if they were international," Claire said as she scribbled away. "They managed to send me flowers in Paris on my second day."

Jack pursed his lips. He tugged at his collar but didn't comment.

She exhaled again, trying to stay calm. Footage of police dramas she had watched flooded her mind. "How do you think I should approach this? Should I act large-and-in-charge like the type of woman he hates and wants to destroy to set him off? Or should I act the victim, meek and mild, to fool him into a sense of security?"

Jack looked pleasantly surprised, almost pleased, at the question. "That's a great question. Ultimately, that choice is up to you and what you feel you're able to handle that day. If you act confident, you may provoke anger and encourage him to give something up. If you show him how little his attempt affected your life, that would really set him off. Or, if you act like a victim, you may lull him into a monologue where he'll reveal more information. Either way, he said he will only speak to you. He barely even speaks to his lawyer —whom I have heard you already know."

"Of course he doesn't. She's a powerful woman." A contemptible crone, too, but powerful woman nonetheless. "Why would he want a woman arguing for his fate?"

He nodded deeply and leaned forward. "I suspect he knows your connection to her and did it to get under your skin. It's the only thing he can control from prison. Unless, that is, he still has some pull with the group. Additionally, you may want to aim for a few personal questions to get him talking. Serial killers typically have troubled childhoods, bed wetting behavior, aggression toward animals, and profound hatred for either their mother or father."

"Well, he already confessed to murdering his dad, so that should be easy enough." Claire added a bulleted list to her notes. "Why aren't you guys concerned about that case? Surely that should be easier to prove than a national serial killer ring."

"It's on the To Do list. Do you have any other questions for me?" he asked, closing his notebook and sliding it into his briefcase.

"Why didn't you ever call? Or write? Why did you never come back?" Claire blurted out. She hadn't even intended to bring up her family history, but the questions poured out of her.

He froze. "Claire, this isn't really the time to talk about it." He crossed the room and nudged the door closed.

"When will be the time, Jack? In case you forgot, I'm being targeted by a network of serial killers." She yanked a copy of the latest note from her murder binder and slapped it down on the table. "I could be abducted and stuffed in a trunk tomorrow. Again."

"I would never let that happen."

"Really? Because you didn't do anything about it the first time. You only bothered to contact me, to come into my life at all, because you saw this," she said, gesturing to her scar. "You only wanted to talk to me when I could do something for you. You're just as bad as they are."

Her temper flared like a match striking a rock. Every thought she'd had for the last twenty years was threatening to pour out.

She jabbed a finger into the metal table. "We had a yard sale to get rid of you. Did you know that? We sold your ties, your vintage record collection. We used the money for a security deposit on a crappy apartment because that was all we could afford when you abandoned us. I was in our front yard, six years old, haggling with people who wanted to take pieces of you away from me."

He leaned against the wall in the corner of the room, arms folded, and painfully silent.

"Thank god Mom married Roy. He was there for every father-daughter dance, every field hockey game, even though I wasn't biologically his. He loved me as he would have loved his own daughter. He's a real man."

Jack's face was flushed, and his hands had curled into fists. "Do you want to know why I never came back, Claire? Your mother never allowed it. She threatened restraining orders. Returned every birthday card I ever sent. She got full custody of you and denied any visitation rights, claiming abuse."

"Bullshit." Claire slapped the table. "You left because you got another woman pregnant. You started a new family and wanted nothing to do with your old one. Were the words 'till death do us part' just a suggestion to you? Marriage is a promise, a binding, lifelong commitment. Or were we just practice while you waited for your real family to start?"

Rosie stood rigid at Claire's side, growling softly.

"No, Claire. I loved your mother, but we had our problems. Most of them were my fault. I was trying to make my way into the Bureau, so I was never home. I didn't give our marriage the time it needed. And your mom had to stay at home with Charlie and never got to finish school. We fought almost every day, over all kinds of things, but especially money. I was so tired of the fighting. I sought solace outside of our marriage, and that's on me. But don't blame me for being gone all those years. I tried to be a part of your life."

She paused. Was any of this the truth? She hadn't inherited Alice's psychic abilities, but she could tell a very uncomfortable conversation with her mother was coming.

"And how about after I turned eighteen? When I sent you an invitation to my wedding last year?"

Jack sighed. "It had been too long. I didn't know what to say. I knew you wouldn't believe me, that you assumed I was just some deadbeat who went out for a pack of smokes and never came back."

"That is the prevailing narrative." She crossed her arms rigidly in front of her.

"How is your mother?" he asked quietly.

"She's good. She's happy."

"I'm glad. Listen, Claire. Tanya—my wife—would really like to have you over for dinner. She wants to meet you."

Claire froze. Unbelievable. Dinner with the deadbeat and the home-wrecker. Who could turn down that invitation?

"And I'd like to talk more about this all in a more appropriate setting." He gestured to the interrogation room.

There was probably a small battalion of cops on the other side of the glass, taking bets and passing tubs of popcorn. But that was the least of her worries.

"I'll think about it. But I have a meeting to get to. Goodbye, Jack." She hurried out of the room, Rosie following in her wake.

Claire plowed through the front door like she had stolen something. Her fists were clenched so tightly they hurt.

How dare he show up after a decade of absence and just expect her to welcome him with open arms? That dinner invitation had only been extended because *Tanya* had requested it. Not because Jack wanted to get to know his estranged daughter. Claire nearly banged her shin against a metal bench as she hustled to her car. With all the pent-up rage threatening to erupt, she was pretty sure she could have ripped it straight out of the concrete. She forced herself to breathe and hurried to her car, mouth clamped shut. The scream trapped in her throat would have shattered windows. Jack wasn't worth the spike in her blood pressure.

CHAPTER TWENTY-THREE

"I don't know how you do it," Nicole said, carrying four tote bags over the threshold of Claire's apartment.

"Do what?" Claire took the bags from her and set them on the bar. One tipped over, and a ream of coral-colored origami paper fell out.

She yawned so wide that it hurt. After her altercation with Jack the previous day, she had barely slept. Something about the abduction had left her untethered and uninhibited. She was yelling at authority figures, confronting someone who had been dead to her for twenty years. Lying to her ex-boyfriend. She barely recognized herself when she looked in the mirror.

"Deal with the freakin' press all day," Nicole said. "One of the reporters outside recognized me from the courthouse and asked how I knew you."

Claire rolled her neck from side to side. She had tweaked it earlier when Sawyer had shown her how to climb into the driver's seat from the passenger side to avoid suspicious vehicles. "I know. Things have gotten so much worse since word leaked about the copycat."

"I'm going to find the bastard who told them and punch him right in the nuts." Nicole began organizing the origami paper into neat stacks.

"I will gladly help you. I hope you plugged your studio when they talked to you, at least. This bullshit attention should do someone some good." It seemed like every time Claire got a note, the press knew about it a day later. But who was telling them? She popped the cork on a bottle of cab sauv and poured a generous amount into two glasses. She handed one to Coli.

"I didn't speak to them. I don't even need the extra business. I can't keep up with the requests that are coming in now."

"Really? That's amazing." Claire took a sip. She was going to need it if she was going to help fold one thousand paper cranes before Nicole's wedding in the spring.

"I guess. I might need to hire another photographer, or at least a receptionist to manage the appointments."

"Look at you. The soon-to-be Mrs. Nicole Collins, small business owner, photographer extraordinaire, and totally killing it. I'm so proud," Claire said and reached over to hug her best friend.

"Enough about me. Who the hell was that guy at your car on field day? Don't think I forgot about it. I've been sensitive to your needs since Luke drop-kicked your heart, but I expect you to be honest with me."

Shit. Another honesty lecture. Claire had forgotten she hadn't told Coli what was going on. She really didn't want to get into the specifics of Barney's potential network of serial killer friends when she had a mountain of maid of honor duties. Maybe an abbreviated version of the truth would be best.

"That was Jack. My biological father. He wants to have dinner."

Rosie trotted over, and Claire bent down to pet her.

Nicole's eyes bulged. "Dinner? Why? And why now?"

"His wife has been bugging him about it."

"The Whole Foods home-wrecker," Nicole muttered and took a large sip of wine.

"Apparently, her name is Tanya." The name was like an ice chip on Claire's tongue.

"Are you going to do it?"

Claire shrugged. "I don't know. I've done just fine without him all these years. I'm not particularly inclined to let him in now just because he broke into my apartment claiming to be in the FBI."

Nicole rolled her eyes. "FBI. I bet. He's probably dead broke and coming after your money. Or maybe he needs a kidney. And when are people going to stop breaking into your apartment?"

"You know, I ask myself that every day. Maybe I should move. Anyway, should we get started? I don't think my fine motor skills are going to improve if I keep drinking."

Nicole waved one hand and drained what was left in her glass. "Who cares? They don't have to be perfect."

Claire raised her eyebrows. Nicole stared back. There was silence.

"It's for your wedding day. They're going to be perfect." Claire crossed to her drunk drawer and pulled out a ruler and protractor.

Nicole opened her mouth to speak, but someone knocked on the front door.

Excellent, another visit from an uninvited guest. Claire sighed and pulled a kitchen knife from the butcher block. Who would it be this time? She pressed a button on her security console, and a man she didn't recognize flickered into view.

Her heart leapt in her chest, and she nearly dropped the knife. Was this the copycat? Would he really be so bold as to ring her doorbell?

She pressed the intercom button. "Who is it?"

"Ma'am, I'm Tom from Chucky's Custard. I'm here to deliver an order for Claire."

She and Nicole looked at each other. Chucky's Custard was Claire's favorite ice cream place. The only problem was the store was located in Delaware, easily five hours away.

"I didn't order anything."

"Order came from a Luke Islestorm and is to be delivered with this note," the man onscreen said, pushing his glasses down the bridge of his nose to stare at the front of an envelope. He held it up to the camera. "He must have messed up real good."

And indeed he had. Claire opened the door despite Nicole's protests. "He paid you to drive ten hours round-trip to deliver me ice cream?"

"He sure did," the man said, handing her a Styrofoam cooler and an envelope. "There's dry ice in there, so you be careful. There's some other feller behind me too." He jutted a hitchhiker's thumb over his shoulder.

Claire handed the cooler and envelope to Nicole, who moved it to the bar.

"Thank you, sir," she called to the man as he disappeared down the hallway. "And you are?" She addressed a second man who wore a bright red shirt with Donatelli's Pizzeria written on it.

"Bayani, Donatelli's Pizzeria in Los Angeles." He glanced uneasily at the butcher knife that still dangled from her right hand. He handed over another large, square cooler. "Cook it for four twenty-five for eighteen minutes on the dot. I wrote it down for you," he said, gesturing to a sticky note.

"I'm guessing this is pizza?"

Bayani scoffed. "It's not just pizza. We have the best pies in the entire country. Google us. And while you're at it, go easy on Luke. He's a good guy. He wanted me to give you this too." He handed over an unmarked DVD.

"Not creepy at all," she muttered, transferring the cooler to the already-crowded bar. When she turned back, both men were gone. She shut and locked the door behind her.

"Well," she said, "should we get to folding?"

Nicole stared blankly at her. "Are you kidding me? Luke sends a pizza delivery boy two thousand miles one way and you're not even going to look at it?"

Claire sighed and walked over to the oven. She stabbed the preheat button and set it to Bayani's instructed temperature. But only because she was going to order a pizza anyway. She flipped the lid on the pizza box. "I apologize" was spelled out in half-moons of pepperoni.

"Well, at least he's becoming more self-aware," Nicole commented behind her.

Claire grunted and took another sip of wine.

"And the ice cream?" Nicole prompted.

Claire sighed and cut the tape on the cooler. Fog rolled out of the box. Inside, nestled in a confusing apparatus of carefully arranged toothpicks were two perfect vanilla soft serves in cones. Why would he send two? If he was outside her door ready to beg for forgiveness, she was heading for the fire escape.

"It's...beautiful," Nicole said, plucking one from the box.

"No sense in wasting it," Claire admitted and pulled the other cone out. It was exactly as she had remembered. Creamy, cold, perfect. She was usually a chocolate girl, but there was something about Chucky's vanilla custard. If she closed her eyes, she could practically smell the salt spray in the air and feel the rough wood of the boardwalk beneath her feet.

"You almost have to forgive him after this," Nicole said in a reverent tone. She had a small ice cream mustache.

Claire straightened up. "Food can't make up for the fifty thousand lies he told me. Can we talk about something else?"

"The awards are in two days," Nicole said over a mouthful of cone. "Are you nervous?"

"Why would I be? You've seen her proposals. They're super dull and generic. And she only had five this year—the restaurant one, a football game, amusement park, Santa's lap, and that one where she staged the groom getting arrested. None of them compare to your proposal. Even with the sabotage."

It hadn't been officially proven, but there was a ninety-five percent chance that Wendy had been responsible for loosening a carriage wheel during Nicole's proposal, causing the bride-to-be to spill out onto the roadway.

Nicole shuddered. "Why is she even still in this business?"

"To beat me. To try to take everything I have. That's the only thing I can think of. She might have gotten Jason, but she won't take anything else from me."

Nicole fiddled with the blank DVD. She held it up to the light as though that would tell her what was on it. "Kyle said your first mediation meeting is next week."

The oven beeped, and Claire tossed the pizza in harder than was necessary. "Yes. Trapped in a room with two lawyers, a mediator, and my ex-fiancé's new girlfriend. It's going to be another fun week."

Nicole reached across the island and squeezed Claire's hand. "It'll be ok. She's going to lose, and things will go back to normal. She flipped a table on live television and openly admitted to stalking you. Anyone with a pair of functioning eyes can see that she's unhinged."

Claire sighed and picked up their wine glasses. She walked them into the living room and set them on the coffee table. "I hope so. Maybe I'll put the award in a glass case and bring it with me to the meeting. Really rile her up."

Nicole followed her and sat cross-legged on the rug. "You should absolutely do that. What's this? Another proposal?"

"Oh," Claire said, quickly snatching a binder off the table. "Yeah, just some notes for the escape room proposal. It's going to take a lot of planning."

But it wasn't the Escape Room binder. Early that morning, she had done a couple of hours of fruitless Googling. She tried searching for the symbol on her neck, antifeminist groups in the United States, anything that could be relevant. Nothing but some scary forums had come up, but there were countless empty sleeve protectors in the Murder Binder 2.0 waiting to be filled with information on Barney's secret group.

"What are you doing?" Claire asked. Nicole had crawled over to her gaming console and put something in the disc tray.

"Come on, you can't tell me you don't want to know what's on the DVD."

"We have pizza to eat and literally one thousand paper cranes to fold." And, frankly, Claire wasn't sure she was ready to confront these feelings. There was enough going on.

"Sweetie, I'm going to need you to put on your big girl panties and read this." Nicole paused, slapping Luke's letter into Claire's hand. "And watch the damn DVD. Because I'm not going to be able to focus on origami until you do."

The letter fell from Claire's hand. "You knew he was going to do this, didn't you? That's why he sent two ice creams."

Nicole bit her lip. "He knew I was going to be here tonight. I didn't know what he was going to do. I haven't spoken to him. It's all been through Kyle."

Claire frowned. She couldn't stay mad at Nicole. "Kyle and I are going to have to have a serious discussion on boundaries. This is exactly what I was afraid of, and why I didn't want to get involved with Luke. He and his stupid lying tongue have compromised the sanctity of our entire friend group."

"He did a really shitty thing," Nicole agreed. "He clearly regrets it and is trying to make up for it, but that doesn't excuse what he did."

"Thank you," Claire said. She ripped the envelope open. The oven timer went off. "Will you get that?"

Nicole nodded and left the room, leaving Claire to confront the contents of the envelope. She wasn't in the mood to read more apologies from the career-driven-to-the-point-of-insanity Luke. Words meant nothing coming from him.

She pulled out a single sheet of Luke's stationery. His cramped handwriting barely covered a single line.

I'm just trying to give them a voice. Watch it and you'll see.

"Holy crap," Nicole said from directly over her shoulder.

Claire shrieked and dropped the paper.

"He must have sent you part of the documentary. He's never done that for anyone, ever. Kyle's mentioned it a million times. He's so secretive about his work."

"He must really trust that pizza guy." Claire tucked the paper back in the envelope and slid it under the box of origami paper where she wouldn't have to look at it. "I guess we're having some true crime with dinner."

"Hell yes." Nicole set two plates on the coffee table and rejoined Claire on the floor.

Claire took a bite of the steaming slice. "Oh my god."

Nicole took a bite too. "Holy shit."

It was the best pizza she had ever tasted. The sauce was perfectly flavored—not too sweet, not overly tomato-pasty. The crust was thin and crunchy, not soggy or doughy. The blend of cheese was elegant. And it had traveled two thousand miles to get here. How good would a fresh one be?

Claire flopped the slice back onto the paper plate like it had personally offended her. How dare Luke exploit her love of carbs? She glanced at her phone with half a mind to send him a video of the pizza frisbeeing out the window. But wasting this pizza would have been a borderline criminal act.

Nicole reached across the table and pressed the play button, startling Claire out of her introspection. The documentary rolled.

Forty minutes later, Claire and Nicole sat side by side on the couch, stack of origami paper untouched.

Nicole blew her nose loudly into a tissue. "And she just —she—the garden. And her dogs. And all the little babies she watched over."

Claire hugged Rosie to her chest and drew her softest blanket around them like a cocoon. The documentary had wiped all of her energy. "I remember Kayley from freshman biology. She partnered with me during a lab. She handled the micropipettes when I was ready to throw them across the room."

"And her wife loved her so much," Nicole choked out, wracked with sobs.

Claire reached over and pulled her into the blanket cocoon. The three of them sat in silence, staring at the blank TV screen. Even though it was a rough cut, every frame had something beautiful in it. The family and friends Luke interviewed had gushed over Kayley's hobbies and interests. She had watched over two hundred NICU babies in her short career as a nurse. Her lovingly tended flower garden had been featured in West Haven's Parade of Homes three times. She had left behind a wife, two dogs, two cats, and a ferret. The entire episode had been more a beautiful memorial for Kayley than a true crime documentary. Barney was barely mentioned until the last ten minutes, when Luke had recreated the timeline of the day she had gone missing.

The documentary had sucked the fight right out of Claire. Luke had asked her something incredibly insensitive —there was no denying that. But the documentary wasn't about making money. It was telling a story, reclaiming the identities of the women as individuals, not just victims. In its own dark way, it was beautiful.

"I think I need to make a call." Claire extricated herself from the cocoon. She handed Nicole the box of tissues and walked back down the hall to the bedroom.

She held her breath as the phone rang.

"Hey. Thanks for the pizza."

CHAPTER TWENTY-FOUR

To Do:
- *Practice acceptance speech*
- *T&E blog post*
- *Update cost spreadsheet for Aaron*

It was go time. Claire stepped out of her black convertible and let the car door shut with a snap. The beads on her clutch glittered under the streetlight. She tugged at the hem of her emerald-green cocktail dress and smoothed her hands over the bodice. All she could see was the wrinkle she couldn't get out with the steamer. At least it would be behind the podium when she accepted her award.

A diamond tennis bracelet, a gift from her mother, covered a mark on her wrist from her homemade restraint system. She really needed to come up with a better sleep-walking prevention solution. Her scarves weren't going to take much more of this.

Her black pumps nearly snagged the hem of her dress as she stepped onto the sidewalk. She recovered and hustled up the steps to the entrance.

"Claire! Over here." Hurried footsteps rushed across the parking lot toward her. What fresh hell?

A blinding light suddenly turned on. The vague shape of a woman appeared in front of her. "Diane Lang, *Channel Four News*. Claire, what is it like to be the only living victim of the West Haven Widowmaker?"

Claire turned around and marched straight for the doors. She thrust them open and disappeared inside without a backward glance. The foyer of the community center was empty. She started to walk through to the ballroom but stopped.

On this exact night one year ago, she had entered the building as a blossoming event planner with a fiancé and a plan for her life, and she had left it heartbroken but more determined than ever to succeed. Tonight, Wendy would pay for what she did. Wendy had taken her fiancé, tampered with Nicole's picture-perfect proposal, and threatened Claire with a lawsuit. But she wasn't going to take anything else. All she needed was a little deep breathing and she was going to kick this award ceremony's ass.

Her heels clacked as she walked down the hallway on the left. She passed the men's bathroom where Wendy had lured Jason into a stall and shook her head. If Wendy hadn't done that, she could be married right now. In a way, Wendy had saved her. For someone who was supposed to be a romance expert, Claire hadn't seen the lack of compatibility in her relationship until it blew up with a (quite literal) bang.

An open doorway revealed an empty classroom. She ducked inside and closed her eyes, planting her feet firmly just wider than hip-width. Her fists planted on her hips, she elevated her chin as though she were balancing a wineglass on her head. She breathed deeply in through her nose and out through her mouth.

"Whatcha doing?" A very long, shadowy torso leaned into the room.

Claire screamed and grabbed the nearest object—a whiteboard eraser—and flung it at the intruder. She put her fists up in a fighting stance. If the press had followed her in here, she was going to punch a bitch. Lawsuit be damned. She took a step forward and her heel caught on a snag in the rug, pitching her forward.

A muscular arm reached forward and grabbed her. Ah, shit.

"Sawyer," she said, gripping his arm as he steadied her. "Well, that was embarrassing. You caught me doing my power stance."

"Your power stance." He raised his eyebrows.

"Yes, it's supposed to help you feel more confident. Fake it till you make it, that kind of thing. I saw it on a TED talk."

"Is it working?"

"It was until I nearly fell on my ass."

He smiled and offered his arm. "This might be safer."

"Thank you," she said, grateful for Sawyer's large, comforting presence.

"Press try to get you on the way in? I saw the anchor from *Channel Four News* moping around the parking lot."

She nodded. "Just one this time. I think they're finally getting bored."

He guided her into the hallway and through the ballroom doors. Dozens of round tables covered in white linen tablecloths littered the room. A gleaming row of awards sat on a table onstage. Had she dusted her award shelf this morning?

"You look nice," she said as they found their table. Sawyer had shed his usual company polo for a well-tailored black suit. He positioned himself with his back to the wall and tugged at his collar.

"Thanks. You look nice too. I hope you have your speech ready? No offense to the other candidate, but your proposals are clearly better."

She smiled. "Thank you. I think so too." She leaned closer to Sawyer and lowered her voice. "It's never been proven by the police, but I know Wendy tampered with Nicole's proposal. She's the reason the carriage wheel broke. She almost ruined everything."

"And now she's suing you." His eyes narrowed, and Claire followed his gaze.

Speaking of Satan's bride. Clearly already drunk, Wendy stumbled into the room in a purple sequin evening gown. She looked as though she had just walked the red carpet at an adult film festival instead of the short flight of steps in front of a venue that didn't even crack the top fifty in Claire's list of favorite West Haven event spaces. Wendy squinted at the seating chart like it was written in another language.

Claire shrank down in her seat, attempting to hide behind Sawyer. It wasn't a difficult task.

"Is that her?" he asked.

"Yep, that's Wendy. Oh good, and there's my ex-fiancé," she added as Jason stumbled into the room and grabbed Wendy's hips, miming a thrusting motion against her behind. They both banged into the easel that held the seating chart. It fell to the floor with a muffled thump, and a white-gloved waiter set it upright.

"I don't like to judge a book by its cover," Sawyer said with narrowed eyes. "But she might have done you a favor."

"They deserve each other." Claire took a sip from her water glass. There was usually an open bar at the awards ceremony, but she needed to stay sharp tonight. Plus, Rachel easily could have spies here ready to report on her public drinking. What she would give for just one glass of chardonnay for these nerves.

The intoxicated couple seemed to have found their table at last. Fortunately, it was at the opposite end of the ballroom. Instead of settling in her seat, Wendy surveyed the room before sprawling into Jason's lap and kissing him full on the mouth. Her leg popped up, and she kicked the owner of a local cat café in the ribcage.

Claire turned her chair toward the stage so she wouldn't have to watch. A white-haired couple settled into seats next to them.

"Bert! Good to see you," she said. "How are the renovations coming on the restaurant?"

Bert, the owner of the West Haven Country Club, reached over to shake her hand. "Just fine, Claire. Should be done early next month. Have you met my wife, Eunice?"

They exchanged pleasantries before another elderly couple arrived and monopolized the conversation with talk of golf. Claire joined in momentarily. She knew nothing about golf, but there was always a chance for a golf course proposal.

"Incoming," Sawyer whispered in her ear.

"Hmm?" She turned and nearly got a face full of sequined boobs.

"Oh, hello, Claire," a sickly sweet voice said from a cloud of tequila.

"Wendy. Here to sue me for something?"

She was mercifully alone. Claire wasn't sure she could handle her ex and her nemesis in her personal space at the same time without stabbing one of them with her butter knife.

"Maybe later," Wendy said, tossing her long brown hair over one shoulder. Her boobs were dangerously close to popping out of the sweetheart neckline. "That's a nice outfit —where did you find it, the grandma section of the thrift store?"

"Yes, that's exactly where I found it. And while I was there, I could have sworn I saw your dress in the D-List Celebrity on Her Seventh Trip to Rehab aisle."

"Cute. Where's your fiancé? Oops, I mean your boyfriend. Your fiancé is with me, obviously." Wendy laughed. "I'll have to take Jason on a little trip down memory lane to the men's bathroom. It's our one-year anniversary, you know."

Claire pushed her chair back, but Sawyer laid a firm hand on her shoulder.

"You can leave now," he said, glaring at Wendy.

Wendy seemed to size Sawyer up for a moment before walking off in a huff and immediately crashing into a chair.

"What a psycho," Sawyer said as she picked herself up and walked away. "And as the child of a psychologist, I shouldn't even be using that word."

Claire shrugged. "That was actually pretty mild for her. She barely mentioned the lawsuit, and only one jab at my love life. Maybe she's growing up."

"Doubt it," he said, scanning the room. "I don't trust her. She's up to something."

Claire glanced up. The she-devil was now sitting smugly on Jason's lap with a dirty martini, clearly making a couple

Claire recognized from a small business seminar uncomfortable.

An emcee came onstage and welcomed everyone, but she barely heard a word. She pulled notecards out of her clutch and went over her brief acceptance speech. Rubbing her win in the drunken harlot's face was going to feel better than a week-long spa trip. Or a seven-day sex bender with Luke. Not that she was thinking about him right now. Even though their post-pizza phone chat had been the most productive conversation they'd had since Paris. Some things took time to forgive, and while she had softened, she wasn't there yet.

Several awards were passed out to thunderous applause. Best Customer Service had been awarded to a local, independently owned pharmacy. They certainly deserved it—Claire had witnessed one of their pharmacy techs snowshoeing down Beaumont Street in a blizzard to deliver medication to a shut-in. Start-Up of the Year was given to De-Stress, a BYOB rage room, despite an alarming number of reported patron injuries.

Claire's gut lurched when Event Planner of the Year appeared on the projector screen. She rubbed her hands over the wrinkle in her dress. "And now, before the presentation of the Event Planner of the Year award, we'll see submissions from two of our best and brightest—three-time award winner Claire Hartley from Happily Ever Afters, and Wendy Flutter of The Yes Makers."

The lights in the banquet room dimmed, and the room quieted. Could everyone hear her heartbeat? Sawyer rested a hand on her arm and squeezed.

Wendy's proposal played first. An overly cinematic narrator droned over B-roll of chopsticks being unsheathed. He narrated the couple's love story and the events as they unfolded as if it were a nature show, adding unnecessary enthusiasm.

"Crikey," Sawyer whispered in Claire's ear. "The wild female sits unaware in a two-star pan-Asian restaurant as the male prepares to make her his mate for life. Little does she know her engagement ring is almost as microscopic as his genitalia."

Claire snorted, earning a disdainful look from one of the country club gentlemen next to her. Oops.

As the rest of the video unfolded, the groom-to-be predictably slid the waiter the ring. The waiter brought it out, baked into a brownie on top of a sundae. The bride bit into the brownie, clearly thought she broke a tooth, and drew out the fudge-covered ring. She immediately started crying. Her boyfriend got down on one knee, and everyone in the restaurant turned to stare.

Just as the on-screen participants began to clap, a smattering of polite applause littered the banquet room.

Across the room, Wendy preened, stroking her hair and laughing loudly at something Jason said. Claire, ever the professional, fought the urge to roll her eyes and leaned forward as her submission began to play.

Nicole and Kyle's engagement unfolded onscreen, a brief super-cut that Luke had put together. Her stomach clenched again. Every second was expertly edited, each frame beautiful and poignant. Luke might have been an asshole, but there was no denying he knew what he was doing behind a camera. Each detail was expertly captured, from the long-awaited "yes" to the B-roll that artistically captured the details—the shoes, the carriage, even the way Nicole's dress swirled around her in slow motion when she twirled.

When the video ended, the applause was thunderous. Claire wiped her sweaty palms on her skirt, preparing to stand up. Eunice reached across the table and patted her on the arm. "Beautiful, dear," she said.

"And the winner of the Planner of the Year Award is…"

Why did the announcer pause? Was he doing this dramatic effect, or was he genuinely confused? Hartley wasn't a difficult name to pronounce.

"Wendy Flutter?" He looked offstage and cocked his head.

What. The. Fuck. How was this possible? It couldn't be. Who could have possibly preferred a generic restaurant proposal to Claire's beautifully crafted and hand-tailored expression of love and friendship? Her hands clenched into fists. Her face must have been the color of a fire hydrant. She was going to schedule a meeting with the town council who voted on the entries. Something had clearly gone wrong. Wendy was not going to win. She couldn't.

The room fell silent as Wendy stood. Someone coughed, and eventually some applause broke out, but it died before she even made it to the stage.

Sawyer rubbed Claire's back, but no amount of comfort was going to calm her down. She was going to explode. She was going to stand up, smash this chair over the table, and stage an impromptu cage match with Wendy. Who needed one lawsuit when you could have two?

Wendy tripped over the hem of her dress as she climbed the stairs to the stage, overhead lights glaring off her purple sequins and blinding the front row. She grabbed the diamond-shaped glass award from the presenter and fist pumped with it.

"Look who's Planner of the Year now, Claire," she slurred into the microphone, brandishing the award.

Claire moved to stand up, but Sawyer pushed her back in her seat.

"Not yet. Breathe."

She froze even though every muscle in her body screamed for her to flee. Okay, so this wasn't the Oscars. There probably wasn't a camera zooming in on her face to showcase her humiliation to the world. But dammit, she was a professional. And she cared about her reputation in the small business community. She fought to fix a pleasant, neutral expression on her face as the treacherous, fiancé-stealing, carriage-tampering sewer rat began her monologue.

"You look like you're trying to hold in a sneeze. Try again." Sawyer whispered.

She un-pursed her lips.

"I'd like to thank everyone who helped make this possible. My parents, for giving birth to an event planning genius." Wendy giggled. "My boyfriend, Jason, for always being so supportive and having the biggest dick this side of the Mississip—"

The award fell from her hand and hit the floor with a thunk.

Unlike Claire's hopes and dreams, it refused to shatter into a thousand pieces. Great.

"Oopsie," Wendy said, bending over to pick it up. When she rose, her sweetheart neckline had dipped even more dramatically, leaving one breast completely exposed.

A gasp split the room. The country club owner at Claire's table leaned forward intently. His wife swatted him with a program. One balding man at the next table removed his glasses and cleaned them to get a better look.

Wendy appeared to be so intoxicated that she didn't notice her wardrobe malfunction. Her eyes were slightly crossed as she continued. A lone camera shutter clicked.

The emcee approached and tried to whisper in her ear, but Wendy fought him off with the award.

"Get off, I'm not done. And thank you, Chamber of Commerce," she said, waving her arm grandly, "for recognizing my potential and my true talent in the field of event planning. I guess the best woman finally won this year," she said, turning on her heel and walking offstage.

"Uhhhh. Next up, Best Food Truck," the emcee continued. He pulled an antibacterial wipe from a tub and wiped down the microphone and podium.

"Let's go," Sawyer said, pulling Claire to her feet and laying one hand protectively at the small of her back.

She should stay for the rest of the awards. It wasn't a good look to duck out before all the winners had been recognized. But she didn't care. Her entire body burned with the fire of a million suns. She held her head high and took short, measured steps on the way out despite the desire to scream until the entire remaining row of awards shattered. She waved goodbye at a few business owners on her way out.

"Miss Hartley," someone called as she had her hand on the door. "Could I bother you for a quote for the *Standard Times*?"

Claire whirled around, ready to explode. How had the press gotten inside? Officer Shiccitano was failing miserably at his job. She would have been better protected by half a ham sandwich.

"He means for the event." Sawyer nudged her with his elbow, and it was like the beak of a dolphin crashing into her rib cage at thirty miles an hour.

Claire winced and set her gaze on the reporter with a pad of paper and press badge. "Sure. I would like to extend a formal congratulations to Wendy and The Yes Makers. That restaurant proposal was really...unique. I'm sure we both have a lot of exciting proposals in the works this year. Check out my blog for more Happily Ever Afters." She whirled and pushed through the double doors to the outside, not waiting for a response.

Sawyer followed close behind her. "Are you okay? Do you need anything? Froyo?"

She exhaled noisily and turned to face him. "I'm good. I'm just going to go home. Or maybe drink a fifth of vodka and run a 5K. I haven't decided. See you later?"

"Okay," he said slowly. "See you later."

She climbed into her car and flung her clutch into the passenger seat. She pulled out of the parking lot, waving at Sawyer, who still hadn't moved. Her grip was so tight on the steering wheel that her hands ached.

A single parking spot was open on the corner by her third-favorite bodega, and she whipped into it without thought. All at once, she was overwhelmed by every negative feeling she had harbored for the last four months. She emitted a scream that was so loud she could have sworn she saw the glass shudder. Was screaming therapy a thing? If not, maybe it should be.

Her phone vibrated, and she pulled it out of her purse. Ignoring the text that had just popped up from her mother, she went straight to her group text message with Mindy and Nicole. Her hands shook as she typed a message.

Claire: *Code Purple. This is not a drill. Bring your college yearbooks and meet me at the warehouse tonight at 10.*

CHAPTER TWENTY-FIVE

To Do:
- Update Code Purple protocol
- Nail that skeezy fiancé-stealing twat to the wall

"Thank you for coming tonight. I know I've never called a real Code Purple before, so great job on the quick and organized response. Although next time, Nicole, try to remember the freeze-dried meals and guide to edible plants in the Northeast that I stashed in your cupboard. I called you here tonight for two reasons." Claire paced back and forth in front of the whiteboard, opening and closing her collapsible pointer. "I have to tell you both something. Try not to freak out."

Mindy and Nicole sat at the conference table. Nicole was in her PJs, and Mindy's hair and clothing were so disheveled it looked as though she had just climbed out of a wind tunnel. Rosie had flopped dramatically into her bed in the corner of the warehouse. Mindy was taking notes on her tablet, and Nicole was trying and failing to stifle her yawns.

"First, the slightly less terrible thing. Wendy won tonight."

Nicole stopped yawning and looked scandalized. Mindy slammed the table with two fists before standing and putting her coat on.

"Are you freaking kidding me? Where is this bitch? Let's go, right now. I'm going to drive my car through her house."

"It's okay, Min. Sit."

"It's not okay. You *own* that award. They literally made that award category because of you. What was her proposal? Let me guess, that generic-ass restaurant one from the blog." Mindy still had one arm in her coat.

Claire paced back and forth. "Bingo. That proposal didn't even need a planner. I don't know how she won. But I know she didn't do it honestly. This insane, disease-riddled koala bear has taken too much from me. At some point, you have to stop waiting for the universe to dole out your karma. Today, I'm going to be the karma. I'm going to find out how she did this. And then I'm going to use that information to get her to drop the lawsuit. Who's down for a stakeout?"

Nicole put her hand up.

"Did you have a question or are you committing to the stakeout?" Claire asked.

"Both. Will there be snacks?"

"Obviously. Next question," she said, pointing the rod at Mindy, who also had her hand up.

"When do we start?"

"Tomorrow night. Saturday is Jason's poker night, so if she's going to do anything nefarious, it'll be while he's gone. Now what do we need for a proper stakeout?"

Claire put down her pointer and picked up a pink white-board marker. She wrote "snacks" on the board.

"My camera," Nicole said. "To capture any evidence."

Claire wrote it down.

"I've been meaning to re-think my stakeout wardrobe. Last time I went with a leather miniskirt, and that really wasn't conducive to sneaking around the park at night," Nicole said thoughtfully.

Sneak-appropriate outfit went on the board below "camera."

"How about a box of live snakes to fling at Wendy?" Mindy suggested.

"I'm trying to avoid more lawsuits, remember?" Claire capped the marker and set it on the tray. It was time to stop avoiding the bigger problem. "We can worry about the list a little later. There's something else I need to tell you about. Slightly more terrible."

"Okay, what's the more terrible thing?" Mindy took off her coat and slung it over the back of her chair. A white handprint was imprinted on the back of her skirt.

Claire took a deep breath. "So, you both know my biological father has made an unwelcome re-appearance."

Nicole and Mindy grumbled.

"What you don't know is that he didn't show up to make sure I was ok after my stabbing and near-death inci-dent. No. He showed up to pressure me into helping the FBI coerce information out of Barney so they can get closure for the families of the victims. Oh, and he thinks Barney was part of a big, murderous cult that hates women."

Nicole gasped. "He wants you to *what*?"

Claire rehashed the story of the suspected cult, the body locations, and Barney's insistence on speaking only to her.

Nicole's mouth had dropped open. "When do you go see him?"

Claire pushed back from the table and rose, beginning to pace again. "Soon, but I feel like I need to do some research before confronting him. Maybe I can get him to slip up a little or piss him off enough to give me something. Have any of you ever seen this symbol?"

Claire pulled her sleeve and bra strap to the side and revealed the figure carved into her chest.

"What is it?" Nicole asked, standing up and coming closer to get a better look. "Oh, it looks kind of like a hiero-glyphic. I've never seen it before."

"This symbol was found on over a hundred bodies recovered all over the country. I'm the first live person with the mark. They think it's the cult's symbol."

Nicole's eyes watered. "I can't believe he branded you. Stabbing is bad enough, but this is worse, somehow," she said, staring at it. She dabbed at her eyes with her sleeve.

Mindy walked over to Claire. Her nose was centimeters from Claire's skin. "What the hell is it? It looks like a three-legged stick figure."

"I don't know. And neither do they. I've Googled every-thing I can think of."

"You should go talk to Professor Burke," Nicole chimed in.

"Who?"

"The archaeology professor from Venor. Remember we almost took her historical symbology class because it sounded cool?"

"I forgot about her. I'll email her and see if I can drop in on her office hours this week. She should be doing a summer term. Nicole, is that your yearbook?"

Nicole slid it across the highly polished table.

"Let's see, Barney would have been two years above us… Ugh, here he is." Claire shuddered as she looked into the soulless eyes of the man she had known as Bernard Twigg before he legally changed his name to Barney Windsor. He had been probably fifty pounds heavier in college, and a shaggy mop of hair nearly covered one eye.

Mindy peeked over her shoulder. "Activities: business club, whittling—boy, he's not kidding—Future Entrepreneurs of America, and something called ESA. What the heck is that?"

Claire shrugged. "Extreme Sociopathic Assholes?"

Nicole tilted her head to the side like a confused puppy. "Wasn't there a frat called ESA?"

Mindy nodded. "A super lame one next to the football house. I think they kicked you out if your GPA dropped lower than a 3.8. They only had like one party a year."

Claire rolled her eyes. "It makes sense that Barney would have been in the lamest frat."

As Mindy typed on her tablet, Nicole came over to Claire and put her arm around her. "How are you, really?"

"A little pissed, if I'm being honest," Claire said, making circles on the table with her pen cap.

"I'm sorry. Have you heard from Luke?"

Claire shook her head. "Not since I spoke to him after the ice cream and pizza incident. He's trying. The documentary was beautiful. I get what he's trying to do, I really do. It's not just a career thing for him like I thought. He really wants to tell their stories. But I've got enough going on. I'm not ready to dig into the most traumatizing event of my entire life in therapy, let alone on camera."

"And he will respect that. Or I will murder him," Nicole said while stroking Claire's hair.

Mindy snapped her tablet case shut. "Okay, I emailed

Professor Burke to see if she can do a meeting. I'm sure she'll be happy to help. As for the stakeout, I will bring chocolate chip cookies and juice boxes."

"Do the cookies have anything to do with the giant flour handprint on your ass?" Claire raised an eyebrow.

Mindy spun several times, staring at her rear. "No comment."

Nicole laughed. "Cheesy puffs. And baby carrots. The orange essentials."

"Good. I'll get the wine and soft pretzels for debriefing at my place after the mission."

They reached out to stack hands.

"Karma on three," Mindy said. "One, two—"

"Karma!" they called in unison.

CHAPTER TWENTY-SIX

To Do:
- Buy soft pretzels
- Pack stakeout bag
- Call safe company about custom safe

"So, you're sure the guest list is set for the gallery proposal? All the family members RSVP'd?" Claire munched on a chocolate chip cookie in the front seat of her car. Mindy sat next to her holding a giant tub of cheese balls. A single overhead light flickered a few parking spaces down.

"Yes, they're all coming, and they all know not to approach until after Aaron proposes."

"And the caterers are prepping some certified gluten-free hors d'oeuvres for Aunt Muriel?"

"Claire," Nicole said, popping up in the back seat where

she had been taking a light snooze. "Is this a stakeout or a board meeting?"

"You're right, sorry." Claire glanced at her watch. "It's 7:45. He should be leaving any second."

"You really think she'll do something shady when he leaves?" Nicole reached a hand into the front seat and fished around in the cheese ball barrel.

"I just have a feeling. I know she cheated. I just need to know how she did it." Claire tightened her grip on the binoculars she had borrowed from Kyle. There was movement in the window of Wendy's apartment. It had only taken five seconds of Googling to figure out where the award-stealing hag lived.

The back of Claire's neck prickled. It just wasn't fair. What kind of universe allowed a woman to steal a fiancé, sue her competition, *and* unfairly win an esteemed professional award? She tightened her grip on the steering wheel. Luck hadn't been on her side this year. But maybe—just maybe—the universe would throw her a bone tonight.

The front door of the apartment opened, and they all jumped, slinking down into their seats. "See you later, babe," a masculine voice called through the crack in Claire's window.

Jason walked out into the moonlight, wearing a sports jersey and baggy blue jeans. Claire rolled her eyes. He was off to his poker night with the guys from his college frat, same as every Saturday night.

"Oh, wait," he said, turning around. "Do you have an extra twenty? I just remembered I'm short."

"Yeah, in my wallet. But just take one, not four like last time. I know when you steal from me, Jason." Wendy's shrill voice penetrated the night air like a tornado siren.

Jason's dramatic eye roll was clearly visible from their hidden position. Claire smirked. There had been many occasions when she'd check her wallet at brunch on a Sunday only to find a handful of ones.

"See you later." He reappeared and strutted down the sidewalk, humming a song that Claire immediately recognized from Mindy's preference for pop radio.

"Right on time," Claire said as his car disappeared around a corner.

"What do we do now?" Mindy asked in a hushed whisper. "Sneak up to the window and try to listen?"

"Too risky. There's not enough cover," Claire said, gesturing to the flowerbeds outside Wendy's windows. "We'll just have to wait to see if she leaves."

As if she had been summoned, Wendy's head poked out the front door. Her beak-like nose swung from side to side as she surveyed the parking lot. Seemingly satisfied, she shut the door and disappeared back inside.

"She was one hundred percent making sure that Jason's car was gone," Nicole said, grabbing the binoculars that were slung around Claire's neck and leaning into the front seat.

Claire gagged and pulled them off. They all pressed forward, staring at the curtains that covered the windows. Was she about to come out? Where would she go?

Suddenly, Claire's car horn honked.

"*Shit shit shit*," she said. Betrayed once again by her oversized breasts. How was she supposed to have a covert operation when they were sabotaging her at every turn?

Claire and Mindy pulled the levers on their seats and flew backward. If Wendy came out and caught them like this, it would only add more ammunition to her lawsuit. Claire said a silent prayer as the seconds ticked by.

"Maybe she didn't hear," Nicole whispered. Her leg was trapped underneath Mindy's headrest.

Claire raised herself slightly off the seat. "Shit, I think she's coming out. What the hell is she wearing?"

Mindy and Nicole popped their heads up.

Nicole gagged. "I think I can see her cervix."

Wendy was wearing a black dress that looked part bandage dress, part catsuit. It was so short it would make an adult film actress blush. She had thoughtfully paired the outfit with thigh-high boots. Claire would have bet her last dollar that there was a riding crop in her purse.

"Is she going clubbing? Or maybe to one of those underground rich person sex parties?" Mindy whispered.

"There's only one way to find out," Claire murmured. She slid her keys into the ignition.

"Shh, she's coming," Mindy hissed.

"Yeah, I'll meet you in the lobby in a few minutes. Yes, I'm wearing what you asked." Wendy opened her car door and tossed her purse inside. Claire shut her eyes as Wendy swung her legs into the car. She didn't need to know if Wendy was wearing underwear beneath the skintight dress.

"Ohmygodshe'sanescort," Nicole said all in one breath.

"She can't be talking to Jason, he just left," Claire said. Every nerve in her body was tingling head to toe. What was this feeling? Vengeance? "I almost feel bad for the guy."

Wendy checked her makeup in the mirror for what felt like an eternity. Finally, she threw her car into reverse and careened for the exit.

"Follow her!" Mindy cried out and pointed out the windshield.

Claire turned the car on and stomped on the gas. She swung out onto Bramble Drive and followed Wendy at a distance. They were heading northeast, back in the direction of downtown.

"Shit, that car is about to cut us off—" Nicole gestured to a car pulling out between Wendy's car and Claire's. "We'll lose track of her."

"Nah," Claire said, gently applying her brakes. "It's better to keep a car between us so she doesn't recognize us. We'll see if she turns."

"You're weirdly calm," Mindy observed. She popped another cheese puff in her mouth.

"It's kind of fun being the stalker and not the stalkee for once. Do you think my stalker's here too? Following behind us? Maybe he'll be a witness for us at the mediation meeting."

Nicole turned around. "No one's following us. Where's Officer Shiccitano?"

"I told him I was spending the night with two friends. Apparently, I can't be in danger with you guys around. Oh, she's turning!"

Wendy's red Mercedes turned right onto Hawthorne Road. Claire activated her turn signal and slowed down. When Wendy was far enough down the road, she turned to follow.

This road seemed extra familiar for some reason. "Aren't we pretty close to—" Claire began.

Oh, no. A hotel loomed out of the night. Its bright, Vegas-like scene half blinded Claire. The Heirloom Hotel.

Wendy's convertible swung up the inclined drive and headed for the back of the lot. Claire's knuckles tightened on the steering wheel. Of all the goddamn hotels in West Haven, Wendy had to meet at the one where Claire had been abducted.

"We don't have to do this," Mindy said in a rush.

"Forget it, Claire. Let's just go home." Nicole reached through the gap in the front seats and squeezed Claire's arm.

Claire paused. They were at a dead standstill on the road outside the hotel. She flicked her turn signal on so violently that she scratched her leg.

"No. This ends tonight. Get your camera." She swung into the lot and parked on the opposite side. Wendy, tottering in her thigh-high boots, hadn't reached the entrance yet.

"Disguises," Mindy ordered, pulling a bag into her lap. She passed out wigs and accessories.

Claire became a redhead with a star-spangled hair scarf. Mindy was a platinum blonde with a press badge, and Nicole had waist-length black hair and an empty gun holster.

"There she goes," Nicole hissed. "Let's go."

As Wendy disappeared through the revolving door, they piled out of the car and slunk like cats through the night. Claire slid into the revolving door. Nicole and Mindy followed right behind her.

"Wait—" she said, but it was too late. The three of them were crammed in a single section of door. They had to shuffle together like a small herd of turtles until they broached the building. Not exactly the covert entrance she had been hoping for.

Her blood chilled as they stepped into the lobby. The hallway to the left seemed to yawn darkly at her. A short way down that hall was the restroom where Claire had been abducted just over a month before.

"You ok?" Nicole asked. She squeezed Claire's hand.

Claire snapped back to attention and nodded. She

scanned the room and found Wendy (or, more accurately, Wendy's underbutt) bent over at the bar, waving at a bartender.

"Let's sit," she said, collapsing into a low loveseat that faced the bar. She snatched the newspaper from the coffee table and opened it. Nicole and Mindy jammed themselves in on either side of her. Not suspicious at all.

"Elevator's opening. Is that—" Mindy hissed.

Claire's mouth dropped open. The paper crinkled in her hands. Dustin Foltz, a member of the town council, had just walked into the lobby. Was he here for Wendy? Was this how she had won?

"Camera," she whispered to Nicole.

"On it." Nicole drew her camera from her bag. Claire stabbed a large hole in the newspaper with the Swiss Army knife in her purse, and Nicole slid the lens into the hole. She snapped a couple of pictures as Dustin approached the bar.

"He's totally going to talk to her," Mindy whispered. She elbowed Claire in the ribcage as though she wasn't sitting there witnessing the exact same event.

Claire frowned. "Do you think she's sleeping with him? But that still wouldn't turn the tides enough. There are five judges for the categories."

"She didn't put on that dress to have a business meeting. Maybe she's sleeping with *all* the judges." Nicole pressed her eye against the viewfinder. The shutter snapped as Dustin put a hand on Wendy's thigh.

"Not even Wendy could be that low. Shh, they're talking. Let's move closer."

The three of them stood up and moved as a single unit behind a large art installation in the middle of the lobby. From here, Wendy and Dustin were just barely audible. The clerk behind the check-in desk stared at them.

"Is this what you wore for Councilman Hobart?" Dustin asked as he slid a finger from the top of her boot to the hem of her dress. If you could even call it a dress. It was more of a belt.

"No, you know I picked out something special just for you. You might be more interested in what I'm not wearing." Wendy sipped her drink and spread her legs apart on the bar stool. Welp, mystery solved.

The councilman's hand, complete with a gold wedding ring, disappeared under the hem of her dress. "How about we take things upstairs?"

Wendy bent down and retrieved something from her purse. She dropped it into Dustin's hands. "First, I want you to touch me with this."

"Is that—" Nicole hissed.

"My freaking award." Claire gritted her teeth. Her stomach lurched. It was bad enough that Wendy had cheated. The fact that she was using the award as a sex toy made things a thousand times worse.

"I could do that," Dustin said, dragging the tear-drop shape down the front of Wendy's dress. "Or maybe we could..." He moved closer to whisper something in her ear.

"If you want that, you're going to have to guarantee your vote for next year too." Wendy laughed, a shrill, nasally sound.

"Did they forget that they're in public? In a town full of the very married Councilman Foltz's constituents?" Nicole shook her head.

Mindy popped her head up from behind the newspaper. "I'm gonna go say something to them."

Claire grabbed her arm and forced her back behind the newspaper. "No. We need something more concrete. Just wait."

Wendy moaned on her bar stool. A couple seated a few seats away cast scandalized looks in her direction.

The Councilman seemed to notice, because he helped Wendy off the chair. "Let's head upstairs."

She grabbed him by the hand and dragged him to the elevator. His hand rested on her ass as they waited. When the doors slid open, the couple immediately grabbed at each other.

"Bingo," Nicole said, snapping a picture of Dustin cupping Wendy's ass while she seemed to be plundering for gold behind his back molars.

"Excuse me," a very prim voice said.

They all jumped. Claire folded the newspaper and tried to look calm.

"You're excused," Mindy said, flashing a brilliant white smile at the front desk clerk. "Shall we, girls?" They turned to go.

"Hold on a minute. You can't be taking pictures of the guests." There was a stain on the satin ascot the clerk wore.

"Oh, we weren't. We're location scouts for a new show on MTV, Murderous Business. We travel to businesses owned by accused and convicted murderers. Such as this one," Nicole said, gesturing at the lobby. "Do you have any comment on the allegations against Mr. Windsor?"

The clerk sighed. "I don't get paid enough for this shit." She walked back to the desk, a bit of toilet paper stuck to the heel of her pumps.

Claire grabbed their hands and they ran out of the lobby, cramming into the same section of revolving door again and practically tripping over each other in their bid for escape.

"Oh my god," Mindy said as soon as they were in the

parking lot. "I can't believe she really did it. She slept with at least two of them."

"Do you think it's enough to get her to drop the lawsuit?" Nicole tucked her camera back into its bag.

Claire climbed into the car and slammed the door. Her heart was beating staccato in her chest. "I'm not sure. But it's the best shot we have."

CHAPTER TWENTY-SEVEN

To Do:
- *Iron court outfit*
- *Look over opening remarks*
- *Get Aaron's final choice on caterer*

"WE'RE GOING TO CRUSH THAT DRIED UP, ONE-DIMENSIONAL sycophant," Mindy said as she crossed the threshold of Claire's apartment and flung her overnight bag into the living room. The blonde wig from earlier poked out through the zipper.

"Kyle sounded pretty confident," Claire conceded. They had called him on the way back from the stakeout. She threw a pile of mail onto the bar and let Rosie off her leash. Kara, her downstairs neighbor, had agreed to doggysit during the stakeout. Not that she knew about the stakeout.

Rosie sprinted for her latest favorite chew toy, a fish taco.

"I can't believe the mediation meeting is on Monday." Claire rubbed her sweaty palms on her jeans.

"Everything will be fine," Mindy said. "Kyle is going to threaten to counter-sue for intentional affliction of emotional distress, and if that doesn't work, you'll drop the bomb about her sleeping with the councilmen and threaten to go public with it."

"I do feel a little bit bad for Jason. Should I tell him?"

"Don't," Mindy said, pulling two wine glasses from Claire's cabinet. "He deserved it. He cheated on you, then he stalked you for almost a year while living with Wendy. He's the textbook definition of trash."

Claire groaned and pulled a bottle of pinot grigio from the fridge. She dumped some into their glasses and retreated to the living room. "I'm so ready for things to go back to normal."

Mindy snorted. "Are you kidding me? With Wendy? It'll be months 'til this thing is sorted out. But at least we can look forward to drinks tomorrow night."

Claire frowned. Right. Mindy's blow-off-some-steam night. She would be surrounded by couples and fifth-wheeling it with Sawyer in tow. "Right. Want to go over some finishing touches for Aaron's proposal?"

"Definitely. I have some thoughts about the lighting."

An hour later, every detail was hammered out for the gallery proposal. It was going to be magical. Claire carried their wine glasses to the kitchen and put them in the dishwasher. She picked up her stack of mail and flicked through it. Bill, bill, spam.

Oh, hell. A plain white envelope with no return address was nestled between a bridal magazine and her water bill.

Her hands shook, and it fell to the floor. She bent to get

it, and her elbow slammed off a cabinet door. She stared up at the ceiling. Why was she being punished?

Mindy's head popped up from the couch. "What's wrong?"

"Pretty sure my friends sent me another note." Claire opened a drawer and pulled out a pair of rubber gloves. She slid them on and ripped open the envelope. For once, she wasn't full of dread. She was sick of this childish game of notes and empty threats. If they wanted her, why hadn't they come to claim her?

Mindy stood and wandered into the kitchen. Her face was grim. "Want me to call Officer Shiccitano?"

Claire skimmed the contents and rolled her eyes. She tossed it onto the bar. "I'll give it to him tomorrow. It's just the usual, we're watching you and we're going to cut out your liver and make cookies with your spine, etcetera. Get in line, bitches. They'll have to get past Wendy first."

Mindy bent over the note and read it. She didn't laugh. "Claire, this is serious. We should tell the police."

"It's just another stupid message saying the same thing as always. Trust me, this can wait until the morning." And if the delay irritated her father, even better. "For a supposed organization of female-hating serial killers, their threats are incredibly underwhelming. Let's go to bed."

"If you say so," Mindy said, but she was still looking at the note. "Have you told Luke about all this? The cult and everything?"

"Nope." Claire pulled a sandwich bag out of her drawer and deposited the note and envelope inside.

"You don't think he'd want to know?"

"Of course he'd want to know. That's exactly why I'm not telling him. I'm not going to write his next documentary for him." She flung the bag into her purse.

"He'll find out eventually, though. I'm sure Nicole told Kyle."

Claire shrugged. "I don't care if it makes him angry."

"You know what? You're right. Fuck him."

Finally, they agreed on something.

Claire whistled for Rosie, and the three of them collapsed onto Claire's bed. The note intruded into Claire's thoughts as she settled down to sleep, but she pushed it away. Every minute of this week was already accounted for, and "worrying about notes from murderous idiots" was not on the agenda.

IT WAS MONDAY, AND THAT ONLY MEANT ONE THING—mediation.

"So, what are we not going to do this morning?" Kyle asked as he held the door of the courtroom open.

"Get angry and flip the table over," Claire muttered like a chastised child. How was she going to sit through an hours-long meeting with the woman who was determined to make her life hell without inflicting some kind of bodily harm? It would take a miracle. "You're sure we shouldn't even offer to cover her copays from the emergency room visit?"

"I really don't think we'll need to. I know John. He's a good guy and a great mediator. He'll see right through her circus. It's going to be fine. Chances of achieving a favorable resolution in mediation are much higher than going in front of a judge."

"I hope you're right," she muttered. If she had to pay Wendy a shitload of money on top of watching her sabotage her life on the daily, she was going to lose her mind.

"It's the meeting room down the hall. Third door on the

right. I'm just going to grab a coffee." Kyle veered off in the other direction.

"Okay." Claire wandered down the hall. A shiver went down her spine as she passed the annex where she'd awaited news from Barney's preliminary hearing. Her prison visit was scheduled for next week, and she would be face-to-face with Barney Freakin' Windsor. Not to mention his lawyer, Luke's velociraptor of a mother, who was also sure to be there. She pushed the thought from her mind as she entered the meeting room. One crisis at a time.

The mediator, someone Kyle knew from law school, was already there.

"Hi, John," she said, reaching out a hand to the portly, brown-haired man. His pants were an inch too short, and he wore blue socks with bulldogs on them. "I love your socks. I have a corgi at home."

"Miss Hartley," he said, returning her handshake and turning back to the material in front of him. Apparently, he wasn't much of a talker. Or maybe as a mediator he wasn't allowed to chat.

Claire settled into a swiveling office chair and put her purse in the one beside her. She pulled out a notebook with an elaborate "Mediation" label. If only Rosie were here. Mindy had taken her to the office.

Kyle walked in a moment later and sat next to Claire. He spread his notes out in front of him and glanced over them once more. "Remember," he whispered to her, "you're doing most of the talking. Stay calm and speak your heart. Don't let her get in your head."

"Thank you," she whispered back.

Someone screamed in the hallway. Claire and Kyle jumped.

The door banged open. Wendy strutted into the room,

clad in a fur shrug and a skintight blue dress. She wore a floppy-brimmed sun hat and sunglasses, like a celebrity avoiding the paparazzi. Her left arm was in a sling even though it surely hadn't been when Claire had spotted her at the hotel. Interesting. "What do you mean we're only going for half a mil? You promised me five mil."

Claire's heart thudded in her chest and her stomach twisted. *Half a million dollars?* While it wasn't as terrifying an amount as five million dollars, they couldn't seriously believe she had that much liquid cash on hand. She would lose everything.

"And I told you we had to be more reasonable about our expectations, Miss Flutter." A harried-looking man in a suit followed her into the room and shut the door.

"I'll fire you, you know. My dad says I can have whoever I want." Wendy lowered her sunglasses and stared at her lawyer.

"Let's just get this over with," he muttered. His shoulders slumped like he was already resigned to a very long day. "John," he said, extending a hand to the mediator.

John shook it. "Miss Flutter, I assume?"

"Yeah," Wendy said, collapsing into the seat directly across from Claire with a humph. She didn't bother to shake the mediator's hand. Hopefully, that would work in Claire's favor.

"Thank you both for joining us today. Miss Flutter and Miss Hartley, you haven't participated in a mediation before, correct?"

The women both shook their head.

"Great. So, my name is John Garcia. I'm simply here to help you reach a resolution. If we can't reach a resolution during today's meeting with the two-hour time limit, we'll continue to schedule individual and joint meetings until everything is resolved. You can confer with your attorneys, but generally in my mediations I like to hear directly from the participants so I can understand your unique situation. And on that note, please do not interrupt each other. You'll each have a turn to explain your side. Understood?"

Claire nodded. It would take an act of god to prevent her from interrupting Wendy's unending spew of lies, but she would give it her best shot.

"All right. It looks like we're here to discuss an altercation that occurred on May 25th, which resulted in injuries for Miss Flutter. Miss Flutter, would you care to make your opening remarks?"

Wendy spit a wad of gum into her coffee cup. "Yeah. So, Claire here beat the shit out of me—"

"Miss Flutter," her lawyer warned.

Wendy sighed. "Me and my boyfriend went to leave this party and Miss Hartley attacked me. She owes me reparations for my medical bills and pain and suffering. Every night when I go to sleep, I have nightmares of her just sitting on top of me, hitting me. I had to go to therapy. Oh, and she got my boyfriend arrested." She stood up and slammed her hands on the table. "I want five million dollars for the trauma."

Her lawyer sighed. Claire gripped the edge of the table. *Don't flip it.*

"Okay," the mediator said, "it looks like I have some itemized medical bills here. Mr. Collins, you've got a copy as well?"

Kyle nodded and slid a sheet of paper between him and Claire.

"I don't see anything on here about an arm injury, Miss Flutter." He gestured to the sling on her arm. "Was that something you sustained during the altercation?"

Her lawyer cleared his throat, but Wendy plowed on. "Oh, yeah. The doctors missed it at the emergency room visit, but it's really been acting up."

"Noted," the mediator said. "Miss Hartley, would you like to make your opening remarks?"

"Sure, thank you." Claire flipped to the first page in her notebook and took a deep breath. "So, in order to fully understand the situation that led to the altercation, I think it would be beneficial to tell you about our shared past." She looked at the mediator. He nodded.

Claire dove into her years-long professional rivalry with Wendy. She brought up the previous year's Planner of the Year awards and Wendy's seduction of her fiancé.

"And that brings me to our terms," she said. Her insides twisted. "If Miss Flutter isn't willing to drop this lawsuit, I'm prepared to counter-sue for intentional affliction of emotional distress. I have a few documents for you." She slid a small stack of paper from a manila folder to the mediator.

Wendy leapt up from the table. "Me? You're gonna sue me? After you beat the shit out of me?"

"Miss Flutter," her lawyer warned.

"Yes," Claire said calmly as she slid a DVD down the table. "I have copies for you as well." She slid them to Wendy's lawyer. "You'll find a timeline of stalking behavior dating back three years, including security footage from outside my office."

She glared at Wendy. That's what she got for sitting outside the warehouse with a camera.

A sheen of sweat appeared on Wendy's lawyer's forehead.

"Also on the DVD, you'll find the television interview where Wendy committed libel and accused me of sleeping with an employee," Claire continued. "And in the same interview, she became so enraged over questions about her relationship with my ex-fiancé that she flipped a table on live TV."

The mediator raised his eyebrows.

"And all of this evidence doesn't even take into account the incident of professional sabotage that's still under police investigation. A hooded figure loosened a wheel on the carriage we were riding in, causing the carriage to fall apart and injure my best friend in the middle of her marriage proposal. Wendy brought up this incident during the night of the altercation even though it was never publicized. How did she know about it if I never advertised the problem? Unless she was the one who did it."

Take that, bitch.

Claire cleared her throat. "And that brings me to the night of the altercation. It was the evening of my best friend's engagement party, an event I had painstakingly planned with very little time to prepare. Imagine my surprise when Wendy and Jason showed up uninvited and threatened me for turning him in to the cops. She then proceeded to insult my best friend's life work. I'm not proud of my actions that night. But twenty minutes after the altercation, I was chloroformed and abducted by the West Haven Widowmaker. So, my memory of the events right before aren't perfect."

"Blah, blah blah, we get it." Wendy slapped the table again. "Poor little Claire, kidnapped by an ex-boyfriend. Stop playing the victim card and take responsibility for your actions."

Claire moved to stand up, but Kyle laid a hand on her shoulder.

The mediator frowned. "Miss Flutter, please don't interrupt Miss Hartley when she's speaking."

"I almost died that night," Claire said rigidly. "You think I owe you something after what happened. I almost paid for that mistake with my life. If I hadn't been alone in the bathroom cleaning up after our disagreement, I wouldn't have been abducted."

"Cry me a freakin' river, Claire. You're alive. And you have to deal with the consequences of what you did to me." Wendy leaned across the table. There was cold hatred in her eyes.

"And one more thing regarding your alleged arm injury." Claire stared back at her as she fished a glossy 8x6 picture out of a folder. She slid two copies across the table slowly. "This picture was taken two days ago. As you can see, Miss Flutter was not utilizing a sling at the time of this entanglement with a married man who conveniently serves as a judge for the award Wendy recently won. But I'm sure those events are totally unrelated."

Wendy's mouth dropped open. She immediately ripped the picture in half and stuffed it in her mouth. She ran down to the other end of the table and snatched the other copy from the mediator.

"You have no proof," she said over a mouthful of photo paper.

"We have more copies," Claire said, leaning back in her chair. "We haven't released any of this to the press out of respect for you as a colleague. But if the lawsuit remains, we may re-evaluate."

"We need a recess," Wendy's lawyer declared, grabbing his client by the elbow and dragging her out of the room.

The mediator let out a long, slow breath and leaned back in his chair.

"You nailed it," Kyle whispered to her.

Claire took a sip of water. Rehashing her past with Wendy had taken a lot out of her. She would kill for a quick yoga flow and a brief nap.

"No!" Wendy shouted in the hallway. Through the window, Claire noted her gesturing with both hands despite the sling. "I'm not dropping it. She owes me."

Apparently, the courthouse couldn't spring for sound-proofing in their mediation rooms.

"Every injury you sustained during the fight was superficial. It even says it in your visit notes in the emergency room. At best, she might owe you a couple hundred bucks in copays. And this isn't even a receipt from a therapist, it's from some nail place on Broad Street."

"Jolisa is my therapist," Wendy shouted. "I tell her everything."

"That's not how it works. If they counter-sue in front of a judge, they will win. You could lose your entire business. Then you won't even have a platform to challenge her. Is that what you want?"

"I'm not giving up!" Wendy let out a frustrated scream. Suddenly, a fire extinguisher crashed through the window into the conference room. Claire gasped. Acting on instinct, she turned and threw herself across Kyle. Shattered glass scattered everywhere.

"Oh my god, are you okay?" Claire asked. Blood dribbled from a cut on Kyle's cheek. She pulled a tissue from her purse and dabbed at it.

"All good," he said, brushing a shard of glass off his lapel. "Mondays, am I right?"

"John?" Claire glanced at the head of the table. John had scooted his chair back until he hit the opposite wall. He looked terrified, but no worse for the wear.

Kyle failed to suppress a grin. "What the hell was she thinking?" he whispered to Claire.

Claire shrugged. She would rather light herself on fire than delve into the bag of angry cats and strap-on dildos that was Wendy's mind.

Wendy's lawyer poked his head through the now glass-less window. "On behalf of my client, I'd like to request that we schedule individual meetings. Thank you for your time."

John shook his head. "I think that's best."

CHAPTER TWENTY-EIGHT

To Do:
- Triple check Nicole's remote camera system
- Buy more dusters for gallery

"THANKS FOR PICKING ME UP, GUYS," CLAIRE SAID AS SHE SLID into the back seat of Mindy's Mazda. "I'm pretty sure the press knows what car I drive. Yesterday I was in the grocery store and a reporter jumped out from behind a wall of paper towels to take my picture. I thought they were finally backing off. But ever since the news broke about the notes, they're everywhere. They're driving me insane." She shook her head.

"Nasty buggers," Gavin said from the front seat. His British accent was honey to her ears. The sharp lines of his haircut suggested he had had a trim that day, and his warm brown skin was flawless. Maybe Gavin had a single brother.

"You still don't know who leaked the information to the press?" Mindy asked as she pulled away from the curb.

"No. My money's on a dirty cop, though. An officer got fired just last year for taking bribes."

"Wouldn't surprise me," Mindy said. "Gavin, you should have let Claire sit up front. She's had a hell of a start to her week."

"We can switch." He tugged at his seatbelt.

"No way," Claire said. "I'm already third-wheeling. I don't want to throw off your date night vibe. Does Mindy ever let you drive, Gavin?"

He shook his head and looked over his shoulder. "I keep pulling out on the wrong side of the road. Old habits."

Mindy rolled her eyes and pulled to a stop at a red light. "You've lived in the United States for a year, babe. It's time to accept our freedom units and customs."

"Inches. What bollocks," Gavin muttered, staring out the window.

"Mindy," Claire said, "Did you see Aaron's print? Coli framed it today."

"Yes, it's perfect," Mindy said with a smile. She turned down Electric Avenue. They were less than a mile from tonight's bar of choice, a country bar called Yee Haw's.

"Hey," Gavin said, whirling away from the window and pointing an accusatory finger. "We said no work talk tonight."

"You're right, sorry. Claire, tell us more about the mediation meeting."

Claire groaned. "Only in America could you destroy government property during a mediation and still think that I'm the problem."

"That can't have won her any points with the mediator. You said she stuffed the pictures in her mouth?"

"Yes! It was crazy. I wish Luke had been there to—" Claire stopped. As much as he would have appreciated Wendy's antics, Luke was not invited to take up space in her brain.

Mindy's eyes flashed to the rearview mirror.

Claire turned to stare out the window. "Anyway, I'm looking forward to a drink."

"And drinks you shall have," Mindy said as she pulled into a parking spot. "Let's do this."

Claire shuddered as she crossed the threshold into the bar that exclusively played country music. Getting through this night was going to require a large volume of whiskey.

Luke loved whiskey. She glanced at her phone. No messages from him today. What was he up to right this minute? It was early in Los Angeles, not even dinner time. He was probably busy lying to someone and/or bossing someone around.

"A warm-up before everybody gets here." Gavin turned away from the bar with three tall shot glasses. A bright green liquid sloshed inside, and there was a spoon on top for some reason.

"Thanks." Claire said, clinking and knocking it back without asking what it was.

Ugh. Black licorice hit her tongue like an electric shock. "What the hell was that?"

"Absinthe! You said it was a rough day."

Was this how people in England got through a rough day? Her whole body shuddered.

"Water," she begged the bartender. "And a beer." She slapped the tall shot glass on the counter. On her list of all-time least-favorite flavors, black licorice came in right below candy corn.

"Hey guys," Nicole called as Claire's beer arrived. "Oh, started without us?"

"You didn't miss anything," Claire grumbled.

"Great. Let's get six shots of cinnamon whiskey, please," Nicole said to the bartender. Oh, boy.

Claire stared at the amber liquid in her hand. Mixing whiskey and absinthe was sure to be a terrible idea. But it really had been a spectacularly bad day. And at least it would get the licorice taste out of her mouth. And maybe the thought of Luke out of her head.

"Where's Sawyer?" Kyle asked, turning around.

"Here," a voice said as the sound of cowboy boots rang out on the wooden floor. Sawyer emerged from the crowd wearing a denim shirt with a bolo tie, jeans that were entirely too tight, and a white cowboy hat that practically brushed the ceiling.

"Are those spurs a tactical weapon?" Claire raised her eyebrows. She pressed her lips together, fighting the laugh that was dying to come out.

"If you think I'm going to come to a country bar and leave without line dancing, you are sorely mistaken," Sawyer said, taking the shot of whiskey from Kyle. "Cheers."

They clinked and drank. The cinnamon burned all the way to her stomach. She really needed to slow down. If she wasn't careful, she'd end up riding the mechanical bull again. And no one wanted that.

"So, how was the rest of your week?" Sawyer asked. He ordered a water from the bartender.

Claire picked up her beer. "Well, the press are hounding me worse than ever since the news about the notes got out."

Sawyer put his hands up in the air. "It wasn't me."

"I know it wasn't you. And as if that wasn't bad enough, Wendy also tried to assault me with a fire extinguisher during our mediation appointment but still thinks she has grounds to sue me."

Sawyer shook his head. "That sounds about right. Oh, I love this song."

What was there to love about it? It sounded like every other country song—twangy chords interspersed with lyrics about a truck and a bottle of whiskey.

"Come on." He grabbed her wrist.

She snatched her arm back. "Where are we going?"

"To dance," he said, gesturing to the dance floor. People had lined up in two rows. Claire wasn't wearing nearly enough flannel for this.

"Absolutely not." She picked her water up and took a large sip. No one could force her to dance if she was hydrating. "I can't leave my drink unattended, Mr. Safety Expert."

Sawyer picked up her glasses and dropped them next to Mindy. "Watch these," he said before dragging Claire into the fray.

The whiskey and absinthe had met in her stomach. It gurgled angrily. Tomorrow was not going to be fun.

Sawyer shuffled her into the line next to him. "Here." His massive hands planted on his hips. "Like this."

The floor shook as he stomped his right boot twice and then clapped.

She glared daggers at him. If this had been a 90s party song, she would have danced him under the table. But line dancing was another beast entirely.

"Come on," he said, nudging her with his elbow.

She begrudgingly copied his movements. Oh no, there was spinning involved. She whirled to the left and to the right. The gurgling in her stomach was intensifying. Somewhere between the stomping and clapping, a trio in the corner of the bar caught her eye.

Two men in cutoff tank tops had cornered a girl in a yellow sundress. She looked terrified. On autopilot, Claire began cataloging the details—two white males, between 5'8" and 5'10", one with a backward facing Phillies cap and the other completely bald. The bald man wore a Venor University tank and neon pink shorts. The other had a tattoo on the back of his left arm. She stomped and spun around again. Were those letters? It was too dim in this bar to tell. She needed a closer look if she was going to prevent a crime.

The song mercifully ended, and she set off in the direction of the men, but they had moved. The girl in the sundress had slipped past them and was headed toward the door. They followed her.

"Not today, assholes," Claire said. She followed them outside without turning back for her purse. The ankle holster for Taser #4 hadn't gone with her outfit, so she hadn't bothered to put it on. She was wandering straight into a potential kerfuffle with no weapon. What was the plan? Shit, maybe she should have gotten Sawyer first.

The douche in the baseball cap walked underneath a streetlamp. His tattoo was finally visible and Claire gasped. The Greek letters epsilon, sigma, and alpha were inked into his skin. Tingles shot through her whole body, and the hair stood up on the back of her neck.

ESA. Barney's frat. And they were pursuing a helpless girl. The Solo cup didn't fall far from the keg, apparently.

"Where do you think you're goin', huh?" the one in the hat asked. He grabbed the girl's wrist and tugged her several feet down the alleyway, pressing her against the brick wall. "I said we're going back to my place." He leaned in and planted one hand above her head.

Claire's blood ran cold. Faint strains of country songs were still audible. She was not going to let this girl get attacked in an alleyway next to a country bar. But how would she save her? She scanned the dingy alley. Other than two dirty trashcans, a dumpster, and a discarded wood pallet, it was empty. She could turn back and grab Sawyer, but what if they attacked while she was gone? She hesitated with one foot on the sidewalk and one in the alley.

"N-no," the girl said. She couldn't be more than five feet tall, and she wore the same wedges as Claire. "I'm supposed to meet my friends."

"You can meet them later," said the other one. "You're coming with us. We're gonna have some fun."

"The fuck you are," Claire yelled in a much deeper voice than usual, yanking the lid off a metal trash can and marching down the alleyway. She stood in the shadows and held the lid in front of her. "Get away from her."

The douche brothers whirled around. They made eye contact with Claire and burst into laughter. "Oh, look, Josh. Another taker."

The bald one cracked his knuckles and took a step toward her. The absinthe and whiskey roiled in her stomach. She held the lid in front of her like a shield. She could throw it, but then she'd lose her only protection.

Lumbering footsteps echoed behind her, and she spun around. Was there a third one? She had only had two physical self-defense lessons, and none of them focused on fighting off three attackers at once.

Sawyer, who had thankfully taken off his cowboy hat, marched down the alleyway. His spurs rang on the asphalt.

"Problem, gentlemen?"

The douche brothers looked at each other. They seemed to be sizing Sawyer up.

"I said get away from her," Claire yelled. The one in the hat still had his hand planted above her head.

"You heard the lady," Sawyer growled.

The bald one took another step forward. Lights came on behind them and illuminated the alleyway. A car must have been turning down a neighboring street. Now was her chance.

"*Run*," Claire screamed at the girl. She pulled the metal trash can lid toward her and released it like a Frisbee. It sailed down the alley and clanged straight into the bald one's nose.

"You fucking bitch!" Blood poured from his nose like a spigot. Claire's stomach heaved.

The girl in the yellow sundress ran back out to the street.

"Claire! Claire Hartley!" an unfamiliar voice called from behind her. The alleyway was still illuminated. What the hell was happening now?

The men turned and sprinted down the alley. They jumped the fence at the end and kept going.

Relief flooded her for a split second. Sawyer was talking to someone behind them. Hopefully it was the police. She was fairly certain she could give a good enough description to track the men down.

Her stomach burned and lurched. Oh, no. She was going to—

"Get the shot! Get the shot!" A male voice called behind her. "Doug Schroff, *Channel Eight News* reporting live from the scene where the only living victim of the West Haven Widowmaker appears to have just assaulted an innocent bystander outside a bar. Miss Hartley, do you care to comment?"

"Hey," Sawyer's voice boomed behind her. The reporter ignored him.

An innocent bystander? She couldn't hold it in. It was no

use. She bent over in the alleyway and vomited spectacularly onto the ground.

"Miss Hartley! Are you drunk? Did you just assault that young man? What do you have to say for yourself?" Something soft bounced off her head. She glanced up. A low-hanging boom microphone. She groaned and whirled toward the camera.

"I didn't assault him. He was going to hurt that girl!" She gestured in the direction that the girl in the sundress had gone.

Doug reeked of aftershave. "Is that really what was happening? Or did we just witness the violent, alcoholic streak referenced by Rachel Islestorm, Mr. Windsor's attorney?"

"That's enough." Sawyer stepped into the shot and pulled Claire out of the alley.

"Not everything is as it seems in the Widowmaker trial," the reporter said into the camera as Sawyer dragged her back toward the bar entrance. "Claire Hartley is currently the defendant in a civil case for assaulting renowned local business owner Wendy Flutter after a drunken confrontation at an engagement party. An incident like this surely makes you wonder, is she really a victim? Or is the Happily Ever Afters moniker covering up something much darker?"

Sawyer marched her inside and stood in front of her to block their shot.

"Sawyer, no, I have to tell them—"

He grabbed both of her arms. "Look at me. They're not going to listen to you."

"But we saved that girl from getting attacked or worse." She gestured at the sidewalk outside.

"I know you did. But if you go back out there, they're going to twist whatever you say. Trust me. Stay put. Mint?"

"What? No, I don't need a—well, yes. Thank you." She took the offered breath mint and popped it into her mouth. What an awful night. She glanced back out at the reporter, who was still standing in front of the bar.

She turned to Sawyer. "Did you see that guy's tattoo?"

"The one of the hotdog surfing?"

"No, the Greek letters on his left arm. Epsilon, sigma, alpha."

CHAPTER TWENTY-NINE

To Do:
- Research ESA
- Upgrade pepper spray
- Escape room – combo locks

"ESA. LIKE BARNEY'S FRAT FROM THE YEARBOOK!" CLAIRE waved her hands. Why were they not getting it?

The gang had piled into a booth at the back of the bar. The droning country music was quieter back here, but she still practically had to shout to be heard.

Nicole shook her head. "Are you sure? Those two don't sound like guys who could meet a 3.8 GPA requirement. And just because they were in the same frat and are both douchebags doesn't necessarily mean they're in cahoots with Barney. He graduated like six years ago. They wouldn't have even met."

"Think about it," Claire said, gesturing wildly. The

absinthe was still coursing through her system despite the soft pretzel Sawyer had procured seemingly from nowhere. "Barney has to be working with someone on the outside. Or at the very least, whoever's doing all this has an in-depth knowledge of his methods and they're repeating them. Flowers, creepy notes, mail that's not postmarked."

"But you said they didn't react when they saw you? They didn't seem to recognize you?" Nicole shivered.

Claire shook her head. "I was mostly in the shadows. It's just a feeling I got. Like I was face-to-face with evil. I think they're the ones who are stalking me and leaving notes. You should have seen them with that poor girl. I don't know what would have happened if we hadn't shown up."

"Lots of frat boys are aggressive douchebags," Kyle chimed in.

Claire groaned. Why didn't anybody believe her? Internal alarm bells were going off like crazy, and they were all telling her the same thing—ESA and Barney were connected. Sawyer put a hand on her shoulder, and her knees almost buckled. He handed her a fresh glass of water.

"I'm going to tell Jack." Surely her FBI agent deadbeat father would be intrigued by this turn of events even if no one else was. She dialed his number.

"Claire? Everything okay?" Jack asked. He sounded startled to hear from her.

"Listen, Jack. Something happened tonight." She launched into the story of finding Barney's frat in the yearbook and running into the ESA brothers downtown.

When she finished the tale, several seconds of silence followed.

"As interesting as that is, it doesn't mean they're working with Barney. I doubt a bunch of nineteen-year-old fraternity brothers have the organization and time maintenance necessary to stalk and murder victims all across the country."

Claire sighed. "Okay, I don't know if they're related to what's going on across the country. But my gut is telling me there's a connection. We can't ignore this."

Jack paused. "I'll mention your theory to my superiors, but I don't know that they'll look into it. Thank you for bringing it to me."

"Great. Talk to you later." He wasn't going to tell his superiors shit. Why did no one believe her?

"Claire, before you go. My wife wanted me to ask you again about coming over for dinner. We live in Scranton, you know. Not far."

She paused for what felt like an eternity. Maybe she should run up to Scranton, rip his door off its hinges, and club him with it until he agreed to follow up on her lead. Spending more time with her absentee father was the last thing she wanted. And yet, she was curious. What had caused him to give up his life, give up being a father to her? Who was Trampy Tanya, and what did she have that Alice didn't?

Finally, she shook her head. "If you insist on doing this family thing to appease your guilty conscience, we'll do it on my turf."

"You want to have dinner?" The surprise in his voice was clear.

"Friday night, seven o'clock, my apartment. Bring your wife and whatever other miscellaneous family members you have that I don't know about."

"Great," Jack said, clearly surprised. "I'll tell her."

Claire hung up the phone. Maybe if she got Jack in front of her, she could make him believe her. In the meantime, she would do her own investigating. Who else was going to look out for women in West Haven? Apparently not the police.

She slapped at the phone in Mindy's hand. "Who are you talking to? Everyone you care about is here."

Mindy pursed her lips and turned the phone toward Claire. A news headline in bold red letters came across the screen. Drunken Widowmaker Survivor Assaults Innocent Bystander.

"Oh no." Claire grabbed the phone. The article had only been posted twenty minutes ago and already had two hundred shares. This was bad.

She skimmed the article. It mentioned everything—the name of her business, the lawsuit with Wendy, Rachel's accusations about Claire being an alcoholic. A video of her whipping the trash can lid and vomiting on the ground accompanied the article. The girl in the yellow dress had been conveniently cropped out of the clip. Claire glanced at the comments and quickly gave the phone back to Mindy.

"They're smearing me for stopping an abduction attempt." She laughed, but the end of the laugh broke into a sob. What patriarchal bullshit was this? She looked down at her hands like they had acted of their own accord. Two shots and half a beer and she had lost control to the point of assaulting someone on live television. It wouldn't matter if she came forward with the truth. The story was already spun.

She pulled her phone out with shaking hands and Googled the name of her business. Happily Ever Afters was a company formed around the idea of true love. Now the first ten search results were either about Barney or Drunk Claire assaulting a "bystander."

"What have I done?" she whispered.

How had the press even known where to find her?

Maybe someone in the bar had tipped them off. She scanned the crowd, but no one seemed to be paying attention to her. Maybe it had been the ESA brothers? But then why did they not react when she confronted them in the alleyway?

"You did nothing," Mindy said, grabbing her by both shoulders and startling Claire from her thoughts. She looked remarkably composed for someone who had drunk absinthe. "It's this asshole from *Channel Eight News* who spun the story to make it look like you went on a drunken rampage when actually all you did was save some girl from being assaulted. I notice they didn't mention anything about her in the article. As soon as I can see straight again, I'm going to find out where he lives and burn his house down."

"Lower your voice," Claire hissed, casting a glance around the bar. Someone in here must have ratted her out to the press.

Claire's phone vibrated in her hand. She glanced down at it and gasped. It was Alex, their newest client. They had just begun brainstorming his soccer-themed proposal.

"Hi, Alex. How are you?" She probably shouldn't have picked up the phone in a country bar with a fuzzy head. But when the clients needed her, nothing else was more important.

"Hey, Claire. Uh, I've been thinking. I don't think I need your services after all."

The bottom dropped out of her stomach. His girlfriend, Molly, was a pilot in the Air Force. "Oh, no! Did something happen? Is Molly okay?"

"Yeah, no, she's fine. I'm still going to ask her to marry me. I just don't think I need your help anymore."

Shock hit her like an icy fist. Her breath caught in her chest. Alex absolutely did need a planner. The coordination alone was too much for one person to handle, let alone the other elements they had discussed. He did need help. He just didn't want *her* help.

"Oh. Did you see the article? Because I assure you that's not what actually happened," she said hurriedly.

"Can you just send me the bill for what you've worked on so far, and we'll call it even? Thanks, Claire." He hung up.

She stared at the phone in her hand like it had transformed into a live snake.

"What's wrong?" Nicole laid a hand on Claire's arm.

"He fucking fired us," Claire said over the honky-tonk song currently playing. Her cheeks were hot. How had a simple night out with friends turned into something that threatened to destroy the business she'd sacrificed everything for? And why did saving a girl from assault warrant having her name dragged through the mud? It wasn't fair.

"He did *what*?" Mindy shouted. She whipped her coat out from behind her like she was trying to lure a bull. Several patrons turned around to stare.

"Alex fired us. He wouldn't say, but I think it was because of the article." Her hands clenched at her sides.

"I have his address. Let's go."

"Stop," Claire said, glaring at her. "First of all, driving buzzed—absolutely not. Second of all, driving a car through the home of a client who fired us isn't exactly going to help my image in the media."

Mindy scowled. She pulled her tablet out of her purse and crashed it onto the bar. "I'm going to send his mother those pictures I found during our surveillance phase. Bad news, Mrs. Palmer. Little Alex used to hide weed in the angel on top of the Christmas tree."

"Babe." Gavin yanked her tablet away. "Don't do something you'll regret."

"You want to talk about regret? Alex is going to be full of it. If he tries running to Wendy to plan this, she'll ruin everything."

"Maybe Wendy's sleeping with the newscaster too," Claire muttered and chugged the rest of her water. This night was over. "I need to go home. I'm calling a car."

Mindy and Nicole put their coats on and stood next to each other at the bar. They each held out one hand and made a fist with the other.

"What are you guys doing?" Claire asked.

"Just checking to see who's staying with you tonight," Mindy said, eyes narrowed in concentration. "Rock, paper, scissors, shoot."

Claire cringed. She had accidentally trashed her reputation. Her best friends didn't even want to spend time with her. They had to resort to children's games to decide who had to stay.

"I'll make it easy for you," she said. "Neither of you are staying. I'm a grown woman. I'm going to be fine."

"Aha! I win. Claire, I'm staying with you tonight," Nicole said, sucking down the last of her glass of water. "And I don't want to hear any arguments. You just stopped an abduction attempt. And if they were your stalkers, and they did recognize you—since that reporter so thoughtfully called you out by name as they were running away—they're going to be pissed, and they might come for you. And frankly, I would love to punch someone in the face tonight." She swung her purse over her arm.

Claire bristled. Company was the last thing she wanted tonight. "I can handle it. I have a fancy security system and an attack corgi."

"I'm happy to stay with you, Claire," Sawyer interjected. "Give your friends a break for the night. I'm probably the most qualified person here to provide private security."

"See? Sawyer will do it," she said. And he would be much easier to manipulate into leaving her alone. "Ready to go? I'll call a car."

"Sure." He stood. "I can drive, though. One shot in an hour is literally nothing when you weigh two hundred and fifty pounds."

"Great. Let's go."

"See you at the office tomorrow?" Mindy called after her, one eyebrow raised.

"Yes. Let's have the escape room brainstorm session at ten instead," Claire said, pressing a hand to her throbbing temple. "Maybe eleven. If they haven't decided to fire us too. We're going to need to run through the puzzles and time everything out to see if we need to add anything. I'll text you."

Sawyer and Claire walked to his car in silence. He pulled out onto the street and headed toward her apartment, dark shapes and neon streaks flashing as they drove. Claire rested her forehead against the cool glass and closed her eyes. The nausea was finally starting to subside.

How could Alex have fired her? Happily Ever Afters was the best in the business. One humiliating news clip and she was losing clients? She couldn't afford to lose clients with Wendy breathing down her neck. This wasn't like her. She never should have taken that second shot. She needed to get her head back on straight. No more booze.

The car ran over a small bump in the road, and she jolted upright, heart pounding.

"Just a bump," Sawyer said, giving her leg a reassuring pat. "Potholes, you know."

Claire clutched a hand to her thumping heart.

"Are you okay?" he asked after a beat. "After everything that happened tonight, I mean."

"With the creepy douches? Yeah, I'm fine. I just hate that people like them are out there, targeting women with zero consequences. Who knows what would have happened to that girl if we weren't around to intervene."

"I think you're right about them. They had a sinister vibe. It would make sense for Barney's old fraternity to have his back. But I guess the only way to know for sure is to talk to him. We'll just have to wait and see what Barney gives you and go from there. The police can't ignore something that comes straight from his mouth," he muttered as he parked outside her apartment building.

"You don't need to stay." She laid a hand on his arm. "I'm going to be fine. I'll deploy my anti-sleepwalking device and be good as new."

"Yeah, we're not doing that," he said, getting out of his car and shutting the door. "Nice try, though."

Damn it. He pulled a bag from his trunk and came around to the passenger side. He opened Claire's door and helped her out.

"Thanks. Wait, do you need to let Doozer out?" Maybe there was still hope for a night alone.

"He's at my mom's. She loves to babysit him."

Drat. Claire checked both ways before crossing the street. Even with Sawyer lumbering along behind her, the hair on her arm stood up. She paused in front of her apartment and looked up and down Beaumont Street. The only pedestrians were an old woman on a Jazzy scooter toting a bulging bag of cat food and a handful of teenagers in hoodies on a street corner. No one appeared to be looking at her, and yet she couldn't shake the sensation of being watched.

The Venor douches had left her ill at ease. Had they gone after another girl? Were they her stalkers? Even if they hadn't heard the reporter call her out by name, they had probably seen the article by now. Were they waiting in the shadows? Maybe having an overnight companion wasn't the worst thing.

"I feel it too." Sawyer put a hand on the small of her back. "Let's get upstairs. You're safe with me."

They trudged up the stairs to the fourth floor, casting backward glances the whole way. She slid her key into the lock and opened the door to a sleeping corgi sprawled on the floor.

Sawyer dropped to his knees next to Rosie and rubbed her belly. Rosie opened one eye and stared blearily at him, offering a brief *arf* before climbing to her feet and wandering over to Claire.

Claire gathered the dog into her chest. Thank god nothing had happened to her. Her downstairs neighbor Kara had watched Rosie while Claire was gone for drinks, but there was still a ten-minute window between Kara returning Rosie to the apartment and Claire arriving home. She wouldn't risk that again in the future.

Sawyer removed his shoes at her entrance and laid them neatly by the door. "Mind if I use your restroom? I'm a little sweaty from the line dancing."

"Of course," Claire said, waving a hand toward the farthest room. "Oh, if you want to brush your teeth, I have new toothbrushes in the medicine cabinet next to the toothpaste. You're welcome to take a shower, though I don't think I have any manly soap. There are clean towels in the linen closet. I'm sorry I didn't give you a chance to bring anything from your house."

"I have some essentials in my stakeout bag." He smiled and disappeared into the bathroom. He looked comically large going down her hallway, head level with the row of Planner of the Year awards. She frowned. That empty spot was going to haunt her forever.

When he disappeared, she took Rosie out for a quick pee. She spent the entire time probing every dark corner around her apartment building, but no tank top-wearing douche lumbered out of the shadows to kidnap her. Back upstairs, she took all the throw pillows she had and fluffed them on the couch. She added a pile of blankets and set a glass of water on the coffee table.

The refrigerator door creaked when she swung it open. An expired bottle of coffee creamer and an empty water pitcher stared back at her. Time to start a grocery list. She grabbed a pen from her purse and pulled a notebook toward her.

Why was this pen so heavy? She rolled it in her hand. It was the expensive silver pen she found in the woods while sleepwalking. Initials were engraved on the back end. She squinted at them. Her eyes flew open wide, and she screamed and chucked the pen across the apartment like it was crawling with ants.

There was a crashing sound from the bathroom, and Sawyer slid into the kitchen, completely naked and covered in suds. There was some kind of scar on his abdomen, a set of three gashes that were six inches long. Had he pissed off a demon?

The scar was less distracting than his mammoth-sized—

"What is it?" he asked, pivoting. He pulled a knife from the block on the counter. "An intruder? A note?"

She was so shocked by the sight of his naked body that she almost forgot to respond. "No, sorry, everything is fine. It's just a pen."

"A pen?" The knife clattered onto the countertop. Sawyer covered his junk and moonwalked backward out of the room and into the hallway. "Why did a pen make you scream?"

"The initials on it. ESA. Actually, Epsilon Sigma Alpha." Her whole body tingled from head to toe. She had surely just uncovered a clue. She could feel it. "I didn't notice the letters were Greek when I first found it in the woods outside Luke's house."

Sawyer swore. "So, unless the Toilet King was an extremely careless frat boy, someone from Barney's fraternity was in the woods outside Luke's house."

"Exactly. I was right. I'm being targeted...by a bunch of frat boys."

CHAPTER THIRTY

To Do:
- Escape room puzzle double check
- Grocery shopping – lasagna ingredients

CLAIRE WOKE THE NEXT MORNING TO SOMEONE POUNDING ON her door. She sat up, heart rate skyrocketing. Her arms were still tied to the bedframe with scarves. Pins and needles ran the whole way down them. She frantically twisted her wrist until she freed one and tossed the covers onto the floor. Rosie barked and whined at the bedroom door.

Claire freed her other wrist and grasped blindly on her bedside table for Taser #2. She left her room and stepped cautiously down the hallway.

Sawyer was already up and pressing a button on the security monitor. Claire's breath hitched when she saw Luke's hooded and sleepless eyes.

Sawyer turned to her, a question in his eyes.

Claire exhaled noisily. She set her Taser on the bar and ran a hand through her wild hair. It wasn't a murderer, but the conversation was sure to be almost equally as uncomfortable. "It's okay, he'll understand."

She threw the door open. The two stood and stared at each other, silent for a moment.

Rosie barked and leapt for Luke immediately, jumping at him and trying to lick his face. Luke bent down to pet her. She put her paws on his thighs, panting happily.

"You're supposed to be in California." Claire was almost surprised by how cool her voice sounded.

"I'm not. Can I come in?"

She slid the door open another few inches to reveal Sawyer, who had mercifully put his shirt back on.

Luke glanced at the crumpled blanket and pillow on the couch. His normally playful and confident eyes were stormy with anger, but he didn't say anything.

"I was just leaving. Claire was freaked out after we stopped an abduction attempt last night," Sawyer said, holding up both hands as if to proclaim he was innocent.

Claire shot a warning look over her shoulder.

"Yeah, Kyle mentioned that. And I saw the article. And the video. It's kind of why I'm here."

Damn it, Kyle.

Sawyer nodded. "See you tomorrow for class?" he said to Claire, slinging his overnight bag over his shoulder.

"Yes, see you then. Thanks again."

Sawyer stepped past Luke into the hallway, leaving a ringing silence in the apartment.

"Coffee?" she asked, turning to walk into the kitchen.

"Here." Luke offered a cup carrier with two dark roasts from her favorite coffee shop. He pulled a bag out of his backpack, revealing the tantalizing smell of buttery scones.

"Thanks," Claire said. She took the bag and popped the scones in the microwave.

"Are you okay?" Luke asked, standing in an oddly formal way. He shut the door behind him.

"I'm fine. Just a little shaken up."

He leaned against the back of the couch and crossed his arms. "Why didn't you tell me about the abduction attempt?"

She picked up the coffee to give her hands something to do. "Because you smashed my heart into a million pieces in Paris and then I fell off a boat into the river."

"Wait—you fell off the boat? Is that why I couldn't find you?"

She nodded. "And then I left, of course."

He crossed over to her and took her hand. She tried to snatch it back, but he gripped harder.

"Did you watch what I sent you?"

Claire nodded. Of course he wanted to talk about the documentary. He barely made it thirty seconds into a conversation without bringing it up.

"Do you understand what I'm trying to do here? For the victims and their families? For me, this isn't even about the documentary. I could care less about how many streams it'll get or how the critics rate it. This isn't a career move for me anymore. Maybe it started out that way when I moved here, but then I heard their stories. I care about them, Claire. Ariel, Shawna, Jennifer, Kayley, Courtney. They're not here to tell their stories. The media just treats them as a unit, an unfortunate set. But they lived whole, beautiful lives before he took that from them."

Claire held a hand up. "I get it. I really do. I'm just not ready to tell my story."

"I don't want you to." He cupped her face gently. "I'm

sorry for even asking. I will give everything up for you—the whole project—right now. I don't care who backs out. I'll find something else. The only thing that matters to me is you."

She met his eyes and sighed. "You can't give up the project. What you're trying to do is beautiful. Other than exploiting your ex-girlfriend, anyway."

"Ex?" His face fell. He stepped back and collapsed on the couch. Rosie jumped into his lap and started licking his chin. He pressed his face against her fur.

"You didn't get the message when I told you it was over and then fell into a dirty French river?"

Luke stood and walked over to her. His clothes were rumpled from the flight. A day's worth of beard growth shrouded his jaw. His eyes were red, and his shoulders slumped. "You can't tell me you don't feel this," he said, gesturing between the two of them. "Like a magnet drawing us together. A year ago, I would have never considered dropping a project for anyone, let alone an ex-girlfriend. But you mean something to me. Something I can't explain."

"Luke, I don't know what to say." She sipped from her steaming cup and set it on the end table. Maybe an earthquake would crack her apartment in two and she could just fall into the center of the earth.

He caught her wrist and pulled her into him, met her mouth with his own. Claire tensed, half-ready to test out some of her new self-defense moves, but then her body sank into the familiarity of his arms, simultaneously charged with energy and completely exhausted. Their tongues danced together, and she pressed herself against him, barely even worried about her mouth and how it probably tasted like a Starbucks dumpster. As much as she didn't want to admit it, he felt like home. Something in her bloomed, but she took a step back, placed a hand on his chest.

"Look, I know I don't deserve another chance with you," he said. "But honestly, at this point, I'll do anything. I can't believe I'm saying this. I've never groveled before."

She opened her mouth, prepared to shoot him down, but stopped. An idea had struck her like lightning. If he really wanted to show some remorse, she had the perfect solution. If she had to suffer through an awkward family dinner on Friday, so did he. She'd invite him. But she wouldn't tell him that she was also going to invite his brother, George. Drunk Claire had found him on Facebook the night before.

"Come to dinner on Friday."

"Done. Anywhere you want." The storm in his eyes lifted.

"Here. With my biological father and his home-wrecking wife." She stared him down.

Luke looked confused, but he evidently decided not to comment. "Huh. Okay. What can I bring?"

"Wine," she said, taking another step back. "I have a feeling we're going to need it." Surely alcohol wouldn't get her into any more trouble if she stayed in the confines of her own apartment. She'd start her cleanse the day after.

"I'll be there."

"Great. I'll see you then. Seven o'clock, don't be late." She crossed to the front door and held it open.

Luke wiped a hand over his tired face. He walked halfway out into the hallway. "Claire? About Sawyer."

She sighed. "What about him?"

"I don't trust him."

Of course. Her hands clenched at her sides. "Just to clarify, you don't trust the man who saved my life? The one who you hired to install a security system in my apartment?"

"That was before. Think about it. Whose company managed security for Barney's hotel?"

"Sawyer's," she said slowly.

"Exactly. And why wasn't there any footage from that night?"

"Barney tampered with the hallway feed."

"We don't know that it was Barney. And Sawyer conveniently showed up just in time to save your life and play the hero. Why bother having a security system in a hotel that's not even finished?"

"I don't know, vandals? Squatters? Sawyer wouldn't hurt me. He's giving me self-defense lessons. Why would he teach me how to most effectively kick people in the balls if he planned on trying to kidnap me?"

"He was in the building the night of the fire alarm when you got the note."

Claire bit back a sigh. He didn't know about ESA. He had no idea she had already uncovered who was responsible for stalking her. She had the answer to his question. But she didn't owe him anything.

She tossed her empty coffee cup at the trash can. It missed and bounced into the dining room. Rosie jumped on the cup. "There was video footage of the person who entered the apartment. Unless Sawyer shrunk a foot and lost a hundred pounds climbing up the steps, it wasn't him. He's literally testifying against the man who tried to kill me. Why would he be doing that if he was involved? I never took you as the jealous type, Luke." She lifted her chin. "I don't like it."

He glowered. "Just be careful."

She stepped behind the island to put more distance

between them. "Dinner party. Friday. Be there at seven with wine, or don't come at all."

Finally, he backed out the front door and left.

She wrestled the coffee cup from Rosie and slammed it in the trash can. How dare he storm in here and insult the man who saved her life?

Rosie whined. Claire slapped herself on the forehead. In all the craziness, she hadn't even taken her out to pee. Now she was failing as a dog mom. She pulled her hair out of its ponytail and snapped the leash on.

A warm breeze blew through the streets of West Haven as Rosie trotted down the sidewalk. Smells of fried bacon and pastries emanated from the café across the street. A pair of elderly men sat at a table in the park playing checkers. The city seemed far less sinister during the day. Still, she couldn't prevent herself from constantly sweeping the area. The park was clear of press and douchey frat boys, at least for now.

Oh, hell. The press. She yanked her phone out of her pocket and frantically checked the local news website. The article from last night was up to five hundred shares. Scores of comments either chastised her or praised her. Some people, at least, seemed to question why she would have attacked a pair of frat boys in an alleyway. But a fearful number of people were calling her a chronic domestic abuser. A pit formed in her stomach. *Channel Eight News* was going to pay for trashing her reputation.

Back in the safety of her apartment, Claire opened her laptop. She pulled up Facebook and typed George Islestorm into the search bar. There he was. Luke's older brother. There was no denying they were related. But while Luke must have looked just like his deceased dad, George was all

Rachel. His flat smile, the slightly pinched-looking nose. She clicked on the message button and began to type.

What were the odds that George was A) Local, and B) Available for dinner with his estranged brother on such short notice? She wouldn't know until she tried.

Luke deserved to suffer for what he did to her, didn't he? And what better way to make a secret-keeper suffer than keeping one from him? Besides, it was too late now. The message was already sent. And maybe she'd even be doing him a favor. His patricidal brother was one thing, but how could he ignore his niece and sister-in-law forever?

CHAPTER THIRTY-ONE

"You're distracted today," Sawyer said as he held a punching pad in front of his body.

Claire threw her weight into the next hit, a sheen of sweat on her forehead. She bounced on her toes, delivering a solid right hook. She grunted. "Can't imagine why."

"Come on, harder," he encouraged as she threw a jab. "That's more like it, I felt that one." Despite his words, his mountain of a body didn't budge an inch. "Want to talk about it?" he asked, voice lowered.

"It's probably more of an after-class kind of discussion," she said, nodding at the blinking security camera in the corner of the practice room.

"Understood."

Claire unloaded all of her frustrations into the next punches—frustration with Luke, anger with her father and herself. Unbridled rage at the press.

"Whoa, killer. You're going to wear yourself out. Slow and steady," Sawyer said.

"You're giving conflicting messages." She glared at him and blew a flyaway hair from her eye.

Rosie yawned in a corner and rolled onto her back, watching curiously as Claire beat the crap out of the punching bag.

"All right, that's enough for today. Your form is improving," Sawyer said, releasing the bag.

"Is it really? Or are you just saying that because my life is in shambles?" Claire tugged her hair from its ponytail. Honeysuckle shampoo warred with pit sweat.

"Both," he said, cracking a smile. "Froyo?"

"Definitely."

The three of them left the building, blinking in the sun after the windowless practice room. It was in the 80s today. Sweat dampened the back of her neck. The dreaded back sweat had returned. At least this time, no one would be erotically pressing their body against it.

Rosie trotted along happily, chasing discarded coffee shop napkins and wrapping herself around Claire's ankles.

"No wonder you trip so often," Sawyer noted.

She shoved him. "She lacks focus." Her phone beeped, and she reached for it, expecting an email from Mindy with the finalized catering menu from the gallery proposal. Aaron, at least, had understood Claire's explanation of the news article. She stopped when she saw Sawyer's side-eye.

He sighed. "It's ok, check your email. I'll keep an eye out. But tell me what's going on."

She glanced suspiciously over her shoulder. "Is this a

pop quiz? Is that guy reading the sports section at the bus stop going to jump me?"

"No, but nice observation skills."

"That's nothing. I've been practicing. There's a pregnant woman wearing yoga pants pushing a double stroller, but there's only one kid in the stroller. There's a watermelon wearing a diaper in the other seat. And then there's the little old lady pushing a rolling grocery cart with an unusual number of green beans, but not the right bulk to be anything dangerous," she said without turning her head.

"Wow. You don't need me anymore. See ya," he said, abruptly turning off down a side street.

"But froyo!" she called after him. He came back seconds later, laughing.

"Enough deflecting. What's really bothering you? Are you worried about next week?" Sawyer asked.

Claire stared at him blankly.

"Interrogating Barney? In prison?"

"Oh, no. Not that. I mean yes, obviously I'm worried about that. I'm still not sure that he'll give me anything of value and his buddies could be kidnapping women left and right for all I know. More things to weigh on my conscience."

He raised his eyebrows and kept staring at her.

She sighed. "It's Luke."

"Surprise, surprise. How was he after your discussion yesterday?"

Claire tugged Rosie away from a discarded hotdog. "He apologized. We talked. But then he said something that really bothered me."

"What's that?"

"He thinks you are somehow involved in my kidnapping

and the stalking situation," she said, shooting him an apologetic glance.

Sawyer stopped walking. "What?"

She tugged Rosie to the edge of the sidewalk, allowing a stream of business people to pass.

"He pointed out that you were in the building the night I got the first note. And that Sanctum was conveniently in charge of the security at the Heirloom Hotel. I told him he's crazy. We had video footage of the first intruder, the second note arrived in Paris, and you were with me for the third. I told him to stop being crazy. Honestly I think he's just jealous of the time we're spending together."

Sawyer's expression did not lighten.

"For the record, I know you have nothing to do with what's going on. I already Googled you. You weren't in ESA."

He started walking again. "You're right. I was never a frat boy. What does Luke think about the whole ESA thing?"

"I haven't exactly told him about it."

"Hmmm." Sawyer took a moment to scan the surroundings. Was he expecting to see Luke hiding behind a minivan?

"He hurt me," she continued. "Like more than I thought it was capable to be hurt by someone, especially after what I went through with Jason. I know it's stupid and immature, but I'm really enjoying keeping a secret from him for once. I'm actually inviting his estranged brother to dinner at my house on Friday. He accepted last night. Anyway, speaking of secrets, tell me about the redhead in all those pictures in your house."

The girl's identity had been a constant question in her mind since she had stayed over.

He didn't respond, so she glanced at him.

A black hole seemed to have opened in Sawyer. The

light was gone from his eyes, his jovial smile was gone, and he tripped on the sidewalk. She had never witnessed him trip before. Oh, hell. She had somehow made things even worse.

He was quiet for almost an entire block. Claire remained patient, tugging Rosie along behind them. He was still headed in the direction of froyo, so at least he hadn't changed his mind about their plans. All she could do was wait.

"Her name was Laura," he said, shoving his hands in his pockets despite his no-hands-in-the-pocket rule.

"Was?" Oh crap, was she dead?

"Well, is. I assume. We dated for three years, and on the night I was going to propose, she dumped me to go study penguins in South Africa."

"Well, that's just next-level shitty," Claire said, stopping in the middle of the sidewalk to touch his arm. "I'm so sorry."

Sawyer shrugged. "It doesn't help that I have a daily reminder of her every time I look in the mirror." He lifted the hem of his shirt. Three long, wide scars slashed his midsection. Right, the scar. She had seen it when he dashed into her kitchen naked but promptly forgotten about it in the wake of the large naked man in her personal space.

"Please tell me she didn't attack you." Did Sawyer have some kind of kink?

"No, nothing like that. I was hiking a few years ago. Ran into a black bear. Tried to escape up a tree."

She hit him on the shoulder. "Never try to escape a black bear up a tree! They can climb."

He sighed. "That's what she said too. She was a forest ranger. She chased it away and somehow managed to piggyback me back to the ranger station."

Claire's mouth dropped open. "That's the best meet-cute I've ever heard."

He shrugged. "It's too bad it amounted to nothing."

She shook her head. "Do you still hike?"

Sawyer shook his head. "I'm more of an urban explorer now."

"Guess it only takes one bear attack to ruin the woods for good." Claire wound the leash around her wrist just in case a black bear came lumbering down the street to snatch her dog.

They finally arrived at the frozen yogurt shop. Sawyer got their orders while Claire waited outside with Rosie. Since her stalker was getting progressively more ballsy, there was no chance of her tying her up outside businesses even for a minute.

She settled at a small, round table and pulled a binder from her purse. Maybe it wasn't smart to openly read her bedazzled cult binder in broad daylight on a busy sidewalk. But if they were watching her, she wanted them to be scared.

Sawyer set their cups on the table. "Find anything new last night?" He nodded at the binder.

"Nothing really. I did another deep dive on Google, but the only thing that comes up for ESA is their shining track record for GPA requirements and community service."

What she really wanted was to break into the frat house on Venor's campus and surveil them, but something told her Sawyer wouldn't approve.

"I ended up spiraling into some pretty terrible forums full of woman haters," she continued. "Maybe it'll give me some psychological ammunition to poke at Barney, but it was not the healthiest way to spend two hours." She yawned. "However, thanks to your meditation techniques and barricading my bedroom door, I didn't sleepwalk across the state last night. I did wake up in the closet wearing a barmaid costume from last Halloween, but better there than Hazelton."

Sawyer nodded. "That's an improvement. What was the sleepwalking snack du jour?"

"Half a protein bar that may or may not have been expired." Rosie stiffened at her side, and Claire glanced down.

"Hello, Claire," came a deep male voice from behind her.

In a flash, she was standing with her keys threaded through her knuckles.

Jack Hartley stood a couple feet away next to a waist-high planter, hands in his pockets. He clearly hadn't taken Sawyer's self-defense classes.

"Oh. It's you." She dropped her keys and glanced behind her. Sawyer had picked up the entire table they were sitting at and held it like a battering ram. He set it back down with a gentle clatter.

Jack took a step closer. His eyes flashed up and down the street. "I'm worried about your routine."

She raised her eyebrows. "My routine?"

"Every Wednesday for the past three weeks you go to Sanctum, then you come here for frozen yogurt. You're being too predictable. It's dangerous, especially considering your current troubles."

How the hell did he know that? Was he keeping tabs on her?

"I'm pretty sure you lost a say in my personal safety habits about twenty years ago, Jack. And stop spying on me. Sawyer, let's go."

"See you Friday," Jack called after her.

She fought the urge to flip him off. "Who does he think he is?" she grumbled to Sawyer when they were half a block away. "He ignored me for twenty years and then thinks he can come back and boss me around. Not today, Satan. I might even put laxatives in the lasagna. Happy freakin' family dinner."

Claire's phone rang, and she glanced down. It was her mother. "Do you mind?" Sawyer nodded.

"Hey, Mom."

"Hello, darling. Is your father bothering you?"

How could she have possibly known? Was she enlisting help from Brian, the PI she had hired to follow Claire during the height of the Widowmaker hysteria? Claire glanced in every direction, but the Red Sox-cap-wearing PI was nowhere to be found. In fact, she hadn't seen him since she had inadvertently gotten Jason arrested on suspicion of being the Widowmaker. To be fair, though, Mindy had almost assaulted Brian in an alleyway because she thought he was following Claire. He was probably screening Alice's calls.

"He is, as a matter of fact," Claire conceded. A niggling thought that had been on her mind for a week tumbled out. "By the way, I've been meaning to ask you. Did you by any chance hide like fifteen years' worth of birthday cards he sent?"

There was silence on the other end. Sawyer shot her some serious side-eye. Claire held her breath. Her mother had only just forgiven her for withholding information on her current stalking situation. Perhaps it was unfair to delve into this family chapter so soon afterward. But wasn't it hypocritical of Alice to hide something like this?

"Yes, I did." Alice's voice was breathy with a tinge of sadness. "I'm sorry about that, Clairebear. I may have taken your father's betrayal a bit too hard and forcibly prevented you from having a relationship with him."

A loud sob burst out from the other end of the call. Claire shot a pained look at Sawyer. Great, now she had made her mother cry. Was she seriously feeling guilty because her mother cried after hiding all evidence of her father reaching out to her during her formative years?

"Mom, you know that's not okay. That should have been my choice." This was shaping up to be the most emotionally exhausting week she'd had since she was brutally stabbed.

"I'm so sorry. I don't know what I was thinking. I didn't want you to get hurt like I did."

Claire sighed. "Mom, can we talk about this later? I have a meeting to—"

An explosion rocked the street.

Glass shattered in storefronts, and Claire hit the sidewalk hard, then rolled to cover Rosie, who quivered in panic. Sawyer hit right next to her. Car alarms whistled. Her ears rang like a thousand gongs had just been rung.

What was it? A gas explosion? A wall of fire was climbing ever higher a block down. She climbed unsteadily to her feet. Her knees and palms were scraped to hell. Everything was muffled.

"Are you okay?" she asked Sawyer. Her voice was muffled, as if she was underwater. He was still on the ground.

He nodded and clutched his heart.

She took one look at the shattered storefronts and picked up Rosie. The dog burrowed her snoot in Claire's hair. Her entire body was shaking.

"Come on, we have to see if we can help." She put out a hand for Sawyer and helped him up.

She jogged across the intersection and down the next block. The explosion must have happened right next to Sanctum. What if Sawyer's staff had gotten hurt? What if—

Oh, hell. She stopped in her tracks. Smoke roiled from a burning carcass of a vehicle directly outside Sanctum. The vehicle was in the same spot she had parked her Audi an hour ago.

Sawyer put a hand on her shoulder. He pointed to the sidewalk.

"You're dead, Claire Hartley," was scrawled in still-wet spray paint.

CHAPTER THIRTY-TWO

"WHO CLEANED THIS WINDOW LAST, A BLIND MAN COVERED IN Vaseline? Honestly." Claire opened a stepladder with a flourish and spritzed Nicole's storefront window with glass cleaner. The fairy lights strung inside the display stubbornly illuminated every smudge. The gallery was far enough from the blast site that the windows hadn't shattered, or Claire would have been dealing with a whole new crisis. Small miracles.

Luckily, aside from her main vehicle, Claire had only lost a scarf and a bag of dog treats in the blast. She had taken all her work and client property out of the car before she had left for Sanctum. Her guardian angel must have been looking out for her. She was temporarily driving the

Happily Ever Afters company van until her insurance could replace her vehicle. She mourned her little black Audi. ESA was going to pay, but they would have to wait until after Aaron and Jane had the perfect proposal.

A door in the back slammed, and Claire jumped like a gun had fired. Okay, so the car bomb had bothered her a little more than she had admitted to friends and family. The fact that someone out there hated her enough to go to such great lengths to scare her chilled her blood. All this because she had gently rejected a guy from her business class nearly a decade ago? And now his buddies were punishing her for putting him in prison? It was insane.

She sprayed the window again and scrubbed with a new paper towel. Why were they just continuing to threaten her, anyway? Surely her security system and one measly cop who didn't even watch her full-time weren't enough of a deterrent to keep them at bay. Why didn't they just come take her? Were they waiting for something? Jack's professional opinion was that they were just trying to scare her, but she wasn't convinced.

There was time to worry about all this later. Aaron needed Business Claire, not Emotional Baggage Claire.

The gallery teemed with Aaron and Jane's friends and family. The excitement was palpable. Nicole stalked around with her camera, capturing the family members. A couple of uncles were arguing over one of the paintings on the east wall, shaking fistfuls of cash at each other. A notoriously sloppy cousin was dumping something from a flask into her glass of Coke. Claire made a mental note to watch her like a hawk.

A harried-looking server slid through a crowd of Jane's relatives and ran up to her. "Claire, there's a problem in the kitchenette. Do we have a fire extinguisher?"

Claire craned her neck toward the back of the gallery. She didn't see any smoke, at least. "First cabinet on the left toward the door. Do not burn down my friend's gallery, please."

The front door opened, and Aaron walked in. A sheen of sweat covered his forehead, and he was paler than the last time she had seen him.

"Aaron! How are you feeling?" She quickly moved to intercept him before the family caught sight of him.

"Great," he croaked. He was now green as well as pale.

"Let's get you some air," Claire said, grabbing his elbow and bringing him back outside. The last thing he needed was an interrogation from Uncle Joe.

The heat of the day had died down into a cool evening. Stars twinkled pleasantly against an inky backdrop.

"Do me a favor. Breathe in for seven counts, okay? One, two…"

As she continued, Aaron breathed deeply until his chest expanded like a barrel.

"Okay, now for the tough part. Out for eleven." She counted down again. He slowly exhaled. "Let's do it two more times."

By the last breathing exercise, he was starting to look less green. He wasn't her first nervous groom-to-be. Hopefully, he was nervous because he was about to ask a life-altering question and not because he was planning to kidnap her and stuff her in a trunk later. But she had gone back through his criminal background check and skimmed all of his social media a second time. He wasn't in a fraternity in college. He wasn't out to get her. He was just a guy who wanted to marry his girlfriend. She needed to learn to trust her gut again.

"I know it's a lot," she said. "It's a big day. But it's going to be amazing. When the night is done, you'll have a beautiful, talented fiancée and a new life chapter to start together. Do you want to see what we did with your drawing?"

Aaron nodded. She led him quickly through the gallery to the back, where a closed door that was usually Nicole's darkroom had been transformed into a proposal nook. Aaron and Jane would have complete privacy for the big moment until they chose to share the happy news.

"See? It's quiet, secluded. It'll be just the two of you." She gestured to the bouquets of roses and the false greenery they had introduced to disguise the darkroom. "Nicole will capture the 'yes' from her strategically placed camera hidey-holes. Now, her family will surely stampede you with love the second you open the door, but you can stay in here as long as you want. And afterward, there's an open bar."

"Thank you," he said on an exhale. He seemed to still be following the breathing exercise.

She adjusted the spotlight below the print. Although his fiancée was the real artist, he certainly knew his way around a sketch. It was roughly drawn, but the similarities between the caricature and the real-life people were undeniable.

"You did such a great job," she said, patting him on the arm. "And that's a perfect rendering of the ring."

He shrugged. "It was no big deal. I took a picture and tried to make it as realistic as Jane would have. She could draw a better sketch in a coma."

Claire laughed and swatted at him. "She's going to love it. She should be here any minute," she said, glancing at her watch. "I just have a couple of things to check on. Don't forget, I have the ring. I'll pass it to you when you're about to go to the back room. Do you want to stand outside until Jane gets here? It's a little crowded in here."

He let out another slow breath and nodded before

disappearing outside. He cut through the throng of family and friends, wringing his hands and taking deep breaths. Jane's father clapped him on the back as he passed.

Claire took another glance around, adjusting a frame that was slightly tilted.

Hors d'oeuvres—check. The waiters were passing spinach dip crostini, mini crab puffs, and tiny shooters of tomato soup and grilled cheese. Jane's favorites. Champagne—check. It sparkled in glasses at the bar, ready to be passed out. The storefront was now gleaming, so Mindy must have finished the glass cleaning job while Claire was with Aaron. Claire had done trash pickup and some light power washing on the sidewalk only an hour ago, so surely it hadn't gotten out of control since then.

Her phone beeped. Jane had pulled up out front. A thrill ran through Claire. "Faces to the wall, everyone! Talk among yourselves. It's showtime!"

The guests whirled to face the artwork on the walls. Aunt Muriel pulled out her compact and trained it on the door. Claire shook her head.

She planted herself in the middle of everything, quickly swiping a crab puff that was about to fall from a tray and crumpling it into a napkin. She stuffed it into her pocket. Hopefully, she would remember to throw it out so it wouldn't become a sleepwalking snack later.

"This is so nice, Aaron," a woman's voice said as the couple crossed the threshold. "I never knew there was a gallery here. I wonder if they ever accept local artists for shows."

Jane stepped confidently inside in a purple kimono romper and combat boots. Her shock of red hair was peppered with streaks of green. A pearl clutch dangled from one hand.

"Couldn't hurt to ask," Aaron said, sweating under the overhead lights. His voice cracked.

Friends and family glanced at the couple out of the corner of their eyes, barely concealing wide smiles.

"Oh, it's my favorite concerto," Jane said as Beethoven's "Piano Concerto No. 5" played softly overhead. "This is my kind of place. Oh, and spinach dip crostini!" She accepted one from a passing waiter. "I want to live here," she said as a glass of champagne was pressed into her hand.

"Shall we look at some of the art?" Aaron asked.

"Of course," Jane said, taking a sip as they walked to the nearest wall. "Wait a fricken second—" Her systematically plucked and groomed brows knit together. "This is my painting."

Aaron stood next to her and feigned ignorance. "Are you sure? Maybe someone else just painted the same spot in the park as you."

"No, these are definitely mine. That's my niece," she said, gesturing to a young girl with cornflower hair giggling under a sun hat. "What the hell?" She turned, clearly searching for someone in charge to begin asking questions.

Nicole stepped in out of nowhere. "Hi, Jane. My name is Nicole, and this is normally my photography studio," she said, gesturing at the structure. "Your boyfriend wanted to surprise you for your anniversary, so he asked me to host an exhibition for you. It's an honor to display the work of someone so talented."

Jane turned to Aaron and hit him on the arm. "You did not."

He shrugged, still sweating, and managed a smile.

"I did."

"Oh my god," she said, pulling him into a hug. "I don't even know what to say."

He kissed her tenderly on the forehead. "You're the most talented artist I know. Your work deserves to be seen."

Claire sidled up to Aaron and slid the ring box into his pocket.

"You should really check out the piece in the back room," Nicole said, gesturing to the darkroom. "It's one of a kind."

"Sounds great. Let's go," Aaron said, a tremor in his voice.

Jane and Aaron walked slowly to the back of the studio. She clearly wanted to stop and look at some of her paintings, but Aaron guided her with a hand on the small of her back.

Finally, they walked into the darkroom. There was a soft gasp as Jane stepped inside and snapped the door shut.

Nicole sprang into action, picking up a tablet, and opened the program that was linked to a number of Wi-Fi-capable digital cameras inside the darkroom. False camera shutter noises came from the screen. It wasn't as good as having free range over the angles, but it would have to do for a couple who craved privacy.

Claire stood on tiptoe to peer over Nicole's shoulder. Even with the limited angles, the lighting was flawless. Jane's eyes sparkled. Aaron's smile was much more relaxed now that he wasn't in the middle of a throng of aggressive relatives.

Claire flailed her hands above her head, trying to draw everyone's attention. The relatives, who had clearly been waiting with bated breath for this moment, stormed across the wooden floorboards like a herd of cattle.

She held out one hand, certain that they would press their noses against the closed door if she allowed it.

"Shhhh, give them their space," she hissed, shooting a

pointed glance at Aaron's Uncle Joe, who had a GoPro on his forehead and a DSLR camera in front of his face.

The relatives reluctantly retreated a few feet, glancing at Jane's artwork but still focused on the door. It was so quiet in the studio that rain tapped audibly against the storefront. Thankfully she had counted on the rain and secured a very photogenic umbrella for their impromptu engagement photo shoot.

A loud squeal sounded from behind the closed door, and everyone crowded around again.

"Oh my god, yes!" Jane said, sounding slightly muffled.

Claire waved the waiter over, and he began distributing champagne. She took a glass, then immediately set it back down. If the press happened to stumble by the gallery tonight, she would surely end up on the front page of the paper. *Hartley the Harlot Dares to Sip Champagne.*

It was all Rachel's fault. If she hadn't accused Claire of being an alcoholic during the preliminary trial, the press would have had no ammunition. And now she was going to have to see Rachel's stupid, smug face this weekend when she visited Barney in prison. Ugh. There was time to worry about that later. She still needed to make sure the family didn't stampede Aaron and Jane when they came out.

Nicole's warm presence arrived at her shoulder, camera poised to capture the happy couple's exit, and Claire smiled at her best friend.

The antique knob turned slowly, and Jane and Aaron stepped out, not paying attention to anyone or anything in the room but each other.

"*Surprise!*" various family members yelled.

"*Jesus Christ!*" Jane panicked, screaming and flinging her pearl-studded clutch into the audience. It hit Uncle Joe in the cheek and knocked his GoPro off.

Claire snatched up the GoPro and returned it, retreating as the bride-to-be profusely apologized and was swarmed by family. Nicole, clearly grateful to be back in charge of the camera, whipped out the stepladder Claire had used earlier and climbed it, aiming her camera at the mob of joyous family.

"So," Mindy said, a spinach dip crostini in her hand.

"So?" Claire said, leaning against the wall and fighting the urge to take her phone out and jump back into the next proposal. They had a meeting in the morning with their client, Dr. Weaver, for the escape room proposal. Her head was buzzing with ideas.

"You're going to Venor tomorrow to meet with the professor about your mark."

"Yes, after the meeting with Dr. Weaver."

"And then on Friday you're having a dinner party."

"Yes."

"With the guy who smashed your heart and his mysterious estranged brother." Mindy raised her eyebrows.

"Yes. But he doesn't know his brother is coming."

"Right. I'm sure that won't backfire. And your biological father, who abandoned you two decades ago."

"That's correct."

"And his family, who you know nothing about."

"Just his wife, as far as I know. Trampy Tanya." Claire shrugged.

Mindy tilted her head. "You're sure they're not bringing your alleged half sister?"

Claire glared at her. "I can only handle two new family members at one time. I can barely even get Charlie to take my calls. The half sister will have to wait."

CHAPTER THIRTY-THREE

To Do:
- Pack disguise(s) and murder binder
- Pay cell phone bill

"You're sure we can get a custom safe in time? I can't believe he wants to do this proposal in just two weeks. It'll take a miracle for us to get everything done." Claire gathered her curly hair into a tight bun at the base of her neck. She pulled a brunette wig from her passenger seat and yanked it onto her head.

"Ooh, you look hot," Mindy said. They were video chatting from Claire's spot in the Venor parking lot. She was headed into the lion's den to meet with the professor. "And yes, I already called them while you were driving. They'll move us to the front of the line."

"You're a godsend, Min." Claire slid on an oversized pair

of sunglasses and added a mauve lipstick—a shade she would never normally wear. It made her complexion look like a beached tilapia.

"That's what you pay me for. Call me when you're done. I'm dying to know what this mystery mark is."

"Okay. Remember, if I go missing, this is what I was last wearing," Claire said, panning the camera over her outfit—a Venor University tank top and leggings. "Call you later." She ended the call and took one last look in her rearview mirror. She didn't look like herself. Hopefully, if the press was hanging around somewhere, they wouldn't recognize her either. And if her stalkers really were in ESA, Venor was probably the last place they'd expect her to show up.

Her alma mater looked and smelled exactly as she had remembered it. Claire rubbed one hand over a cast iron bell next to the art building. The bell was worn where decades of students had rubbed it for good luck. She walked to the quad, bending down to touch the vibrant flowers in the school colors—blue and gold. She, Nicole, and Mindy had laid out here for hours, studying for exams and tanning. The bush that Nicole had thrown up in after one particularly crazy kegger looked no worse for the wear.

She ached to be back in those crappy dorm rooms, where her greatest worry was getting an A from a particularly annoying sociology professor.

Claire turned and took a picture of the quad sprawled out in front of her, sending it to the girls with a simple caption: "Home."

Swallowing her nostalgia, she pointed herself west and headed for the academic center and Professor Burke's office. A handful of students were in the library, probably studying for their summer session classes.

They had changed the carpet in the business classrooms. The desks were still the same, graffitied with profanity and drawings of boobs. She went down another hallway, passing rows and rows of offices for various faculty. Venor was a small liberal arts school, so most of the non-STEM offices were crowded together. She knew the path well from chasing down her business professors. She found Professor Burke's door and knocked tentatively.

"Come in," a dreamy voice called.

Claire opened the door hesitantly, poking her head in before fully committing. "Professor Burke?"

"Yes, dear, can I help you?" An owlish-looking woman sat in a chair, sipping a steaming cup of tea. Her blue eyes were comically large and set close together, but the rest of her was tiny, almost frail-looking. It was hard to get a good look at her because her office was so dark that Claire had to remove her sunglasses. The window was covered by a heavy drape, and a gauzy scarf shrouded her lamp. Was that a fire hazard?

Claire entered slowly, wringing her hands. How in the hell was she going to broach this subject?

"Thank you so much for agreeing to meet with me, professor. I'm a Venor alum. I was hoping you could help me with something. It's kind of...confidential," she said hesitantly.

"Oh my, we don't get to help in a lot of confidential situations in the archaeology world," Professor Burke said, laughing and setting her teacup down on a saucer. "Most of the people we concern ourselves with have been dead for centuries. Please, call me Sharon. What can I do for you?"

"I was wondering if you could tell me something about a symbol."

The professor leaned forward in her chair, clearly excited at the prospect. "What kind of symbol, dear?"

Claire pulled a glossy 4x6 photo out of her purse and slid it across her desk. She had grown tired of yanking her bra strap every time someone wanted a look at her mark. Plus, it was starting to heal and lose some of its definition.

Professor Burke reached into her desk drawer and withdrew a magnifying glass, making her eyes even larger. She peered at the photo for several seconds. Suddenly, she burst out laughing.

"Oh, dear, you really had me going there for a moment. Who put you up to this, Professor Hummel?"

"What do you mean?" Claire asked.

"Come, now. You can stop pretending."

"I really have no idea what you're talking about."

"The figure in this picture is from ancient Greece. It's rather crudely drawn, but the resemblance is undeniable."

"Okay," Claire said slowly. "So, what is it?"

"This is the symbol for the Greek god Priapus."

"Priapus." Claire repeated. Why did that sound familiar?

"Yes. He was a fertility god. Protector of male genitalia and livestock, among other things."

Oh. Priapus, like priapism. Jason had once gone to the emergency room with a priapism that had lasted six hours. Served him right.

"You're sure about the symbol?"

"It's unmistakable. I have a vase at home with the same insignia."

"Thank you for your help, Professor Burke." Claire shook the professor's hand and hurried back into the hallway. She closed the door and leaned against it. The professor was still chuckling behind the door. Of course her almost-killer carved a symbol for a protector of dicks into her skin permanently. Why not?

She clenched her fists. What was she going to do with

this new information? She needed some retail therapy, stat. The student store had a modest makeup selection. Maybe switching out this dreary mauve lipstick would provide clarity.

She trotted down the four flights of stairs to the lobby and pushed open the doors to the courtyard. It really was a beautiful day. She desperately wanted to pull her phone out and check her email, but Sawyer's incessant stream of personal safety instructions echoed in her mind. She set off toward the student store.

Was it her imagination, or were those footsteps behind her? Students milled here and there, but campus population during a summer session was minuscule compared to a regular semester—maybe two hundred students max. The footsteps probably just belonged to someone heading to their dorm, but hair stood up on her arms. She stopped in her tracks and dug through her purse. Footsteps behind her continued for an extra second. Her stomach clenched. Someone was definitely following her. But how had they recognized her with the disguise? Her whole body tensed. What would Sawyer do?

She pulled earbuds out and popped them in but didn't turn on any music. Hopefully, her mysterious stalker would think she was totally unaware of her surroundings. She pulled her phone out of her purse and pretended to check her messages while walking. She activated her front-facing camera and zoomed in behind her. There was definitely a man in a camo shirt behind her, maybe forty yards away. He was following cautiously, ducking behind trees and lamp-posts. He was shorter, maybe 5'8", but jacked. His bald head shone in the afternoon sun.

Her heart thudded in her chest. Thank goodness Rosie was at the studio with Nicole today. Claire took several photos as she passed the science building, but they were grainy and poor quality. She sent them off to Mindy and Nicole before tucking her phone in her bra and pulling Taser #4 from her purse. She slid it into the side pocket of her leggings. If this idiot was toting a chloroform rag, she was going to make him choke on it.

She sped up as she approached the campus store. But the store wasn't safe—there was only one exit. She walked straight past it and rounded the corner of campus. Where could she go? She racked her brain as she walked. The man was still behind her, keeping his distance but following intently. Should she make a break for it?

As she rounded an upperclassmen dormitory, she spotted it. The communications building. Claire had written for the student newspaper in that building, and the office had a keypad. What were the odds that they had changed the lock combination? It might be her best shot.

She glanced behind her. The man had yet to round the corner. He disappeared behind a clump of bushes, and she took her shot. She set off in a dead sprint, pounding the pavement. She was so close. A low-hanging branch slashed at her cheek and ripped her wig from her head. Bobby pins hit the sidewalk with a series of metallic tinkles. She winced but kept running.

She slammed against the doors to the building, pushing them open with so much force that they nearly banged off the wall. The newspaper office was down the hallway on the right. She sprinted down it and slid to a stop outside the door.

Oh god, were those heavy footsteps approaching the building? She stabbed the last combination she remembered into the keypad. 5926. There was a beep, and the light flashed green. She wrenched the door open and closed it behind her just as the doors to the building crashed open. The lock clicked loudly. Had he heard it? Was he coming this way? She leaned against the wall, trying to quiet her breath. Her heart was beating out of her chest, and her legs might as well have been an elaborate, fleshy Jell-O mold.

In the hallway, there was a frustrated grunt, and something shattered. Footsteps came down her hallway. Door handles rattled. Her vision pulsed with her heartbeat. Was this going to be how she died? Next to an eight-year-old PC and a crudely drawn cartoon of the school mascot making a political speech? She hadn't had time to forgive Luke. Or have dinner with her deadbeat dad. And neither Nicole nor Mindy was really ready for the responsibility of adopting Rosie. This couldn't be the end. She pulled the stun gun from her leggings and held it at chest height.

"Hey, it's me," a gruff voice said.

Oh shit, was he talking to her?

"I lost her," the voice continued.

Claire froze. Who was he talking to?

There was silence for a few seconds, and the man sighed. His voice was young, masculine, angry. "I know, I know. I didn't expect her to show up on campus. No, I don't know what she was doing here."

Her pulse raced. Claire slowly approached the door, ear turned toward the wood.

"It's getting harder. She has a cop tailing her sometimes again. No sign of the boyfriend at least, but lately she's been hanging around with some huge dude. He's in private security. That's not going to make the eradicators happy."

Eradicators? Her heart fell into her butt. What in the actual hell was an eradicator? She pressed her ear against the crack in the door.

The voice was growing fainter. The doors to the building

creaked when they swung open. Shit. She was going to lose him. This had to be one of the people who was stalking her. She unlocked the newspaper office door as quietly as possible and peeked into the hall. Her hands shook as she grasped her weapons. Was he lulling her into a false sense of security? Would the Taser be enough to bring down the giant bowling ball of a man?

Shit. A shadow was moving away from the building. There was no telling what kind of intelligence she was missing out on. She had no choice. She had to follow him.

Claire crept down the hallway, low to the ground like a cat. She approached the front doors of the communication building and paused. For a member of a secret society, he sure wasn't trying to keep his voice down.

She inched the doors open just wide enough for her to leave and stepped out into the sunshine. She peeked around a large bush and glanced down the sidewalk. The man was maybe ten yards in front of her, wearing a camouflage T-shirt and cargo shorts. Her brunette wig dangled from one meaty fist.

Shit. If he turned around, she was screwed. She dug through her purse with one hand and pulled out a red wig and a hot pink T-shirt. She threw the shirt on over her tank top and yanked the wig onto her head. Thank god she had kept a secondary disguise just in case.

His voice was quieter. "I know, you should have seen her face when we torched her car. It was perfect. The cops still have no idea. Maybe I'll send her another message this week. Can't have her getting complacent." He laughed cruelly and stopped in the middle of the sidewalk.

Claire leaped behind a bush, heart hammering against her ribcage. After a second, the footsteps resumed. She poked her head out cautiously and followed, leaving more space between them. Her ears strained to pick up his lowered voice.

He swung his head from right to left, but thankfully didn't think to look behind him. "Yeah, I think we can mark the vehicular sabotage category as complete. The newbies did good."

What the hell was this? Vehicular sabotage category?

"Yeah. I think Master is gonna love this new training method. So, we've done psychological, property, animal, career, family, travel, and vehicle. What else?"

Oh god. There were so many categories. What did it mean? A prickle of fear danced along her spine.

"Right, we'll get started on that and run some ideas by you. I'm almost going to miss her after we kill her. These training exercises have been great." He chuckled darkly.

Training exercises? Shock hit her like a lightning bolt. Was this why they were constantly toying with her? They were using her to train new recruits in their tactics?

"I know, man," he continued. "We really could use some psych guys to help us pick out what's working best. There's a lot of people on campus for summer session, so we might try to set up a recruitment event. Me, Logan, and Rafael will be doing some light recon, looking for potentials. This school is full of them. Just yesterday, I heard a guy in my psych class complaining about some bitch he tried to get with at this party. She was dancing on him, grinding. She was wearing a skintight dress. You know how sluts work. Anyway, when he tried to take her home, she refused. And when he tried to encourage her by showing her his dick, she punched him in the face. But do you think that bitch is going to get charged with battery?"

Claire bristled. What in the unholy neckbeard was going on?

"Yeah, don't worry," the stalker continued as he walked toward a row of Greek houses. "I bet we can get ten this year. I'll keep you posted. You coming to the Friday meeting next week? It's at ten." He paused in the middle of the sidewalk, and Claire ducked behind a large shrub. She peered between the branches. Apparently, he was incapable of walking and speaking at the same time.

"Nah, you're right. We don't want them to know who's in charge before they've proven themselves. I have the target all picked out. It's going to be a fun Saturday night. Cool. Later." He hung up the phone. A tabby cat ran across his path, and he kicked at it but missed.

Claire pursed her lips and brought her Taser up. She wasn't sure if she was going to fire it or throw it at his stupid bald head.

He turned suddenly and jogged up a set of porch steps. Claire leaped into a yard and ducked behind the porch. Had he spotted her? Keys jingled loudly. A door opened and slammed. Claire collapsed onto the weed-covered ground. Her stomach lurched, and she dry heaved.

When her head stopped spinning, she crawled back out to the sidewalk on her hands and knees, craning her neck at the house Bowling Ball had disappeared into. From her position on the ground, she could just make out a worn set of Greek letters hammered into the siding above the porch.

Epsilon Sigma Alpha. ESA.

JACK HARTLEY PEERED OUT THE WINDOW OF HIS MAKESHIFT office, arms folded and brows furrowed.

"Are you really sure they were talking about you?" He turned, dirt-brown eyes boring into her.

Claire stared at him blankly. "You're joking, right? He followed me, called somebody up to talk about leaving me another note and complain about women refusing to sleep with men on campus, and then discussed recruitment, eradication, and even fricken training exercises. How does that not sound like a toxic masculine cult to you? And where the hell was my police escort today?"

"Claire, you overheard half of a phone conversation. I can't go to my superiors with the word of an amateur sleuth who's probably suffering from post-traumatic stress disorder. I'll be laughed out of the Bureau."

Her mouth dropped open.

He cleared his throat and continued. "This organization isn't populated with beer-swilling frat boys. While this revelation is interesting, I'm not convinced it has anything to do with Barney or with the organization. As for your police escort, there was a staff meeting this morning."

"You're joking, right? A group of men recruiting women-haters at the same university the only known offender attended? You're not even going to check to see if Barney was a member of this fraternity? Even though it was listed as an activity in the yearbook?"

Jack straightened his tie. "We'll look into the incident at Venor, but we still believe that the best chance we have in cracking this case lies with you speaking to Barney at the prison."

Claire stood, scraping her chair over the linoleum. "You know what, Jack? This? What's happening right now?" She waved her hand around his office. "Shit like this is the reason that there are over forty thousand missing women in America. That's enough for today." She turned to leave, biting her lip and trying to hold it all together. What good was running to the police if they refused to help? She was clearly on her own.

"See you tomorrow," Jack called as she left. Shit. The dinner party. Storming out lost some of its weight knowing she was about to make lasagna for his smug, ungrateful ass. At least her booze embargo would be lifted for one night.

CHAPTER THIRTY-FOUR

To Do:
- *Prep lasagna*
- *Practice deep breathing*
- *Quote on greenery rental*

CLAIRE YAWNED AS SHE TORE OFF A SHEET OF ALUMINUM FOIL and covered her freshly made lasagna. Her mother's recipe had carried her through countless potlucks and dinners with glowing reviews. Claire could have made it in her sleep. It was the lowest amount of effort she could put in without setting out cold cuts and calling it a day.

She leaned against the kitchen island and took a sip of wine, fanning herself with the oven mitt. In classic Pennsylvania fashion, the temperature had soared up to ninety. Her tiny window air conditioner was chugging along doing its best, but it was definitely warm in her fourth-floor apartment. Maybe the heat would scare people away sooner.

What would this dinner be like? She was starting to get a handle on Jack, but Tanya and George were complete unknowns. What if Tanya was another Rachel? What if George was a serial killer? At this point, nothing would surprise Claire.

She ripped off sheets of paper towels and tucked them under the forks at the place settings. She wasn't trying to impress these people. She hadn't even made a dessert. They were lucky she made them a meal at all. Really, she was only doing it to shut Jack up...and to satisfy her curiosity. With the bonus of torturing Luke.

Claire took another sip of her wine and jumped when the doorbell rang. Rosie went crazy, barking at the door as her stump of a tail wagged vigorously.

Claire blew a strand of hair out of her face and opened the door.

Her father, clearly already uncomfortable, stood in another one of his famous nondescript suits, his arm around an earthy, ethereal-looking woman.

"Oh, Claire!" The woman exclaimed, rushing forward and wrapping her in a tight hug.

Claire shrank into herself like a hermit crab scuttling into its shell. Why was the home-wrecker hugging her?

"I am so pleased to meet you," the unsolicited hugger added. "Let me look at you."

She drew back and held onto Claire with both arms, her meadow green eyes poring over Claire's features. Claire leaned backward as far as she could manage without tipping over.

"You have your dad's eyes. And his chin," Tanya said with a dazzling smile. "You are every bit as beautiful as I imagined."

"Uh, thank you," Claire said, taking a small step back

into her apartment. "It's nice to meet you, Tanya." A realization hit her like a sack full of day-old scones. Tanya had a label beyond home-wrecker. She was Claire's *stepmother*.

"Please come in." She opened the door wider and tried to covertly take another deep breath.

"Your home is lovely," Tanya said, floating around the room in her gaucho pants and Birkenstocks. Gold bangles clanged against each other on her slender, tanned arms as she skimmed her hands over the spines of Claire's books as if she was reading by touch. Apparently, her father had a type.

Jack thrust a gift bag in Claire's direction. His posture was rigid.

"Gifts," he said simply.

"Thanks," she said. The bag definitely wasn't big enough to hold twenty years of birthday and Christmas gifts. She reached inside and drew out a bottle of top-shelf wine. At least he was good for something. "This will pair well with the lasagna."

Tanya's smile faltered for a moment.

Jack cleared his throat uncomfortably. "Tanya is a vegan. Sorry, I should have mentioned."

Of course she was. Claire's smile was so cemented on at this point that her cheeks ached from the effort.

"That would have been good to know. But it's okay, I have several vegan-friendly side dishes. Sorry, Tanya, I wasn't aware of your dietary preferences."

"It's fine, darling girl," she said, cupping Claire's cheek with her hand. She stared intently into her eyes again.

Ugh. Why was this woman so touchy? Claire squashed her neck back and gave herself a double chin.

"I actually brought a vegan chocolate cake." She leaned

in close, and Claire's skin crawled. "It's made with nutritional yeast," she whispered conspiratorially.

"That sounds delicious. There's nothing I love more than nutritional yeast."

"Me too! We have so much in common. Did you see the other gift?" Tanya asked in the same manner that someone would have asked what their wildest hopes and dreams were.

Claire reached into the bag again and pulled out a bag full of tiny glass bottles and a diffuser. "Oh, a diffuser. Thank you."

"It will change your life," Tanya said earnestly. "I used to have crippling migraines and an awful immune system. I started using these oils and I feel twenty years younger. If you like these, there are dozens more. My friend from ceramics class—"

Jack put a hand on Tanya's shoulder, and she stopped.

"Tanya, we talked about the oil thing," he hissed through gritted teeth.

"I know, I just thought after all the poor girl's been through, she could use some relief," Tanya said.

"Great. I'll just set this over here." Claire slunk further into her living room and placed the bottle on her coffee table. She sneezed immediately, overwhelmed by the smell of star anise.

The doorbell rang again, and Claire almost sprinted to it. The door swung open, revealing Luke dressed in a navy button-down with the sleeves rolled up.

"Luke," she said in relief. Butterflies swarmed in her stomach.

He stepped over her threshold, smiling and holding two bottles of wine. He stepped forward and kissed her on the cheek.

"Come in," she said, backing away to let him enter. "Dinner will be ready in a couple of minutes."

The secret of George perched on her tongue, but she swallowed it. He should be here any minute. Luke would know soon enough.

Rosie, who had been dancing on two legs trying to get Jack to pet her, sprinted for Luke and nearly took him out at the knees.

"Jack, this is Luke." Claire nudged him toward her father. If she had to deal with the awkwardness, so did he.

"Nice to meet you, Special Agent Hartley," Luke said, giving what looked to be a firm handshake.

Jack seemed to be sizing him up. Luke flexed his fingers when the handshake broke.

"Something smells good," Luke said, turning back to Claire.

"Lasagna." She gestured at the oven.

"Sounds great. Anything I can do to help? I see you already set the table." He scanned the place settings. "Are we expecting someone else?"

As if he had summoned it, there was a knock at the door.

"There might be one teensy surprise," Claire said. Her heart rate quickened. Maybe this had been a bad idea. Luke was making an effort, and she was intentionally pulling the wool over his eyes.

She opened the front door and stepped back.

A man strode into her apartment. "You must be Claire. George Islestorm, attorney at law," the man said, putting a very confident hand forward.

So, he had taken after his mother. This was true in more ways than one. In addition to Rachel's steely, commanding demeanor, George also had her fierce cheekbones. Although Luke had clearly inherited more traits from his dad, there was no denying they were brothers. Their movements were the same, the "nice to meet you" fake smile was the same. George was an inch or two shorter than Luke, and his sandy blond hair was carefully molded into place.

"Hey, man," George said, crossing into the dining room and sticking a hand out to Luke. "It's been a while."

Oh, boy. A vein stuck out in Luke's forehead. He opened his mouth to speak, but only a strangled sound came out. His hands turned into fists at his side.

Luke had never acted like this before. Not when she was bleeding out on the ground in front of him, not when strangers had broken into his house. Bamboozling him with George's presence may have been a mistake. He hadn't seen him since their father's funeral, after all. Blinded by her rage, she may have gone too far in her quest for revenge.

George's permasmile faltered, and he pulled his hand back to his side.

"Jack, this is Luke's brother, George," Claire redirected. Jack reached over and shook George's hand. "George, this is my biological father, Special Agent Jack Hartley."

"George Islestorm, attorney at law," George parroted, administering another bone-crushing handshake. "FBI, CIA, or something in between, Jack?"

"Why don't you all go into the living room and have a seat for a few minutes?" Claire interjected.

Tanya led the charge, floating from the dining room to the living room. George and Jack followed. Luke did not.

Claire nearly dove into the kitchen, pouring glasses of wine. She hid behind her refrigerator so she didn't have to make eye contact with Luke as she downed her glass in one gulp before refilling it. Press be damned, she wasn't planning on leaving her house. This wine was warranted.

This dinner may have been her dumbest idea ever. What

had possessed her to invite into her personal space her estranged father, her home-wrecking stepmother, and the man who had effectively killed her sort-of-boyfriend's father?

Luke was still standing wordlessly at the dining room table. She put a glass of wine down for him and walked out without saying anything. It served him right. Didn't it?

"Nice digs," George said when she appeared in the living room. "A renter, I see. I'm sure your landlord appreciates you paying his mortgage."

Awesome. George was a douche. She had suspected it the moment he walked in, but now red flags were falling out of the sky like a freakin' ticker tape parade.

"I'm sure he does," she agreed. "Almost as much as I appreciate being able to call him anytime something breaks."

She handed a glass to him, and he took it, sniffing it. "Is this wine gluten-free?"

Oh, boy. He really was a Rachel.

"Are grapes gluten-free?" Claire said, unable to clip a hint of sarcasm from her voice.

George set his glass down and said nothing.

She passed glasses out to the remainder of the attendees. Fortunately, Tanya didn't ask if the wine was vegan.

Claire quietly excused herself. She shut her bedroom door and picked up her pillow and screamed into it for a few seconds. Then she picked up the flask she had stashed on her nightstand in case of such an emergency and took a small swallow. Maybe she should pull out Taser #3 too.

Her bedroom door opened unexpectedly. She whirled around, whiskey dribbling out of the corner of her mouth.

Luke stepped inside and shut the door with a snap. Wordlessly, Claire handed him the flask and turned back around. She studied the sword hanging between her bedroom windows. For some reason, she couldn't bring herself to look Luke in the eyes.

The flask rattled. Luke sighed.

"You invited my brother," he said, his first sentence since George had walked in.

"I did," she began.

Luke cut her off midsentence.

"Why, Claire? You invited the asshole that I told you was responsible for ending my father's life. For taking away my last chance to see him alive. To say goodbye. And you didn't think I deserved a heads up."

"I wanted to punish you," she whispered to the sword. Her entire body tingled with shame. "I wanted you to hurt, like you hurt me."

She turned to look at him.

"Well, you did a great fucking job." Luke set the flask down on her dresser with a clunk.

She flinched.

"Listen, I get why you would want to hurt me. I did a shitty thing, and I've been trying to make up for it. I have never tried this hard in my life, do you understand that? I have bent over backward for you, sending pizza boys across the country and talking about my feelings and missing the shit out of you when you're not in the same room with me. And every second of it has been worth it, because I hoped that at the end of this rough patch, you'd remember what we have and come back to me. But this," he said, gesturing to the bedroom door. "Miss Happily-Ever-Afters and True Love. I had no idea you were capable of something like this. Honestly, after today, I feel like I don't know you at all. How could you keep something like this from me?"

She reeled like he had slapped her. The bed creaked as she sprang to her feet.

"Oh, you mean like when you didn't tell me you thought I was being targeted by a serial killer?" She pointed forcefully in his direction. "Or when you told me twice that you didn't have a brother, but George was douching around this earth the whole time? Or when you covered up the fact that your entire documentary hinged on getting me to agree to an in-depth interview about the night I was almost murdered?"

Luke took a step back. "How long are you going to keep rehashing the past, Claire? I've apologized for all of that. I have fought for you. I've done everything I could conceivably think of to make this up to you. I even checked Google to see if professional apology planners were a thing. They aren't, by the way. There might be a market for that. Anyway, if you can't accept my apologies and my promise to do better—to be better—in the future, there's nowhere to go from here. I can't make you forgive me. I think I need to go. This was a mistake." He put a hand on the doorknob.

Her heart launched itself into her throat.

"I'm sorry," she said. She had known this was a mistake from the moment George walked through the door. It was time she owned up to it.

He paused.

"You're right. I went too far. I thought maybe you were being dramatic with the whole estranged brother thing. I didn't realize how much I'd actually be punishing you by inviting him tonight. This was a terrible idea." She sat back on the edge of her bed and turned away from him again. She couldn't watch him leave.

There were footsteps on the hardwood floor. Luke sat next to her and took her hand. "You've had better ideas."

"I don't know what the hell I was thinking. I was so angry at you. I'm still angry at you, if I'm being honest. But you're right, inviting your brother was needlessly cruel and didn't help solve anything. This night is a disaster. Your brother's an opinionated dick. My stepmother is a multi-level marketing hippie. My father is even more uncomfortable than I am."

Luke passed her the flask again. She took another small sip, vowing to abstain from alcohol for at least a week...after tonight.

"Should we get this over with?" He offered his hand.

She raised her eyes slowly. "You're not leaving?"

Luke shook his head. "I'm sorry for threatening that. That's the kind of shit my mom used to pull on my dad. If you're willing to work on this—us—then I'm not going anywhere. I'm willing to talk, and to work this out like adults. Leaving in the middle of an argument isn't healthy."

Wow, how mature of him.

"Thank you." Claire stood, steeling herself.

"We can do this," he encouraged.

She caught his arm before he opened the door. Maybe it was the whiskey, or the fact that they had talked—really talked—for the first time since Paris. Or maybe it was the apartment full of attack-hugging and occupation-dropping strangers. Something in her ached for him. She tugged him back to her, hungrily drawing his mouth to hers.

Luke pulled her in as though he would never let go. The smell of sunshine and freshly cut grass enveloped her. His thumb grazed over her cheek, and she nearly moaned. There was more than passion in this kiss. There was longing, frustration, and an apology. His fingers fisted in her hair, and her hand snaked around to cop a feel. She had missed that glorious butt.

A titter of laughter sounded from the living room.

Claire broke away. She blinked slowly, slightly dazed after the kiss. "We should get back out there." A true smile blossomed for the first time that evening.

"One more." Luke drew her in again.

"Maybe they'll have all killed each other," she said breathlessly as he kissed her neck.

"We can only hope."

THE SALAD AND SOUP COURSE WERE LARGELY UNEVENTFUL. The salad had come from a bag, and the soup from a can, but that didn't stop Tanya from raving over it. Jack and George had an uncomfortable political conversation. Tanya said what seemed to be a pagan prayer, offering thanks to the "Earth Mother" for their bounty. George refused to eat anything with carbs in it and informed everyone he only ate 1,200 calories a day.

"You know, Claire, you have a half sister," Tanya said in her irritatingly positive way.

"I heard rumors."

Tanya plowed on. "You might actually know of her. Her name is Brianna. Brianna Hartley."

Claire's fork tumbled out of her hand.

"You're joking. The Brianna Hartley from—"

"*Fool's Silver*? *For the Love of Frosting*? *Aidan's Peak*?" Luke interrupted with a rapid-fire list of movies. All those titles were in the "guilty pleasure" section of his floor-to-ceiling DVD cabinet in the screening room.

"The one and only," Tanya said, laughing again. "We don't get to see her very often because she's usually in Los

Angeles or New York, but I'm sure she would love to meet you."

"That would be...nice," Claire said, sitting back in her chair. She would rather set herself on fire. Of course her half sister was a young, beautiful, famous actress. Probably a vapid narcissist too. She should have brought the flask to the table.

"Your lasagna is delicious, Claire," Luke said, laying a hand on her knee under the table. He squeezed it once.

"Oh, thank you. It's my mother's recipe."

There was a beat of silence after she spoke. Whoops.

"It's actually my recipe," Jack said with a small smile. "You did a great job."

"No," Claire politely corrected. "It's definitely mom's recipe. She got it from a friend. Here's a picture of the recipe card," she said, getting ready to pass her phone to her father.

"Oh," she said, sitting back down. She had never noticed that the top of the card had a monogram at the top that said JH. "I stand corrected," she said.

Great, he even ruined her sacred family lasagna recipe. Everything was a lie.

"My Jack is a marvelous cook," Tanya said. "Just the other day he made a delicious aquafaba meringue."

"My dad had the best recipe for chili," George spoke up, setting down his fork with a few leaves of spinach still wound through the tines. "Remember, Luke? He would make it on football Sundays."

"I remember," Luke said quietly. He was systematically ripping his garlic bread into tiny pieces.

George, who had clearly decided the wine was gluten-free, judging by the four glasses he had consumed, stared Luke down.

"You still won't talk about Dad."

"You don't know that. You're not a part of my life anymore. You don't know what I talk about."

"I know you're still a pussy," George said, sitting back and crossing his arms, a dare in his eyes.

"And I know you're still a murderer," Luke said in a matter-of-fact way.

Claire, Tanya, and Jack froze. Claire's eyes widened.

"You shut your mouth," George said, fist clenching his wine glass. "I did what I had to do. I was the medical power of attorney. He put that on me, not you. I made the hardest decision I have ever made. And I had to make it alone, because you were gone. You were always gone."

"I was in Afghanistan," Luke said, voice raising. He shoved his chair back, stood up abruptly. "It's not like I was on spring break in Miami."

George threw his chair back too. He stood, and they stared at each other. "It doesn't change the fact that you weren't there."

"Oh, boy," Claire said softly.

"You should have waited," Luke said with a darkness that Claire hadn't heard in a long time. His voice wavered ever so slightly. "I was at the airport."

"You know that's not what Dad would have wanted. He always said if he was ever a vegetable that we needed to—"

"Pull the plug. Yeah, I know. Except you and Mom got to say goodbye. The last time I saw Dad was when they saw me off when I was getting deployed. I missed most of the last two years of his life." Luke's mouth had hardened into a solid line. His hands were clenched into fists at his sides.

"Oh, yes," George said loudly, looking around as though he were addressing an invisible audience. "All hail Luke, the golden boy. The American hero. Too busy serving his country to be there when his dad's in a fucking coma. Too far away to take any responsibility."

Claire's mouth dropped open.

Luke leaned forward. "I almost forgot. It's Friday. Isn't there a church somewhere you should be drunkenly plowing your car into? Or do you need to have Sophia with you in order to take that errand off the To Do list?"

Uh-oh. The dirty laundry was out. The shit was officially hitting the fan.

George reared back with his fist cocked. Claire leapt up from the table, between Luke and George.

George, unable to stop the momentum of his punch, staggered forward with force. Claire ducked her head to the right and dropped to the floor, sweeping George's legs out from under him. Sawyer would have been proud. Where was a camera when you needed one?

George banged off the table and fell heavily to the floor, wheezing and moaning.

"Get out of my house," Claire said, hand shaking as she pointed to the door.

A loud click came from the table.

Claire glanced back for the first time. Luke was gaping at her with an open mouth. Jack was standing, gun drawn, and Tanya stood next to him with her hand on his arm.

"Jack. You know the rule. No guns at dinner," she hissed.

It was possibly the first sensible thing Tanya had said the entire evening.

George high-tailed it out the front door and slammed it behind him. Silence rang in his wake.

"Who wants cake?" Claire asked after a moment, lifting the lid on a meticulously decorated chocolate cake. The sooner everyone ate cake, the sooner they would get the hell out of her house.

As much as she hated to admit it, the weird vegan cake was pretty good. Maybe she really did like nutritional yeast.

Tanya cleared the dessert plates and left Claire with a hefty, cling-wrapped chunk of cake. Luke washed the dishes and Jack dried. They exchanged a few words about the upcoming football season. For such a strange collection of people, it was eerily normal.

Claire served coffee, and the four of them sat around the table for another few minutes.

"Claire?" Tanya asked.

"Yes?" Good lord, what now?

"Thank you so much for having us over. I know it can't have been easy for you. You must feel like I took your father away and disrupted your entire life."

Claire shrugged. "It was a long time ago."

Tanya reached over and touched her hand. Her hands were soft, like unbaked dough. Claire cringed but didn't withdraw.

"I don't regret the life your father and I created together. But I regret the way it started."

Yep, a child born of adultery while half of the couple was still legally married to someone else was not exactly a recipe for a classic fairytale romance.

"And most of all," Tanya continued, "I regret not being able to be in your and Charlie's life while you were growing up. Do you think she would ever agree to meet with me?"

Claire exhaled. Charlie was a badass publicist who did not have time to suffer fools. She had written her father off the day he had walked out the door. "Maybe. Someday."

Tanya smiled and withdrew her hand. "Jack? We should get going. It's a flower moon tonight."

"We should do this again sometime," Jack said, awkwardly sticking his hand out to Claire.

"Sure," she said, shaking his hand. What a tempting offer.

"Did you have any questions for the procedure tomorrow?"

Oh, hell. Tomorrow she was going to the prison to grill Barney. She had purposely put it out of her mind, but time was running out. She needed a plan.

"I'm good, thanks," she said to Jack.

"Oh, Claire," Tanya strode over to the bar, where Claire had abandoned the diffuser and bottles of oils. "If you're feeling nauseated, just lift the cap off the peppermint oil and take a deep breath. It'll fix you right up. And if you find yourself having anxiety or trouble sleeping, just run a nice hot bath and add a few drops of the lavender oil."

Great. Then she could sleepwalk in the streets of West Haven while smelling like an apothecary.

"Thank you both. Take care," Claire said as she opened her front door.

The moment they left, she collapsed on the floor. Rosie sprinted over and licked her cheek. Luke came to lie beside Claire and sat down a glass of water with a straw.

"Thank you," Claire said, sipping noisily. Was this blossoming headache from the stress or the alcohol? "That could have gone worse."

He smiled and rolled onto his side, propped his head in one hand. "I will always cherish the memory of you sweeping my brother's legs."

"Shit, he's not going to sue me, is he? I'm already in the middle of trying to low-key blackmail my way out of a lawsuit. It's not a good time to add another. And then there's the fact that I flung a trash can lid at a cult member's face on live television." Good lord. How many lawsuits could one person have? Maybe she really *did* have a violent streak.

"Unlikely. He'd have to admit he got his ass handed to him by a proposal-planning badass."

"He deserved it," she said, sitting up and draining the rest of her water. "Luke?"

"Yeah?"

"There's something I need to tell you."

"Oh god. What now? Did you schedule a brunch with our moms tomorrow?"

She glared at him. "Don't even speak that into existence. No, I need to tell you something about Barney." It was time he knew the truth. The whole truth. Punishing him had solved nothing. If they were going to rebuild whatever this was, honesty had to come first.

"Okay. Go ahead." Luke sat up and stared at her patiently.

Claire took a deep breath. "It's a long story. Let me start from the beginning."

CHAPTER THIRTY-FIVE

To Do:
- Plan a vacation. For real this time.
- Email Dr. W for clarification on anniversary date

A BARBED WIRE FENCE SURROUNDED THE WALLS OF THE penitentiary. A line of crows huddled together on the guard tower, cawing wistfully into the humid afternoon. A handful of inmates stood on a cracked asphalt basketball court. They stared, utterly still, as Luke's car entered the grounds. Claire had not yet acquired a new car, and something about the idea of driving a van promoting "Happily Ever Afters" to a prison seemed a little too macabre.

After the explosive family dinner, Claire had decided to try honesty with Luke. She told him the truth about her visit to Barney in prison and her fears about ESA. He hadn't taken any notes or even mentioned the documentary in light of her revelation. Maybe he had left the real Luke in California.

Her palms grew sweaty, and her heart throbbed in her throat. She slid down in her seat, avoiding the gaze of the inmates. There was no use in pretending this wasn't going to happen. She was minutes away from facing her almost-killer. Was she ready? Could someone ever really be ready for something like this?

"It's okay," Luke said, reaching across the gap and squeezing her knee. "He'll be in cuffs. The guards will be in there with you."

She stared at him. "Yeah, and so will your mom. It's bad enough being in a twelve-by-twelve concrete room with one person who wants me dead, let alone two."

"She doesn't want you dead." He cracked a smile. He had shown up that morning with a new haircut that, in spite of the current state of affairs, kindled something below her belt.

"That's comforting." She hurriedly checked her hair and makeup in the mirror. It was no use; she still looked like a sleep-deprived banshee. She had planned to face Barney looking calm and unaffected, but apparently that wasn't in the cards.

Luke parked by a line of black sedans and unmarked police cars. Claire stepped out and slammed her door. Several of the prisoners whistled, but she didn't acknowledge them.

"Well, if it isn't Officer Absentia," Luke muttered, waving at Officer Schiccitano. He sat in the front seat of a cruiser, pretending to read the newspaper. He nodded at them. A barely visible earpiece nestled in his ear.

Claire nudged him. "Hey. He does his best. The police have limited resources. He can't watch me all the time."

"Claire." A masculine voice came from behind her.

She jumped. How did her father move so silently? And why hadn't she inherited that ability? Dishes rattled in her kitchen when she walked by. He was like a panther.

"Jack."

"Thank you for being here today," he said, reaching for a handshake. She returned the gesture without comment. He had neglected to mention his wife's dietary restrictions and drawn a gun during her dinner party. There was no need to be overly nice. "You'll be in a conference room with Mr. Windsor and his attorney. A couple of guards will be present, too, but that's it. The rest of us will be observing remotely."

"Including Luke? You promised."

Jack sighed. "Yes, including Luke. Here's a tablet and pencil if you want to take notes, but you'll want to keep all other belongings in the car. Phone, keys, wallet. Visiting rules are strict."

Luke popped the trunk, and Claire tossed her purse inside. Leaving her lifeline to the world in a hot trunk surrounded by prisoners. No big deal. Their current clients had been instructed to contact Mindy for the day if needed, but you never knew when a proposal disaster might strike.

"Deception, control, body locations," she whispered to herself, averting her gaze from the inmates on the basketball court. "Should have done my power stance."

"Shall we?" Jack asked.

She nodded. Luke placed his hand on the small of her back and walked her to the entrance of the prison.

Jack opened the doors. There was desperation in the stale air. Cheap cleaning supplies mingled with high school gym smell. They were immediately faced with a metal detector. Claire walked through. She had diligently studied the visiting guidelines on the website and purposefully worn a bra without an underwire. She didn't have time to be aggressively patted down by a handsy guard.

The rest of her crew passed through without incident. A bored-looking guard sat at a desk underneath a flickering fluorescent light.

"Name." He was so gruff that it didn't even sound like a question.

Claire identified herself, provided her ID, and signed in. Her heart rate climbed the deeper they went into the prison. They walked down a dimly lit hallway. A guard at another desk met her and escorted her to a small conference room. She turned back to look at Luke as she passed through the door. He nodded at her, and then she was alone.

Claire sat on the edge of a conference chair, gripping the yellow legal pad in front of her like a shield. Her heartbeat thudded in her ears. Her foot tapped incessantly, echoing in the small room.

The sound of stilettos came from the hallway. *Ugh.* She was coming. The dragon lady herself. The door opened, and Rachel Islestorm stalked into the room. She dropped her briefcase onto the table and pulled out an identical yellow legal pad.

"Claire," she said simply. At least she had gotten her name right this time.

"Rachel," Claire responded. Neither of them moved to shake hands. Claire sat her notepad down and crossed her arms over her chest.

The door opened again, and Claire flinched. Two uniformed security guards walked in wearing night sticks and stun guns. Each had a stoic expression. There was only one person left to arrive.

Outside, chains clinked together. Her heart rate went

from galloping to full-on hummingbird, and the pencil she held snapped in half. She forced herself to breathe. She would not give Barney the satisfaction of dissolving into a full-blown panic attack just because his stupid ass walked down a hallway. Maybe she should have tried some of her stepmother's hokey lavender oils. Or vodka.

The clinking and shuffling grew closer. Her fingers gripped the conference table as she breathed and tried to rearrange her facial expression.

Finally the shuffling feet dragged themselves around the corner of the doorway, and Claire came face-to-face with the man who stalked, abducted, and tortured her. The prison orange hung from his gaunt frame.

What was that smell? Fresh drywall and a dirt floor? But this prison was old. The memories of that night in the parking garage swamped her. She flinched, expecting the scratch of wedding dress lace against her skin, the burn of her arms bound in rope. The walls were closing in, weren't they?

She gripped the arms of her chair so tightly that her knuckles ached.

"Claire," he said with a skeevy smile.

"Bernard." Her voice didn't shake. Ha, suck it.

She forced herself to loosen her grip and erase what must have been a pained look from her face. She could do this. He had already failed to kill her once. And she knew more than he thought.

"Thank you for agreeing to meet me today," he said, shooting a glance at his lawyer. "Ah, Rachel. I would introduce you, but I guess you two already know each other?"

So he *had* hired her because she was Luke's mom. That was underhanded even for a psychopath.

Rachel grunted and leaned back in her chair. Barney sat

next to her, directly across from Claire. He smirked, but it didn't reach his cold, steely eyes. He trained them on Claire, and a lead fist dropped into her stomach.

Rachel cleared her throat. "Mr. Windsor, as we previously agreed, you're not to discuss the trial or the event leading up to it."

Barney gave Rachel a passing glance before turning his dead fish eyes back to Claire.

"You're probably wondering why I've asked you here."

Claire leaned back in her seat, drummed the stub of her pencil against the notepad. "I don't really care why you asked me here. I'm only here because the FBI strongly suggested it."

"A pawn, of course. How true to your nature."

She bristled, leaning forward again. "You know nothing about my nature."

"Oh, but I do," Barney said, inspecting his fingernails. "You forget, I watched you for months. I know which orange juice you buy, your favorite ice cream shops, which video game your nephew is currently playing."

"Mr. Windsor," Rachel interrupted.

He glared at her with cold fury in his eyes before shifting back to Claire. "I know your clothing sizes. I probably paid more attention to you than that boyfriend of yours ever did. Not that you were worthy of it."

Even though he wasn't in the room, Claire could swear she felt tension radiating from Luke. She stared right back at Barney. "Congratulations on your complete lack of hobbies. What's this about, Barney? I don't have time to listen to your weird brags. In case you haven't noticed, I've won."

Barney laughed, and Claire jumped. The sound was unnatural, almost animal. She clenched one fist under the table.

"You haven't won at all. You know as well as I do that this is far from over."

Aha! He had basically admitted to knowing that she was still being targeted.

"Please. There's a mountain of evidence that's going to land you major prison time for trying to kill me. And then, while you're incarcerated, they'll come up with a plan to charge you with six other murders." She took a sip of water from the plastic cup the guard had brought and sat back in her chair. "Pretty sure that means I've won."

Barney raised an eyebrow. "In case you haven't noticed, I haven't been tried for any of them. It's pretty hard to charge someone with murder without a body or a murder weapon." He leaned forward and stared at her intently.

Her skin crawled, but she met his unforgiving gaze.

"Have you felt safe in your bed since that night in the parking garage?"

"Mr. Windsor," Rachel said sharply.

He ignored her and continued. "Do you sleep soundly? Can you walk down the street without looking over your shoulder?" His voice was quiet, dangerous.

Rachel sighed and tossed her legal pad back into her briefcase. She sat straight as a nail and stared at something on the table. Her expression wasn't as severe as it had been on entry.

He smirked, leaned closer, and propped his elbows on the table. "Do you still like to read for an hour before bed?"

Claire bristled. That was enough of this shit. "Tell me why I'm here, or I'm leaving. Did you just want to observe your greatest failure up close and in person, or is there something else?"

The mask of calm had started to slip from his face. His eyes bulged slightly, and his face was turning red. His gaze moved from her face to her collar. They were probing desperately.

"I want to see your scar," he said.

Gross.

"Why?" Claire said flatly, crossing her arms over her chest.

"I just need to see it." His hands reached as if to tug her collar aside himself. One of the guards rapped on Barney's chair with his nightstick.

"If you show it to me, I will give you one body location," he added.

"Mr. Windsor," Rachel warned.

"Shut it," he hissed at her.

Claire glanced at the camera blinking in the corner of the room. Images of Kayley Herrold's family weeping on camera, begging for information, sprang into her mind. Barney was definitely trying to manipulate her, even as he sat in chains. But this was what she signed up for. Closure for the families was worth more than a moment of lost dignity.

"How do I know you won't lie?"

"What's the point in lying? You're so confident that I'll be in prison for the rest of my life," he said, gesturing to the handcuffs that bound his wrists.

She didn't believe him for a second. But she had to try. Since it looked like he was willing to cooperate with a body location, maybe it was time for her to extend a small olive branch to Luke. Not much about Barney's childhood was public record. Some probing questions could make a real difference in the documentary.

"All right. I'll let you see the scar. But first," Claire began, holding her stub of pencil to the notepad, "I'd like you to tell me about your mother."

Rachel looked up from the table and narrowed her eyes. Barney blinked in surprise, finally breaking his unwavering eye contact.

"My mother? Why?"

"I'm just trying to understand why you are the way you are." Claire tried to sound nonchalant as she scribbled on the legal pad. "Call it a morbid curiosity. What was your childhood like?"

Barney stiffened, eyes still probing her collar.

"I answer your questions, and then you show me the scar."

"You answer my questions, you tell me the body location, and then I'll show you the scar," Claire ordered. "Was she a nurturing mother?" She continued, broken pencil poised. She shot a glance at Rachel, who was busy rolling her eyes at the concrete walls.

He scoffed. "She was too busy working to be a nurturing mother."

"What does she do?" she asked even though she already knew the answer.

"She's a nurse."

"That explains why she worked so much. That's a very demanding career."

"I suppose. It's one of the Acceptables," he said, sounding as though he was questioning everything he knew.

Acceptables? What fresh hell was this? "What do you mean, one of the 'Acceptables?'"

"One of the five acceptable feminine careers."

Claire steeled herself. The misogyny was already taking center stage. "There are only five?"

"Yes. Hospitality, teaching, nursing, secretary, and retail," he said, ticking them off on his abnormally long fingers.

"And being a stay-at-home mother, of course. Telling men how to woo women is not on that list, incidentally."

Claire rolled her eyes. "Remind me. Who hired me to plan your proposal?"

Barney glowered and declined to respond.

"Who decided these were the only acceptable careers for women?" Maybe a different tactic would get the answer she wanted.

"Someone much wiser than you."

Time to twist the knife. "Did your mother teach you to sew?"

"I don't sew." He looked offended by the very thought.

"Sure you do. I vividly remember the charming quilt you made out of your victim's undergarments. I specifically remember you zooming in to show me the pair that said 'Slut' in sparkly gold letters. I'm going to take a wild guess that those belonged to Courtney. Was the quilt hand stitched or machine quilted? Either way, really unique work. It must be hard to get those patches just right."

His cold eyes burned, but he didn't say anything.

"So, your mother was a single mom."

"Yes, and I was a child born out of an affair with a married man. He paid her to terminate her pregnancy, but instead she took the money and lied. She kept me. Lucky me."

"You didn't have a happy childhood?"

"I found some joy here and there. I liked animals. I liked killing them more. It was good practice."

Rachel pursed her lips. It could have been Claire's imagination, but it seemed like she had shifted an inch away from Barney.

Claire raised her eyebrows, made a checkmark on her tablet, and consulted the next criterion Jack had given her.

"You used to wet the bed," she stated. It was not a question.

Barney bristled and straightened. The handcuffs on his wrists clinked together.

"Nocturia is completely normal in childhood, even in adolescence."

"Sure, it's normal if you're a serial killer," Claire muttered.

"What was that?" he snapped. His eyes bulged even wider.

"Nothing," she said with a smile. She slowly, deliberately unbuttoned the top button of her shirt.

His hands twitched. He stared at the spot where he knew her scar was.

"Here you go." She swept her hair off her shoulder and instead showed him the symbol of Priapus that he had carved into her neck.

"Cover it. I don't want to see that one," he hissed through gritted teeth. He clenched the edge of the metal table so tightly that the tension radiating across it was almost palpable.

Interesting. Maybe he and his ESA pals were less than *simpatico* at the moment.

"Oh, you mean the *stab* wound," she said and let her hair fall back into place. Her fingers paused at her buttons. "You left me with so many charming body decorations it's hard to pick the right one."

She leaned forward and stared directly into the cold, hard eyes of her almost-killer.

"Tell me where the bodies are."

"I'll never tell."

She glanced at her notepad. It was time to deploy some deception. Would this risk pay off, or would it be a disaster? "That's right. You won't. Do you want to know why?"

"What do you mean?"

"The feds have one of your friends. You know, from ESA."

Rachel glanced up from the table. Somewhere in the building, Jack Hartley was probably throwing a chair through a window.

Barney's nostrils flared. "I don't know what you're talking about."

"Sure you do. Epsilon Sigma Alpha. The lamest frat on Venor's campus. But anyway, the feds have picked up a—oh, what do you call them? Incinerators?"

"Eradicators," he hissed.

Bingo. Idiot.

"Right, an eradicator. Turns out he's taking credit for your kills."

She held her breath. This was a gigantic, risky leap. All she had was circumstantial evidence. Was it going to pay off?

His face went from red to purple. "That's impossible."

Claire leaned forward. Her fingers were poised on her buttons. "As it turns out, it is possible. He's claiming all of them. I sure hope you didn't tell anyone where the bodies are, or nothing will stop him from taking your legacy and becoming the West Haven Widowmaker."

Barney's expression darkened. Silence stretched between them. The clock in the corner was practically screaming as the seconds ticked by.

"You recall Kayley Herrold," he said.

"I do," she said calmly, hands still on her buttons.

"Her head is buried in the state park between Victoria's house and the West Haven Heirloom location."

Her stomach lurched. Victoria was Barney's fiancée. The feds had tried to use her television interview to guilt Barney into revealing body locations, but no dice.

"Where in the park?"

"I've given you enough." His eye twitched.

Claire withdrew her hands, crossed her arms.

"Why so close to Victoria's house?"

"I passed that spot every day when I drove to work. I got to relive every moment. And now I can't because I'm in a fucking *cage*," he said, almost shouting the last word.

"Where in the park is she?"

"About seventy yards off the highway, straight out from mile marker 107 on Route 45."

Holy shit. She had done it. It was time for her to hold up her end of the bargain. She unbuttoned a second button and pulled her top to the side, exposing the place where Barney had thrust a knife into her chest.

His demeanor changed immediately. He zeroed in on her wound, then threw his head back, eyes closed for a moment. When he opened them, she recognized the same look he had had in the parking garage. Bloodthirsty. Evil. And totally sweaty.

"Get on your knees," he spat at her.

"Excuse me?"

"On your knees. Beg me not to hurt you. And I'll tell you where the rest of her body is."

"Not a chance," Claire said, standing up and pushing her chair back. She held the notepad protectively in front of her.

As the guards reached for Barney, Claire turned. Maybe there was time for one more quick probe about ESA. The feds couldn't ignore her forever if Barney admitted to being part of the cult. Could they?

"They're not happy with you, you know," she said suddenly, staring at Barney.

"The feds? No, I can't imagine they are," he said nonchalantly. He was still staring at her collar.

"Not them. Your friends. ESA," she said. She would show her father just how devastating a group of frat boys could be. "I caught one of them following me. What an idiot. All I had to do was tail him for a quarter mile and he gave away everything. They're ashamed of you, just like your mother is." She put both hands on the conference table and leaned forward. Her voice was low, but everyone in the room trained their eyes on her.

He crossed his arms over his chest. "Bullshit. You wouldn't have caught them."

"I know they said you went rogue, ruined everything with a personal vendetta. Killed a couple of women in one of the 'acceptable feminine careers,' even."

Another wild guess. Ariel had been a waitress.

"You were sloppy, and your targets were personal. You didn't stay true to the mission. You betrayed the brotherhood and all that it stands for. No wonder they're letting someone else take credit for your kills."

Barney's eyes suddenly blazed in a way that she hadn't seen since the night of the kidnapping. His face was full-on scarlet now, and his hands shook.

"I don't know what you're talking about," he said, hissing like a cat backed into a corner.

"That's why they haven't visited you." More assumptions —though she'd bet it was true. Her tone was mocking, though her knees were shaking. "You're dead to them. It's going to be awfully lonely in here without any of your buddies."

She turned and walked to the door. "No friends, no

hotels, no legacy. No power. I feel bad for you. Toodles. Don't drop the soap."

The knob was cold in her hand. Just a thin door separated her from freedom.

"Claire," he shouted, trying to get out of his seat. The armed guards, who had been standing in the corner the entire time, hastily restrained him, pressing his face into the conference table.

Her stilettos struck the concrete floor as she exited the room without a backward glance. She had some misogynists to catch.

CHAPTER THIRTY-SIX

To Do:
- *Test fairy lights*
- *Vomit in a bush somewhere*
- *Bring ESA down*

CLAIRE WALKED OUT OF THE DEBRIEFING WITH HER HEAD spinning and her father two steps behind. She would give her right kidney to be out of these poorly lit hallways. She was ready to be done with this dark world of serial killers and get back to her happily ever afters. But there was something left on her To Do list before she could hang up her sleuthing hat for good. ESA had to be brought down.

"You did a good job," Jack said as they walked toward the entrance. "It was smart to let him think someone else was claiming his kills. I'm surprised he gave up as much as he did."

Apparently, he wasn't going to scold her for bringing up ESA. Did that mean he believed her now? "Thanks. Let's hope it was the truth."

Jack turned to her just before the doors. "I really appreciate everything you did. It can't have been easy. You're going to be bringing some much needed closure to Kayley's family if his intel was good. But it's time to leave things to the professionals, Claire. No more investigating."

"I wasn't planning on it," she said. He didn't need to know that there was already a binder dedicated to infiltrating the meeting the Bowling Ball guy had mentioned.

"Until next time," Jack said, holding the door open for her. Next time? If he thought she was going to come back here and show off her scar again so that a psychopath could manipulate her, he was sorely misinformed. She walked outside and took a deep breath. Someone had definitely just spread manure nearby, but any fresh air was better than the stink of the prison. She paused at the corner of the building and bent over, waiting for the wave of nausea to pass.

"Are you okay?" Luke's familiar voice soothed.

"I'm doing great. Like a charged crystal in a tranquility garden."

"You were amazing in there." He sounded genuinely impressed as he pulled her in for a quick hug and squeezed her tight. "I don't know how you held it together. I would have jumped over that table and dropkicked him."

"I probably would have if I could have gotten away with it," Claire said, then pulled back and continued her yoga breaths.

"Do you think he's telling the truth? About the body?"

"I really hope so."

He put a hand on her cheek. "Let me make you dinner." As usual, it wasn't a request.

"Sure. Your place?" She was too tired to argue. Wide open country spaces and a kitchen that was hopefully filled with food and not just out-of-date coffee creamer? Sign her up. The four walls of Luke's house had come to feel more like home than she'd care to admit. Even if they were owned by a pathological liar.

She retrieved her purse from the trunk and immediately checked her messages. No proposal emergencies. Thank god.

Luke started up the car and rolled out of the prison gates. He turned Claire's favorite metal album on without asking. The passenger seat was still angled exactly where she liked it, and a strand of her hair clung fast to the glove box. The familiarity brought a sense of peace, and she reached across the console to lay her hand on his leg.

Something had been bothering her since Luke had addressed walking out in the middle of an argument. "I'm sorry for running away in Paris," she told the windshield. "Instead of talking to you. That's something I need to work on."

"You have nothing to apologize for," he said, gripping her hand tightly. "I was being an idiot and letting my vision of the perfect documentary compromise everything. And letting the pressure from Pete get to me. He dropped out. I didn't want someone like that trying to tell me how to produce my project anyway."

"I'm so sorry, Luke. I know how important this documentary is to you."

"Nothing is more important than you."

A thrill ran through her belly.

"And there will be others, if I still decide to go through with it," he continued.

"You have to. Their stories need to be told."

Luke smiled and squeezed her hand. Butterflies tickled her stomach.

"Do we need to pick up Rosie?"

"She's having a sleepover at Nicole's."

"Perfect. Let me just make a quick call." He pulled over into a gas station and got out of the car to talk to someone before topping off his gas tank.

"All set," he said, climbing back into the driver's seat and buckling his seat belt.

"What exactly do you have planned?"

"You'll see." He smirked at the frown on her face. "I know how much you love surprises."

Claire rolled her eyes and slid on a pair of sunglasses. "There had better be food."

She drifted into a light sleep as he drove through the countryside.

He shook her awake a few minutes later. "Put this on." A blindfold fell into her hands. They were in his driveway, and a mysterious van was parked next to them. Who else was there?

"Why do you just have a blindfold in your car? I know we joke about me getting kidnapped again, but it's kind of creepy."

"For emergency surprises," he said. While she situated the blindfold, he got out and rounded the car. He opened her door and walked her onto the driveway, then into the house.

"Upstairs," he said, taking her elbow and gingerly leading her up.

"What smells so good? Is someone cooking in your house? Please tell me it's not your mom."

Luke declined to comment.

"If there is a puppy up here, I am gonna lose my damn mind,"

He laughed. "No puppy. Here," he said, pulling off her blindfold.

A massage table and her favorite masseuse from Reflection Spa stood in the bedroom.

"Jade!" Claire squealed, giving her a squeeze. "Thank you—" She turned to thank Luke properly, but he had disappeared into the bathroom.

With the help of some soothing music and Jade's unparalleled masseuse abilities, Claire was able to banish Barney from her mind for a full thirty minutes. She staggered into the master bathroom after her session and collapsed into the steaming whirlpool tub.

Here, surrounded by pulsating water and lighting she had adjusted to her exact specifications, the reality of her day crept back in.

She had stared into the cold, steely eyes of the man who tried to kill her. It hadn't broken her. She hadn't projectile vomited or had a panic attack, but she had debased herself to get information out of him. Would it be worth it? Had he told the truth? Would she help bring Kayley's family closure, or would this all have been for naught?

He had basically admitted to ESA's involvement, which was huge. But the revelation didn't bring her any comfort. How was she supposed to protect herself against a legion of homicidal frat boys? Her only option was going on the offense. She couldn't just wait around for them to kidnap her. She needed a plan. But there was time to worry about that later. For now, she had a date that deserved her full attention.

She drained the water in the tub and dug under the sink in the bathroom, pleased to find her emergency makeup bag still stashed below.

When she emerged, she found a beautiful black dress, matching diamond bracelet and necklace, and heels displayed on the bed. Claire slithered into them, secretly wishing it had been a new pair of yoga pants instead.

She opened the bedroom door and was greeted by a trail of rose petals. Holy crap. Mr. Tough Guy No Time for Romance had pulled out all the stops. Was he trying to seduce her, or was he about to admit to something terrible?

"Luke?"

Claire followed the trail of petals down the stairs, chasing the smell of bacon. She wobbled her way down the hallway, all the way to the double doors of the ballroom. She opened them hesitantly.

Luke stood next to a tiny, candlelit table set for two. Classical music came from somewhere in the room. Sunlight streamed through the row of floor-to-ceiling windows.

She approached hesitantly, footsteps echoing in the otherwise empty room.

He pulled her chair out for her wordlessly, smiling in his infuriating Luke way, accented by the candlelight.

"This is beautiful," Claire said, gesturing at the ballroom where Nicole and Kyle had gotten engaged. "Are you about to admit to something terrible? Because if you killed someone, I'm not going to be your alibi."

Luke shook his head. "I wanted it to be like Paris. Before I screwed everything up. Is this romantic enough for you?" He raised an eyebrow but continued without letting her respond. "I thought about a harpist, but the acoustics in here aren't suitable for string instruments."

"Well, it's better than falling off a boat into a river. Thank you."

He grabbed her hand and kissed it, and shivers ran up and down her spine.

"How are you feeling?" he asked, placing her napkin on her lap before sitting down. "You've had a hell of a day."

"I've had better days. Now I have to pencil in bringing down ESA along with throwing together the escape room proposal. Logistically, it's the most complicated one I've ever planned."

Luke unrolled his silverware. "Tell me about it."

"Really?" She raised her eyebrows. He always had an opinion if she asked for it, but he had never just asked her to tell him about an upcoming project outright.

"Yes. I'm always interested in your work." He took a sip of water.

"Okay," she said slowly. Had she stumbled into some kind of alternate dimension where Luke respected her career? He really *was* trying to make it up to her. And maybe it would be helpful to have a male perspective during the planning phase.

Claire launched into the escape room. At Dr. Weaver's request, they had landed on a stranded-on-a-desert-island theme for the actual escape room, and a Parisian theme for the proposal to represent their two-part honeymoon: Paris and the French Riviera.

Luke shook his head. "Fixed overhead cameras will ruin the entire illusion. You're just going to see their backs half the time. And please tell me you're going to swap out the overhead lighting. Fluorescent strip lights are a crime against humanity."

She sighed. "Well, how do you propose I make a convincing escape room and have a cinematic record of it? I can't very well throw a camera man in there with them."

"Easy. All you have to do is—"

The door opened behind them, and Claire screamed, turning with her butter knife clenched in her fist.

Luke put a hand on her stabbing wrist. "It's okay, this is my friend Mario. He owns—"

"Mario's. The Italian place on Seventh Street. Of course. Thank you," she said as he set a Caesar salad and a basket of bread in front of her. It smelled like heaven.

"So," Luke said as soon as Mario closed the door behind him. "Let's talk about the proposal later. I wanted to talk to you."

Claire stopped buttering her bread. She put the roll down and sat up straighter. Was he still mad about the whole George thing? Damn it. She should have made an apology basket.

"Communication seems to be a problem between us. I'm a big part of that problem." He reached underneath the table and pulled out a binder.

Her mouth froze in an O of surprise.

"What?" he asked. "It's a good way to organize your thoughts."

"Nothing," she said and took a sip of wine. "Please continue."

He flipped to the first page of the binder. "It's not easy for me to talk about the hard stuff. You've met my mom. My family is painfully stoic. We barely had a family dinner once a week. Talking about feelings was not expected or encouraged, especially after the divorce."

Claire bit her lip. Alice and Roy had all but dragged her feelings out of her on the daily after school. She wasn't one to conceal how she was feeling anyway, but with a psychic for a mom, Claire's emotional state was never a mystery for long.

He stared at his napkin and shuffled the silverware until they were neatly lined up. "My dad was the only one I ever really felt like I could talk to. He'd sneak me a beer while we worked on the '76 Corvette he was restoring in the garage. He would ask me about school, life, what I wanted to be. He bought me my first camera and books on filmmaking. When he died, I closed myself off to a lot of things." Luke flipped to a new page in the binder.

Claire leaned forward, drawn to him like a moth to a flame. This was the most information he had ever shared with her. She should have brought a notebook. Maybe he would let her photocopy his notes.

"As soon as I got out of the Navy, I jumped straight into school for film and never looked back. I threw myself into work. Work was the only thing I could talk to my mom about. It's still the only thing she takes any real interest in."

She reached across the table and grabbed his hand. Their mothers couldn't have been more different.

He took a deep breath. "And finally," he said, glancing down at the binder, "after he died, I dated the wrong women. You mentioned before you heard rumors of me being a ladies' man. That's not entirely untrue. I was looking for something simple, easy. Someone who wouldn't challenge me. I found plenty of that, and even got pretty close to marrying one of those girls—"

Claire's eyes grew wide. Luke had almost proposed before?

"But it didn't work out, and it didn't take long to realize that wasn't what I actually wanted. What I want is you. Claire. You challenge me. You drive me crazy. You make me a better, more empathetic, less frigid human being. You make me laugh. You've shown me there's value in expressing feelings instead of burying them where no one will ever find them. Hell, you've made a whole successful business out of it."

He closed the binder. "So, this is me, trying to work on our communication and explain where I'm coming from. It doesn't excuse what I did to you, but I thought you had a right to know. I'm going to do better in the future. If you'll still have me."

He withdrew his hand and took a big sip of water. "Can you talk now? I think I hit my quota for the month."

Claire sat up straight. She was woefully unprepared to respond to this avalanche of information.

"Of course. Uh, thank you for being so honest with me. I wish I would have prepared something to say."

Luke shoved a hunk of bread in his mouth and nodded encouragingly at her.

"Let me just try to put into words exactly what I'm feeling. This isn't exactly easy for me either."

She took a sip of wine and closed her eyes. Where to begin?

"Just to recap the past three months of knowing each other, you have neglected to tell me that I was likely the target of a serial killer, lied to me about having a brother, forgotten to mention until the worst possible moment that your producers wouldn't go through with your documentary without an interview with the only surviving victim of the killer, who happens to also be me, and—"

She paused, taking a deep breath and another big sip of wine.

"You didn't tell your mother that you had a girlfriend. Do you see the pattern?"

"I do," Luke said, making intense eye contact with the cutlery that he was arranging yet again to be perfectly flush with the edge of the table.

"However, I also suck," she said in a softer tone. "I don't deal well with conflict. I ran away in Paris. I didn't tell you about my biological father. I invited your idiot brother to dinner to punish you. I didn't tell you my suspicions about ESA because I was angry with you. I won't talk with you or

Mindy or anyone else about the idea of expanding the business because it terrifies me, and I'm using Barney as an excuse. Hell, speaking of Barney, I told him he was a great friend in college." She flung one hand toward the ceiling. "The man who tried to murder me. That's how bad I am at communicating."

She stretched across the table and took his hand again. "I'm sorry for my failures. I'm a guarded person. Damaged goods. I don't always tell you what I'm thinking or how I'm feeling because I'm not used to having someone to rely on. Obviously I have some abandonment issues, daddy issues, control issues, and probably a whole slew of other things I haven't even recognized. Maybe I do need therapy," she muttered to herself.

Luke pursed his lips. He didn't nod or acknowledge her statements in any way. Smart man.

She plowed on. "Anyway, I appreciate so much that you were willing to talk to me about what you were feeling. So, starting today, I want to be completely, painfully, open and honest with you. Since you left, you missed some things."

Luke leaned forward and maintained eye contact. The salad sat untouched between them.

She ticked items off on her fingers. "My bio-dad came back into my life just so he could use me to talk to Barney. A bunch of frat boys blew up my car. I learned self-defense, and it's helped a little with managing some of my fear. I developed what Google says is probably an anxiety disorder. Or maybe it was always there. My sleepwalking problem is way worse than you know. I straight-up sleepwalked into a lake after Paris. Sawyer has been a huge help to me these past few weeks," she said, wincing at his tightened grip.

"Sorry," he said, relaxing his hand. "Go on."

"First of all, there's nothing going on between us. We're

friends. I know you still don't fully trust him, but I want you to try. For me. ESA is the one doing all of this to me. He's been a really good friend. And, if it puts any points in his column, Kyle trusts him too."

Luke sighed, leaning back in his chair.

"I'll try. I'm grateful you had someone to look out for you while I was gone."

Claire took another deep breath, trying to calm the heart that seemed to be beating in triplicate against her ribcage. Why was telling the truth so cringey?

"The last thing that happened while you were gone genuinely surprised me. I didn't want to admit it to myself. In spite of everything we had been through, in spite of how angry I was at you"—she paused, searching for the right words—"I missed you," she said quietly. "Something would happen, and I would immediately want to know how you would feel about it. How you'd react, what you'd say."

"I missed you too," he said, taking her hand again, pressing it to his lips.

Warmth tingled in her fingers. "So, if you're willing to try this again, I'm willing."

He stood, knocking his chair onto the floor. He pulled Claire out of her chair and crushed his mouth to hers. Her hands snaked around his waist. Every familiar muscle rippled under his suit jacket.

Apparently, he had had enough of talking.

He picked her up and wrapped her legs around his waist, sliding the hem of her dress up her thighs.

Her body viscerally ached for him. She wrestled with his jacket, wrenching it off and tossing it onto the floor. Her back arched as he slid down the sweetheart neckline of her dress.

She ripped at the buttons on his shirt, yanking and

pulling as she tried to keep her balance. Finally he was free, bare chest bathed in the dying light.

They stopped for a moment, looking at each other, and then at the door to the ballroom.

Luke gripped her tighter and carried her across the marble floor, banging the door open and stepping down the hallway.

"Keep it warm for us, will you?" he called down the hallway before carrying Claire up the stairs. She wasn't going to be able to look Mario in the eyes for weeks.

They crashed into the bedroom. She held him so tightly that her fingertips would probably leave bruises. He laid her on the bed, peeling her dress away and revealing more of her body, inch by inch until she was completely exposed. She reached for him, and they collided.

They held each other, for once perfectly in sync, holding nothing back. Luke's eyes were unreadable. Relief, fear, lust, all mixed together in a storm of blue and green.

There were no rats, no rank dumpster, no pile of crates. There was only the two of them.

They rose and crashed together, holding each other as though they were the last two things tethered to the earth, in danger of falling and spiraling into the sky.

Luke collapsed next to Claire, a sheen of sweat on his stupid, perfect forehead.

"I guess that's a yes," she said weakly.

CHAPTER THIRTY-SEVEN

To Do:
- Fix stupid lighting issue for Dr. W proposal
- Call the florist

WHEN LUKE ARRIVED IN THE BEDROOM THE NEXT MORNING with a breakfast tray, Claire had her hair in a bun, notepad in one hand, cell phone in the other.

"You've got your concentration face on, but you seem surprisingly calm this morning," he said, setting the tray with a plate of eggs and bacon on the bed.

"That looks amazing, thank you," she said with a genuine, relaxed smile. "All this banging must be great for my stress levels."

"What are you doing?" he asked as he slid back into bed next to her, then planted a kiss on her bare shoulder.

"A few little things for the escape room proposal. We

have the whole flow figured out, but I still need some artwork and a few more candles and—" She sighed and pressed her palms to her eyes.

He squeezed her leg. "I'll leave you to it. Unless you want to talk about it," he said, pausing half-crouched on the bed.

"I'm good. Thank you." She offered a quick kiss and a smile before he walked out of the room. It was amazing how quickly they had fallen back into their old patterns. After their talk the night before, she had lain awake in his arms, glowing from the inside out.

Finally, finally, he was being honest with her. Even about the hard stuff. She could hardly believe it. They had more to work on—it wasn't like her daddy issues had disappeared overnight—but what a step in the right direction.

Her phone rang, and she groaned at the caller ID. Speak of the devil.

"Yes, Jack?"

What did he want now?

"They found part of Kayley's remains. Right where Barney said she would be."

"They did?" Claire leapt out of bed and nearly toppled the breakfast tray. Her stomach twisted violently, and she clutched the nightstand for support. Nothing about this felt like a victory. She sank to her knees beside the bed. "So, he was telling the truth. Her poor family. What a bittersweet day this will be for them." Her heart ached. "Thanks for the update."

She ended the call before Jack could ask her to go back to the prison for more information. Her forehead pressed into the mattress. Sure, she had helped coerce a killer into telling her where he hid a body. Maybe being able to lay her to rest would bring her family some comfort in time. But she had just effectively erased the last bit of hope the Herrolds had. They would never see their daughter alive again.

"Claire?" Luke's voice came from downstairs, an edge of panic cutting his words.

"What? What's wrong?" She crossed the room in seconds and flung the bedroom door open. Her heart hammered in her throat. Surely he hadn't heard the news about Kayley already.

"I need you to stay upstairs. Lock the door."

The tablet fell from her hand. The edge of her vision went dark for a moment as she slammed the door, leaning against it and clutching at her heart. Had ESA finally come to take her? There was no time for panic attacks. She needed to act.

Claire threw on her clothes haphazardly. She tore the room apart until she found a hockey stick that Luke kept underneath the bed. Saying a silent prayer, she flung the bedroom door open, hockey stick held like a baseball bat.

"Yeah, I need an officer at 204 Stone Bridge Road. Someone dropped something off on my porch that looks a lot like a human heart." Luke's voice carried up the stairs. "I have a security system. No, the alarm didn't go off. I don't think they're in the house. Listen, my girlfriend is Claire Hartley. She's here. Send Detective Smith."

Claire crept down another hardwood step, still holding the stick aloft. The step creaked, and Luke turned around. He gestured at her wildly, attempting to shoo her back up the stairs. She shook her head, coming to stand next to him.

Outside the windowpanes, a trail of tiny red droplets led up the stamped concrete sidewalk. They stopped on Luke's doormat, where a human-looking heart rested with a knife plunged through the left ventricle.

Her stomach rolled. Who or what had this heart belonged to?

Luke hung up and glanced at her. "The bedroom, now. We don't know for sure that there isn't anyone in the house," he said, grabbing her arm and steering her toward the stairs.

She yanked her arm back. "No. Let's check your footage. Then we'll know."

Luke swore and walked into his office. He slid his computer chair down a row of monitors until he got to the last one. He pulled up the footage from his front door camera and began scrolling through the evening, starting when he and Claire had arrived.

"Before we do anything, back the whole night up and email it to me and Detective Smith," she instructed sternly. "I will not stand for any more technological failures in catching bad guys."

"Done. Nothing, nothing," he mumbled to himself as he fast forwarded.

"There," Claire said, pointing to the screen.

Just after 3 a.m., a figure dressed entirely in black emerged from the dense clump of oak trees by Luke's driveway. The figure swung a backpack off their shoulder and set it on the driveway, digging for something. A plastic bag holding a dark shape emerged. The figure, who already had gloves on, reached into the bag and drew out what could only be the heart. They seemed to stop and listen for a long moment, still crouching on the ground.

They walked up the sidewalk and onto the porch, taking care to arrange the heart exactly in the center of the welcome mat. The figure took a steak knife out of their back pocket and considered for a moment before plunging it into the heart.

Just then, Luke's phone rang.

"Detective Smith?" he asked, hitting pause on his desktop. "The back door? Why? Fine."

Claire followed him out of his office and down the hall to the ballroom. They pushed open the patio doors and took the long way to the front door, passing several officers examining Luke's land.

Another policeman was cordoning off the front porch with yellow caution tape. A half dozen police cars parked at haphazard angles on Luke's driveway.

Detective Smith, an unremarkable-looking man who seemed to carry the weight of the world on his shoulders, turned to them with grave seriousness in his ice blue eyes.

Claire gasped, staring at the front door. She clutched Luke's hand so hard that she thought she felt something pop.

There, in foot-tall, blood-red letters, was a simple message.

You're next, bitch.

Luke turned to her, gathered her into his chest as though he could shield her from the message.

"Well," she said into his shirt, "you have to give them points for the correct comma usage. Villains are not usually known for being sticklers for grammar."

The police combed Luke's entire yard and the surrounding woods for hours before leaving. Yellow caution tape still stretched across the porch. They had taken the heart with them as evidence, and a call had been placed to a crime scene cleanup company.

"Do you think things will ever be normal?" Claire asked as she stood by the breakfast nook, staring at the tree line.

She had just checked all the locks in the house for the fortieth time that day.

Somehow, the heart on the doorstep was worse than torching her car. They had come onto Luke's land while they were sleeping and utterly unaware, just to leave a horrifying message. How much longer could this go on?

She had scoured the internet daily ever since learning the truth about ESA. There weren't any new reports of women going missing in the greater West Haven area. What were they waiting for? Were they so afraid of Luke that they wouldn't try to breach his house to get to her? Or was this just another cruel training exercise like Bowling Ball had mentioned?

"With you? Unlikely." Luke slid an arm around her waist and pressed a mug of coffee into her hand. Bags had formed under his eyes. He kissed her just below her earlobe, sending a shiver down her spine.

"I have to go to the office," she said, turning to look at him. She took a big sip from her mug and handed it back to him. Work might be the only thing that could save her sanity.

"Right now?" he asked.

"I have to go make sure every detail of the escape room proposal is perfect. I can't afford to lose focus on my clients just because a bunch of idiots are hell-bent on killing me."

Twenty minutes later, Mindy looked up as Claire entered the warehouse. "What the hell are you doing here?"

"What do you mean what am I doing here? This is our office."

"I mean what the hell are you doing here when a psychotic person just left an organ on your doorstep? Go home."

Claire shot her a dirty look and dropped her purse on

the conference table. "Am I supposed to throw in the towel and curl into a ball and cry every time these psychos do something to me? No. They've ruined enough things in my life. Like our business's reputation, for example. I would bet anything one of them called the press on me at Yee Haw's." The thought had been rolling around in her mind for a while now. She had no proof, but it felt true.

"Why do they keep doing this to you?" Mindy asked quietly.

Tears burned unexpectedly and she sniffed them back. Emotions were not invited to this work meeting. But if Luke deserved honesty about how she was feeling, so did her best friend. "I don't know. When I followed that guy at Venor, he said something about training exercises. He named a whole bunch of categories—vehicular, psychological. I can't even remember them anymore. I think they're torturing me to train their recruits. And eventually, they're going to run out of training exercises."

Maybe the heart had been their final warning.

"I'm tired of waiting for them to escalate," she continued. "I honestly wish they would just hurry up and try to kidnap me already. Every time they do something else, all I can think about is you and Nicole and the guys and Rosie. And what will happen when they hit the end of their list? What will they do when they really want to hurt me? What if they go after someone I love? I'm putting every single one of you in danger, just by virtue of being associated with me."

"Stop it," Mindy said. "If any of those assholes tried to hurt one of us, we would destroy them because we're not a bunch of idiot frat boys with suspicious access to dead body parts."

Claire bit her lip. "I think they're capable of more than we think. There's no doubt in my mind that the idiot who stalked me on Venor's campus would have taken me if I hadn't locked myself in the newspaper room."

Mindy reached across the table and grabbed her hand. "We're not going to let anything happen to you."

"Can we talk about something else?" Claire dabbed a tissue under one eye.

"Of course." Mindy bit her lip and stared around the room as though expecting to see a new topic of conversation crowded between the tablecloths and sconces on the shelf behind them. "Did you see the article about you finally stopped gaining traction? A state senator had an affair, so it's yesterday's news now."

"It's still out there. Every time somebody Googles us," Claire said bitterly, setting her laptop on the table. ESA would pay for this. And in the meantime, she was going to cut back on the drinking.

"I will increase our budget for search engine optimization next month." Mindy turned on her tablet and tapped away. "So, you stayed with Luke last night."

"Yes." Claire drew her hair back into a bun.

"Does that mean you're back together?" Mindy peered over her screen.

"I think so. We actually had a really good talk. He brought a binder and everything. He told me about his dad and more about his past than I ever expected to hear."

Mindy whistled. "A binder? He must really like you. I can't get Gavin to talk about his feelings to save my life."

Claire smiled. "Maybe you should try screaming at him and then falling off a boat in Paris."

"Excellent advice. So, should we talk about the escape room?"

"Yes. I had some ideas this morning." Finally, some talk she could handle without having an emotional breakdown.

"Oh my god, she's okay. Claire, what the hell is wrong with you?"

Someone grabbed at her arm. Claire blinked. Where was she? Why was it so cold? What was on her hands? And why were her nipples on fire? The last thing she remembered was a meeting with Mindy at her apartment that stretched almost to midnight. They had headed straight to bed afterward. But this wasn't her bedroom.

She was standing barefoot in some damp grass. An unfamiliar house was in front of her. A hot pink "female" symbol on the siding was still wet.

"We need to go, now." Someone tugged her backward, and she stumbled.

"She's still coming out of it. I got her," a masculine voice said.

The porch light of the house turned on. Suddenly she was upside down. Something fell from her hand.

"Shit. Grab that," a gruff male voice ordered.

"Got it." That was definitely Mindy. A ball rattled in a metal can. What were they doing outside?

Oh, shit. She hadn't handcuffed herself to the bed. She must have sleepwalked again. There was no telling where she had ended up.

"Go, go, go," another male voice ordered. Claire bobbled upside down like a rag doll, smacking her face off a very broad back.

Angry voices came from behind them. The group moved quickly down the block, then cut left. They paused at the corner of Walnut and College Ave. Claire listened intently. More lights had snapped on at the house that was barely visible from the street corner.

"Let's keep going," Nicole said. She jogged across the crosswalk. Everyone else followed. They ran another three blocks and collapsed in the parking lot of a Rite Aid, bent over and breathing heavy.

"I think we lost them." The voice rumbled in the chest of the person carrying her. It had to be Sawyer.

"Guys, what's going on?" Claire asked, still upside down. "Why is everyone carrying weapons?"

Sawyer gently set her on her feet. Luke laid down an axe and glared at Sawyer. Mindy dropped what looked like a medieval flail onto the asphalt. She crossed to Claire and got right in her face.

"What's going on? I'll tell you what's going on. I woke up, and you were gone. I called your phone, and it was still plugged into the wall. Then I checked your location with the watch"—she gestured to the GPS watch she had gifted Claire the month before— "and I saw that you were at the ESA house. I thought they had taken you. How could you do this?" Tears sparkled in Mindy's eyes. She pushed Claire's shoulders with two hands and released a frustrated scream.

Claire bounced into Sawyer. Her heart pounded in her chest. How in the hell had she gotten all the way to Venor? It was easily five miles from her apartment.

"It's not her fault," Sawyer spoke up. "She was sleep-walking."

"Sleepwalking?" Nicole, who had been silent until that moment, dropped her bat in a parking spot where Kyle was sitting, sword at his side. "Since when do you sleepwalk?"

Claire sighed. "For a few weeks now. Since the incident. I had a handle on it, but I forgot to tie myself to the bedframe last night. I didn't want Mindy to ask questions. But I didn't know I could drive." This was very bad. The press had only just decided to move on from the story of her vomiting and whipping a trash can lid at someone. If they got wind that she was sleep driving, her business would never recover.

"So, instead of being honest with your friends, you drove the company van five miles *while asleep* and spray painted a female symbol on the house of the crazy misogynists who want you to *die*?" Mindy had stepped up to Claire again.

Sawyer stepped between them and put a hand on Mindy's shoulder. "She can't control it. She sleepwalked at my house too. Right into a lake."

Mindy peeked under Sawyer's arm and jabbed a finger at Claire. "I am so angry at you. Why didn't you tell me about this?"

"I guess it was one of those things where if I pretended it wasn't happening, it wasn't real. Usually I take a snack with me, but I must have opted for spray paint this time. Oh wait, my nipples."

"Your nipples?" Nicole came to stand next to her and wrapped a hand around her elbow. She sounded like she was speaking to a toddler who just had a nightmare.

Claire dug a hand into her bra and grabbed a handful of mystery bumps. She dropped them onto the parking lot.

"Are those buffalo cauliflower bites from JP's?" Kyle asked from the ground. JP's was the late-night student restaurant on campus.

"Apparently, I made a pit stop. I'm so sorry, guys. This is so stupid."

Claire plopped down onto a concrete parking block. She was wearing both of her Taser ankle harnesses. At least if the ESA brothers had come to confront her, she could have incapacitated two of them. Mindy and Nicole sat down next to her. They put their arms around her, surrounding her in a cocoon of Paul Mitchell shampoo and Tide detergent. Kyle was still panting on the ground. Luke crossed his arms over his chest, brow furrowed. Sawyer stayed on his feet, eyes fixed on the university in the distance.

"Guys?" Claire asked.

"Hmm?" Nicole responded as she stroked her hair.

"Where's my car?"

CHAPTER THIRTY-EIGHT

To Do:
- Make this the best proposal yet
- Find a way to sneak into ESA meeting

A CRAMP TWISTED CLAIRE'S SIDE AS SHE RAN FROM ONE END of the previously vacant storefront to the other for what felt like the fortieth time this hour. She arranged the freesias again, rotating them so that they caught the glow of the Edison bulbs strung in a crisscross pattern above.

The custom designed West Haven Escape Room sign had come down. The reception desk where Claire had checked the couple in had been disassembled and hidden. An eight-foot replica of the Eiffel Tower had been quickly hefted into the room. False greenery was arranged to mimic the *Parc du Champ de Mars*. The reminder of Paris didn't sting quite as much now that she was on better terms with Luke.

The false ceiling was broken down, revealing pictures of the couple over the years hung from the rafters, slowly spinning in the breeze from the HVAC system. Mindy was fighting with dozens of white pillar candles that refused to stay lit. If no one ended up on fire by the end of this, it would be a miracle.

Speaking of miracles, there hadn't been any retaliation from ESA after Claire sleep-tagged their frat house. Either they were regrouping and planning something truly horrible, or they didn't know she was responsible for it. Every day that inched by since the attack was a small eternity. What would they do next? She really needed to infiltrate the meeting to find out what they were up to. But how?

There was time to worry about all that later. For the moment, she had a happily ever after to create. Even if it was in danger of catching on fire and/or collapsing into a pile of trash at any moment.

Nicole stood in the corner, remotely monitoring the cameras they had stashed in the escape room and snapping pictures at opportune moments.

"Everything's going to be okay," she whispered reassuringly to Claire.

Claire nudged a fire extinguisher behind the fake greenery. Every part of this proposal had been a chore. The venue had sprung a leak and sustained significant water damage the week before the proposal. The groom-to-be had gotten a black eye from a charity softball game. Mindy had tripped and knocked the Eiffel Tower over. They had superglued the two halves back together, but it was leaning precariously despite the fishing wire that Claire had secured it with.

And yet, despite all the aggravation and chaos, it was lovely. Easily one of the most creative proposals they had done to date. The puzzles were carefully thought out, every detail designed with the couple in mind.

She and Mindy had spied on the clients, Dr. Jerry Weaver and Sarah, while they had a date night at Dave and Busters. The couple was fun-loving, sweet to each other, and very clearly in love, if a bit over-competitive at Skee-Ball. As an added precaution, Claire had also called the state board of medicine. Luckily, Dr. Weaver didn't have any open investigations into his license. She had done everything she could to make sure this couple was the real deal. And they were. She could feel it.

Behind the locked door, Dr. Weaver, an emergency department physician at a local hospital, was helping his soon-to-be fiancée crack open a safe.

"We only have four minutes left," Sarah said from one of Nicole's monitors, glancing anxiously at the clock in the corner of the room.

"Plenty of time. What were the numbers from the periscope again?"

"Four-eight-nineteen."

"Wow, our anniversary date. What are the odds?"

The odds were very good indeed.

"Why don't you try those on the safe?" Jerry asked.

"Good idea." Sarah deftly twisted the lock back and forth with her long fingers. She was the first chair cellist for the West Haven Orchestra. "This is the best date night ever, by the way. I didn't even know this place was here."

"It's new," Jerry said as he paced behind Sarah. He had grown steadily paler over the last hour.

"It opened! We found the key!"

Sarah leapt into Jerry's arms. He smiled.

"Let's make sure it works." He gently set her down and gave her the key.

Nicole sprang into position, crouching to the side to make herself as inconspicuous as possible, camera at the ready. Claire sat the ring box on top of a table and scuttled underneath it, hiding behind the tablecloth. Mindy joined her a second later, still clutching a candle.

When the door swung open and Sarah cried out in victory, Claire watched through a hole in the cloth as Jerry picked up the box and tucked it in his pants pocket. Mindy peered out a hole next to her. Unlike most of the proposals they had done this year, everything was perfectly intimate— no family, no friends, just the couple and their magical moment.

"Oh, man, that was crazy. What an adrenaline rush. We should do another—wait. Was all of this here when we came in? Is this like part two of the escape room?" Sarah asked, spinning around and walking back to the door they had just come out of. She walked as gracefully as she played, as though she were gliding on air.

"This is the only door. Miss?" Sarah called, clearly looking for Claire.

Sarah spun around and finally noticed Jerry kneeling under the Eiffel Tower.

Her hands flew to her mouth, and the look of surprise was unmistakable.

Claire's gaze was glued to the Eiffel Tower. Surely it would hold. It had to. If it broke apart and concussed the couple, she could kiss whatever was left of her career goodbye.

"Sarah," Jerry said simply, holding one hand out to her.

Sarah ran across the room. "Yes. Yes, a thousand times yes."

She dropped to her knees and threw herself into his arms.

"But I didn't even ask you yet," Jerry laughed, glasses askew from the impact of his now-fiancée. "You have to let me ask."

Sarah stood back up, wiping at the happy tears that had sprung up. "Okay, okay, fine."

Jerry launched into a story about the first moment he knew he was in love with Sarah, which involved a lost patient and a large tub of water balloons. Was it her imagination, or was the tower leaning a little more? Hurry up, Jerry.

Claire's phone buzzed in her pocket. They had forty local applicants to look over. Although they had lost a client and a potentially beautiful proposal over the alleyway incident, couples were still applying. It had been days since she'd seen a reference to herself as an alcoholic in the West Haven Times. Maybe the press really had moved on.

Wait a minute, was something burning?

She glanced at Mindy. The candle in her hand had seemingly re-ignited. The ends of her willowy black hair were on fire.

"Oh my god," Claire whisper-screamed.

Mindy's mouth was frozen in an O of surprise. Claire took off her shirt and beat Mindy with it until the flames receded. The smell of burned hair was growing stronger, and it did *not* fit Claire's vision for a Parisian proposal. She pulled a perfume tester out of her purse and squirted Mindy with it.

She slapped Claire's hand.

"Would you do me the great honor of becoming my wife?" Jerry asked, apparently unfazed by the kerfuffle unfolding behind them.

"Yes!" Sarah called.

Claire's heart grew in her chest. She had almost missed

the "yes." Damn faulty pillar candles. These were going straight back to the trading company.

Claire shuffled back into her shirt, elbowing the underside of the table and almost swearing. When the couple broke apart, she stepped out from under the table and gave them another minute before walking over with their coats and Sarah's purse.

"You have a reservation in twenty minutes at Barrel Twenty-One," she said, handing over their personal effects and a bouquet of freesias. "And congratulations."

The happy couple wandered off to dinner, leaving a void in the room. As the front door closed, the Eiffel Tower fell over and snapped into two pieces. At least it waited.

"Get some good shots?" Claire asked Nicole as she texted a member of the crew she had hired to help set up and tear down.

"Amazing ones," Nicole said, coming over to Claire and quickly flipping through a few on her camera. "They're going to look great on the blog."

"You are so good at what you do, Coli."

"Thank you. So are you," she said and gave Claire a hug. "Do you have any good candidates coming up?"

Claire climbed a stepladder and cut the fishing wire from the wall. Mindy stood by the entrance, frowning at the ends of her hair. "We do. Sorry, Min. Can you grab the Tupperware boxes by the door? Thanks. She turned back to the task at hand and addressed Nicole. "There's a hiking-themed one, a Christmas village flash mob, a luxuriously decorated rooftop proposal. I would love to do them all."

"Maybe once all this settles down, you'll be able to take on a few more clients at a time," Nicole said, shoving some fake greenery into a storage bin.

"I really hope so. I'm tired of men blowing up my cars

and threatening me. They're not going to be happy about my midnight spray painting escapade. One way or another, this is going to end."

"It sounds like we need to schedule another Code Purple." Nicole met Claire's eyes over a clump of freesias.

"I think you're right. Girls only. Thursday night."

CHAPTER THIRTY-NINE

To Do:
- Invest in better bedtime restraints
- Send candidates screening test

CLAIRE PACED IN FRONT OF THE WHITEBOARD. HER FOOTSTEPS echoed in the cavernous warehouse. "Thank you for joining me for another girls-only Code Purple. With your help, I'm going to infiltrate ESA's meeting on Friday."

Mindy raised her hand.

"Yes?"

"We're coming with you. Obviously." Mindy had trimmed a couple of inches off her burned hair and looked more beautiful than ever.

Claire sighed. "I had a feeling you'd say that. Fine. So, what I can't figure out is how we're going to spy on the meeting. Breaking into the house is too risky. We don't know how many there are. And if we linger outside, any number of neighbors could see us and call the police. I'm thinking about shipping them some kind of surveillance device that could transmit what they're saying to us, but what if they threw it away?"

Mindy shook her head. "The audio wouldn't be admissible in court anyway. Can't record them without their knowledge."

Claire harrumphed.

Nicole glanced up from her laptop. "Spying is going to be the easy part. We'll use the tunnels."

Mindy and Claire stared blankly at Nicole.

"You know, the tunnels. The ones that run underneath all of campus and connect the buildings to West Haven's underground bomb shelter? Built during the Cold War?"

Claire tilted her head. "This is literally the first time I'm hearing about them. Are you sure this is at Venor?"

Nicole sighed. "Come on, guys. I made you go on my tour sophomore year. Were you even paying attention?"

"She's right," Mindy said. She stopped tapping on her tablet. "In the basement of the chapel, there was a door that was padlocked shut. I always wanted to go fool around in there."

Claire stopped pacing. "How do you know what the basement of the chapel looks like?"

"It's where the practice rooms are. Band, remember?" Mindy was a surprisingly accomplished clarinetist.

Claire turned back to Nicole. "You're sure they connect all the buildings on campus? Even the frats?"

Nicole nodded. "There was a framed map in the registrar's office. ESA probably has a door in their basement."

Claire added two items to the whiteboard—bolt cutters and dust masks. It was going to be an awkward trip to the hardware store.

"ESA doesn't strike me as the kind of frat to leave a door bolted. So, we'll have to hope that we can quietly break in through the basement door and then hear well enough from downstairs. Ugh, I never thought I'd spend another Friday night in a frat basement." The smell of stale beer and body odor washed over her.

Nicole shrugged. "It's our best option."

Claire sighed. "I don't love it, but it'll have to do. Remember, no one tells the guys anything. We're just having a normal, run-of-the-mill girls' night."

She bit her lip. She was already going back on her promise to be completely honest with Luke. But surely this was different. If he knew about the ESA meeting, he would probably handcuff her to the headboard to prevent her from leaving. If she could pull this off, she could find a way to get ESA out of her life forever and keep everyone she loved safe. There had to be exceptions to every rule. She'd tell him when it was over.

"At this point, this *is* a run-of-the-mill girls' night. Is this our third stakeout this year?" Mindy raised her eyebrows.

"Whatever. Let's meet back here tomorrow at seven."

THE SUN WAS BEGINNING TO SET AS THEY PULLED INTO THE parking lot of Alabaster, a local coffee shop. Claire stared longingly at the espresso machine inside, but if she had one now, she would be up all night. Getting older sucked.

She unzipped the backpack for the millionth time. Bolt cutters, masks, and disposable gloves were still inside. She wasn't sure exactly how many laws they were about to break, but surely they had collectively given Venor enough money to justify their actions.

"Ready?" Mindy said from the driver's seat.

"Let's do this." Claire pulled on a new brunette wig and slid on a pair of glasses. Mindy donned a platinum blond wig and a Coach backpack, and Nicole paired her new waist-length black hair with a letterman jacket she had borrowed from Kyle.

They climbed out of the car and bent forward to examine their reflections in the window.

"Nothing to see here, just Chloe Patterson on her way to the library to study for the LSATs," Mindy said.

"I like that you gave your character a backstory," Claire said as she again applied a shade of lipstick that didn't suit her.

They set off toward campus.

Mindy pressed the back of her hand to her forehead and adopted a Southern accent. "She just wants to save her family farm from the clutches of the evil land developers who want to pave over it and turn it into a mega strip club."

"If the land developers were smart, they would leave it a farm and call it 'The Hoe Down.'"

"It's my backstory, Claire."

"Sorry."

They crossed an intersection and hit the eastern edge of campus. The chapel rose in front of them, a stately, three-story brick structure. Loud music thumped from one of the dormitories nearby. The ghost of the taste of cheap vodka seared Claire's tongue.

"Are we really doing this?" Mindy whispered, staring up at the chapel.

"I have to. You guys don't." Claire looked at her foolishly dressed friends. "I told you from the beginning I'm completely fine with you guys staying home or being lookouts."

"We're not leaving you alone." Nicole nudged her in the ribs.

"Or missing a chance to take down a bunch of woman-hating sociopaths," Mindy added.

"Okay." Claire turned to face the chapel. "Let's do this." She slid on a set of gloves and wrenched open the chapel door. "Mindy, lead the way."

They wound their way down a narrow set of steps into the basement. It was eerily quiet. They passed the sound-proof music rooms Mindy had mentioned and came to stand in front of a nondescript metal door with a padlock.

Claire glanced around. There didn't seem to be any cameras down here. Hopefully, there weren't any in the tunnels either. The last thing they needed was campus security blowing their cover. She pulled the bolt cutters from her backpack and clamped them onto the lock.

"Help me," she whispered, and they all grabbed the bolt cutters. They grunted and squeezed until the shackle snapped in half. The padlock thunked onto the floor, and Claire tucked it in her backpack. There was no sense in leaving evidence behind.

Mindy pulled the door open. The tunnel walls were rock. Everything was damp and smelled like a cave. There was no light switch on the inside. Claire pulled flashlights out of her backpack and handed them to her friends. She clamped on a headlamp and turned it on.

"Only one way to go," Nicole said, stepping inside. The hallway ended in a wall on their right. An abandoned tuba sat just inside the door on the left. They walked another couple of feet, and Claire nearly banged her shin off a cello case. Communion trays were stacked haphazardly on a lopsided table.

"It'll be a miracle if we make it to ESA without breaking our ankles," Mindy muttered as she climbed over an old TV.

"How are we going to know which door is theirs? These all look the same," Claire said, gesturing at another identical metal door that evidently led to another campus building.

"My GPS is still working." Nicole waved her phone in the air as she led the way. She was like Indiana Jones in a wig. "We should probably try to be quieter in case someone is outside one of these doors."

They descended into silence as they weaved through the tunnels. They passed piles of old computers, overflowing file boxes, and a full-blown papier-mâché dragon. Finally, after what felt like hours of walking, Nicole held up one hand. They stopped. In front of them was another metal door, and a blow-up sex doll lying face down in the corridor. Voices came from the other side of the door.

She touched her finger to her lips, and they crowded around the door. A soft light flickered through the crack in the frame. The three of them leaned in and pressed their ear to it. If someone jerked the door open, they would all fall into the frat and probably be murdered.

"I can't believe someone tagged the house. I bet it was that bitch," one voice said.

Claire's heart thumped in her chest.

"But how would she know to put up that bullshit symbol? She's not smart enough to figure out what we're about," a gruff voice answered.

Someone else spoke with measured pauses. "Gentlemen, welcome to your last meeting before you're officially made members. It'll be a short one. Each one of you has shown loyalty and commitment to the cause. Your training efforts with terrorizing Miss Hartley have been truly heartwarming. You've mastered the basics of intimidation, all the way up to internationally coordinated threats and explosions. Well done, gentlemen."

Mindy's knuckles cracked. Claire nudged her.

"But before you can become an official brother, you must prove yourselves."

"How do we do that?" a deep voice asked.

"Our two most sacred duties as members of Epsilon Sigma Alpha are identifying women who have opportunities they do not deserve or are unsuitable for and restoring the natural order. Your initiation ritual will be your first chance to pay homage to our practices and figure out your strengths. You, collectively, will be assigned a target," the guy that seemed to be in charge answered.

Claire exchanged a worried glance with Mindy and Nicole. Were they finally going to come for her?

"Who's our target?" someone new asked.

There was the sound of a latch being undone and a shuffling of papers.

"She is your target. She is a business owner and, even worse, has been identified as a manipulator of local male officials. She's not a high priority, which is why we're saving her for the new recruits. However, every target is important. Each win brings us closer to restoring order."

"What's her name?"

"Wendy Flutter."

Holy shit.

Claire's mouth dropped open. Mindy flailed her hands beside her.

"What do we do with her?" another voice asked.

"You have twenty-four hours to find Miss Flutter and bring her here. Tomorrow night at ten p.m., we'll show you what the eradicators do. And, as always when you're in public, remember your cover. You are a member of Epsilon

Sigma Alpha, a fraternity with unparalleled requirements for GPA and community service. You are bold, you are righteous, you are alpha. Go in justice."

There was a shuffling on the other side of the door, and footsteps padded across the concrete floor. The flickering light went out. There was silence. Claire's heart was going to beat its way right out of her body.

"Do you think it's safe to go?" Mindy whispered.

The door opened.

They leapt away from the opening. A man walked into the corridor and blinked in surprise.

Claire grabbed Taser #3 from her purse and fired it. The prongs jumped the short distance in the blink of an eye. The ESA member went rigid and started to fall forward. Mindy nudged the sex doll over to break his fall, then hit him in the head with a hardcover romance novel from her purse.

Something rolled out of his pockets. Claire shined the beam of her flashlight over it. It was an expensive-looking silver pen, identical to the one she had found in the woods. She shuddered.

Nicole eased the door shut, then they turned and ran like hell. Claire made it about eight feet before jerking backward like a caught fish. Her heart leapt into her throat.

"Shit! The prongs are still stuck in him."

Mindy whipped open her purse and pulled out cuticle scissors. She snipped the wires.

"Wait!" Claire called. An idea had struck her. She pulled out her tube of unflattering lipstick and uncapped it.

"Claire, what the hell are you doing?" Nicole hissed. "We need to go."

Claire leaned over to the wall and dragged the lipstick across the surface. She glanced nervously at the body on the ground, but he didn't move. Mindy must have really clocked him.

"Done!" She stepped back and admired her handwork.

TKE RULES

"Smart to try to blame it on another frat, but why would a TKE brother have lipstick?" Mindy whispered.

"Never mind. Let's go." They followed the beams of flashlights down the hallway all the way back to the chapel. Claire turned around no fewer than seventy-two times, but no lumbering ESA brother followed them. They snuck back through the basement and outside without incident. Once they had piled into Mindy's car, they let out a collective sigh of relief.

"So. Wendy," Nicole said. There was a cobweb in her wig.

"Right. Option A: we let them take her," Mindy offered as she turned the car on. Air conditioning and pop music blasted simultaneously.

"We can't let them kill her. Can we?" Nicole said thoughtfully.

Claire sighed. They had no choice. "You know what we have to do."

"Call the police and let them handle it?" Nicole suggested.

"No. We have to kidnap her first."

CHAPTER FORTY

To Do:
- Assemble Code Purple Task Force
- Kidnap Wendy

"YOU DID *WHAT*?" LUKE SHOUTED.

Rosie popped her head up from a new dog bed in Luke's living room—undoubtedly another apology purchase from him.

"Yeah, I know," Claire said sheepishly. She took a sip of hot cocoa and leaned back in the breakfast nook. "But everything was fine. Only one person ended up unconscious, and it wasn't any of us, so I call that a win.

"That was so stupid and dangerous." He looked ready to flip the table. "Did we not just have a conversation about honesty?"

"Yes, we did, and I'm sorry. That's why I'm telling you now. Listen, we can debate later about how stupid it was," she said. "But right now, we need to come up with a plan. Wendy is in imminent danger. We need to kidnap her before they can."

"You know if you kidnap her, she's going to sue you even harder," Kyle said over a steaming cup of tea.

Nicole and Mindy nodded and yawned. It was almost midnight.

"If it's between Wendy getting murdered and getting sued again, I pick the latter. So, we need a two-fold plan. We need to kidnap Wendy, and then we need to lay a trap. Who's got ideas?"

She glared at Kyle when he popped his hand into the air. "And for the record, any suggestions of calling the police and letting them handle it will not be entertained. They don't believe me about ESA, so they surely won't send someone to watch out for Wendy. I refuse to have her death on my hands."

Kyle put his hand down.

Claire whirled on Mindy. "And where the hell is Gavin?"

Mindy shrugged. "He couldn't make it. He has an exam tomorrow."

"He's forfeited his option to be on the Code Purple Task Force, then. Good to know we can't count on him in an emergency." Claire scribbled in her notebook and closed the cover. "Someone just lost their spot in the bunker."

"Is there really a bunker?" Sawyer whispered to Kyle.

"Don't worry about it," the other four said in unison.

"I have an idea for the second half of the plan," Luke said suddenly.

Apparently, he was on board now.

"Go on."

"Throw an event in her honor. That will draw them out."

Claire glared at him. "You want me to throw another

event to honor the psychopath who threw a fire extinguisher at me during mediation? Besides, we have less than twenty-four hours. Where am I going to get a venue? And a reason to honor her?"

Sawyer cleared his throat. "Surely one of the couples you've planned proposals for could help out. A lot of people owe you."

"That could work," Mindy piped up. "What about Sally? She works for *West Haven Magazine*. They have a monthly column about women in business. We could ask the magazine to throw together a small reception celebrating local female entrepreneurs and get her to invite Wendy for a speaking role."

"Okay...maybe." Claire stood up to pace. Could they really pull something this elaborate off in less than a day?

"But a venue?" She turned back to the table.

"What about the historical society? Remember Mei said they owed you a favor after that proposal we did at the Walker house quadrupled their donations and foot traffic," Nicole suggested.

Claire looked out the window into the dark night and sighed. It was too chaotic, too messy, but it was the only plan they had. "It's worth a shot. Okay, triage time. I'll call Sally. Mindy, you leave an emergency voicemail for Mei at the historical society. Luke, Sawyer, and Kyle are on security detail. Nicole, we need you to photograph the event and take pictures of anyone who looks suspicious. We need to know who these demented frat boys are."

Luke stood up and disappeared down the hallway.

"If it's a reception, won't we need light refreshments? Maybe some booze?" Mindy said. "It has to look legit."

"Good point. Boys, here's my vendor book," Claire said, digging a small black book out of her purse and flinging it onto the breakfast nook. "Divvy up the list and start calling people until someone says yes. The ones marked with purple stars usually answer their phones after hours, so start there." She turned away from the group and gripped the side of the kitchen island. She took a couple deep breaths and tried to get her heart to stop galloping.

A wave of rose hip shampoo hit her. Mindy. "I know you're freaking out right now, but don't. We can do this. Remember when we took four finals in two days and still managed to co-chair Whiskeypalooza? This is nothing compared to that."

There was a thwack of plastic hitting wood. Claire turned around. Luke had laid an empty binder on the table. She could have kissed him, but there wasn't time.

She pulled her phone out and scrolled through her contacts. When the phone started ringing, she held her breath.

"Sally? Hi. Sorry for calling so late. I need you to help me save someone's life."

"This is torture." Mindy moaned from the back seat of the company van.

"I know, but it has to be done." Claire eyed the sun that was slowly peeking over the mountain. "Wendy's bragged about being a runner five million times, and if ESA's been watching her, they already know that. I would bet my last dollar that they're staking out her running route right now and finding a quiet spot where no one will overhear a struggle. We have to get to her before they do."

"If the cops would happen to investigate our car right now, we're going to look sketchy as hell." Nicole held up a blindfold, a pair of fuzzy handcuffs Claire had been using to shackle herself to her bed frame, and a ball gag that Mindy had thoughtfully donated.

Claire shrugged. "It's nothing illegal. Any word from the boys?"

Mindy pulled out her phone. "Luke just texted. Yuffie committed because someone cancelled on her last night. So, we'll have the pastries and hot and cold apps that were supposed to be for that group."

"Good enough." Yuffie had catered during Nicole's proposal. Her pastries were divine, but her manners left much to be desired.

"The only thing is, it was a bachelorette party. So, all the food is shaped like penises."

"Oh, boy." Claire bowed her head. "It's ok, we'll cut them up into different shapes. Put small star-shaped cookies cutters on the shopping list. We'll make it fit the theme somehow."

Nicole glanced at her screen. "Kyle says we have a bartender. One of his friends from law school knows a guy."

"The guy knows how to make more than Irish car bombs and lemon drops, right? This is a high-class event honoring women in business."

Nicole turned to Claire and raised her eyebrows. "This is a fake event fakely honoring the girl who is suing you."

"Right. Sorry. I got caught up in the cover story. Shit. Here she comes! Everybody out."

Wendy had just stepped out into the early morning light. Her shoulder-length brown hair was tucked back in a ponytail, and earbuds were already in her ears. She was practically a sitting duck.

The three of them approached as Wendy grabbed her right foot and pulled it up into a quad stretch. She leaned against the wall away from the girls. Sawyer would have been ashamed of her obliviousness.

"Hey," Claire said when they were just a few feet away. Wendy didn't seem to hear.

"*Hey*," Mindy said even louder. Nothing.

Claire crept up and tapped her on the shoulder.

Wendy screamed like she had been shot and crumpled onto the ground.

"Jesus Christ," she said, pulling out one earbud. "What the hell are you doing here?"

Claire fought the urge to mock her by surveying the parking lot for Jesus. "We need you to come with us."

"No way. I'm about to go on my run. Some of us like to say in shape," she said, looking Claire up and down.

Bold words for a woman marked for dead.

Claire sighed. "You're in danger. Someone's planning to kidnap you. The only place they won't expect to find you is with us."

"Bullshit. You're just messing with me because of the lawsuit."

Claire turned to the other two. "We don't have time for this. If they have to wait too long on the trail, they're going to come looking for her."

"You don't have to tell me twice," Mindy said. She grabbed Wendy by the back of her sports bra and shoved her against the side of the apartment building.

Nicole sprang into action and slapped the furry handcuffs on Wendy's wrists. Mindy grabbed Wendy's cell phone and turned it off before putting it in her own purse.

"Ouch! You stupid whores will pay for this. Do you know who my father is?"

"Yeah, yeah," Mindy said, turning her around and frogmarching her across the parking lot. "We're all very impressed."

"Help! I'm being abducted!" Wendy screamed.

One of the apartment doors opened, and a bleary-eyed old woman in a dressing gown stepped out onto her porch.

"Surprise bachelorette party! We're going to Atlantic City!" Claire called merrily over her shoulder. "Have a nice day!"

Nicole slid open the van door, and Mindy forced Wendy inside. Wendy grunted like an angry pig and thrashed around in her seat as if the seatbelt was burning her.

Claire turned around and held up one finger. "Listen up. I know you don't want to be here. And trust me, I would rather be anywhere else in the world. But someone is trying to kill you, and I don't want that on my conscience. So, you're staying with us in a safe location until the danger has passed. Deal?"

Wendy rolled her eyes. "No wonder Jason dumped you. You're such a psychopath."

Claire sighed and locked all the car doors. She started the engine, and they shot out onto the highway then turned toward downtown.

"Have you felt like you're being watched lately?" Claire asked. She glanced in the rearview mirror. Wendy stopped wiggling like a trapped feral cat for a minute.

"I always feel like I'm being watched. People love to look at me. Men especially." She attempted to flick her hair over her shoulder, but she looked more like a horse trying to chase away a fly than a diva.

They pulled to a stop at a red light. "I'm serious. Have you noticed anything strange over the past couple of weeks?"

"I don't know," Wendy said quietly. "There was one

weird thing. I checked the mail one day last week and had a plain envelope with a note that said, 'I know what you did.' I thought it was from you."

"Not unless it was written in calligraphy on mono-grammed stationery," Nicole said. "You should have seen the wedding invitations."

Claire shot her a dirty look as she turned onto Market Street.

"Sorry," Nicole mouthed.

"It sounds like them," Claire said to Mindy and Nicole. They nodded. "Did you get any weird flowers? From no sender?"

Wendy's eyes narrowed. "Jason said he sent them."

Claire snorted. "He didn't send them. They did."

"Who's they?" Wendy leaned forward in her seat. "And how do you know?"

"ESA," Claire said as she turned into the warehouse parking lot. "And I know because they're doing the same thing to me."

CHAPTER FORTY-ONE

"THAT WAS MEI." CLAIRE SLID HER PHONE BACK ONTO THE charger. "She said everything is a go for the Walker house. One of the historical society members will meet us there to get things set up."

Rosie walked out of the rows of warehouse shelving dragging a ten-foot garland of silver tinsel.

Mindy looked up from the conference table. "I don't want to jinx us, but this might actually work."

Nicole walked out of the office. "The magazine just confirmed the event. They're scrambling to put together some marketing, so I offered to help. Can I use your laptop?"

"Go for it. It's on the desk in there." Claire glanced at her watch. "Where are the boys? They're behind schedule. It's like they've never planned an event before."

"Excuse me," a snotty-sounding voice interrupted from behind the closed bathroom door. A bookcase, a life-size statue of the Venus de Milo, and half of the broken Eiffel Tower barricaded the door.

Claire groaned. "What, Wendy?"

"This yogurt is lemon flavored. I hate lemon," Wendy whined.

"You know what you'll hate more? Being brutally murdered by a cult of homicidal frat boys."

"And the only thing on TV is *Stepwives of Secaucus*. I've already seen this season. And this beanbag chair smells like a dog."

They ignored her.

"I'm going to sue all of you, you know," she called again. "You can't just hold me here against my will. It's false imprisonment."

Nicole waved a hand. "Don't worry, false imprisonment is only a misdemeanor."

"And kidnapping?" Claire said grimly.

"Let's not worry about that right now."

Claire turned up the brainstorming music and drowned Wendy out. There was a very real chance she would face jail time for kidnapping Wendy. But at least her life would be spared.

Claire reached into Mindy's purse and pulled out Wendy's phone. There was no passkey for her phone, which seemed a bit risky for someone who was cheating on her boyfriend with half of the town council. But what did Claire know? She scrolled to Wendy's message with Jason. A surprise dick pic elicited a full-body shudder.

Wendy: *Working late tonight babe. Keep the bed warm for me.*

Sending that message was only slightly less nauseating than that time she and Nicole had ridden the Vomit Comet four times in a row during Campus Carnival freshman year. The last piece of the puzzle in making this a believable lie meant impersonating Wendy on social media. She navigated to Wendy's Instagram and posted a gushing message about being honored at the Women in Business networking event. It would have to be enough. She turned off the phone and set it on the conference table.

The door banged open. Claire screamed and unstrapped Taser #2 from beneath the conference table. Was it ESA? Had they somehow found out where Wendy was hiding?

Kyle burst into the room, bouncing on his toes. "All right, ladies, what can we do? Give us a job."

Claire breathed a sigh of relief.

"He had four lattes," Luke explained. Five-o'clock shadow had spread across his sharp jawline, and he looked exhausted. Sawyer pulled up the rear.

Luke dropped the rapidly filling binder onto the conference table. He had even added a label. His bedazzling could use some work, but his preparation skills were definitely igniting something beneath her belt.

Claire looked at Mindy. "What do you think, blush and champagne? Lilac and lavender? Navy and sage?"

"I was thinking cobalt and coral," Mindy said, brows furrowed.

"Tie breaker?" Claire called to the office.

"Champagne and blush. Make it glam," Nicole yelled.

"I would have gone with watermelon and lemon," Wendy called from the bathroom. "It is a summer event."

"Nobody asked you," Claire and Mindy said.

"Okay, boys, follow me." Claire walked down one of her rows of shelving. She pulled carefully labeled totes down from the shelves and slid them across the concrete floor. "We're trusting you with an incredibly important job. I need you all to go to the Walker house and start setting up for the event. Someone from the historical society will meet you there. They already have chairs and banquet and cocktail tables, but you'll need to add tablecloths, vases, and floral arrangements."

She dropped several more boxes and shoved them toward the boys.

"You want us to...decorate?" Luke asked.

"I want you to decorate for a trap that will help us catch a ring of serial killers," Claire clarified.

"Let's do this!" Kyle shouted, picking up three boxes at once and sprinting headlong toward the exit.

"Don't let Kyle hold anything breakable," she whispered to Luke. He nodded.

"Sawyer, were you able to borrow those nanny cams from your inventory?"

Sawyer nodded. "I have six. I'll do front and back entrance, event room, and anywhere else that looks like it might be a point of entry. They're a little spotty with outdoor service, but I think they'll work."

"Perfect. Thank you. The police might be able to ignore our theories, but they can't ignore a 911 call from an event with multiple witnesses and video evidence. I couldn't do this without you guys."

"You sure we shouldn't be telling the police what we're up to?" Luke raised an eyebrow.

"I have barricaded the woman who's suing me in my company bathroom. I think we're gonna skip giving them a heads up this time."

"You should at least let Jack know."

Claire groaned. "Fine. Give me a minute." She stomped back along the row of shelving to the far end of the warehouse. Rosie followed her and sat on her foot.

Her heart rate kicked up a notch as the phone rang.

"Hello?"

"Hi, Jack. Listen, I can't explain how I know this, but that frat I was telling you about? Turns out they are definitely Barney's homicidal besties and they're going to try to kidnap someone today. There's an event at the Walker house this evening. The intended victim is the keynote speaker. I know you think this frat isn't related to Barney and the missing women with the mark, but you're wrong. Anyway, just thought you should know." She hung up the phone without waiting for a reply.

Her phone immediately rang, but she silenced it. She had work to do. She walked back up the aisle, straightening a box full of extension cords on her way.

"Boys are gone?" she asked when she emerged at the conference table.

"Yes," Mindy said. Her previously unkempt hair was swept into a bun, and she was wearing lipstick. She totally had the hots for Sawyer. He was a way better choice than Gavin the non-participator.

Claire took a deep breath. "So, there's one other part to the plan that I didn't mention."

Nicole groaned from the office. "What now?"

"I'm going to impersonate Wendy at the event."

Mindy slammed her pen down. "Absolutely not. You've already been abducted this summer. Let someone else take a turn."

Claire shook her head. "You guys have risked enough for me. This is my plan, and I have to see it through. I'm not putting either of you in any more danger than I already have. Besides, you're both too tall. They're going to notice when 'Wendy' grew five inches overnight. That's final," she said when Mindy opened her mouth to undoubtedly argue.

"You and Wendy don't look super similar," Nicole said slowly.

"I'll wear a short dress and a wig and sunglasses. Maybe splash on a little eau de tequila. No one will notice the difference."

"How dare you!" Wendy screamed from inside the bathroom. The door handle rattled. "No one in their right mind would mistake you for me."

"I think that's the nicest thing you've ever said to me," Claire called back. She rolled her eyes.

"I don't like this," Mindy said.

"Me neither. But it has to be done. If 'Wendy' isn't physically there, they'll get suspicious. They have to be stopped."

"Done!" Nicole walked out of the office. "I did some quick graphic design and sent over some images for them. The event should be looking legit in just a few minutes."

"Nice job, Coli." Claire collapsed into a chair and dropped her head to the table. This was shaping up to be one of the longest days of her life. Would things ever go back to normal?

"What are you going to do with yourself when you can just focus on planning proposals instead of preventing murders and taking down cults?" Nicole asked, apparently reading her mind.

Claire's head popped up. "I'm going to start accepting out-of-area proposal inquiries."

Mindy's tablet fell over. "You are?"

Claire nodded. "If we can pull together all of this in less than twenty-four hours, we can totally plan something a couple of time zones over. Big-ticket proposals only for now, though. We're going to need the capital if we're going to expand."

Mindy clapped her hands together. "Oh my god, I'm so excited. I have a couple emails flagged that we should start with—"

"Later, Min. One thing at a time."

"Fine," Mindy grumbled.

A LINE OF CARS WOUND AROUND THE CIRCULAR DRIVEWAY IN front of the Walker House. The house was built in the 1800s by wealthy merchants and had stayed in the family for several generations before it was left to the Haven County Historical Society. The house backed up to Skylight Lake, and forest shrouded it on every other side.

Claire pulled the company van up to the service entrance. She, Nicole, and Mindy unloaded a couple more boxes, then Mindy parked.

They walked through the house to the ballroom.

"Holy shit," Nicole said, taking a step back and bumping into Claire.

"I know. It looks..."

"Amazing," they said in unison.

A fleet of cocktail tables cloaked with glittering champagne tablecloths were scattered through the room in a half circle. Gold bunting hung from the stage. Star-shaped pastries were already laid out along a banquet table in the back of the room. Sawyer and Luke were in the heart of it all, seemingly having a heated conversation.

"I really think the Pacific rhododendrons would be best for the cocktail tables," Luke said, holding a vase full of trembling faux flowers. "It adds violet tones and a pop of interest."

Sawyer shook his head fervently. "No way. The blush peonies are more elegant, and they fit the color scheme without being too loud."

"Are you calling my flowers too loud?" Luke thunked the vase down onto a table.

"Gentlemen," Claire interrupted, stepping between the two of them. "They both look great. Why don't you do both and alternate tables?"

Luke and Sawyer both humph'd and went to opposite ends of the room. Glittery gold ribbon was hanging out of the back pocket of Luke's Levi's. Never a dull moment.

Claire followed Sawyer, half-jogging to keep up with his gigantic steps. "Hey. Where's Kyle?"

Sawyer pointed to one of the long banquet tables lined with pastries. "He crashed. He tied a tablecloth around his neck like a cape, said he was going to Birmingham, and laid down under there."

She nodded. "That sounds about right. Did you have a chance to plant the nanny cams?"

"We're all set. They're hooked up to the network, so I can monitor them from the van outside later on."

"Perfect. Thanks again." She scuttled across the room to Luke. "You didn't bring your camera?"

"For what?"

"I assumed you would want footage of a chapter of ESA getting brought down."

Luke shrugged and picked up a pair of scissors. He measured the gold ribbon from his fingertips to biceps and cut. "I told you, I quit the documentary. I'm going to find something else that doesn't bring back the worst memory of your life."

Claire put her hand on his. She gently tugged the ribbon from his grasp and turned him to face her. "Luke. You have to do the documentary. This isn't about me. It's about the victims. And tonight, we're going to get a little bit of justice for each of them. Bring your camera."

CHAPTER FORTY-TWO

To Do:
- *Impersonate Wendy*
- *Catch the bad guys*
- *Shove it in Jack's face*

"I look freaking ridiculous," Claire said as she tugged on a shoulder-length wig with pin-straight brown hair. A red sequined cocktail dress with a sweetheart neckline dragged on the floor. A gaudy costume necklace adorned her neck.

Mindy stood next to her in the small mirror on the drawing room wall. She got to wear a sensible black pencil skirt and button-down blouse.

"You do," she said, "but at least you don't look like yourself. This is definitely the kind of thing Wendy would wear to a professional networking event. She'd storm in and threaten to sue everyone for not bringing out the red carpet."

Claire groaned and slid on a pair of sunglasses. "Are people starting to arrive?"

Nicole opened the door to the drawing room and stepped inside. "Yep. I don't know where Sally drummed up all these women on such short notice, but I'm impressed. Even the mayor's here. Falsies," she said, tossing fake eyelashes and some glue at Claire.

"Who's going to see falsies under my sunglasses? By the way, who brought the tequila? I need to dump some on me."

Mindy pulled a flask out of her purse and handed it to Claire. She dabbed it on like eau de parfum and handed it back. She smelled like a bar bathroom after Cinco de Mayo.

Her phone rang, and she jumped.

"Hi, Mom. Thanks for the care package. You know you don't have to keep apologizing."

Alice had sent several packages with empanadas, bath bombs, gourmet chocolates, and apothecary jars since their discussion about Jack.

"I know, darling. I just feel guilty. What are you up to tonight?"

"Oh, nothing much. Just a networking event," Claire said, rubbing one hand on her incredibly tense neck. Definitely not kidnapping her nemesis and impersonating her to draw out a homicidal mob of morons.

The door opened again, and Kyle and Luke walked in wearing nicely tailored suits. Luke's leather shoes shone under the overhead light, and his hair was smoothed back. Despite not sleeping, he looked alert and ready for anything. There were literal lives at stake, but *damn* if he didn't look good.

"That sounds nice. So, you aren't planning on doing anything dangerous? No midnight swimming?"

"No, Mom, it's too cold for any midnight swimming tonight. It'll only be in the 60s."

"You know my intuition doesn't lie, Clairebear. I just woke up from a nap and I had a dream that you were floating under the stars, bleeding. Just stay away from bodies of water, okay?"

Claire laughed, but her stomach lurched. Dying sunlight glittered on the lake outside the window.

"Your imagination is amazing, Mom. Don't worry. I'm safe."

"I'm not convinced you are. Keep Luke close. He has such a soothing aura. He's good for you."

"Will do, Mom. I love you. I'll talk to you later." Claire hurriedly hung up the phone.

"Is Mercury in retrograde tonight?" Luke asked seriously, taking a big sip of water.

She shot him a dirty look. "Even better. My mom said she had a vision of me floating in some water and bleeding. So, that's encouraging. Who's ready to get things started?" she said, clapping her hands together and feigning enthusiasm.

"Did Sawyer give the all clear?" Kyle asked.

Luke frowned.

"He did," Mindy chimed in. "His van is parked across the street. He set up a command center in there where he can see all the cameras."

"Great. I just want to check in with him quick before we get started." Claire went through the drawing room to the kitchen and escaped out the side door. Nicole and Mindy followed despite her protests.

They stepped cautiously down the rocky driveway in

their stilettos. At the windowless black van, Claire knocked six times in a pre-defined pattern on the side door. Mindy smoothed a flyaway and straightened her posture.

The door slid open, revealing Sawyer in a headset and on a chair before a row of dimly lit monitors. Rosie sat in a bed in the corner of the van, happily panting. She also wore a miniature headset.

"I didn't want her to feel left out." He grinned.

Claire squealed and took a picture with her phone before re-focusing.

"Any activity so far?" Mindy asked.

"Nothing suspicious," he said, shaking his head. "There are a lot of people going in and out, but they're mostly women. Zero college douchebags. Here." He handed over five tiny, clear earpieces.

"Thank you, Sawyer," she said, installing one in her ear and covering it with the wig. Nicole and Mindy installed theirs too.

"I'll keep a close eye on all of you. Let me know if you see something I don't."

"I will, thanks." Claire bent over to kiss Rosie between her furry eyebrows and slid the van door shut. "Let's get back to the drawing room."

They hustled back to where they had started. The circular driveway was packed with cars, and classical music and warm, ambient light spilled out from the building. The sun hung low on the horizon. The first speaker had already gone on. There were a couple more before Claire/Wendy would make her speech.

"Okay." She turned to her friends, who had gathered in the middle of the room. She pulled a small, spiral-bound notebook out of her sequined clutch. "Here's the plan. First of all, take these." She passed out the remaining earpieces to

Kyle and Luke. "Call out if you see anything. The safe word is 'queso,' but please don't use it unless you are actually in danger."

The other four nodded.

Claire continued. "Great. So, we keep our eyes open. It shouldn't be difficult to spot a bunch of frat boys at a networking event for professional women. I'll deliver Wendy's keynote speech at nine and make it look like I'm super drunk. I will then stumble out the back door toward the lake in full view of the nanny cam. By that time, they'll be on a serious time crunch—they'll have to kidnap me and make it back to campus by ten. They'll be desperate, and they'll be sloppy. The boys will be watching from the trees. You two will stay inside the house."

Mindy and Nicole groaned.

"I'm serious. Don't take a single step off that patio. I don't want you anywhere near those maniacs. Everyone have your pepper spray? All right, let's do this." She took a deep breath and opened the double doors that led into the foyer.

She wrote Wendy's name sloppily on a name tag and slapped it onto her chest. It barely stuck to the sequins. It was time to mingle. Who would Wendy talk to at an event like this? Or would she just camp out at the bar and look for a penis to sit on?

"Club soda with a lime, please," she decided, sidling up to the bar. Kyle's bartender friend seemed competent. Maybe this fake event wouldn't be a total failure after all.

She crossed the room with her drink. The sunglasses made it difficult to tell, but it didn't look like any ESA members were present just yet.

Oh, there was Sally. She better go say thank you.

"Sally," Claire whispered loudly, tapping her on the shoulder.

Sally tuned around, and her smile faltered for a moment when she took in the apparel of the person tapping her.

"It's okay, it's me. It's part of the trap," Claire said, lifting her sunglasses. She had been forced to give the bare minimum of details to Sally so that she understood the gravity of the situation, though she had tactfully avoided revealing the abduction.

"Oh, Claire. I didn't recognize you in that getup." Sally splayed one hand with inch-long ballerina nails over her chest. Her permed blonde hair didn't budge a centimeter when she shook her head.

Claire cringed. "I don't recognize me either. I just wanted to thank you for throwing this all together so quickly. You are quite literally a lifesaver." She reached over and squeezed Sally's shoulder.

"It was nothing. Frankly, I love it. I might steal this event from you in the future and do it for real. Oh, my sister-in-law is about to start her speech on work/life balance. You be careful now, okay?"

Since twenty-four hours wasn't exactly a lot of notice, Sally had leaned heavily on family members and colleagues to fill the speaking slots.

"Of course. Thanks again." Claire walked off with her drink and surveyed the party. Everyone was staring at her. If she really was Wendy, she would love it. But Claire just wanted to take the dress off and hide in her all-black event uniform.

The boys had done a surprisingly great job with the decorating. It was as elegant as Claire had imagined. She sighed when she walked past the pastry table. Yuffie's staff really should have put more space between the cream puffs and éclairs. They weren't joined up in the shape of penises anymore, but there was definitely still some dick energy emanating from the table.

A woman she vaguely remembered from the Chamber of Commerce Awards took the stage and began talking about the struggles of being a woman in the corporate world. Claire glanced at her watch. 8:45 p.m. She had a few minutes to scope out the rest of the house.

She walked from the ballroom to the hallway and opened doors as she went. Maybe the ESA guys were hiding until the last possible moment. Or maybe her plan had totally failed, and she had just spent upward of $3,000 for nothing.

"Claire, I see them." Sawyer spoke in her ear.

Her heart rate skyrocketed. "Shit, what should I do?"

"Go back to the ballroom and surround yourself with people. If they catch you on your own, they'll try to take you early. And if they get too close, they might notice that you're not actually Wendy."

"Got it," Claire said, hustling back down the hallway to the ballroom. She stepped inside and into the throng of women.

"Oh, love your blazer. Where did you get it?" she asked a black woman with diamond studs and royal blue Manolo Blahnik pumps.

She listened halfheartedly to the woman's response while sweeping the party. Nicole and Mindy were stationed at the back of the ballroom doing the same thing. Luke and Kyle stood with their backs to the bar.

"Thank you so much, ladies," the speaker said as she walked off the stage to applause.

Mei from the historical society stepped up to the podium in a powder blue dress and lowered the microphone. Her dark hair shone under the lights. "And now we have a special guest speaker who recently won the coveted West Haven Planner of the Year Award for the first time. Please welcome Wendy Flutter of The Yes Makers."

There was a light, scattered applause, and Claire picked up her hem and walked to the stage. She nearly made it all the way to the top before remembering she was supposed to be drunk. She stumbled up the last stair and nearly plowed headlong into the podium.

"What's up, party people?" she called into the microphone. There was dead silence in the room. "My name's Wendy Flutter, proposal planner extraordinaire. You've probably seen my proposals on YouTube." She tossed her hair over one shoulder.

"Anyway, I'm here to talk to you about taking risks." This topic had come to her at the last second. It had been on her mind since her impulsive decision to start accepting out-of-area proposals. "Too many people live in a safe little bubble all their lives. But I'm here to tell you that there are things worth taking risks for. Whether it's seeking a small business loan to expand your business, or—"

Someone in her voice interrupted. "You're being too Claire-like," Mindy hissed.

"Or maybe you gotta go after this hot guy from your spin class. You can't live your life in a bubble, ladies. You need to go out there and go after what you want. To hell with anyone who tells you differently."

"They're inside," Sawyer said in her ear. "Some are approaching the ballroom, others are standing by the exits. I count twelve."

Her heart rate doubled. Twelve? They were hopelessly outnumbered. Luke and Kyle left the ballroom to take their positions.

Right, she was supposed to be giving a speech.

"As ladies, we're supposed to be like solid and predictable and boring. Plod along on that well-traveled road, never deviating or surprising anyone. Leave the risks to the men so they get all the rewards. But not anymore, girls. We're going to get what's ours."

The back door cracked open. Her heart stuttered. Three men who had to be members of ESA slunk inside. One was exceptionally tall with a hooked nose and a band T-shirt. A short guy, squat but muscular, with an ill-fitting button-down shirt, walked in behind him. And the third had cold eyes with a penetrating gaze that made her shudder even from thirty yards away. They weren't doing much to fit in. Her heart beat even faster. Evil was crossing the room like a dense fog. Goosebumps formed on her arms. Was she really going to make it out of this alive? Or was she going to die trying to protect the yogurt-judging shrew who slept with her fiancé?

Her hands trembled, and the water bottle fell from the podium. It landed on the stage with a loud thunk.

"You look like you need a water," Claire slurred, picking up the bottle and tossing it into the crowd. It struck the mayor of West Haven in the temple. Good, another lawsuit.

"Sorry, Madam Mayor." She curtsied. "The world is a scary place, right? We all have fears. I'm afraid of Beanie Babies and artichokes, for example. Most women in business are afraid of failure. But we can't let fear run our lives. We can't let fear stop us from taking chances, from changing lives. How will you know what you can accomplish if you never try? You're capable of more than you think. If you work hard, spend wisely, and curate a solid foundation of devoted clients, you can do anything. You can change the world. You can implement a 'green' policy. You can sell that new product. You can shove your success right in the face of the patriarchy."

Mindy cleared her throat. Shit, she was slipping back into Claire again.

A couple of women applauded. Her anxiety ticked down a notch.

"In conclusion, ladies. You are capable of greatness. Today, I encourage you to find the courage to do whatever it is you need to take things to the next level. Apply for a loan. Launch that new online store."

Nicole sighed in her ear.

"Ask out that guy from spin class. Don't wait for permission. Stop waiting on the world and go seize it by its balls."

She dropped the microphone on the floor and walked off the stage. There was more applause than before. It was almost heartwarming. She made a detour to the bar and grabbed another club soda. The penetrating gaze of the ESA members came from just behind her. It was time to lure them outside. Maybe she could use the glass as a backup weapon.

"There's one on the patio. Be careful," Sawyer muttered in her ear.

She stumbled through the room to the set of double doors behind the stage and pushed through them to the patio. It was a pity this wasn't a real event because it was a lovely evening. Cool, but not cold. The sun had set, and the lake glittered with the light of the full moon. Even the mosquitoes seemed to have taken a break.

"They're almost on you. Luke and Kyle, keep your eyes open," Sawyer said.

Footsteps followed her. She hustled to the edge of the lake and pretended to be looking for fish. Her sunglasses were too dark, so she dropped them to the ground. She needed every bit of her night vision if she was going to make it out of this alive.

"Hey. You're coming with us," a male voice behind her grunted.

"Queso," she muttered into her comms unit. It crackled in her ears. Had they heard her? What was the range on these things anyway?

She whirled around and pretended to be surprised. "No, thanks. I have a pool boy at home."

The short one cracked his knuckles. "I said, you're coming with us."

"Oh, I'm sorry, I didn't realize you're hard of hearing. Go. Fuck. Yourselves," she enunciated carefully. "I'm not going anywhere."

The tall one pulled a rag out of his pocket and dabbed something from a small bottle onto it. Oh, no. Not chloroform again.

"Seriously? Chloroform? Are you guys twelve?" Why was nobody coming? Had they not heard the queso?

"I don't think this one's going to come quietly, Corbin," he said, passing the rag to the short one. "We're almost out of time."

"I don't need it," the short one who must have been named Corbin said, dropping it on the ground and pulling a handgun from his belt.

Claire's heart rate skyrocketed. The edges of her vision were going blurry. She had been prepared for knives and chloroform. A gun had somehow never occurred to her. Barney had never used one.

"Come with us, or I'm going to shoot you in the fuckin' head." The short one jabbed the weapon in her direction.

Claire took a step back. Her heels brushed the edge of the lake and sank into the mud. It was freezing, and her mother's words of warning rang out in her mind. Was this the end?

She bent down and slipped off her shoes in case she needed to run. Her wig slipped, and before she could secure it, it fell into the water. She whipped her Taser out of her ankle holster and pointed it at them.

"Hey, wait. Isn't that—"

"Claire fuckin' Hartley," Corbin said, bringing the gun up. The safety clicked off. "Just my lucky day."

A gunshot rang out. The Taser in Claire's hand exploded, and she screamed and staggered back into the lake.

Several things happened at once. The double doors on the patio banged open, and the real Wendy Flutter stomped out screaming. Her hair was wild and tangled, and her crop top had a massive tear in one side. Several other event attendees followed behind her. How the hell had she escaped?

"Claire Hartley, I am gonna kill you!" she screamed.

Every ESA brother but the short one whirled and turned to look at Wendy.

"Dude, it's her," one said.

Dark shapes ran around the corner of the house. Luke and Kyle sprinted toward them from the woods, and on the side of the house, Nicole and Mindy approached the fray. Her breath hitched. They were too close.

"*Gavin*?" Mindy's voice rang out in the night.

What? What the hell was Gavin doing here? Unless—

She didn't have time to focus on the chaos unfolding around her. She needed to survive. Claire whipped her shoe at Corbin's head.

Another gunshot rang out.

She braced, waiting for the impact. Someone dove in front of her, and something stung her hip. She cried out in pain and fell backward into the lake. The frigid water stole her breath. Her lungs burned. For a moment, she was stunned and could only look up at the stars. But she needed to keep moving.

Then Corbin was on her. He had a face like a shovel, and a vein was ready to pop in his forehead. She staggered to her feet, dripping with lake water.

He dove for her, and she thrust the heel of her hand upward and into his nose.

He cried out and dropped to his knees, clutching his face while blood poured out around his fingers. She gave him another punch for good measure, and he collapsed backward into the lake. If she made it through this, she was going to tell everyone he peed his pants.

"Claire!" Luke yelled, but she couldn't tell where it was coming from. She scanned the yard and looked up just in time to see Mindy punch Gavin in the face.

Someone grabbed Claire from behind. She went rigid, Sawyer's words echoing in her mind like someone was fast-forwarding a tape recorder. She tucked her chin and blocked the attacker from getting a grip on her windpipe.

He lifted her up. How strong was this frat boy? Did they have special kidnapping workouts? Maybe a HIIT-style class where they dragged blow-up dolls filled with sand?

Her feet flailed. She couldn't touch the ground. Panic flared inside her like a flame.

Her captor dragged her backward, away from the fray. She wiggled and thrashed, but her aimless kicks at his legs didn't delay his progress. Static crackled in her ear. Could Sawyer see her?

A tree branch scratched at her cheek, and the light of the full moon dissipated. They were in the forest now. Crickets chirped on each side of her. The lawn was getting farther away. Help was all but gone.

Her heart beat so hard and fast that her smart watch vibrated on her wrist with a warning to breathe. Darkness started closing in on her vision. Her head was fuzzy. Nausea twisted her insides.

What was that sound? Was that a belt buckle coming undone? Was he going to tie her up with it, or was he preparing for something even worse?

Fuck it. There was no time for officially sanctioned self-defense. She wrenched her neck to one side and sunk her teeth into the man's arm.

He cried out and dropped her like a sack of potatoes. She fell to the ground, knees nearly collapsing, and whirled to face him.

"You stupid bitch!" Stringy hair hung in his eyes as he clutched at his arm.

Claire cocked her arm back and smashed the heel of her hand into his greasy nose. He cried out and stumbled against a tree. She took a couple of steps back and then ran straight at him like a freight train. She swung her foot up and directly into his crotch like she was kicking a field goal.

The man crumpled to the leaf-scattered earth and moaned. She aimed another kick at his ribs for good measure.

"Claire?" Nicole called from far away.

Claire turned and ran toward the voice. Her hip stung like she had wandered over a yellow jacket's nest. Something wet and red was dripping down her side, splattering into the grass. Great, now she owed Mindy a new dress.

Someone had jumped in front of that bullet for her. But who? She scanned the grass. Kyle and Luke were duking it out with two brothers. She breathed a sigh of relief and swiveled. Mindy stood over Gavin's crumpled form, scream-ing. Nicole was talking to Wendy and gesturing at the kerfuffle with exaggerated hand movements. Several women from the event had crowded around and were frowning at the scene on the lawn.

Sawyer walked by, dragging an unconscious ESA brother in each hand. "Police are on their way," he said calmly before depositing the bodies in a pile.

A cry rang out to her left, by the dock. A man in a suit fought an upside-down triangle shaped frat boy in a cutoff tank top. What the hell was a man in a suit doing here? This was a women's networking event.

She squinted at the pair. Hang on, she knew that perfectly molded hair.

"Dad?" The word tumbled from her lips before she fully comprehended what she was seeing.

Jack met her eyes for a split second. His entire torso was drenched in blood. An unnatural pallor had spread across his face. Her stomach clenched like she had been walloped in the abdomen. So, he *had* listened to her.

He was losing steam, barely holding his hands up in defense as the triangle guy swung at him. Moonlight glinted on something in the grass. From here, it looked like Jack's FBI badge. Apparently, cults weren't afraid of the FBI. She took a step in his direction, heart in her throat.

Another cry came from her right. Luke clutched at his arm. Blood was spreading rapidly from a new wound. She gasped. The tall, hook-nosed man from the ballroom darted back and forth in front of him. A blood-stained knife was clutched in his hand.

Everything around her moved in slow motion. She tore her gaze from Luke to Jack. Back and forth. Her deadbeat dad and her newly reformed pathological liar of a boyfriend. They were both in danger. Jack dodged another punch, but he bent at the waist, wheezing with effort. Luke's attacker raised the knife again. Luke raised a blood-drenched fist.

Claire let out a strangled cry and sprinted across the lawn. She jumped onto the back of the knife-wielding man and wrapped her arms around his neck. A seam ripped in the dress. His elbows flailed, and the tip of the knife jabbed into her forearm. Another day, another scar. It wasn't even as deep as the self-inflicted one she had from her sword. What a pansy.

Luke ducked and swept the attacker's legs, sending them both crashing to the ground. Claire gasped, the wind knocked out of her. She rolled to her side in time to see the mayor of West Haven pepper spray a frat boy. All around them, women from the meeting were descending on the brothers. There were cries of pain in every direction. If it wasn't so terrifying, it would have been empowering as hell.

Nicole kicked a knife out of someone's hand, and Kyle punched him in the face. Sawyer calmly passed out zip ties from his utility belt to secure the brothers. Even Wendy had just kneed someone in the balls.

Claire froze. Luke was safe, for the moment at least. But she had abandoned her father. Her gaze swung back to the lake. The man who was attacking her father was gone. A clothed mass drifted at the edge of the shore.

She sprinted back to the beach and staggered knee-deep into the water. Crimson trails of blood swirled into the lake from a bullet hole in Jack's shoulder. He floated face down. She grabbed an arm of his navy suit and tugged him back to shore, flipping him onto his back. His eyes were closed. She shook him, but he didn't stir.

What had she done?

CHAPTER FORTY-THREE

To Do:
- Forgive Jack
- Google how to get blood out of sequins
- Grade the questionnaires from new prospects

THE VENDING MACHINE HUMMED LIKE A FIFTY-YEAR-OLD refrigerator in the otherwise empty hospital waiting room. It had eaten a handful of Claire's quarters an hour earlier. Her stomach growled like a feral cat. She hadn't even had a chance to sample a reformed penis pastry.

The surgical floor was dead this time of night, save for the occasional custodian pushing a squeaky cart. Forty-two ceiling tiles. Seventeen earth-toned squares of carpet. Eleven recessed lights. Three stitches in her side and one large wad of gauze to close the wound where the bullet had grazed her hip.

She glanced at the clock for what must have been the

thousandth time since Luke had been taken away for questioning by the police. The sky outside was starting to lighten from an inky black to a deep purple. She hadn't slept in forty-eight hours, and her visual field seemed to lag a little when she changed focus. What she would do for a nice nap. She picked up her tablet and flicked through some proposal candidates, but the hospital's Wi-Fi was spotty, and she couldn't concentrate anyway.

Footsteps came from the hallway, and Claire's head snapped up.

"Sorry, they kept me forever." Luke dropped heavily into the chair next to her. "They insisted on having a PA check me out." He gestured to a pucker in his shirt where they must have applied gauze to his stab wound.

His dress shirt was covered in grass stains, and there was a massive tear in his pants.

"You're okay?" she asked hesitantly.

He nodded. "Thanks to you. You jumped on the back of a knife-wielding idiot for me. Don't ever do that again," he said sternly. He took a deep sip from his coffee cup and winced. "Any updates on Jack?"

Guilt twisted her stomach. "He's still in surgery. Shoulders are tricky."

"He'll be okay," Luke said, sliding his arm around her. He planted a kiss on her forehead and offered her a bag of chips from an apparently less irritating vending machine.

"Did you get any good footage?" she asked over a cheddar and sour cream chip. She tucked her legs under her. Her red evening dress was soaked and in tatters, so she was wearing sweatpants and a T-shirt Luke had found in his car. The ensemble didn't really go with her gold stilettos, but hopefully no one had noticed.

"I don't know. I had to turn it over to the police."

Claire nodded. It figured. "So, what did they ask you?"

"The same things they asked you, I'm sure. Why we were at the event, what made me hide in the woods in the backyard, why you were impersonating someone else? They weren't happy when I reiterated that we reported ESA to the FBI, and they neglected to follow up on it."

She snuggled under her his arm. After the worst spring and summer in the history of time, this horrible, dark chapter of her life might just be coming to a close. "Bet they feel stupid now."

He kissed her forehead and stroked her arm. She was home.

"Luke?"

"Hmm?" He stifled a yawn.

"There are other chapters of ESA out there." The victims Jack had shown her had come from all over the country. How many members were there?

"I assume so."

"Do you think the FBI will finally take care of it?"

"Probably. Unless there's a mole in the Bureau."

"Don't even joke about that." She nudged him in the side.

Footsteps came from the hallway again, and she cringed. Were the police coming back to talk to her again?

"Oh, Claire," Tanya said as she swept into the room in a tropical-print muumuu. She gathered Claire and Luke in a tight hug that smelled like patchouli. Her eyes were swollen and red.

"The nurse said about half an hour ago that he's still in surgery," Claire reported dutifully. "They think he'll be fine."

"I'm so relieved," Tanya said, wiping at her eyes with a tissue.

"It must be hard to be the wife of an agent." Claire was entirely too tired for this conversation.

"But you were hurt too." Tanya eyed the lump of gauze under Claire's too-large shirt. She dug through her purse until she found a small stone. She placed it in Claire's hand, and she opened it to reveal a small, sparkling amethyst.

"For healing," Tanya said, stroking Claire's hair.

Another woman stood a few feet behind Tanya, hesitating in the shadowy doorway.

"Brianna, sweetheart. Will you come here? I want you to meet someone."

Claire stood. Could it be?

When Brianna walked under the recessed light, Claire almost gasped. She had seen Brianna in a couple of movies, but until this moment she hadn't noticed that their eyes were exactly the same. Her teeth were toothpaste-commercial white, and there wasn't a single blemish anywhere on her tanned skin. She wore a tank top with ripped jeans and flip-flops. Beachy waves ran down to her mid-back. Hadn't she seen that same purse in Target the week before?

Tanya took their hands as though they were about to play a rousing game of Red Rover.

"This is Claire. She's your half sister from your dad's previous marriage," Tanya said, gently tugging them toward each other.

"Claire." Brianna smiled as she studied her face. Suddenly, she dropped her mother's hand and drew Claire into a tight hug. She clearly had inherited her mother's friendliness.

"My sister," she said, pulling back and holding both of Claire's arms. "I have a sister."

Realizing that she was supposed to say something,

Claire opened her mouth, not sure what was about to come out.

"Two, actually. My—uh, *our*—sister Charlie lives in Los Angeles. It's nice to meet you. I've seen you act. You're wonderful."

Brianna flippantly waved one of her long, graceful hands. "The movies are garbage. But I've seen *you*. I mean, aside from all the Widowmaker stuff. Sorry. You do those crazy proposals, right? So romantic. I caught Dad re-playing your interview from that morning show like a thousand times. You're amazing."

Claire blushed. "That's really nice of you to say. Oh, Brianna, this is my boyfriend, Luke."

He hadn't moved since Brianna had walked in, so Claire nudged him with her foot. "Luke."

"I'm a big fan," he said, his voice cracking slightly as he stood up.

"You're too kind," Brianna said with a friendly smile and a firm handshake.

The door to the waiting room banged open, and they all jumped.

"Claire Aurora Hartley!" Alice Alejo whirled into the room in a pink peplum top and pencil skirt.

Oh, boy. This should be fun.

Alice had had a grade-four meltdown when Claire had delivered the news over the phone. She had hopped on the first outbound plane this morning. Would the two decades of etiquette lessons she had drilled into Claire from childhood still stand when she was confronted with her ex husband's mistress and love child?

Alice marched into the room without looking at anyone else and threw her arms around her daughter. She pulled back and gripped her shoulders.

"Hi, Mom," Claire said sheepishly.

"Did I not tell you that you were in danger? Why do you insist on putting yourself in these situations? Am I going to need to hire a private investigator again? I still have Brian on speed dial."

Claire cringed. She had mostly kept her promise to be honest with Luke, but she had failed to do the same with her mother. She really needed to work on that. "Please don't. Anyone but Brian. I promise I'll do better."

Alice huffed and flung her purse onto a waiting room chair. She pulled out a Ziplock bag full of small glass jars. How had she managed to sneak those onto the plane?

She pulled them out and started sniffing them. "Now I know I packed a turmeric and cat's claw poultice—aha!" She tugged at the corner of Claire's shirt. "This will prevent an infection."

"Mom, not now, please. We have company." She nodded in Tanya's direction. "This is Jack's wife, Tanya. And his daughter, Brianna."

Alice turned around and froze. She straightened herself to her fullest height. Her nostrils flared, and her face was so pinched it looked like she was holding in a tremendous fart.

"Nice to meet you," she managed to say. She stuck her hand out. Tanya ignored it and brought Alice in for one of her signature bone-crushing hugs. Alice went rigid under her grasp.

"Alice, so lovely to finally meet you." Tanya pulled back and held onto Alice's hand with both of hers. "You have the most marvelous energy. So much light in your aura."

Alice frowned. "Thank you." She withdrew her hand and turned to Luke. She took hold of his arm and steered him to the other side of the waiting room. They sat down to talk in hushed whispers for several minutes. Claire sat again, leaving a chair between her and Tanya. It was a very strange morning.

At that moment, a fatigued-looking surgeon stepped into the room.

"Mrs. Hartley?"

Tanya nodded, and the doctor walked over and sat down next to the family. "Your husband lost quite a bit of blood, but he's going to be fine. The bullet missed his brachial artery by a millimeter. He was extremely lucky. He's awake and in recovery now. You can see him if you like."

Tanya immediately threw herself at the doctor, bursting into tears. Luke came over and took Claire's hand.

"Do you want to see him?" he whispered.

How could she face him after she chose Luke over him? But she had to. Blood was blood. "I guess I should thank him for taking a bullet for me."

The family followed the doctor back to recovery, where Jack was the only patient. He was sitting up, and he looked paler than usual, but otherwise unfazed. The newspaper on his lap was open to the sports section. For the first time since he had returned to Claire's life, he wasn't wearing a three-piece suit. He was probably already planning to ask the staff if they had a more formal hospital gown available.

Luke and Claire stood back as Brianna and Tanya fussed over him. Alice hovered in the hallway.

"What is this, bullet wound number three? Are you trying to meet some kind of quota at work or something?" Brianna asked, nudging him in the unaffected arm. She slapped a pair of fuzzy socks and a book with a picture of a cowboy on the hospital bed. Jack smiled at her and squeezed her hand.

Tanya draped herself over Jack like a blanket and let out an indiscernible stream of cries and half-pronounced syllables. The pockets of her muumuu rattled and clacked with what was probably more crystals.

"Here—this—" Tanya finally removed herself from her husband long enough to pull out a vial of some kind of essential oil.

"Mom," Brianna said kindly, holding her mom's wrist, "let's hold off on the alternative medicine until Dad leaves the hospital, okay? You know what the doctors said last time. Now what groceries do you need for the house? I'm putting an order in."

"Well, your dad really likes this vegan cereal," Tanya began tearfully, finally climbing off the hospital bed and following her daughter out of the room.

Brianna winked at Claire as they left. It was like a ray of sunshine had just gone behind a cloud. The awkwardness crept back in.

Claire took a step closer. Even with hours to prepare, she didn't know what to say.

"I'm sorry you thought I didn't believe you about ESA." Jack folded his newspaper and rolled it into a tight tube. "I hoped that if you saw an officially sanctioned government agency dismissing them as a threat, you would stop investigating them. For the record, my superiors really didn't believe me when I explained what you overheard."

Claire frowned. "And so you let me believe that I had no choice but to save Wendy on my own."

He nodded. "In hindsight, not the best choice. I had local law enforcement go to her apartment early yesterday morning, but she was already gone."

"Yeah, because we preemptively kidnapped her," she

said. "I wasn't going to let an innocent person be tortured and murdered. Not another one. Not even Wendy."

He unfurled the newspaper and spread it over his lap. "Well, because someone sent a text from her phone and posted to her social media, they didn't believe she was in danger and weren't willing to dispatch officers to the event. But I was there the whole time, staked out in the woods, even though it wasn't an officially sanctioned mission."

It sure would have been helpful if he would have brought a couple of agent friends so the mayor of West Haven didn't have to karate chop a twenty-year-old in the Adam's apple.

This conversation was going nowhere. She sighed. "Thank you, Jack. For saving my life. I'm sorry you got shot by a weird, angry misogynist."

He shrugged, then winced. "All in a day's work. You called me Dad, by the way."

Damn it. A slip of the tongue.

Jack smiled. "It was nice."

"Well, we should go," Claire said, turning to Luke. She grabbed his hand and tugged, but he anchored her to the spot.

"Claire," Jack continued. "Before you go. I know I haven't been a great dad. I haven't been a dad, period. But I'd like to. If you're open to it. Even if it's just dinner once a month. I want to know my daughter."

She hesitated, ready to snap at him for downplaying her fear. But he was trying. Maybe it was time she tried too. She had abandoned him to save her boyfriend, after all.

"We'll try it," she said somewhat stiffly in spite of the tears that welled up in her eyes. Two days of no sleep had rendered her a weepy mess. It was time for a very long nap. And probably some tacos.

A nurse walked in. "Sir, an agent's here to debrief you."

"Good luck," Claire mouthed to him and walked out with Luke. "Coming, Mom?" she asked. Alice was still standing in the hallway.

"In a little bit, Clairebear," she said, reaching over to give her a mini hug. "There are some things I need to say to your father."

That couldn't be good. Claire hustled down the hall with Luke at her side. They walked out into the breezy summer morning. Finally, freedom from the sterile smell of the hospital. Tinges of pink were curling into the sky, but there was still a scatter of stars overhead.

"Let's avoid hospitals for a while, okay?" Luke pulled her close and tucked her into his side.

"Luke, in the amount of time that you have known me, how many times have we been at the hospital?"

"Good point. Let's try to make it at least another month."

"Deal. Hang on," she said, stopping in the middle of the parking lot. "Do you see the stars?"

He glanced up. "I see them."

"They're perfect."

He raised his eyebrows. "Are you suggesting that we star spin?"

She shrugged. "We are right outside a hospital if it goes horribly wrong."

"Race you," he said, spinning furiously in place and counting to fifteen.

Claire did the same, lifting her head to the heavens and laughing as the stars blurred into each other. An entire community of badass businesswomen had banded together to bring down a dozen dangerous people. She had a new sister. And for the moment, everyone she loved was safe.

"Go!" Luke said, sprinting in the direction of his car.

She followed, staggering from side to side. "I'm coming for you," she said, arms outstretched.

She made it several feet before her gold stilettos slammed into an unseen curb. She lost her balance, grasping at the empty air before collapsing, butt-first, into a large plastic trash can.

Damn it. She wiggled her arms and legs, but she was really wedged in there. The sky was still spinning stubbornly above her. "Luke, I need help."

"What?" he asked distantly as he bumped into a car, setting off the alarm. "Ah, shit."

He ran back toward her, almost crashing into the tailgate of a truck, and burst out laughing.

"Hang on." He dug into his pocket and pulled out his phone.

"Luke! No pictures, come on. Help me!" She laughed in spite of herself. The stars still swam above her head, but the world was starting to right itself.

Luke ignored her, snapping half a dozen photos from various angles. At least he hadn't brought his professional-grade camera.

Eventually he grabbed both of her hands and pulled, tugging Claire out of the trash can.

"Ugh, I think I sat in some kind of milkshake," Claire said, spinning around and trying to look at her rear. Thank goodness these were borrowed pants.

He caught her hand and dragged her to him, barely ending his laughter before he pulled her into a deep, warm, familiar kiss.

Heat crept into her cheeks when he pulled back. He gazed at her with an indescribable look in his eyes.

"What? Is there something in my hair?"

Luke reached underneath her mane of hair and pulled out a wadded-up burger wrapper. He looked happier than she'd seen him in a month.

"God, I love you," he said, tossing the wrapper back into the trash and pulling Claire in for another heated kiss.

CHAPTER FORTY-FOUR

To Do:
- Safety tips for California
- Buy Christmas presents
- Hide wine in every room-vases?

LUKE'S HOUSE SMELLED LIKE TURKEY, STUFFING, AND DESPITE Claire's best efforts, burnt gravy on Thanksgiving Day.

"Goddammit, Martha Stewart, how do I carve this bird?" she screeched at her phone. A sheen of sweat covered her forehead, and her hair was getting more frazzled by the second. She picked up a knife and stabbed it into the twenty-five-pound golden brown turkey in front of her. After quickly surveying the room, she pulled a hidden bottle of wine out of the dishwasher and took a hefty swig.

The house was teeming with an eclectic mix of people. Against her better judgment, she had decided to celebrate making it through the worst year of her life by inviting all of her and Luke's families from both sides. Her Thanksgiving binder and food preparation timing spreadsheet lay abandoned on the breakfast nook, covered in flour and breadcrumbs. She had dismissed him from the kitchen half an hour before to corral his relatives.

Luke walked in now, wearing his tool belt and carrying a hammer. Rosie sprinted in after him, looking jaunty in her turkey-themed bandana.

"Everything smells amazing," he said.

Claire pouted. "Your green beans look way better than anything I made."

Luke wrapped his arms around her from behind and kissed her neck. She relaxed a millimeter.

"Just so you know, your mom is offering tarot readings in the ballroom right now." The warmth of his breath on her neck nearly distracted her from the gravity of his words.

She swore. "Please tell me she's reading George's cards and predicting an untimely demise?"

Since arriving an hour ago, Luke's brother had loudly berated everything from Luke's home décor to Rosie's bandana.

"He's probably about to plummet face-first into an Olympic pool full of cash."

"Oh, hi, George," Claire said as he opened the front door and walked into the foyer. Speak of the devil. "What were you doing outside?"

He slapped a legal pad on the kitchen island with zero regard for Claire's ever-shrinking counter space. "Listen, Luke. We've gotta talk about your pool. In the lawyer community, we call that an 'attractive nuisance.' All you need is one neighbor kid hopping over that fence and drowning and you're screwed. That fence has to be at least six inches taller, and you need a couple of signs."

"I just remembered there's a piece of molding in the ballroom that was never fully secured to the wall. I wouldn't want Sophia to get hurt," Luke said, walking straight back down the hallway. George's five-year-old daughter, Sophia, had seemingly inherited nothing from her father. She was sweet and well-mannered and loved to help her mother, Stella, bake. George trailed after Luke, still talking about the pool. He was so not invited to Christmas Eve.

Damn it. The turkey was still whole, and everything else was done. With every second that ticked by, the side dishes were cooling down. At this rate, she'd give everyone food poisoning.

She had half a mind to storm into the basement and pull her stepdad off his ladder. She had witnessed him carve the turkey at Thanksgiving last year. He wasn't a big fan of tense family gatherings and had excused himself to install dimmer bulbs in Luke's theater room while Claire's nephew, Ryan, played video games. When she had last checked on them, Claire's sister, Charlotte, was assisting, holding a flashlight in one hand and a very large wineglass in the other. She was less than thrilled about the prospect of sharing the same roof as Jack.

The doorbell rang. "Don't worry, I'll get it," Claire said to no one.

Rachel, Luke's mother and Barney's attorney, stood at the door. Her posture was so erect that it looked like she had had a pole surgically attached to her spine. Claire let out a long, slow breath. They hadn't seen each other since Claire's visit to the prison. If she was going to kill anyone at this family function, it was going to be Rachel. But Luke had requested they try to make amends. She was the only parent he had left.

"Hello, Claire." At least she had gotten her name right today.

"Please come in." Claire briefly considered sprinting out the front door before closing it behind them.

"Where should I put the salad?" Rachel brandished an expensive-looking wooden bowl.

"There's a couple of banquet tables set up in the ballroom," Claire said, returning to the turkey and gesturing with the carving knife. "Thank you for coming. George and Stella are in the ballroom with Luke. Sophia was looking for you earlier," she added. Even though she desperately needed help carving this turkey, she would rather shut her head in the oven than ask Rachel.

"She's a dear little thing." Rachel moved past Claire to set two bottles of wine on the counter. She didn't make eye contact and instead spoke to the refrigerator. "You should know I am no longer representing Mr. Windsor. I recused myself. He admitted he only hired me because Luke is my son, and he knew it would drive you crazy."

"I'm glad to hear it," Claire said, furiously whisking the gravy. She could only imagine what Rachel would have to say if there were lumps in it.

Rachel continued to avoid eye contact. "Things have been hard since the divorce and George's death. Work was all that I had left. I really thought Mr. Windsor's case would be the defining case of my career. I didn't think about what it would cost. For what it's worth, I'm sorry."

Claire raised her eyebrows. No wonder she had been such a nosey nightmare. Although Rachel was essentially still a vial of nitroglycerin coated in acid and porcupine quills, burying herself in work to avoid personal problems was something Claire was an expert at. It wasn't excusable, but it was understandable.

"I'd like to offer my services, if you ever need them, for your business or personally. Free of charge, of course."

"I did assault a couple of Barney's friends in July, so I may need to take you up on that. Thank you, Rachel."

As Rachel disappeared, Claire's heart rate settled like a ticking bomb had just been removed. That was probably the longest conversation she and Rachel had ever had without threatening or belittling each other. Claire reached back into the dishwasher and took another swig of secret wine before turning back to the turkey.

The front door opened. If that was George coming back in with another complaint, she was going to drown him in the gravy.

Mindy rushed into the room, looking a little worse for the wear. Her raven hair was drawn back in a messy pony-tail, and there were bags under her eyes.

"Hey, Min," Claire said, putting everything down to give her friend a massive hug. "Did you finish hanging up all your art last night?"

"I did." Mindy yawned. "By the way, you left your bar cart in the apartment."

Claire stepped back to the turkey and resumed staring at it. "That was a housewarming gift for you."

"Thank you. And thank you for subletting to me. I know what that place means to you."

Claire shrugged. "I'm glad it's going to someone who will carry on the shenanigans. Plus, everyone in that apartment complex saw me naked. It was time for me to go."

Mindy giggled. "Ooh, top shelf," she said as she pried open a bottle of the wine Rachel had brought. She poured a generous serving into a long-stemmed wineglass.

"I can't wait to see it all re-decorated. How are you doing?" Claire asked with genuine concern.

"I'm fine. It was good to get out of that place. Too many memories of Gavin there."

Claire reached over and squeezed her hand. It had been months since the incident, but Mindy was still struggling. Gavin, as it turned out, had used his connection to Mindy to feed information about Claire to ESA.

"Love you," Claire said, smiling sadly at her friend. "Any chance you know how to carve a turkey?"

"Give me that." Mindy grabbed the knife. "I need to stab something."

Claire began moving side dishes to a bar cart that she had repurposed.

The doorbell rang again. "For fuck's sake!" She dropped a foil-wrapped tub of mashed potatoes onto the cart and whirled around.

Jack and Tanya stood on the porch. Claire let them in, and Tanya immediately began babbling.

"Brianna couldn't make it, sweetheart. She has to be on set tomorrow for *Private Sarah*," Tanya said, rushing in and kissing Claire on both cheeks. "We made a tofurkey for anyone else with dietary restrictions," she added, brandishing it proudly.

"Thank you so much. Could you set it on the cart? And then you can go straight back the hall, double doors at the end. We're almost ready to eat."

"Of course, sweetheart. What a beautiful home. The energy is wonderful in here, except at the front door. You might want to grab a bundle of white sage. Are these floors original? The stonework out front is just breathtaking," Tanya rattled off in one breath, not even waiting for a reply. She walked down the hallway, inexplicably knocking on the walls every few feet and pausing to listen.

"Can I talk to you for a minute?" Jack had not followed Tanya.

"A quick minute," Claire said, setting another dish on the tray as Mindy hacked at the turkey.

"What's up?" she said when they had made their way to the front porch.

"A professor from Venor has been declared missing."

"Who?"

"Dr. William Taylor."

Claire gasped. Dr. Taylor was a notoriously difficult business professor. She and her freshman roommate, Courtney, had taken one of his classes. He had been so upset about a group of test scores that he had thrown them from his fourth-floor office window and told the class they could collect their exams from the courtyard below. Courtney had almost failed the class but had scored a passing grade after the final.

"Do you think—was he—"

Jack nodded. "He was listed as the faculty advisor for the fraternity. The FBI reached out for questioning at the beginning of the fall semester, and he kept postponing. He disappeared right before Thanksgiving break."

A realization struck Claire. "I think he slept with Courtney Stevens. She said she had slept with a professor for a passing grade. She was so close to failing that business class, and she was going to need it to continue her major. It had to be him."

"Every federal agent in the country is looking for him. He can't stay on the run forever."

"And we still don't know how many members of ESA exist?" She didn't really want the answer to this question. Things had been quiet since July, but the fear of retaliation had never quite left.

"We're working on it," Jack said. "And one more thing."

Good Lord. What now?

"The office of Internal Affairs conducted an investigation of your case. A West Haven cop has been fired for leaking information to the press."

"*What*? Which one? Is that how they knew about the notes?"

Jack nodded. "Officer Jordan. He was looking to support his gambling habit."

Claire sighed. "Well, at least he wasn't secretly in ESA. Thanks for the update. Could you help Mindy with the turkey? I really need to get everything on the table."

"Sure thing." They walked back inside. He took the knife and meat fork from Mindy and began expertly carving the turkey.

Mindy grabbed Claire's elbow and dragged her into the living room behind a wall, out of view of the kitchen. She handed her a flask.

Claire guzzled from it and handed it back. What was that? Rum? Tequila? It was so metallic she couldn't even tell. "Why the hell did I think it was a good idea to invite all these people?"

"Because you have a big, beautiful heart," Mindy said and elbowed her in the ribs. "Plus, we're celebrating four whole months with no nonsense from ESA."

"Thank god for that," Claire said, stepping back into the kitchen and loading the last of the food onto the cart. "Ready to do this thing?"

The doorbell rang. Claire froze. They weren't expecting anyone else.

Deciding that there were enough people in her house to take on any enemies who may be at the door, she wiped her hands on her apron and walked over to the front door for the millionth time that day. She froze mid-step.

Wendy and Jason stood outside and appeared to be arguing. If they were here to serve her papers for the kidnapping, this would officially go down as the worst Thanksgiving ever. Strictly speaking, Wendy still had an open lawsuit against her. She had postponed their follow-up mediation appointment a total of eight times, which was really throwing a cramp in Claire's schedule.

Claire opened the door. "Uh, hi."

"Hi, Claire. Could we come in for a second?" Wendy asked. For once, she wasn't wearing anything cleavage-revealing or skintight. There wasn't a single sequin on the sweater dress that hung from her thin frame.

"Okay," Claire said slowly, pulling the door open wide. What in the hell was going on? Had she not suffered enough?

"Oh, you have a lot of company," Jason said, gesturing to all the cars in the driveway and voices coming from the ball-room. "Maybe we should come back later."

"No, I need to do this now," Wendy said, a strained smile on her face. She took a reusable grocery bag from Jason and handed it to Claire.

Claire cautiously opened it and peered inside. She pulled out a teardrop-shaped glass award. The Planner of the Year award. What the hell?

"I don't understand," Claire said.

Wendy looked incredibly constipated. "It should have been yours. I cheated to get it anyway. You saved me from those idiots. I would probably be dead if it wasn't for you. Today is supposed to be a day of giving thanks, so I wanted to give my thanks to you. Even though you kidnapped me and forced me to eat lemon yogurt."

"Well, thank you," Claire said, setting the award on the table and fighting the urge to plunge it and her hands into a pot of boiling water.

"And one other thing." Jason nudged Wendy.

"Right," she said. "I'm dropping the lawsuit."

Claire blinked. "You're what?"

"Yeah, I called the mediator this morning. It's over. It was stupid in the first place."

The crushing weight of potential financial ruin that had stubbornly clung to Claire's back for the past six months lifted. "Thank you," she said and gripped the bar cart for strength. "I appreciate it. Well, thank you for stopping by. Happy Thanksgiving."

"Oh, yeah. We'll, uh, see you later," Jason said, grabbing Wendy's elbow and half-dragging her toward the door.

"Bye, Claire."

"Bye," Claire said, waving at the woman who had tried to ruin her personal and professional life more times than she could count.

Wendy and Jason paused just outside the door and appeared to be arguing again. Jason looked at his phone and shrugged animatedly.

Oh no. *Don't do it, you idiot.* Cursing herself, Claire opened the door again.

"Do you guys want to stay for dinner?" With any luck, they would create such rampant chaos that Rachel wouldn't be able to find anything about Claire's dinner to complain about.

"We would love to." Wendy dragged Jason back into the house.

"You can follow me," Claire said as she pushed the cart back to the ballroom.

"Luke, can you set two more places at the table?"

The next morning, Claire awoke feeling fantastic despite the absurd amount of carbs she had scarfed the night before. She hadn't sleepwalked since moving in with Luke the previous month. She quickly showered, applied makeup, and found a dress that wasn't covered in dog hair.

She tiptoed downstairs, stopping in the small room across from Luke's office that she had decided to claim as her own. She opened her laptop and pressed send on the email draft she had agonized over for the past month.

Then she went into Luke's office and found a ring light, boom microphone, and an expensive-looking camera. She arranged them as best as she could and dragged a bar stool into the middle of the living room.

There were footsteps on the stairs. "What the hell are you doing?" Luke asked, wiping the sleep from his eyes as he entered the living room. "It's like seven a.m."

"I'll tell you what I'm doing. I'm making big changes. I emailed a business consultant on how to expand my business in the United States and maybe break into the international market for proposals in Europe. Maybe."

He stopped mid-step and blinked. "You did? I thought you said you weren't ready."

"As much as I hate to admit it, there may be something to this whole therapy thing after all." Claire smoothed a strand of hair back into her bun. She had been seeing Sawyer's mother, Dr. Goulding, for the past three months.

"Okay, but you said—"

"And—sorry, I know we're working on our communication. But this is important. I'm ready for you to interview me," she said, gesturing to the camera. "It's time to put this behind me."

"Claire, I don't want to interview you. I don't want you to have to relive that, ever."

"Shut up and get behind the camera," she said. "I love you, and I want to do this for you. I know it'll make every difference in your documentary. I'm ready. And, you know, it might help to talk about it," she said, parroting his words back at him.

"What did you say?" He was smiling.

"It might help to talk about it," she mocked again.

"No, the other part."

"Oh. I love you," she said, butterflies in her stomach the same as the day they had met. The words had been on the tip of her tongue since Luke had said it in the hospital parking lot, and she had been planning on saying them for the first time in a dramatic way, possibly with fireworks or a musical group or at the very least a cheese fountain. And now they had tumbled out without her even realizing.

"You admitted it now, you can't take it back," he said with a laugh, drawing her into him. His kiss was passionate, tender, and it filled her to the brim with liquid light.

"Never," she said, looking into the eyes of the man who had changed her life. They were calm this morning, more sea than storm. Sure, he drove her crazy seventy percent of the time. And he was sort of responsible for her plunging into the Seine River. And he had lied to her about a number of important things. But they had grown a lot in the past four months, both as a couple and as individuals. Luke had vowed to tell her the truth even if it was scary or uncomfortable, and Claire had kept her promise to never again hide from him any knowledge about murderous cults.

He disappeared into the kitchen and returned with a binder. "Are you ready?"

"I am," Claire said. And for the first time, she meant it.

Claire woke the morning of Christmas Eve with a grateful heart. Since arriving in Miami three days ago, she had whisked Luke through an increasingly elaborate series of Solstice and Christmas traditions.

Luke had won the annual Alejo family cookie baking competition with an extravagant gingerbread recreation of a scene from *The French Connection*, while Claire had gotten distracted by a work email and ended up burning her *Stepwives of Secaucus* themed sugar cookie crew.

The Christmas tree had been meticulously decorated. Citrus bird feeders were hung in the front yard. Even the house itself had been de-cluttered.

Alice insisted on an annual purge of furniture and decor in order to unblock the energy in the house and welcome the returning sun (even if that meant hauling the dining room table to Goodwill and eating dinner standing up in the kitchen). As a result, the three-bedroom bungalow was decorated differently every time Claire visited. The bizarre clown prints and bold circus colors of the last year had recently been replaced by a calm, sea-inspired theme that celebrated their proximity to the ocean. She had not been sorry to see the clowns go.

Now that the Solstice traditions had been celebrated, they would spend their Christmas Eve the way they always did—prepping Roy's family recipe for nacatamales, volunteering at the local community kitchen, and blasting off fireworks until midnight. It was her most treasured time of the year. And now Luke was an integral part of it.

She rolled over and opened her eyes. There he was, furrowed brow and all. Grumpy even in sleep. Crisp white sheets draped over his lower back. The gray light of early morning washed over him. God, he was handsome.

She glanced at her watch. Crap. It was only 6:00. If Alice's usual Christmas Eve events transpired, there would be no sleep tonight and she had just squandered her last chance to sleep in. But her phone beeped with an email from a January client, and she sighed before sliding to the edge of the bed with a big stretch. Maybe there would be time for a nap after the community kitchen.

Or maybe this year Alice wouldn't drag them on a quest given by some passing spirit. It had happened almost every Christmas Eve for as long as she could remember—most were still festively documented on Alice's original blog. But still. There was always hope.

Phone in hand, she snuck out of the bedroom and crept across the hall into the bathroom. She typed a response to the email as the shower filled the room with steam. Her thoughts returned to Luke. The Islestorms didn't have much in the way of Christmas traditions. His mother was always working, yet she had refused to let his dad take them for the holiday. He and his brother, George, had spent most Christmases alone, playing with their new toys in a big, empty house.

And yet he hadn't let his lack of enthusiasm for the holiday season ruin their trip. He had gone along with every Alejo tradition without complaint. And all the while sporting button-down shirts with the sleeves rolled up—Claire's personal kryptonite.

Desire burned deep and hot inside her. Thanks to Alice's constant, dramatic presence, she and Luke hadn't been intimate the entire trip. Her hand hesitated on the doorknob. Should she kick Rosie out of the room and wake him up while the rest of the house was still asleep? But no, he had already missed too much sleep from cramming in work on his documentary after everyone else went to bed. He should rest while he could.

She released the knob and stepped into the shower, reveling in the warmth washing over her body. Proposals. Think about proposals. She mentally ran through some logistics for an upcoming event, but she couldn't get the curve of Luke's biceps out of her mind. The strength rippling in his shoulders as he lifted her to hang the bird feeders. Beads of sea water glimmering on his stupidly hot abs when he walked out of the ocean waves.

Her hand slid down over her body and slipped between her legs. She was not going to be able to focus on work or making this Luke's best Christmas ever with all this carnal energy swirling around. The warm water mixed with the friction of her fingers as she caressed herself. She gripped the shower rod with the other hand and bit her lip to fight back the moans threatening to escape. What had Luke done to her? She had never been so horny for Jason that she couldn't concentrate. But Luke was a walking aphrodisiac.

The shower curtain flew back, and Claire threw her hands up in front of her, mouth opened to scream. Luke's hand closed over her mouth, calloused and strong.

"Shh," he said. He stepped into the shower next to her.

"You scared the shit out of me," she hissed.

"Sorry. It looked like you needed a hand," he said. "Or maybe something else."

He nipped her bottom lip before dropping to his knees in front of her. The tile wall was cool against her back as he pressed her against it, propping one of her legs over his shoulder. He eagerly found the source of her heat, exploring with tongue and fingers.

Her knees went limp, but the rest of her body went rigid as a board. Heat waves coursed through her as he wrote a symphony with his tongue. Pure light pulsated in her core as he urged her closer and closer to the edge.

She fisted her hands in his hair. His green eyes stared back at her, mischievous in the muted light. Was he going to drown down there?

She clamped a hand over her own mouth. The pressure was building. She couldn't take it. With one final flick of his tongue, she surged over the peak. Her body exploded in tingles and involuntary convulsions, stealing her breath. Her legs utterly gave up, and she grabbed the curtain rod for dear life.

Slowly, Luke kissed his way up her body, trailing his hands along her curves. He lingered on her neck.

"I'll give you a minute, but I'm not done with you yet." He picked up a bottle of shower gel and squirted it into his hands.

Claire, still largely useless after her body-convulsing orgasm, didn't fight when he released her grip on the curtain rod and turned her around. His rough hands caressed her, gently brushing her wet mop of hair over her shoulder. He massaged the soap into her back, gliding his fingers down her spine all the way to her ass.

Something pressed against her. Heat was building in her again. The man was ruthless. When the feeling returned to her legs, she stepped out of the spray and bent forward. She dragged him towards her and aligned them. With one thrust, he stole her breath. There was a hint of pain in this sharp surge of pleasure. He was unfairly well-endowed and knew exactly what to do with it.

She planted her palms on the wall for support. His hand slid to her front and found her apex. Her fingers curled on the wet tile. It was a damn Christmas miracle that she hadn't woken the entire house with agonized moans.

Ragged breaths tore through her. She couldn't possibly do it again. She would fall straight through the floor to the center of the Earth. And still he coaxed her, filling her emptiness and gripping her hips so hard she was sure to have bruises.

She gripped him back—her weekly Core Crusher pilates class had a whole section for pelvic floor muscles—and elicited a small moan. The noise sent her surging forward, approaching the break with blinding speed.

His thrusts came faster. Her head was nearly banging off the tile, but she barely registered it. With a final surge, he buried himself to the hilt.

"Luke—" she barely managed to whisper before the wave shattered over her.

They stood together in the warm spray, still joined, breathing hard like they had just run a marathon. His hands flanked hers on the wall and they caught their breath together.

Finally, when the stars disappeared from behind her eyes, Claire eased herself off and turned to face him. The shower pelted his back. Suds were still trapped in her hair. She had never been so clean yet so dirty at the same time.

"Best Christmas gift ever," she mumbled through numb lips.

He opened his eyes and smiled. "What makes you think that was your gift?"

"It wasn't?" she asked as he kissed her neck.

"No. But I can show you."

Claire cocked her head. "I thought we weren't exchanging gifts until we got home."

"I lied."

A smile curled her lips. "Me too. Come on."

Half an hour later, Luke and Claire were curled up in a blanket at the foot of the Christmas tree. Rosie rolled on the plaid tree skirt before flopping across their laps, a new Santa hat perched on her head.

Claire pulled a box from behind her back and handed it to Luke.

He studied it. "How did you fit this in a carry-on?"

"I told you. I'm a master packer. I'm impressed at you too, by the way." She picked up the parcel he nudged towards her and shook it.

"This sounds like shoes," she said over the muffled rattle inside.

"No shaking," he said sternly. His fingers closed over hers, and a thrill ran through her belly. "You first."

"Fine." She was 85% confident that she was giving the superior gift anyway.

She ripped the paper off with the enthusiasm of an architect revealing new plans. It landed on Rosie, who didn't seem to mind.

A plain brown box with white script lettering appeared. She gasped.

"Luke. You didn't."

"I don't know what you're talking about."

She opened the box and moved aside a layer of tissue paper. The most gorgeous black pumps appeared, red soles blazing in the morning light. Fricken Louboutins?

"These shoes are like fifteen hundred dollars. Are you insane? Rosie's just going to try to eat them."

"I saw you look at them when we went to King of Prussia. It was a face you only make when there's an animal you want to adopt."

He had remembered a longing glance from six months ago? How dare he be so thoughtful? Was there such a thing as shoe insurance? She would definitely be storing them in the farthest reaches of the walk-in closet at home.

She ran a finger over the leather and inhaled the rich scent. Was there a better smell than new shoes? They were too much, but there was no sense in arguing with Luke. He never backed down on a gift.

"I love them. Thank you."

"Do you need a moment alone with the shoes?"

She elbowed him in the ribs and he smiled.

He reached for the remaining box, and her heart stuttered. Was her gift for him really as thoughtful as a pair of dream pumps?

"I would not advise shaking it." She bit her lip.

Luke opened the gift that she had wrapped with borderline surgical precision. The lid popped off, revealing a vintage camera bag. He cocked his head, then undid the buckles and peered inside.

"Is this—"

"The same model as the first camera your dad ever bought you? I hope so." She had pored over pictures from Luke's childhood and consulted a manager at an electronics store in West Haven before making a purchase.

He tugged it from the bag and turned it over in his

hands like he was inspecting an avocado at the grocery store.

"It works," she added when he continued to stare at it. "I tested it. There's some great B-roll of Rosie rolling in squirrel poop on there."

He set the camera bag gingerly on the floor and pulled her roughly to him.

His kiss was tender, and when they broke apart his arms enveloped her like a safety blanket.

"Thank you," he said softly.

"Welcome," Claire said, muffled in his chest.

The sun's rays filtered in through the bay window. The electric fireplace crackled in the corner. It may not have been home, but it was definitely her best Christmas ever.

ABOUT THE AUTHOR

Madison Score is the author of the Claire Hartley Accidental Mystery series (and the younger, weirder sister of Lucy Score.) She lives in Pennsylvania with her husband, son, and perpetually shedding corgi. For some reason, her parents allowed her to get a degree in Creative Writing, which she now utilizes to craft stories with comedy, romance, and sometimes a hefty dose of crime.

When she's not writing, working at her real job in medical billing, or chasing after her tornado of a toddler (seriously, how many times can he upend our rubber tree?) you can find her blatantly ignoring recipes in the kitchen, flailing her body around in the gym, or bingeing true crime podcasts, TV, and movies.

Follow her on Facebook and Instagram if you want to see an excess of poorly photographed foods during her weekly Madison Tries It segment.

Website: madisonscore.com
Facebook: madisonscore
Instagram: madisonscore

ACKNOWLEDGMENTS

Kari March designs for having the patience of a saint while I waffle about background colors and graphics.

TWSS for giving me the chance to turn an unpaid hobby into a career.

The beautiful readers who patiently encouraged me on social media despite the fact that it took four thousand years to launch this trilogy into the world *and* there aren't as many penises as they were probably hoping for.

Luna, whose antics gave me much fuel for the character of Rosie.

Mike, my cinnamon roll hero, for playing Hot Wheels with Oliver for several millennia so I could finish these books.